THE BAD BOX

Also by Harvey Click

Demon Mania

Demon Frenzy

The House of Worms

Magic Times

THE BAD BOX

a novel by

HARVEY CLICK

For my wife, Rose, whose support and help
are priceless

In the beginning
in a place shunned by God
with a word like wind in a graveyard
a ghost of other light flutters
bequeathing seven swords of pain
dealing death in the dark
to the world that waits above.

   -Anonymous, twelfth century
   Translated from Latin by Dr. Raymond Brown

Part One: In the Beginning

Chapter One

The lid of the bad box shut. Cold darkness.

Angel's turn.

***

Angel knew how to escape the darkness. There was a tunnel she had found, a long, narrow, cold burrow in the dirt. All she had to do was wiggle through it like a worm, and before long she emerged from a secret hole beneath the bushes beside the old grade school.

She crawled out from the bushes into the bright sun and brushed the dirt off her knees and dress. It was a beautiful day but chilly, the kind of chill the sun didn't penetrate. She needed a sweater.

She walked slowly from the big grassy schoolyard to the gravel playground. No need to run or hurry—she knew there would be plenty of time to play, more time than she wanted, but she didn't think about that.

There were no other children; there never were. Angel didn't miss them, but she hoped her friend would visit. Maybe he was hidden behind a tree, playing hide and seek with her. He liked to play games.

She sat in a swing, grasped the cold chains, leaned back her head, and gazed at a fat white cloud. She began to swing, and soon she was sailing in a high arc, the sky and trees blurring together.

The motion was soothing, and it helped her not to think, but she was chilly and wanted to go home, not to Grandpa and Grandma but to Mom and Dad, but she knew she couldn't go home to them ever again, not since their accident. In fact she couldn't go anywhere, but she tried not to think about that, tried not to think about anything but the motion of the swing, up and down, down and up, up into the cold blue sky.

Angel started to tell herself a story about Hansel and Gretel and their breadcrumb trail as they wandered lost through the dark woods, but the story made no sense. Why would they leave Mom and Dad to go live with a mean old witch? And why would they waste all that bread? Her tummy ached, and if she were Gretel she would eat the bread instead of spilling it on the forest floor for the stupid birds to eat. The story was right about the mean old witch, but why did it leave out the ogre?

No, it was a stupid story, and Angel didn't like to think of the cage that the witch put them in, and she didn't like to think of Hansel because he reminded her of her little brother, and she didn't want to think about her little brother because he was a bad, bad boy, and it was a stupid story, though she liked the part when the children shoved the witch into the oven, and she thought I'd shove the mean old ogre in there too, but first I'd chop off their heads and then I'd stick their bodies in the oven and cook them up, but I'd keep their heads just so I could look at them and say, "So there! So there!"

Angel shivered. The air on her back felt like cold rain, though the sky was a perfect storybook blue.

***

She didn't know how long he had been sitting there. She had been swinging and shivering and thinking of the witch and the ogre and what she would do with their heads, and when she looked he was sitting in the swing next to hers. Appearing like that was one of his games. She was delighted, but she tried not to show it.

"Hi, Angel," he said, his voice whispery like dry leaves.

"Hi."

She continued swinging, aware of him watching her but pretending she didn't care. He was a handsome man, big and strong, older than her father had been when he'd had his accident, but somehow more like a kid.

She didn't know his real name. She called him Baby Beddybye because he reminded her of a doll she had once owned with that name. His head was bald like the doll's, and his eyes were black and shiny like polished stones.

"Going to ignore me today?" Baby Beddybye asked.

Angel smiled but didn't answer. She swung a little higher and leaned her head back, letting her long blond hair stream out behind her like a kite tail. She knew that Baby Beddybye liked her hair.

"Aren't we friends?" he asked.

"Maybe." Angel kept swinging, staring at the sky and hoping that he was noticing her pretty hair.

"Maybe I'm your only friend," he said.

Angel tried to remember the friends she used to have, but that seemed so long ago, before the accident.

"Maybe," she said at last.

"Are you cold?" he asked.

"Yes."

"Here." Baby Beddybye took off his jacket. "Since we're friends."

Angel stopped swinging. It was a nice dark gray suit jacket like Daddy used to wear when he got dressed up.

"Go ahead," he said. "It doesn't have any cooties."

Angel smiled and put it on. That felt better, warm and cozy. It was as big as a dress on her, and she wrapped it around herself like a blanket and snuggled into its warmth. It gave her a funny feeling, tingly and secretive, like a tent you could hide under and no one would ever find you.

"It's a very special jacket," Baby Beddybye said. "It's a secret jacket."

"A secret jacket?"

"Yes. It's a secret just between you and me. Friends share secrets, don't they?"

"I guess so."

Angel began to swing again, warm in her comfy jacket, her hair streaming out behind her. She thought of the witch and the ogre, how she would hide in her secret jacket and sneak up on them and cut off their heads and shove their headless bodies into the blazing oven.

"So there!" she would say.

"I know one of your secrets," Baby Beddybye whispered.

"No you don't."

"Yes I do. I know what you're thinking. You're thinking about an ogre and a witch."

"Maybe."

"Sure you are. You're thinking of what you'd like to do to them."

Angel stopped swinging. Such a smart man, she thought.

"Now you haveta tell me a secret," she said, "since you know mine."

"I will, if you promise you'll always be my friend."

"Okay."

"Forever and ever" he said. "You have to swear."

"I swear, cross my heart and hope to die."

Baby Beddybye smiled. "Okay then. Now listen very, very carefully."

Chapter Two

Eva Dietrick stared out the kitchen window across the wide weedy yard at the barn nearly hidden by relentless rain. It had rained like that all day as if it meant to wash the whole farm into a ditch, where it could run all the way to hell for all she cared.

It had been dark all day, but now the deeper dark meant night was coming, and the old fool was still out there. For many years she had regretted that she couldn't see what Gus did out there in the barn. It certainly wasn't work, because if the stupid old fool ever lifted a finger except to stick it up his nose, the yard wouldn't be growing weeds and the barn wouldn't be falling down and the bills from the grain elevator wouldn't be piling up like leaves in fall.

"*Narr!*" she muttered out loud, turning her wheelchair so she could see if the old fool was loitering in front of the barn, too stupid to come in out of the rain, but he wasn't. He was still inside the barn, where he had been the whole wasted day since noon, when he had gummed down his chopped bacon and beans and potatoes with his wad of wet tobacco beside his plate staining the kitchen table as always.

Eva had a hunch about what he did out there, more than a hunch, a hard suspicion, but it wasn't her responsibility, and what was she supposed to do about it anyway, stuck in a chair like a bag of sand in a wheelbarrow?

"*Dummkopf!*" she growled, jerking her chair to face the table, where Gus's supper sat cold and could rot with maggots for all she cared. She had already eaten her own supper, and a lot more pleasant it was without his wet wad on the table and his hand going down to the crotch of his overalls to scratch whatever itched down there.

At the thought, her own hand shot up to her scalp and her nails dug deep into the skin. Sometimes it seemed as if worms were crawling on her scalp and every other inch of her carcass. Eva despised her body, despised all bodies, filthy itching things racked with pains and obscene needs of their own, too disgusting to consider.

Let his food rot if he didn't want to come in and eat it. But she turned back to the window, as she had been doing all day, and stared out at the rain.

Dark now, dark as death. Something was wrong. She had known it all afternoon. *Furcht. Sorge.* Fallen from the haymow. Trampled by a heifer. Impaled by his own manure fork—a fitting end.

But who would take care of her? How was she supposed to get by, helpless like a bag of sand in a wheelbarrow?

Eva pushed herself to the hutch, found the thin phone book, and rang the sheriff's office.

"I need help," she said. "Gus has been out there all day, he's not coming back."

"Who is this?"

"Eva!" she shouted. "Eva Dietrick. *Mir helfen!*"

"Sorry. Could you repeat that?"

"Do you not speak English?" she shouted. "I told you. What am I expected to do? A bag of sand in a wheelbarrow. Should I put myself to bed? I tell you, I haven't been to toilet since noon!"

"Please, could you just give me your address?"

"*Furcht! Sorge! Schmerz!* Can you not hear me?"

***

Deputy Joe Miley and Deputy Doug Brown found Gus's body in the barn collapsed over a bale of hay. Joe called for an ambulance, though a hearse would work just as well. They were young men, and neither of them had ever given news like this to a wife before. Finally Joe agreed to do it because he was three years older and a bit more experienced.

"Didn't I say?" Eva said. She glared darkly at Joe Miley. Stupid! she thought. What they tell me already I know.

She was in her bedroom, already mostly packed but still finding a thing or two worth keeping, a few letters in German from someone she had known long before she met Gus, an old pair of galoshes that would be useful if she ever walked again, a broken necklace that might be worth something, though she doubted it since it had been a gift from Gus.

"Now I am expected to do what?" she asked. "Is this house something I can live in now?"

Eva poked through a dresser drawer, found a coin and peered at it. It seemed to be made of tin, some trash from the old country, but maybe someone would buy it. She stuck it in her pocket.

"Somewhere else I have to go," she said.

"Well, there's County Services," Joe Miley said. "We can take you there."

"I don't know this County Services, but here I will not stay. I haven't been to toilet since noon!"

The two young men looked at each other.

"You're older," Deputy Brown whispered to his partner.

"Maybe she better go in the ambulance," Joe whispered. "You know, so there's not a mess in the back seat."

Eva latched her trunk, and Joe carried it to the dining room while Deputy Brown pushed her chair behind him. They looked out the open door, waiting for the ambulance. The rain was even harder now, battering the weeds flat and bouncing off the ground like balls.

Eva stared out at the bouncing rain and thought that maybe she was forgetting something. A bolt of lightning struck a withered tree along the fence row of a field, and the explosion jarred her memory.

Bouncing balls, she thought. Stupid games for stupid children. *Das Kind.*

"*Das Kind* is down there," Eva said. "*Das Kind* is in the bad box."

The young men looked at each other. "What did you say?" Joe asked.

"Can you not hear me?" she shouted above the noise of the rain. "I told you. Do you not speak English? The stupid child is in the bad box!"

Annoyed by the two men, Eva scratched angrily at her greasy scalp. She could feel tiny worms crawling through her hair, burrowing through the skin and bone, digging into her brain.

Filthy worms, filthy carcass, filthy world!

Part Two: In a Place Shunned by God

Chapter Three

Peter Bellman awoke thinking of Sarah. He had been dreaming about her, but all he could remember of the dream was her dented-up Toyota pulling away, muffler roaring, while he chased it down the street and shouted at her to come back. Not a pleasant way to begin the day.

He rolled over and stared gloomily at Emily Larkins, lying flat on her back still asleep, though she should have been awakened by the sun that poured through the curtain to fall in a bright puddle on her not-so-bright face.

She slept like a department store mannequin. One moment she would be chattering and giggling in that perky way that was already beginning to annoy him, and the next moment she would shut her eyes and be fast asleep. She would lie supine and motionless, not even flickering an eyelid to indicate that a dream ever passed through her head, until precisely 8:00 a.m., when her eyes would snap open and that damned cheery patter would begin at once, as if an automaton's switch had been turned back on.

So different from Sarah, who was always a restless sleeper and grumpy as a troll in the mornings until she had drunk enough of her kick-ass coffee to boot up her operating program. Funny, it seemed to be Sarah's imperfections that Peter missed the most, her moodiness, her contrariness, her insomnia. Now he wished he could comfort her after a nightmare or fix her a pot of strong coffee to ease her waking.

I deserve another chance, he thought. I'd do things differently.

The sheet had slipped down, and he gazed at Emily's breasts and tried to feel excited. They had certainly seemed exciting two weeks ago, when he had first seen them, just hours after Sarah had moved out. He had watched Sarah's old car pull away, loaded with books and junk, and instead of chasing her down the street as he had in his dream, Peter had gotten on the phone and invited some people over, including Emily Larkins.

She had been Peter's student the previous quarter in 301, and she had spent plenty of time in his office flirting with him while they discussed the fine points of sociology. If Sarah was going to run out on him because of a few trivial arguments, then fine, he wasn't going to sit around and mope. It hadn't taken much encouragement to get Emily to stay after his other guests had left, and that night she had seemed plenty exciting, especially because he knew that Sarah would soon learn she wasn't the only woman in the world.

Now he wasn't sure his haste had been a good idea. In fact, he hoped that no one had told Sarah about Emily.

He looked at his watch: 8:02. Any second now—and even as he thought it, Emily's eyes snapped open and she sat up and stretched.

"Oh, hi, honey," she said with a sunny smile. "You're awake already. Umm, looks like a nice day. Did you make coffee?"

"No," he answered gloomily.

"I'll make some." Emily trotted cheerfully out of the bedroom, her round pink hips jiggling as if they were happy too. She could have been the model for that damned smiley face emblem, Peter thought.

He sighed, got up and put on a bathrobe. Usually he enjoyed lounging around naked, but he didn't want to give Emily any encouragement. He didn't have to teach until 1:00, and he was hoping to get her out of the house so he could have a few hours to himself.

He trudged to the kitchen to make some coffee. It was the wrong brand, something Emily had picked up. Here just two weeks, and already she was buying groceries. Already she had made herself at home, already his friends were hers, already the whole department seemed to know they were a couple. At first he had been delighted that she was spending the next night and the next, delighted not so much by her as by how Sarah would feel when she learned that he already had another mate.

It occurred to him that Emily's next step would be to give up her apartment. It wouldn't surprise him if she had already given her landlord notice.

"Oh gee, I was going to make it," Emily said. She stood naked in the kitchen doorway, as bright and boring as a daisy.

"You make it too weak," Peter said.

"Oh. Well, I'm glad you told me. How many scoops do you use?"

"Never mind," he muttered.

He stood over the coffee maker, wishing it would hurry up. Emily came over and gave him a big wet kiss, her breath smelling of mouthwash. He pulled away and continued glaring at the coffee maker.

Was there no way to dispel her cheeriness? It seemed to be all over his house, sticking to the furniture like cheap perfume. Now she had her hand inside his robe, stroking the red hair on his chest.

"You going to prance around naked all day?" he asked.

A dark cloud swept over her sunny face. She turned away, looking as if he had slapped her, and headed to the bedroom to get dressed.

"Shit," Peter muttered, feeling a little ashamed of himself. It hadn't been necessary to hurt her feelings.

He told himself that he was just dreading his one o'clock. He hated teaching summer term and hated the classes he was stuck with. The students were unresponsive, almost hostile. But he knew they weren't the problem. His heart just wasn't in teaching right now. He stood dully in front of the class, speaking in a monotone, barely able to focus on the subject and feeling like a fraud.

Until this summer he had been a popular professor. He had always been a master of passionate classroom revelations, holding his arms in front of his chest and flexing his fists to show his muscles, a sinewy workman toiling for truth. Subjects that most of his peers reduced to dry statistics had issued from his mouth as fiery sermons that stirred the souls of even the most apathetic students. Maybe some of his colleagues muttered that he played fast and loose with facts, that he hadn't published anything in years, but they were just envious. He had always dismissed them as dried-up number crunchers, dull scribes in the Temple of Truth, but now he wondered if they were right.

It was Sarah's doing, he thought. A couple years ago, as one of his students in a graduate seminar, she had been swept up in his vision. But as soon as she had moved into his house, her niggling facts and figures had taken over. She was the opposite of him, all numbers and no tongues of fire. Every time he opened his mouth, she would scrunch up her small face in that serious frown that he both loved and hated, and she would cite some dreary statistics to spit in the face of everything he stood for.

"But if that's true," she would quibble, "why is it that such-and-such percent of this or that group are earning X wages just Y years later?"

All kindling and no flame—but after a while her numbers had chipped away at him. Then, as soon as she had wrecked his self-confidence, she had packed her belongings and roared away.

Goddamn her anyway, Peter thought. All her rubbish about how we couldn't get along. We were doing just fine.

He was disgusted that he was thinking of Sarah again, as if no other woman existed. Ridiculous. She wasn't even that pretty. Cute, but no great beauty. Time to get on with his life.

He yanked the carafe from the coffee maker though it wasn't finished brewing and filled a cup. He opened the refrigerator and started shoving wine bottles and pickle jars around impatiently. Of *course* there was no cream. Of *course* Emily wouldn't remember to buy any. He slammed the refrigerator door shut and gulped the coffee black.

He began redoing the past in his head: he should have demanded summer term off; he should have taken Sarah somewhere—maybe Spain or Greece. It would have been a nice way to help her get past her parents' death.

He imagined her lying on a beach in Greece wearing just the bottom of her bikini, a scrap of pink cloth. Her small breasts were bare, and he could see her dark nipples so clearly that he became erect. He thought of her usual costume around the house, a skimpy pair of panties and a T-shirt, thought of how exciting it had been to gaze at her sitting half naked while she read a book, unaware of his attention, thought of how snugly her panties had clung to her . . .

"I think I'll go to my place for a while," Emily said, standing in the kitchen doorway. "I've got some things I need to do."

Peter could tell she was hoping he would ask her to stay. "Sure. That's fine," he said, not turning fully toward her because he didn't want her to notice his erection—she wasn't the one who had inspired it.

She turned and left, doing a pretty good job of showing she was angry without saying so. Peter sat down at the kitchen table and rubbed his temples. He reached for his phone and tried to call Sarah but got a recording instead: "The number you have dialed is incorrect. Please check the number and try again."

What a ball-busting bitch! She had no right to cut herself off from him like that, not after two whole years of living in his house and sleeping in his bed—and just because of a couple stupid arguments. It wasn't fair. It was like sawing off one of his legs and hiding it somewhere.

Pocahontas jumped up onto the kitchen table and sniffed his coffee. Peter pushed it angrily away. Damned cat had always liked Sarah better than him. He should have allowed her to take it. Maybe he had been thinking that if he kept the damned cat, she would be more likely to come back—or maybe he had just wanted to make her miserable.

He rang Howard Goldwin's number. He was annoyed with Howard for helping Sarah move. Howard was supposed to be his friend, not hers. Damned traitor.

"Hey, Howard, how's life and all that? Say, I've got some important mail here that I need to send to Sarah, and I seem to have misplaced her address. Well, yeah, sure, I'd just call her, but the last time we talked, a couple days ago, well, frankly it wasn't very pleasant. I'm afraid she's a little put out because I'm seeing someone else, you know, she's a little jealous, and I'm afraid it will make her feel bad if I call her about a lot of bills and rubbish like that. I'd hate to hurt her feelings, she's, well, you know, she's so sensitive, it may take her a while to heal, if you know what I mean. I'd rather just mail the stuff. Yes. Here, let me write this down . . ."

Peter hung up the phone and stared at the address for a minute. He knew where the street was, not a nice neighborhood at all. At first he thought: good, let her find out what it's like to run out on me without two fucking dimes to rub together—she'll be dragging her ass back here pretty soon, begging me to forgive her.

But the longer he stared at the address, the less happy he felt. She could be mugged or raped, maybe even killed. He pictured the squalid neighborhood, litter everywhere, miserable crack-house apartments, barking dogs, prostitutes and gangs roaming the sidewalks. He looked around his spacious kitchen at the designer faucet and expensive stainless steel appliances, the gourmet skillets and kettles hanging neatly above the gleaming granite counter, the sliding glass doors that led to a pleasant back yard with dwarf fruit trees and a hot tub and a privacy fence.

Time to rescue her, he decided. Maybe I won't even make her apologize.

Chapter Four

Sarah Temple stood in the front room of her new apartment and
watched an ancient Volkswagen bug trying to crawl into a parking
place out front. It was a small sunroom with ten cheerful windows,
perfect for plants, though the only plant she owned was the half-dead
jade that Peter had given her way back when there was still a reason
for them to give each other presents. The street and the tiny singed
lawn that the windows looked out on weren't so cheerful, especially
now that the afternoon shadows were lengthening and gangs of
young boys were beginning to emerge from them like flies from a
rotting carcass.

Really not a bad place, she told herself. She had been telling
herself that for two weeks.

The Volkswagen squirmed back and forth, trying clumsily to
work its way closer to the curb, as it did each evening at 5:15.
Finally the driver shut it off and climbed out. It was the ghost,
Sarah's upstairs neighbor. Slight and pale, maybe thirty years old,
dressed always in the same black suit despite the heat, he looked
more like an apparition than a creature of bones and blood. He
drifted slowly toward the entrance of the building, stepping so
weightlessly that his feet seemed scarcely to touch the pavement, as
if he weren't quite connected to the earth.

Each evening Sarah would hear a few ghostly footsteps above
her and then nothing else, no radio, no TV, no voice talking on a
phone or even to itself. Each weekday morning at 7:45 she would
hear the door above her shut quietly, and then the ghost would drift
down the stairs so softly that she sensed him more than heard him.
She would be sitting in the sunroom drinking her morning coffee,
but he seemed not to notice her or anything else as he emerged from
the building and headed to his rusty old bug.

The landlady had said that the other three apartments were
occupied by singles, the ghost above her and one woman in each
apartment on the other side. But after two hot lonely weeks of living
here, Sarah had met none of them. Her three neighbors all kept to
themselves, and their aloofness seemed to demand that she do the

same.

She could hear a TV behind the door of the other downstairs apartment whenever she was in the landing, but it always seemed to be talking and laughing to itself, and she had never seen anybody go in the apartment to give the poor TV some company.

Last weekend she had caught a quick glimpse of the woman who lived above that apartment. Sarah had seen her creeping down the rear fire escape, peering at her feet through dark glasses, trying to keep her high heels from getting stuck between the iron strips of the steps.

She was nice looking if you like the look of prostitutes, a young woman with sleek blond hair halfway down her back, her tight, short purple dress advertising her slim figure and showing every detail except her price tag.

Sarah was bent over watering the withered jade when someone outside turned on a boom box so loud that the windows rattled. She turned and saw a gang of teenagers in the small front yard, staring in at their new neighbor. One of them grabbed his crotch and gave her a face that said eat this, bitch.

She slammed the windows shut and moved to the rear of her apartment, where she had been organizing the dining room into a study. It was still cluttered with boxes of books and endless piles of paper, which she hadn't the stomach to sort through. She sat at her desk and stared angrily at her computer screen.

Even with the windows shut, she could hear the boys outside yelling above their boom box, their adolescent voices already as hard as gun metal. Crime statistics swarmed unbidden into her brain, as if she had clicked open a computer file, the residue of two years of graduate study in sociology. She knew all too well the crime figures for this neighborhood, but she also knew the tiny figure in her checking account, and it told her she couldn't afford anything better.

She was hot and sticky, the rattling box fan having nothing but hot air to blow around. She wanted to strip down to her underpants, but she hadn't gotten around to buying drapes for the windows, and the old roller-blinds offered plenty of peepshow holes.

Friday, soon to be Friday night, and she had nowhere to go, no one to see, and nothing to do.

Though she had lived in Columbus for over two years, she had been too wrapped up in her graduate studies to make any close friends. Peter had plenty of friends, most of them faculty, and she had accepted them as her own even though she had felt uncomfortable around them, being younger, being just a student, being just a small-town girl from Iowa, being just Sarah while they were all Dr. This or Professor That, the esteemed author of Such and Such. Now that she had time for friends and wanted some, they just seemed like his people. Calling them would feel awkward, a step back into his world, a world that had never really been hers.

She was beginning to wonder if she would ever have a world of her own. A few weeks ago she had been hectically busy with her teaching assistantship and her master's thesis, with Peter's weekend soirees and his burly body beside her each night, with her vague plans to write a book based on the research for her thesis. Each day had bustled by with duties and deadlines and dramas, and now each day crept by with boom boxes outside, a ghost tiptoeing upstairs, and inside just a gnawing, aching void.

The void had been there all along, she thought, but she had been too busy to notice. It had suddenly grown deeper at the end of last fall semester when she got the call saying that the house she would always know as home and her parents who had been asleep inside it were now just ashes, ashes to ashes, and she had been so busy grading final essays and writing her own essays that she had barely found time to fly home for the funeral, much less to make her peace with these two new graves added to the emptiness inside.

And the void had dug itself deeper still two weeks ago, when Peter slammed her head against a wall and slapped her once too often. Sarah didn't intend to spend any more days or years in the OSU sociology building watching the bastard strut up and down the halls with his coterie of coeds, so she withdrew from the doctorate program that would have begun this fall. Now she would have to apply to other schools, and that meant waiting another year to begin her studies, so while she waited she may as well try to write her book. It almost seemed like a plan if she didn't think about it too hard.

So here she sat in the box-cluttered dining room turned study, surrounded by piles of papers and bookmarked books and newspaper clippings, and she strained to see in the gray pixels of the computer screen some inkling of the idea she had once believed she had for converting all these dull facts and statistics into a book just screaming to be written, but the only thing screaming was the boom box outdoors.

Twenty-seven years old, and nothing to show for those years except a lot of boxes and a few bruises.

Friday. No doubt Peter was going to have people over, a few attractive female students among them. In another hour he would be opening a bottle of wine and firing up the gas barbecue grill in his nice back yard so that he could cook the shish kebabs that had been marinating all day in his big kitchen. She thought of his long red hair, his tanned arms, his strong hands that knew every part of her body.

Goddamn Peter and his nice fucking yard! The son of a bitch wasn't going to have any trouble getting into some cute new panties tonight.

Instead of evaporating the sweat on her back, the fan seemed to be congealing it into an itchy second skin. The boom box seemed to be moving away, thank God. Sarah could hear it thumping off into the distance, a giant thug roaming its turf.

She got her address book and thumbed through it. Peter's friends, Peter's friends. How could such a jerk have so many friends? Only one person listed in the book was more her friend than Peter's. She had met Howard Goldwin through Peter, but he'd had a bellyful of Peter's crap a long time ago. She called.

"Oh, hi Sare. How's the place?" He sounded bright and chipper, as always.

"Alcatraz guarded by the Shadow Boys. They roam around out front, make sure no one escapes."

"I told you so. I warned you. My darling, you're lucky you're still alive."

"Thanks."

She pictured Howard, slender and elegant, groomed and cologned and nicely dressed, no doubt wearing a colorful silk tie and sipping a glass of wine.

"Move in here," he said. "At least until you can afford a better place. I told you, I've got an extra room. More than one—I'll give you *two* rooms."

"You're sweet, Howard, but no thanks. Can't even put up with myself in the mornings, sure wouldn't expect you to. But I was hoping we could go have dinner."

"Love to, but not tonight, my dear. I'm gazing at the reason. Adonis, sitting right across the table from me. Chewing a bagel with lox. Poor sleepyhead, he just got up. He needs some babying." A moment's pause, and Sarah could see him making a face at his new paramour. "But soon, darling, soon," Howard said. "Why don't I have you over for dinner next week?"

"I'd like that. I've been talking to myself so much I'm beginning to feel like an old couple." She tried not to let him hear her disappointment.

"By the way," Howard said, "Peter called this morning and said he'd lost your address."

"He can't lose what he never had, and he never had it because I didn't want him to."

"Oh dear. Then I'm afraid I blundered. I was silly enough to give it to him. Sorry, Sare."

Sarah didn't like what she was feeling. Was Peter missing her? Wanting to see her? Wanting to apologize? Wanting her to move back? Why should this excite her?

"I should have known better than to believe his poppycock," Howard said. "He implied that you've been chatting away like old chums."

"Did he say why he wanted my address?"

"He said he has mail for you."

Great. Mail. Ain't that a thrill? Sarah was disgusted with herself—no self-respect. Two weeks on her own, and already she was wanting to crawl back. Probably Peter was seeing some joy-toy by now. If anyone would know, it would be Howard. She tried to think of some discreet way to ask.

"I hear he's seeing someone," she said.

"Oh, really? Whoever told you that, my dear?"

"Someone," she said awkwardly. "Well, no one, actually. I just want to know."

Sarah could tell by Howard's long silence that she was right. At last he said, "Emily Larkins. Do you know her?"

Larkins, Larkins. The name didn't sound familiar, but Peter knew so many women, one could hardly keep track of their names.

"Apparently she has taken up residence in his house," Howard said.

Jeez. Already. That hurt.

"The problem with Peter," Howard said, "is perhaps not his fault. I suspect it may be in his genetic makeup. It's evident he's one of those pre-human primates from the Pleistocene epoch. What are they called? Oh yes, Assholelopithecus. Really, my dear, you deserve someone far better."

The moment she hung up, she remembered a young woman she had met a couple months ago in Peter's office, some bubbly blond student named Emily. Of course. In fact, Sarah had sensed something at the time, something in the way the woman was sitting, something in Peter's too-casual manner.

Bastard! Sarah stomped to the bathroom, pulled off her soaked T-shirt and hurled it angrily into the corner. She turned the old tub faucets, adjusting the water to just barely lukewarm. The mirror, like everything else in the apartment, was old and spotted and stained. She pulled angrily at her long auburn hair. It looked damp and stringy. She should have it cut off, chopped as severely as a boy's, something really ugly. She was sick of looking like some cute little doll baby.

She pulled off her shorts and underwear and eased herself into the tepid water. The old claw-foot tub was large, that much at least could be said for the apartment, and her slender 107 (today) pounds fit into it comfortably.

She lay back with her knees sticking up, trying to enjoy the rush of water against her legs. Somehow she had to get out of this mood. She shut her eyes and drifted. She thought of the small town where she had grown up; she imagined the woods just outside town where she had loved to play, the wide creek that meandered through the trees. She and her little brother Johnny would catch frogs and harmless snakes from the clear, clean water. She could see the green pebbles at the bottom. She remembered Johnny's guileless smile, so wide that it looked almost comical on his round moon-face.

Poor Johnny. Poor Mom. Poor Dad.

She soaped up her washcloth and began to scrub off the second skin of grimy sweat. Friday night and not even a TV set to keep her company. She could almost hear Peter popping another cork from another bottle of wine and pouring a nice glass for Emily Larkins.

There was a knock at her door.

Chapter Five

Peter stopped in the middle of the narrow street with his engine running and stared at Sarah's apartment building. Nestled in a litter-strewn corner of two blighted streets, the building seemed to have four apartments, two on each side, with a row of windows in front of each apartment, though there wasn't anything that anybody would want to look out at.

Not quite ready to confront her, he continued to the stop sign just past the building and turned right. He still hadn't decided what to say. All day he had been running speeches through his head, but at some point each one derailed into a bullying whine.

He had felt nervous all day. His one o'clock had gone badly, a droning lecture delivered to students petrified with boredom. After class, not wanting to go home for fear that Emily might be there, he had stopped at a bar and had a few scotches to steady his nerves. The drinks had been a mistake, especially before dinner. If there was one time he needed his wits, this was it. He believed Sarah would give him one chance, but not two. He knew he should get something to eat to take the edge off the alcohol, but he felt too anxious to eat.

The street perpendicular to hers was wider and busier, still throbbing with traffic though rush hour was over. Peter tried a new speech, saying some of the words out loud, but it began to derail as soon as he imagined her spouting out some hard fact to trip him up.

He noticed a carry out and pulled over. Maybe some wine would soften her up. Then he would take her out to a good restaurant. The side of the carry out was painted with gang graffiti, and its windows were protected with steel mesh. Inside, the coolers and shelves had nothing but malt liquor and rotgut wine. What a neighborhood! At last he located a couple dusty bottles of Merlot on an obscure shelf. Cheap stuff, but it would have to do.

He drove past her place again, turned the corner again, and parked beside her building on the busier street. If she saw his car parked out front she might not open the door. His legs felt weak and rebellious, and he had to force himself to climb the crumbling concrete steps up to the front door and step into the dingy landing.

There was her door on the right, its metal A hanging loose and crooked. He knocked.

Maybe she has a man in there? he thought. Then he heard some splashing: she must be taking a bath. He pictured Sarah sitting naked in the tub. Maybe she would greet him at the door wearing nothing but a towel. The thought brought the alcohol to his head in a dizzy rush.

"Who is it?"

"Peter."

A long pause. At last she said, "Jeez. Wait a minute. Let me get something on."

It seemed to take forever. Finally the door opened, and Sarah stood there frowning and rubbing the damp ends of her long hair with a towel. She had put on a T-shirt and shorts. It seemed unfair to Peter that he was no longer permitted to see her undressed.

"I know what you're thinking," he said. "You think I have no right to be here. You don't even want to let me in. You think I'm a jerk. But you have to let me talk to you."

Sarah stared for a few seconds and then shrugged. "Come in."

He marched past her on wobbly legs, down a short hallway to her living room. It wasn't the opening he had planned, blaming everything on himself like that, but at least it had gotten him through the door.

The living room was a mess, some ratty sofa that she must have found at Salvation Army, some other pathetic junk. A dining room to the left was crammed with books and boxes and her computer sitting on a cheap table heaped with papers. Good. She must want out of here as badly as he wanted her out.

Peter sank into the sofa and stared at the bottles grasped in his fists. He put them on the floor because there was no coffee table. Where was she? In the kitchen, rummaging around. Before long she appeared with a corkscrew and one glass.

"Don't you want any?" he asked. "I brought it for you."

"No thanks. I have stuff to do tonight."

He didn't like the sound of that. What stuff? Did she have a date?

Sarah sat across from him on a cheap old chair and continued drying the ends of her hair, ignoring him. He had nearly forgotten how pretty her green eyes were, how delicately her chin was shaped. Something about the corners of her mouth, the way they turned down even when smiling—like no one else's.

"What stuff?" he asked.

"I'm writing. I'm right in the middle of a section, and I want to get back to it with a clear head."

She put down the towel and scratched her thigh, a mosquito bite or something, and it turned pink. Peter wanted to kiss it. He stared at her legs, thin and smooth as a girl's.

"Really? What are you writing?"

"My book."

Her book? Yes, of course. She had talked about some silly notion, something to do with her thesis, but he had never paid it much mind.

"That's nice," he said at last. "Well, then, I won't have any either. Really, I brought it for you. The bottles are a little dusty— they've been sitting in my cellar, waiting for a special occasion."

"You sound like you already had a few," she said.

It made him feel like a derelict, already potted before dinner time. Sarah had a talent for shrinking him down to the size of a fly spot.

"Do I? Actually I did have a couple—at the faculty club."

Peter didn't like the way she was looking at him, scarcely blinking, her expression unreadable. He felt old and shabby, sweating alcohol in the humid heat, his shirt sticking to his wet armpits. He was holding the glass in one hand, the corkscrew in the other, and he didn't know what to do with them. He placed the glass on the floor but continued holding the corkscrew, feeling foolish.

"Well, how's it coming?" he asked. "The book I mean."

"Not too bad. Took a while getting started, but now it's moving right along."

He thought it was a bluff. He didn't believe she was really writing a book. She was trying to sound as if she had landed on her feet. She was trying to make him feel small, remind him that he hadn't written anything publishable for many years. It was a dirty trick.

"That's nice," he said. "So, what else have you been doing?"

She shrugged. "Not much. What about you?"

"Nothing. Just teaching. Not going so well this summer."

"That's too bad."

But her cool gaze didn't look sympathetic. Peter shifted uncomfortably, wanting to scratch his armpit, which was trickling sweat. The least Sarah could do was bring in the fan that was rattling away in the other room. She wanted him to be uncomfortable; she had him in the hot seat.

She didn't seem to be sweating at all. Something bothered him about her calm gaze, her eyes like still green ponds. She was the nervous type; this serene expression wasn't like her.

"The truth is, I've been missing you," he said, annoyed that he was the only one humbling himself.

"That's natural, I suppose," she said. The green pools of her eyes didn't show a ripple. "I mean when people break up they sometimes miss each other for a while."

"I don't mean for a while or any of that rubbish," Peter said, his tone sharpening to an irritable edge. "I mean I really miss you. I want you to come back. I've been miserable."

"Funny. I hear you've been keeping yourself pretty well entertained."

"What's that supposed to mean?"

"I'm told you have someone named Emily Larkins living with you."

That traitor Howard Goldwin—it had to be.

"Nonsense! Who told you that? She is *not* living with me. She's just a friend, that's all. Who said she's living with me? It's a fucking lie."

Peter realized he was starting to shout. He lowered his voice, but now it sounded weak and unconvincing. "I haven't been seeing anyone, I've just been thinking about you all the time. I know I did a lot of things wrong, but that's all going to change."

He went on and on, repeating himself, pleading. Almost without noticing it, he had removed the cork from one of the bottles and poured himself a glass. He needed it. The wine was too warm and a little sour, but he finished one glass and filled another. Sarah sat with her bare feet on the seat of her chair, her elbows on her knees, her chin resting on her hands, the corners of her mouth turned down in a tantalizing frown, and she looked so sexy, so small, that he could scarcely bear it. He wanted to grab her by the shoulders and shake her.

He kept trying to tell her how he understood so much more now, how he wished he had taken the summer off and taken her to Greece, how profoundly he had changed, but he was having trouble keeping the irritable edge out of his voice.

Sarah's eyes maintained that tranquil gaze, and it occurred to him that she had picked up this new demeanor from some man, the way lovers often borrowed gestures and tics from each other. Who was this man, already impregnating her with his Goddamned annoying mannerisms?

"I didn't realize how much you meant. You're everything to me, everything," and while Peter spoke he kept staring at her legs and hoping that all this would end with them in bed together, tonight, now, he didn't want to wait, he wanted to take that T-shirt off of her now, touch her sweet little breasts, pull down her shorts, and the more urgent this need grew, the more hurt and angry he became that she was not responding to his need, just gazing at him with some bullshit Buddha expression in her eyes that she probably had picked up from her new lover—maybe she was even thinking of that new lover ripping off her T-shirt, enjoying her breasts and her slim legs. He realized that everything was coming out wrong, that he was bellowing at her, blaming her for everything, shaking the corkscrew at her like an absurd weapon.

"So that's that!" he finally shouted. "That's the way I feel!"

"Peter," she said, "you're snot-flinging drunk."

"I'm not drunk!" he roared, though he knew he was. It had been a terrible mistake to drink before coming over. Now he had blown it. He felt like crying. No, he'd be damned if he would let her see him blubbering.

He shut up and waited for her response like an accused man waiting for the verdict. So he was drunk—big deal. Surely she would understand. It was human to get drunk, human to roar sometimes. Humans had emotions, even if Sarah didn't.

The verdict finally arrived: "I'm not in the mood for this tonight," she said.

He couldn't take any more. She loved this, he thought, loved watching him grovel and crawl. Burning with humiliation, he walked to the door, but it was fastened with so many chains and bars that he couldn't get it open, and she had to help him. He felt her small body against his as she undid the locks.

"Maybe we can learn to be friends," she said. "Maybe you could call me when you're sober."

"Fuck you."

Peter stumbled out of the building, and the twilight heat made his stomach reel. Down the street some young thugs were eyeing him. Where the hell was his car? Oh yes, around the corner.

Two years shot straight to hell, he thought. When they had met, he had held all the cards: a prestigious position, a beautiful house, countless friends. She was a student struggling on a paltry TA's stipend, new to town and all alone. He had given her comfort, friends, a nice place to live.

Now she imagined she had the winning hand with some kind of wild joker card stuck up her sleeve, some Buddha-eyed lover-man that she had slipped between her sheets, and that gave her the right to humiliate him. Fuck her.

He had rounded the corner and was nearing his car when a sound caused him to glance at the rear of her building. A woman on the fire escape was locking the back door of the upper apartment across from Sarah's. Peter watched her climb down the stairs. Striking, with dark glasses, a short pink skirt, and long blond hair. She made her way through the scruffy back yard, heading toward him. When she noticed him watching, he looked away and continued to his car.

What an interesting idea, he thought. Sarah's neighbor— wouldn't that be something? Let her see what it feels like to be humiliated. Do the ol' in-an'-out nasties right there under her nose, or rather right there above it.

While he fumbled with his keys, he stole another glance. The blonde was standing at the bus stop. No place for a young woman all alone, he thought. He wondered if she was a hooker. He brushed his hair back with his fingers and walked over.

"Hello," he said.

She pushed a golden strand of hair out of her face and smiled. Very pretty, Nordic maybe.

"Seems like a dangerous neighborhood," he said. "I wish you'd let me give you a ride."

"How do I know you're not dangerous?" she asked. But still smiling.

"Do I look dangerous?" He probably did, he realized. Probably stank of alcohol too.

"One never knows, until it's too late," she said. Nice voice, sultry and low, but with some breeding in it. Definitely not a hooker.

"I'm a professor," he said. "Sociology." Hard word to get your mouth around, and he slurred it a little. "That's as harmless as they come. Where are you going?"

She shrugged, and her loose-necked top slipped down a little, revealing a black bra strap. "Just out for a drink."

Peter thought he could see a bus approaching in the distance behind her. "Good," he said. "I know a great little place. I'll buy you dinner and all the drinks you want."

It worked. As they headed for his car, he found it hard not to laugh out loud. That bitch Sarah wouldn't be gloating much longer. This was going to be rich.

Chapter Six

Angel was above him on the fire escape, but instead of looking up her short skirt as he was tempted, Peter stared at Sarah's rear window. The light was still on, and he thought he could see a shadow moving on her window blind. No doubt staying up late to peck away at her ridiculous book. What arrogance, imagining that she could write a book! She should get a job—probably some nearby restaurant needed a dishwasher.

He made plenty of racket on the metal stairs, hoping she would look out. Suddenly he was inspired. He began to sing "Strangers in the Night."

That did it. The blind moved, and he glimpsed Sarah's face at the window, her Buddha-calm replaced with wide-eyed shock. Her face vanished and the blind fell.

Ha! Popped her stupid little bubble of nirvana.

Luck had been shining on Peter all evening, ever since he had gotten up from Sarah's hot seat. He had taken Angel to a cozy restaurant, and if he hadn't known the maitre-d they wouldn't have gotten in without a reservation. Nice impressive touch of luck there, being slipped in like a celebrity.

The food was the best this town had to offer, and after eating they had enjoyed a lovely conversation. Nice to know that not all women shared Sarah's disparaging opinion of him. Angel had appreciated every joke he had made, every anecdote, every opinion, every glittering gem of wit.

And she was no stupid woman. That was obvious from her manner of speaking—articulate, grammatical, almost bookish. Not that she had spoken much. In fact, she had said next to nothing about herself, but she listened with intelligence, like an ideal student. Sarah could learn plenty from her.

Cheap date too—she had nursed a single glass of Cabernet the whole night, leaving the rest of the bottle to him. But thanks to the food, he now felt lucidly high instead of sloppily drunk.

Angel got her back door unlocked, and he stepped from the fire escape into her dark kitchen. Hot and musty. The kitchen was bare, not even a table.

He followed her nice slender hips into the living room. Just a sofa and a few books, not even in bookcases, but stacked on the mantle. He could scarcely see into the murky dining room, but it looked barer still. Maybe she didn't even live here, maybe the place was her love nest. Maybe she was married.

She went back to the kitchen, and Peter glanced at the books on her mantle. Odd selection, nothing but medical books. *Gray's Anatomy*. Davis and Christopher's *Textbook of Surgery*. Maybe she was a nurse or a medical student. She had said really nothing about herself.

Angel came in with two glasses. God, she was lovely! A goddess from a dream. Made Sarah look like a stick of furniture. She took a small sip from her glass but didn't offer the other glass to him.

"You have to earn yours," she said.

Peter bowed. "Your slave awaits your command, my mistress."

"Remove your clothing," she commanded. "Every stitch. Your mistress wants to see if you are worthy of her attention."

Peter loved games like this. He began with his shoes and socks, then unbuttoned his shirt and pulled it off. Angel sat on the sofa and watched while he undid his pants, let them fall, and kicked them away. He had worn sexy black nylon briefs in hopes that his visit with Sarah would turn out differently; now he slid them down with the slow showmanship of a stripper. His penis began to swell with its own theatrical flair.

"Has your eager slave earned his mistress's approbation?" he asked.

"The mistress is satisfied with the immensity of her subject's devotion," she said, and handed him his glass.

Peter sipped. It was cheap scotch, rather bitter, but at this point in the evening he didn't care.

"Perhaps it would please my mistress to follow suit?" he suggested.

Angel smiled. "For the moment she chooses to look. Then, perhaps, it will please her to touch. And then, if her servant is worthy, she may command him to undress her. Now, stand over here and allow your mistress to examine her servant's body more closely."

He came close to the sofa. Angel's eyes on his body felt even more exciting than hands. She ordered him to turn. Peter drank his scotch and basked in the sun of her eyes, felt them moving down his muscular back to his buttocks, which he tensed for her benefit. Every sweaty hour of working out had been worth the toil. He moved his feet farther apart, picturing the delicious glimpse she was getting of his balls. He gulped down the rest of his scotch.

"Stand there like a good boy," she ordered. "Your mistress shall return anon."

Peter heard her move into the hallway, probably to the bathroom. Getting undressed, no doubt—and he was a little disappointed, remembering her suggestion that he would be allowed to undress her. Well, that wasn't going to ruin his evening. Too bad Angel's apartment wasn't directly above Sarah's so she could hear the bedsprings squeak—rub it right in the bitch's face!

He wandered to the kitchen, found the bottle of scotch on the counter, and refilled his glass. Maybe ice would cut the bitterness, but when he opened the freezer he couldn't see any ice, just some meat or something wrapped in cellophane. No, it looked more like cabbage heads. Who in the hell froze cabbage heads?

He picked one up, looked at it, and felt his legs buckle beneath him. His arms and legs suddenly had no strength, and he collapsed to the floor, unable to move. The severed human head lying on his chest stared at him with frozen eyes. Beneath a frosty black mustache, its thin lips were frozen open in a snarl.

He saw Angel standing above him. She picked up the horrible cellophane-wrapped thing, put it back in the freezer, and shut the door.

She smiled. "What's wrong?" she asked. "Didn't you want me to give you head?"

Chapter Seven

Sarah awoke from a dream of being smothered, and for a moment she didn't recognize the room. For some reason she was expecting her childhood bedroom, and this wasn't it. In a bewildered panic, she raced through her mental files of every place she had lived: Peter's house, the three apartments in Madison, the place—oh yes. Shit. *This* place.

In the same instant, she remembered what had happened last night, Peter singing "Strangers in the Night" while he stumbled up the fire escape with the woman upstairs. No wonder she had slept so badly.

The woman upstairs—Sarah realized she had been dreaming about her. Something creepy, a spectral blonde glowing like a will-o-the-wisp in the moonlight, but she couldn't recall any more of the dream.

She got up slowly, one limb at a time, aching because her second-hand mattress sagged into a circulation-choking rut. She stood naked and stretched, trying to get rid of the kinks and twinges and the residue of her dream. Already hot. She went to the kitchen and discovered a new outrage: she was out of coffee.

As she drove to the grocery store, she saw Peter's Volvo parked around the corner at the side of her building. It was still there when she drove home. The coffee made her feel no better, nor did a bath. She tried to write but couldn't. Peter had pulled some dirty tricks before, but nothing like this.

Yesterday he had started off seeming so contrite, so eager to change, but just when she was tempted to give him another chance he had started bellowing at her, and she knew his bellow all too well. Usually it was a prelude to slamming her up against the wall and slapping her till her nose bled. He weighed twice what she weighed; it wasn't fair.

For two years she had tried to excuse the abuse. After all, he had never punched her with a fist, though sometimes he pounded her against the wall hard enough to leave bruises and an aching skull. Two years of that crap, and she had still wanted to believe him last night. And even after he had started yelling and jabbing a corkscrew at her like a dagger, she had suggested he could call her and they could try to be friends.

So he responded by saying "Fuck you" and going home with her upstairs neighbor.

I'm crazier than he is, she thought. Crazy for ever putting up with him. Crazy for wanting to give him another chance. Crazy for caring what he's doing up there.

In the afternoon Sarah stole out for another look. The Volvo was still there. Unbelievable! Here she was, trying to carve out a little bit of peace in this wretched hellhole so she could write a book, and even that measly scrap of solace he had to steal from her. It seemed like a new way of slamming her against a wall. She had put up with too much abuse from him already. She wasn't going to put up with this.

She climbed the stairs to the second-floor landing and stood at the woman's door, intending to pound on it and demand to see Peter. Or had she in fact come up to eavesdrop? Certainly she was straining to hear them in there, a snatch of baby-talk, a pig-like grunt, a bedspring squeaking, any damned thing.

Sick, she thought. Still, she listened. It was even hotter up here, the air wet and stale and already making her perspire. Was that a moan?

She heard a quiet creaking behind her and spun around. It was the ghost, peering at her from his half-open door, face white as paper, his eyes pale blue.

"Sorry," he said, his voice as faint as his footsteps were each morning. "I thought it was someone at my door."

Sarah just stared.

"Are you a friend of hers?" he asked.

"No. I . . . I just wanted to meet my new neighbors." Sarah was whispering, not wanting Peter to hear her voice through the door. "I haven't met her yet."

The ghost stared at the woman's door, then at Sarah. "Nor have I," he said, "and I've been here a long time. I don't think she's around very often."

"Well, she was here last night," Sarah murmured.

"Was she really? I didn't see her."

Something about his manner, his whiteness, more like smoke or fog than a person. Almost not there.

"Perfect neighbor," he whispered. "Never around, I mean." Then he caught himself and said, "No, I didn't mean I never want to see *you* around."

Embarrassment brought some blood to his face, making him for a moment look more like a human than a ghost. A shy Kafka bug, embarrassed by his own shadow. Someone even weirder than she was.

"My name's Darnell." He gave her a distant smile, not exactly friendly, but gentle. Maybe too shy to be friendly.

"Nice to meet you," she whispered. "My name's Sarah." She started for the stairs.

"You could come in. I could make some coffee."

She could hear how difficult that was for him to say, each word forced through a gauze of shyness.

"Maybe for a minute," she said.

She stepped in, grateful to be out of the landing. Darnell shut the door, and it seemed to her that they both relaxed a little. He led her to the living room and went to the kitchen to make coffee.

His place was identical to hers. The likeness made her uncomfortable; it seemed to make them twins, two ghosts superimposed over each other. Even the contents were similar: books, books, books, and a few sticks of furniture. But one major difference—his place was clean and neat, everything in its place.

She glanced through one of the many bookcases. Every book seemed to be about religion. Lovely, she thought. As soon as he returned with the coffee, he was going to start proselytizing. Sarah was an agnostic, which meant that she couldn't see any reason to believe there was a God, but couldn't see any way to prove there wasn't. She was already dreaming up excuses to get out of there when Darnell drifted in with two cups of coffee, so quietly that she hadn't heard him.

"Can't stay long," she warned him.

"Do you take milk? I'm afraid I only have cream." He placed the cups and a cream pitcher on the coffee table. "Please, sit down."

She perched on the edge of the sofa, ready to bolt in an instant, and Darnell sat facing her in an uncomfortable-looking wooden armchair. He didn't look like someone who cared for comfort. An ascetic, Sarah thought. A weird little monk.

He made coffee the way she did, so strong that without the cream it would strip the skin off your tongue. There was a wooden chessboard at the other end of the coffee table, each piece placed, she noticed, precisely in the center of its square. The game was well underway, and each captured man was neatly arranged on either side of the board by rank, a place for bishops, a place for rooks. Very tidy.

"Good coffee," she said.

"Thanks."

"So you've never seen her?"

"No, she keeps to herself. She always seems to come and go by the fire escape, never uses the stairs." Darnell frowned at his coffee for a while and said, "But I don't like her. Her place gives me the creeps. Sometimes I hear strange sounds."

"Like what?"

"I don't know. It's always late at night, I'm usually asleep. Something will wake me up, maybe her shoes on the fire escape. Then dragging sounds. Thumps, moans . . . muffled cries, like someone gagging. It's hard to get back to sleep."

He looked like a virgin frightened of sex, and Sarah wondered if the sounds of lovemaking were what disturbed him so.

"What do you do?" she asked.

Darnell seemed to be startled from some train of thought. "You mean for a living? I work at the main library. Cataloging."

Silence. Of course he would work at a library. Bartleby the Librarian, haunting the stacks.

When the silence began to sound eerie, Sarah said, "You must be interested in religion," and even as she said it she wondered why she was bringing up a subject she didn't want to talk about.

"Oh," he said. "You mean the books. Religions. Christianity, Judaism, Islam, Buddhism, Hindu, Taoism, Zoroastrianism, etcetera. But I've not yet discovered what I believe."

Darnell rested his elbows on the arms of his uncomfortable-looking chair and placed his chin on his hands. "Christianity seems to come the closest," he said at last. "But you have to read between the lines. And what you find between the lines is the occult. Simon Magus wanting to buy Jesus' secrets of magic from Peter. The Gnostics. The Templars. The alchemists and the mystics."

Another silence. It figured: he looked like a guy who would pore over worthless old books of religion and occultism while other people were out living their lives.

Sarah said, "I guess I don't think about it much. Nothing you can prove, nothing you can see."

"Oh?" Darnell considered this for a while. "Suppose you awoke one day inside a room. There are no windows. No door. You cannot recall how you got there. Let's say there's furniture, lamps and vases, a refrigerator filled with food, everything you need to survive. Some people never wonder what lies outside those walls or how they got there. If they have curious minds, of a scientific nature, perhaps they carefully measure the legs of the chairs, the tops of the tables. If their curiosity is on a grand scale, perhaps they even measure the walls and the ceiling, or rap on the floor to see if it sounds hollow. But they tell themselves that nothing lies outside the walls, and that no one built the room and put them inside it. Doesn't that strike you as odd?"

"I guess if there's no window, then there's not much point in wondering what's out there," she said.

"Maybe not."

He thought some more, his delicate chin resting on his fingers. Really not a bad-looking guy, Sarah thought. With his slender bones and almost colorless hair, he was the opposite of Peter. She noticed that his eyes never strayed to her breasts. He seemed asexual—not gay, not straight, just not.

"But what if there were others in the room who swore they'd glimpsed the outside?" Darnell asked. "Wouldn't you be curious to hear what they said?"

"I dunno. That doesn't prove anything. Maybe they're just lunatics."

"And what about your own dreams?" he asked. "What if you dreamt of the outside again and again? What would you do then?"

"Jeez. Maybe get a different pillow or something."

Darnell smiled faintly. "Do you believe in evil?"

"Sure. People do rotten things all the time."

"No. Evil with a capital E. Something apart from the self."

"No. People do evil things. Squirrels don't. Rocks don't. That's all the word means, lousy behavior, breaking the rules. The rest is baloney."

He thought about this for a minute. Sarah pulled at her sweaty shirt. Darnell apparently didn't own a fan. Nor did he seem to need one: he looked perfectly comfortable in his long-sleeve white shirt and long black trousers. He had probably never worn shorts in his life.

"Don't you believe in souls?" he asked.

It was the kind of question that ordinarily made her uncomfortable or impatient, but Darnell's gaze was soothing, and somehow from his lips the question seemed more compelling than it would from someone else's. Sarah was about to quibble over the word—what did he mean by soul, the personality?—but his eyes reminded her of the cool waters of the creek where she and Johnny used to play.

"I used to have a brother named Johnny," she said. "Two years younger, cutest little guy in the world. I can still remember when Mom brought him home from the hospital, his big round face, little tuft of hair. He was so cute he made me jealous."

She wondered why she was telling this weird wisp of fog about Johnny. His cool blue eyes seemed hypnotic, vague as the sky but never bored.

"I fell in love with him," she continued. "He was my doll-baby, my . . . I can't describe him, such a happy little guy, I mean a smile that would melt ice. When we got older I liked playing with him better even than my girlfriends. He was my best buddy. I don't think I was ever innocent. I mean, I came into this world with an attitude, and I've been on the warpath ever since. But not Johnny. He was like the sun. If I wanted to play hide and seek, then he did too. If I wanted to play school and be the mean old bitch teacher and make him sit in the corner for being a dumb little brat, well then that was okay with him too."

Darnell's eyes seemed to listen as closely as his ears, with the kind of benign caring that one hoped for in the ideal priest, a priest so detached from his body that he felt neither lust nor greed. Though it wasn't like Sarah to open her heart to strangers, she found herself eagerly telling the story.

"So anyway, when I was 12 he ran out in the road and got hit by a car. I was on the front porch tying my shoes—I saw it happen. I ran out screaming my head off. The bumper had hit his head. His face . . . there was blood."

"You needn't picture it," Darnell said. "There's no point in that."

"The person driving the car was an old woman. She hadn't seen him. She sat in the car, too upset to get out. Johnny wasn't dead, not yet."

Sarah stopped. After all these years, she couldn't tell the story without a pain in her throat. Nothing else in her life had ever been so terrible; nothing else ever could be.

"There's a point to this," she said. "That night Mom and Dad and I were sitting around his hospital bed when he let his spirit go. I mean literally let it go—I saw it leave. It seemed to exhale from his mouth. I saw a glow, like a cloud of sunlight. It floated above his body, just hovered there, and I could feel it saying goodbye to us. We all saw it, even Dad. The room felt peaceful, not so sad, though of course we were all crying. And then it left. Ascended. And we knew he was gone."

She met Darnell's eyes. There was something of the same peace in them, though cooler, not radiant as the cloud of sunlight had been.

"So I guess I believe we have souls," she said. "I don't know what they are, maybe some force of the personality, I don't know, that connects people who care about each other, or something like that." She made a face. "I guess that's what's called gibberish."

Darnell watched her thoughtfully. "A force. Yes, I agree. But you believe it fades after one dies?"

"I don't tell many people about this," she said. "But my brother has come to me more than once. Not like a ghost—more like a comforting glow of sunshine when I need it. The last time was when my parents died—Johnny came to me and helped me through. He was a hell of a lot more helpful than my boyfriend, I can tell you that."

Darnell smiled, not a big broad smile like Johnny's, but there was some of the same meekness. "You know what psychologists would say," he said. "That what you describe is wish fulfillment. They'd say when we're distressed, our minds invent whatever will soothe us."

"Sure," she answered. "But I know what daydreams are, and Johnny's presence isn't anything like that. It's palpable. He's not just some dream-kid. There've been a thousand times I wanted him to be there but couldn't conjure him up. He comes when he comes. If I'm just fulfilling wishes, why can't I snap my fingers and make him appear?"

Darnell apparently had no answer for this. He was silent for a minute, no longer watching her but staring at the chessboard instead. The blue of his eyes seemed to flicker, as if a dream were passing through them.

"I envy you," he said at last. "The spirit that haunts you is made of sunshine. What if it were made of something not so friendly?

Darkness . . . dreadful sounds . . . things that groan in the night?"
Sarah saw that he too was sweating.

Chapter Eight

Peter's car was still there Sunday morning. In the middle of the afternoon, Sarah went out for another look, and there it was. Incredible. Didn't he need to go out for condoms or something?

She returned to her apartment, hot and miserable, and didn't even bother to sit in front of her computer. There was no point in pretending she could work. She should get out of the apartment, but that might mean missing his exit. Why was she so interested? Let him screw his heart out, catch syphilis and gonorrhea, why should she care?

But she did. She wished she had a peephole into the woman's apartment. If he was going to be nesting up there like an obscene vulture, she should at least be allowed a glimpse into the nest. Was this abnormal? Probably, but she had no statistics to tell her.

She tried to convince herself that her curiosity was driven by concern instead of voyeurism. The strange noises Darnell claimed to have heard from the woman's apartment—what had he said? Moans, muffled cries? Sounded like sex, and no doubt sex was what she was wishing she could see or hear, maybe just to fuel her anger.

No sense trying to make it sound healthy, she thought. It was masochism, pure and simple. Peter was trying to torture her, and she was eagerly lending a hand.

She ate a tuna sandwich for dinner, sitting by the kitchen window so she could see him if he came down the fire escape, but nothing was descending except the sun. Surely he wasn't going to spend another night! Didn't he have to teach tomorrow? Maybe she had missed hearing him leave? She finished her sandwich and went back out to see if his car was still there.

It was. The sun getting low in the west, and the Volvo hadn't budged. Too fucking much.

All day she had been considering going to meet her downstairs neighbor. No sense in trying to make that sound healthy either, pretending that her chief interest was being a good neighbor. Nope—whoever lived there must have been getting an earful, and maybe she would like to share a scrap of what she had heard.

Sarah stepped across the landing and knocked. She waited and knocked again. She could hear a television's canned laughter, and it seemed to be laughing at her. She didn't blame it. She was about to retreat to the gloomy safety of her own apartment when a faint voice said, "Who's there?"

"Hi. I'm Sarah. I moved into apartment A."

Sarah heard bolts being drawn, a lock turning, and the door came open the two inches that the chain allowed. A bespectacled eye peered out, blinked.

"Hi," Sarah said again. "I just moved in, I thought it'd be nice—"

"Just a minute."

A bony claw moved to the chain, fumbled and trembled, and the door opened to reveal a very old black woman half a foot shorter than Sarah. Her hair was pure white and braided, the braids wrapped and pinned neatly on her head like a cap. She wore a flowered dress that nearly touched the floor.

"Hi, I live—" Sarah started to repeat, but the old woman interrupted with, "I heard you, I heard you. I ain't altogether deaf yet. Sarah, that's a right pretty name. My name's Esther Robison. I was speculating who moved in there. Come in, Sarah, and make yourself at home."

The tiny woman's step was quick and agile. Sarah followed her along the short hallway to the mirror-image of her own living room, but this one was dark, lit only by the TV screen and a single lamp with a dim bulb, and it was cluttered with old chairs and stands and cabinets and vases and photos and knickknacks and a hundred other things half-hidden in the shadowy nooks and corners. The windows were all closed, sealing in hot air scented with lavender and must and old woman.

Sarah could tell that the gooseneck rocking chair in front of the TV was where Esther usually sat, so she chose the sofa covered with worn pink fabric, its wooden arms carved to resemble bunches of grapes.

Esther shut off the TV, making the room even darker. "Would you like some tea? I got a kettle warming."

"Yes, that would be nice."

The old woman disappeared into the kitchen, and Sarah gazed into the dining room, where a table and chairs and china cupboard were not so much visible as suggested in the thick shadows. The silence, the darkness, and the stale air made her feel as if the city were far away. She listened for a sound from upstairs. Nothing, just Esther in her kitchen.

The old woman returned, a large teapot trembling in her hands and tilting so that tea dribbled out of its spout onto the threadbare Oriental rug.

"Let me help you."

"No, no, that's fine." Esther managed to place the teapot onto the coffee table without too much damage, and then disappeared into the darkness of the dining room. There was a clatter of china, and she emerged with cups and saucers.

"D'you like sugar?" she asked.

"No thank you." In fact Sarah did, but she thought the woman's exertions had been enough for one evening.

Esther sank into her gooseneck rocker as lightly as a dried-up leaf. "Just let it steep for a minute and then maybe you can pour it," she said. "Spect you find it a mite warm in here, don't you? Heat don't mean much to me no more, but the cold go right through me. I gotta keep them windows closed count of the neighborhood ain't what it used to be. My daughter tell me, Ma, get outta here and come live with me, but I ain't going nowhere at my age. I lived here ever since my husband died back in '82.

"Awful nice a you to come by. I don't get much company no more, 'cept my daughter Marcy come by every week. Maybe you seen her? She bring me all kind a groceries, everything I need. Never miss a week to visit me, that girl. She getting up, though, I spect she must be, le'see, she must be 76, 77 year old now. She don't look it though, if you was to see her. She always been right pretty, that girl. See how that tea's doing there, will you, honey?"

Footsteps, directly overhead. Someone, at least, was ambulatory up there. The sound was somehow reassuring, taking the upstairs drama out of the theater of sick fantasy and placing it in the real world. The footsteps moved west through the hallway, probably to the bedroom, and dissolved again into silence. Great. Time for another bout of sweaty lovemaking.

"Me, I'm 98, and I sure do look it," Esther was saying. "No, don't be saying nothing flattery, I'm showing my age and that's a plain fact. In the canister there, I mean the one with the roses, you find some sugar. If you just stir four lumps in mine I 'preciate it. Always liked it sweet. Much 'bliged. Marcy, she the only one a my kids still alive. Oh, I got grandchildren and great-grandchildren, and I even got me some great-great-grandchildren. Can't 'member all their names. Most a them live down in Virginia, and I don't get to see 'em more'n once in a blue moon. Coulda swore you said you didn't take no sugar. Now, where was I? My husband Sam, he died back in '82. Weren't no surprise neither, way he smoking them cigarettes every waking hour . . ."

The teapot emptied, and Sarah half-listened to the old woman while keeping her ears alert for another sound from upstairs. Esther Robison could remember when the neighborhood had been filled with flowers and church bells and playing children—"and nice children too, not the kind like to slit your gizzard sooner'n look at you."

At last she talked herself out. "You got folk yourself?" she asked Sarah.

Sarah told her about her parents' death. She started to say something about Peter, how he hadn't been much help, when suddenly there was a loud groan from the direction of the upstairs bedroom.

Esther cocked her head. A few seconds later, there was a low, deep moaning—either the world's greatest orgasm or someone in serious pain. Esther shook her head and clucked her tongue with disgust.

"Have you ever met her?" Sarah asked. "The woman who lives up there?"

"I ain't met her, but I seen her. Pretty thing, I guess. She ain't there too often, and when she come in she like as not be sneaking up the back way, up the far 'scape, always on a Friday. Almost always got a man with her, and always a different one too. I can tell you reliable she don't really live up there. Bet you five dollars she married, and she renting this place on the sly just to take her boyfriends on the weekend when her husband ain't looking."

"I saw her bring someone up Friday night," Sarah said.

Maybe there had been something funny about the way she said it, something in her voice that caused Esther to peer at her through her spectacles.

"He wouldn't be a friend of yours, I s'pose?"

"Well . . ." And Sarah for some reason told her the whole story.

Ester sat frowning and thinking for a while after Sarah finished. "Don't like to poke my nose where it don't belong," she said. "But do I hope, child, that he eventually come back down."

What on earth did that mean?

"I ain't altogether deaf yet, and when you get my age sleep don't come too regular. I guess I hear most everything. You gonna say I'm crazy, and maybe I am, but men go up that far 'scape with her—and sometimes they don't come back down."

Jeez. It made no sense. Probably they came down while the old woman slept.

But when was Peter going to come down?

"But if he do come down, it'll be tonight," Esther said. "Always Sunday night when they leave. Them that leaves, that is."

The two women listened, but there were no more sounds. Sarah looked at her watch: almost 9:00. She thanked Esther and promised to fix dinner sometime soon for her. As she stepped into the landing, it felt as if she were leaving an airless den, but as she entered her own place, silent and dark, it seemed just as stifling.

After midnight, as she lay drifting in and out of sleep on the sofa, she heard footsteps, slow and stumbling, on the fire escape. She hurried to the study window and peered past the blind.

It was Peter. He was alone, shuffling slowly down the iron steps, hanging on to the rail to keep from falling.

He looked very drunk. But this time he wasn't singing.

Chapter Nine

Though Peter was no longer perched over Sarah's head in his love-nest, he still seemed to hover like a vulture over her thoughts. She thought she had known all of his flaws as well as she knew her own, but this raw crudity was something new. She didn't know what to expect next. Every sound upset her, as if he might be at her door or ascending the fire escape steps again to perform another crude burlesque.

As with any Punch and Judy show, there was a touch of the sinister. Esther's words stayed in her mind: "Sometimes they don't come back down."

Howard Goldwin called her on Thursday. "Sare, my love, have I got tales for you. About your sexy-exy."

"Got a few of my own," she said, and she told him everything that had happened.

"You must meet me for a drink," Howard said.

As she turned the corner from her street, she looked to make sure that Peter's car wasn't back. It was an irritating new compulsion, just one other way that he had infected her peace of mind.

Howard was waiting for her at a bar near his house, seated at his favorite table on the patio so he could smoke. Unfortunately, Paul Finney was with him. Sarah had been hoping for a private conversation.

"Sare, my love. You know Dr. Finney, don't you?"

She could tell by his expression that Howard would prefer privacy too, but there was no getting rid of Paul Finney. He was a man who needed a lot of company, people to watch him drink. Short and unattractive, he looked like a fat leprechaun. The department tolerated him because he had tenure and he had published a few important books before the bottle had dissolved his wits.

Finney rose halfway from his chair and smiled. "It is a pleasure to see you again, my dear." He sounded like a fat leprechaun too.

Sarah nodded. A waiter came out as she sat down, and she ordered a cappuccino.

Howard lit a cigarette and stroked his elegant mustache. He was a slender man of about fifty, perfectly groomed, his dyed black hair combed with a fanciful hint of a wave at the sides.

"Well, where shall I begin?" he said. "Let's start with The Gossip According to Karl Hoffmann. By the way, I suppose you've heard that the illustrious Dr. Hoffmann has befriended Emily Larkins?"

She hadn't.

"Well, but of course you know Dr. Hoffmann?"

She didn't.

"My dear! You are the last of the anchorites! Everyone knows Hoffmann. He's a very popular figure at the faculty club because after one drink he's absolutely powerless to stop his tongue. He would describe the condition of his own grandmother's under-drawers if anyone were to ask him. So he recounted a most lurid tale, no doubt related to him in the strictest confidence by Ms. Emily.

"Picture this. It is Sunday night, in fact by now it's the wee hours of Monday morning. Imagine that you are Ms. Emily, lying in Peter's bed in the grips of deepest anxiety because you've neither seen nor heard from your Romeo for days—since Friday morning to be precise. Has he been beset by thugs? Or perhaps by wicked wenches? Can it be that he's suffering amnesia caused by a bump on the head and is now residing somewhere in New Jersey, quite unable to recall the name of the woman who haunts his dreams?

"Ah, but you perceive a sound, a key in the front door, a familiar footstep in the hallway. Your Ulysses has returned from the dark unknown! You hear him approaching the bedchamber. You tremble beneath the sheet, in dread of fainting. Suddenly he is there in the room—but, alas, he seems perfectly oblivious of your presence. He lurches blindly through the darkness, muttering strange words out loud, the most shocking obscenities peppered with utter gibberish. His clothing is soiled, and he reeks of the sewer. The air of the room is overcome with noisome effluvia, the vile stench of loathsome bodily secretions that better we leave unnamed."

Paul Finney began to chortle and choked on his scotch. He gasped for air, his eyes bulging. "Howard! You are positively cruel!"

"At last, in great alarm," Howard continued, "you switch on the bedside lamp and call out his beloved name. He covers his eyes and bellows as if he's been struck by a cudgel. 'Who's there?' he cries, and his voice makes your very hackles rise like quills upon the fretful porpentine."

Howard stopped. "Oh. You've drunk all your cappuccino. Allow me to buy you another." Like Scheherazade, he loved to suspend his stories in mid-climax.

"If I could trouble you for another scotch," Paul Finney said.

Trying to ignore Finney's pathetic eyes, Sarah watched Howard walk into the bar. Usually she found his outlandish performances amusing, but today she was put off by his tone. She wasn't convinced there was anything funny about this story. It sounded as if Peter was suffering a nervous breakdown or maybe slipping into psychosis.

But then, Howard exaggerated everything. He could turn a minor spat at the faculty club into Armageddon. Probably Peter had merely come home with a hangover and a sore pecker.

Howard placed their fresh drinks on the table and reseated himself, carefully adjusting the crease of his trousers as he crossed his long legs. "Well, where was I?"

After Peter had covered his eyes, as if the light hurt them, he had begun to threaten Emily. What was she doing in his house? Did she imagine that she lived there? He had grabbed her roughly and wrestled her to the front door and had thrown her out into the yard—stark naked. A moment later he hurled out her car keys and purse and locked the door. The terrified woman had no place to go; she was allowing a couple of Asian students to stay at her apartment.

"So of course she drove, naked as the good Lady Godiva, to the house of Dr. Hoffmann, who, aroused from his slumbers, found in his heart the commendable charity to give bed and shelter to the hapless nudist."

"Jeez."

Howard looked disappointed. "I thought you would find this amusing."

"What's going on?" Sarah asked. She kept thinking of Esther's comment: "Sometimes they don't come down."

"The old boy's flipping his wig," Howard said. He stroked his mustache and grinned, obviously not sharing her concern. "My diagnosis would be that he's become so full of himself that there's no longer any room for his wits. They have fled, seeking more hospitable accommodations."

"I seem to have missed part of this story," Finney complained. "Where *was* Bellman over the weekend?"

"Visiting Sarah's upstairs neighbor," Howard said. Sarah wished he would keep his mouth shut, but he quickly told Finney everything that Sarah had related to him about the mysterious blonde.

"So every Friday she emerges to find a man," said Finney. He seemed to find this the most fascinating part of the story. As he gazed thoughtfully at his drink, Sarah could discern the hint of a once-handsome face beneath his sagging features. "Every Friday," he repeated.

"Book Two," Howard said. "Shall we call it The Apocalypse? As related—to the office of the Dean, no less—by six or seven young undergraduates enrolled in Soc. 237. It appears that Monday and Tuesday our addled protagonist forgot to come teach his class or even to call in, for that matter. But yesterday he made an appearance, a rather disheveled one I regret to say. I'm told his hygiene was questionable, his clothing less than pristine, his handsome face obscured beneath a scruffy growth of beard." Howard leaned toward Sarah and lowered his voice. "I have it on good authority that his fly gaped open!

"Now, we all know that Professor Bellman is famous for his dramatic lectures, but by all accounts this one quite out-Heroded all his others. Almost in the nature, I gather, of one of those Elizabethan melodramas, *Titus Andronicus* let us say. Perfectly incomprehensible, at least to the bewildered undergraduates, but replete with menacing phrases and ominous declarations, all delivered in the most thunderous voice, a terrible volcanic rumble as if Vulcan himself were standing before them. And as the great man orated, he seemed to become transfixed by one particular young lady who sat in the front row, a mere innocent child, possibly even an unsullied virgin."

Howard let out a thin, deliberate stream of smoke, contemplating this unlikely possibility with obvious pleasure. Finney began to chortle again.

"As I say, Peter seemed to address his every sulfurous word to this young lady, drawing closer and closer to her as he spoke, until he was just inches in front of her—his gaping fly not a foot from her tender face. Holding her eyes with his, he reached out and stroked the side of her face, no doubt seeking to draw her attention more closely to his words. And then . . . and then his hand, perhaps desiring even more astute attention, slid down her slender neck, and from thence to her prim young bosom, slipping inside of her shirt and even, I am told, inside of her brassiere to kindle the ardent flames of scholarship there. The wholesome maiden was for a moment too mortified to move. But then her Christian instincts took over, and she leaped from her seat and delivered a swift knee to his crotch. His agony, I am told, was quite pathetic to behold."

As Howard had neared the end of his story, the gleeful expression had gradually faded from his face. Now he sat and smoked with the same brooding expression that Sarah wore.

"I suppose it's really not so very amusing," he admitted.

"Every Friday she hunts for a man," Paul Finney said. "I wonder . . . do you think she has such a drastic effect on all of them as she had on Bellman?"

"Perhaps she's discovered a lost chapter of the *Kama Sutra*," Howard suggested.

Sarah shot him an impatient look. "I'm not so sure it's a laughing matter." She told them what Darnell and Esther had said.

"Muffled cries," Howard repeated. "Dragging sounds. And now Peter behaving like a madman. God, I would love to know what went on up there."

Finney stared at his empty glass. "So would I," he said. "And this Friday, I believe I shall endeavor to find out."

***

Peter Bellman stared into his refrigerator. Not much there: he hadn't been to the grocery store since his Awakening. Such details as grocery stores and gas bills were hard to focus on, once the big truths were before you.

Still, eating was important, he mused, and he was going to have to learn to attend to the mundane necessities. After the Pentecost had scorched them with tongues of flame, the disciples still must have needed to bother with their purses, their larders, the condition of their sandals. Revelation unfortunately didn't do your laundry for you.

He found some cheese, salami, an onion, and a few pieces of bread. He sat at the kitchen table and began to eat, not bothering to make a sandwich. He would bite a hunk from the cheese, stick a piece of salami in his mouth, then a piece of bread, and chew. The salami had become slimy and the bread had green spots, but this didn't bother him. The most complex and interesting flavors derived from aging and fermentation. Only fools would pay a premium for Stilton but throw away their moldy Swiss.

He wore nothing but a pair of dark glasses. He had hung blankets over the windows and the sliding glass doors to make the place as dark as possible. His eyes still hadn't readjusted to light. Fine with him. Now he knew light for what it was—a distraction from the truths that danced and walked through the dark for those with eyes to see.

The truths of night were all that mattered, Peter reflected, his mouth stuffed with rancid meat and bread. But the mundane details were part of the scheme, and they mustn't be ignored. He had been careless with details all week, clumsy like a weight lifter not yet used to his new strength.

It didn't bother him that he had been excused from his teaching duties for the remainder of the term. Good—he had more important work to do. But he had been foolish to evangelize to his class—as if those callow children would have ears to hear. One girl had given the appearance of understanding, but of course it had been a pretense, pretending to be all ears just to get a good grade, no doubt. She might keep up that pretense her whole life, but to what purpose? In the end, in her box, she would be alone with her F.

Peter washed down his food with a mouthful of scotch, drinking straight from the bottle. Next to last bottle—tomorrow he needed to go to the liquor store. That was one detail he wouldn't neglect.

When the sun went down he carried the bottle with him to the backyard and climbed into the hot tub. He sat in the tepid water in the deepening twilight with his sunglasses on and drank his scotch and meditated on the profound secrets of the shadows.

He thought of the Solitary One who hid in shadows. The Solitary One was a motionless dance of dark enigmas, a sleeping scripture of whispered riddles, the living dead who ruled the living, an inky blot of black fury locked away in a secret place, his anger crackling like midnight lightning in a frenzy to be free. Soon he would be, and then woe to all those who were not his friends!

Something floating on the water brushed up against him. Peter had to reach around and touch it before he remembered. Pocahontas had gotten on his nerves for the last time. He recalled with pleasure holding the cat beneath the water and watching its legs kick. Now it was as stiff as a board. He scratched the wet fur beneath the cat's chin and felt himself getting an erection.

"What's the matter, widdle puddy cat?" he murmured. "Do you miss Sarah? Don't worry, we'll go see her soon."

Chapter Ten

Even after his limbs went numb, Professor Paul Finney still believed it was a game. He was used to strange games.

He knew he was no longer an attractive man, his face having gone to seed and his body to fat. The promises of his younger days— a brilliant reputation as a scholar, a loving marriage—had proven to be lies, and the only redemption for his disappointments he had found not in the chalice but in the bottle. Part of his paycheck went automatically to his ex-wife, now living in Oregon with his three children and a slender, dapper man whom Paul had once trusted as a brother. The other part went to the bartender.

Men with his unimpressive assets sometimes had to play strange games or else go home alone. Finney had played them all, BDSM complete with leather and cuffs, dress-up games with the woman done up like Bo Peep sans panties, or with him squeezing his girth into a servant's livery many sizes too small. He had applied the lash to pink rumps that during the workweek sat in secretary's chairs; he had pretended to sneak like the midnight rambler through the bedroom window of a bored housewife who pretended to be atwitter with fear; he had even, God help him, donned the collar of a priest to hear the randy confessions of a fifty-year-old frump who had all the while tested the good father's chastity in various inventive ways.

He had developed a tolerance for kinkiness, but little taste for it. What Finney most ardently craved in the privacy of his mind was the most extraordinary kink of them all: a devoted, loving, monogamous, ordinary relationship with one lifelong mate. But for some reason it pleased the fates to deny him this extraordinary kink and to make him instead a pudgy jester in the monotonous house of games.

Earlier tonight he had parked beside Sarah Temple's apartment building and watched for her upstairs neighbor to come down. He had waited an hour or more, feeling foolish and wanting a drink, but determined not to back out of his plan. He was doing it because he had drunkenly boasted to Howard and Sarah that he would. And because he was hoping the evening would provide a good story. A good story would ensure that for a week or two people would want to sit at his table and drink with him. And most of all, he was doing it because he wanted to get laid.

The woman had come down at last, and even from his car he could see that she was a looker. She got on a bus, and Finney followed it until the woman got out and entered a bar. He found a parking place, followed her in, and offered to buy her a drink before any of the other men had a chance. There was an odd cast to her face that made her even more beautiful, something childish and mysterious in her smile that teased a deep nerve in Finney's desire.

One drink did it; Angel was obviously out to find a man and apparently wasn't too particular. They had gone back to her apartment, a starkly bare place with a bad smell. She gave him a drink and before long she cajoled him into pulling off his clothes, even though revealing his flabby body was always an embarrassment for him. Angel sat on the sofa fully dressed, teasing him and making him turn in silly circles so that she could see every ounce of his fat.

And then Finney's legs had gone numb, and he had fallen weakly to the floor.

At first it seemed to be just another game, and he lay there barely able to move in a heap on the living room floor, feeling absurd, wishing in his heart that he were instead lying in the arms of a faithful wife, in a bed that required no games to make it exciting.

He saw Angel leaning over him, smiling.

"A nice strong sedative to calm you down," she said. "You'll stay awake but your muscles will feel like wet noodles for a while. You may find breathing a bit difficult for the next few hours, especially with all the booze in your system, but if you concentrate you should be able to manage it."

She was right: breathing was becoming a chore. He tried to yell for help but was able to squeeze out no more than a sickly moan.

She left the room and returned with chains and a set of handcuffs. She bound his arms behind his back with the cuffs, wrapped his legs with a chain, and sat him up with his back against the sofa so she could wrap another chain around his chest and abdomen. She locked the chains with padlocks.

She dragged him out of the living room, down the short hallway, and into the dark bedroom. Except it wasn't really a bedroom because there was no bed or dresser, just some unlit black candles stuck in wooden candle holders that surrounded the one and only furnishing, waiting there in the center of the floor for him with its lid wide open.

A casket.

Angel dragged him up next to it until his head leaned against the side. The wood was weathered and rough, as if the thing had been buried in the ground at one time. Then she grabbed him under the armpits and lifted. He was heavy, and it took some doing to get him inside.

For a while his shoulders lay over the top, his head dangling partway in, and he saw that the cloth lining was torn and filthy. It stank horribly of piss, vomit, shit, and decayed flesh. Then he was inside, flat on his back, and he could see three steel hasps bolted to the lid, heavy enough to lock the casket like a safe.

His panic was larger than he was; he hadn't enough room inside to hold all of it, but there was no way to let it out. He struggled to scream, but his throat was paralyzed like his limbs, and only a ghastly groan emerged.

He saw her looking down at him.

"You'll be able to scream after the drug wears off," she said. "The coffin lining will muffle the sound, so feel free to indulge yourself. But be careful not to use up all your air. There are only six small air holes, down there by your feet, so choose your screams carefully. Don't waste them calling out to God. God shuns the darkness. He's no help when you're locked in the bad box."

Angel leaned forward and kissed him tenderly on the lips.

"But there *is* a friend in there," she said.

She pushed her long blond hair out of her face and gazed at him for several minutes, an oddly gentle expression on her face, curious, probing, as if trying to read the message of horror written in his eyes.

"Befriend the one who can help you," she said. "Remember, in the box black always wins."

The lid closed and he heard the three steel hasps snapping shut. After a long while Finney's limbs and vocal cords regained their vigor, and he screamed and thrashed like a terrified child calling for his mother.

And then eventually the darkness responded.

Chapter Eleven

Sunday afternoon Howard Goldwin called Sarah. "Sare, have you
heard anything from Paul Finney?"

"No. Why should I?"

"*No* one has. He promised me he would call Saturday with all the
lurid details. I mean about his cockamamie plan to debauch your
mysterious neighbor."

"I saw him staggering up there Friday night," she said. "Stupid.
Very dumb."

"Is he still up there?"

"Probably. You know what Esther said. They come down
Sunday night . . . if they come down."

"You don't really think that . . . that . . ."

"Dunno what I think. You know what his car looks like?"

"Yes. A pile of blue dents with four wheels. Let's see, I believe it
used to be a Buick."

"Just a minute." Sarah stepped into the sunroom and looked at
the parked cars. "Think maybe I see it," she said.

Howard sighed. "There's not a woman on this planet who could
keep Paul out of a bar so long, unless she owns a still. Please call me
if you see him leave, my love."

Sarah had been feeling ashamed of herself all weekend.
Thursday at the bar she had made the motions of trying to talk
Finney out of his plan, but not very hard. In fact she had been more
interested in learning what went on up there than in talking a foolish
drunk out of a bad idea. Friday night she had watched from her
window like a voyeur while Finney climbed the fire escape. Now she
was disgusted with herself and worried.

After dinner, she decided to visit Darnell. Maybe he had heard
something from across the hall. Maybe his monkish serenity would
take the edge off her nervousness. She climbed to the hot upstairs
landing and knocked. Darnell opened his door a few inches and
gazed out with a wary look and no greeting.

"Hi," she said. "Like some company?"

He let her in without a word, staring for a moment at the door across the landing before shutting and barring his door. This time he didn't offer her coffee. He sat silently in his wooden armchair and stared at his hands folded in front of him. They were squirming slowly.

"How've you been?" she asked.

"Not well."

"I'm sorry. Are you sick?"

"Just not well."

"Maybe I should leave you alone?"

"No. Stay."

"Something I didn't tell you," she said. "The guy who was visiting your neighbor last weekend—I know him."

Darnell's hands stopped squirming. "You *know* him?"

"I used to live with him. Guess I was sort of eavesdropping when you saw me. That's not all—I also know the guy who's there right now."

She told him about Paul Finney. Darnell stared at her with astonishment. Tonight his blue eyes looked glacial, arctic.

"You sent a friend to her?" he asked. "To that . . . *gorgon*? I find this hard to believe. You have no idea what you're dealing with, no idea. You think she's just a woman like any other."

"I thought you said you didn't know her."

He shot her an icy look. "There are ways of knowing other than seeing with your eyes," he said. "Materialists are idiots. They squint through their peepholes and imagine that the little bit they see is all there is."

At first Sarah thought he was castigating her for spying, but as Darnell ranted on she wasn't so sure.

"Eyes are just peepholes. So are ears. The brain's a wonderful device, but mostly it just processes information from the peepholes. Materialists imagine that without our bodies, there'd be no sounds or sights or thoughts. But we all possess a force more powerful than the peeping Toms can imagine."

"I don't see what this has to do with—" Sarah began, but Darnell cut her off.

"Some people, I tell you, have traveled outside of their bodies. As we all do when we die. As your brother did. And these people see with stronger eyes, not with peepholes. And they realize that the only reason they ever needed those peepholes was because they were trapped inside their bodies."

Darnell placed his hands on his temples and seemed to look at something that wasn't in the room. This was too much like raving, and Sarah wanted to change the subject. She noticed the chessboard on the coffee table, its neatly placed pieces suspended in the midst of a bloody battle.

"Do you play often?" she asked.

"I go to the chess club some evenings," he answered impatiently. "Usually I just play alone."

"That must get monotonous."

"On the contrary. It's very challenging. No matter how well I play, I always lose."

Sarah smiled. "But you must also always win, if you're playing by yourself."

He glared at her as if she were impossibly dense. "I always lose," he said. "I play white. Black always wins."

Jeez, she thought. So much for serenity. She stood and said, "I need to get back to work."

"Wait."

She sat back down, but Darnell didn't say anything for a while. He studied the chessboard, his hands struggling with each other in a slow, grim contest.

"One move from checkmate," he muttered.

"Really, I have to be going."

"She's getting stronger," he said quietly. "I live next door to her, and I tell you I can feel her power like poisonous radiation seeping through the walls. It always happens suddenly—one day all of a sudden she's stronger. It happened again last week."

"What are you talking about?"

"I'm talking about *her*, the one who makes men groan like ghosts in the night. Soon she shall make all of us groan."

He stared intently at the chessboard as if witnessing a battle of flesh and blood. His hands squirmed and wrestled.

Sarah got up again and this time made it to the door before he seemed to notice.

"Wait," he said. He hurried to the door and grasped her wrist. His hand felt feverishly hot.

"I like you," he said.

"I like you too."

"Get out of here. Get out tonight. You can pick up your things later, just get out. You're not safe here. Nobody is."

His grip was stronger than one would expect from such a slender man. Sarah had to unlock his fingers one by one. Darnell seemed hardly to notice; his eyes had become frozen in place. She freed her wrist and hurried down the stairs, her legs rubbery.

When she looked back from the landing, he still stood there, his hand open now like a beggar's, his eyes gazing at the door across from his.

Chapter Twelve

"Have you learned a name?" a voice kept asking him.

To Paul Finney the words were meaningless. He had been hearing many obscure messages, and he had chosen not to make sense of them because he knew they were malevolent and depraved. The words were abominations, so he had taken refuge in madness to keep from hearing them.

"Tell me what you've learned," the voice said, but the words meant nothing to Finney.

Nothing was real except thirst and hunger and pain and madness. His madness was a shelter from the pestilence. And though the madness rendered him a fool, he felt safe and comfortable inside it. It was a loving madness.

Madness was the ideal marriage.

The voice despised his madness and was trying to lure him out of it. So in his mind Finney turned the words into stones sculpted into unreadable shapes. They were harmless that way.

There was a sharp pain in his head again. The pain was light. Mustn't open his eyes—too bright out there. But for a moment he did, and he saw her face. The woman, the game-player. Angel.

She had opened the lid of the casket, and the words made of stone were tumbling from her mouth, but earlier they had tumbled from the darkness itself, from something unspeakably horrible that hid in the darkness.

There was a terrible spasm in his back, and he realized that she was forcing him to sit up.

"You have learned a name," she said. "Tell it to me and you'll live. If you don't tell me I'll cut off your head."

He opened one eyelid just a crack and saw that she was holding a sword.

"This is your last chance," she said. "Tell me the name or off with your head."

But Finney hid inside his madness and turned her words into harmless hieroglyphs.

Suddenly a stark, fiery agony struck his madness away.

"So there!" she said.

An incredible pain had rendered him glaringly sane, and in the sharp light of sanity he opened his eyes and saw her hand reaching down to grab his hair. Then the room tilted and he seemed to be going for a weightless ride up into the air.

She turned his face down so he could see the bloody headless body beneath him. A fat, naked body.

His body.

The decapitated carcass slid out of view as the bright room rotated, and then his eyes were just a few inches away from hers. He was staring at her face, and it wore the same mysterious smile that had teased his desire in some bar one Friday night an eternity ago.

Finney saw her lips move but couldn't hear her words, not because his madness protected him, but because his ears were dying. Then his eyes began to die too, and as the harsh light faded the room began to disappear into a darkening fog.

And then her face began to disappear too, until at last all he could see were her lips smiling.

***

Sarah sat in her kitchen in the dark drinking coffee at the flimsy folding card table. She was peering through her window at the fire escape, watching for Paul Finney to come down. It was after eleven; she had been waiting since she had left Darnell standing like a statue in the landing.

The old refrigerator chugged noisily and the faucet dripped into the stained sink. Stupid to drink coffee this late: the caffeine was making her head spin. Darnell's words whirled around in it like a cyclone.

"I always lose. Black always wins."

"Get out of here. You're not safe here. Nobody is."

"She's getting stronger. I can feel it. It happened again last week."

The faucet dripped. The refrigerator chugged. Last week the woman had gotten stronger, Sarah thought—after Peter was there.

One part of her mind had been making dark conjectures ever since she had left Darnell. The other part of her mind was trying to pay no attention to them.

She was pouring another cup of coffee when she heard the fire escape rattle. She hurried to the window. It was the woman, descending carefully in her high heels, peering at the steps through her dark glasses. She was carrying a package wrapped in plastic. Finney wasn't with her. Sarah watched her pick her way through the litter of the backyard.

Gone every week, Sarah thought, but every Friday she emerges from the apartment. Does she ever go *in* before she comes *out*?

Follow her.

By the time she got the deadbolt on the back door unlocked and all the bars unbarred, the woman had disappeared. Sarah hurried down the fire escape and ran to the side of the building, but the sidewalk was empty. She ran around the corner to the front and saw the woman standing beside Finney's Buick, her package sitting on the car roof.

She was working her way through a ring of keys, trying to unlock the door. She got it open, and as she was reaching for her package, Sarah quickly approached.

"Hey there!" she yelled, a dozen feet from the car. "Doesn't that car belong to Paul Finney? Where is he?"

The woman stared at her for a moment and then got into the Buick.

Sarah darted closer, grabbed the door handle, and for a few seconds the two played tug of war with the car door while the woman tried to fit a key into the ignition. She got it in, started the engine, and tugged again at the door, but Sarah had wedged her knee in it.

The woman stared at her, inscrutable behind her dark glasses. Now what? Sarah wondered.

But the part of her mind that had been making all the dark conjectures already knew what to do.

"Excuse me," she said rather absurdly as she pulled off the woman's glasses.

The glacial blue eyes stared coldly at Sarah. Then Darnell snatched his glasses from her hand, put the car in gear, and drove away.

Chapter Thirteen

Sarah knocked on the door upstairs and called Finney's name. At first she called quietly, afraid of waking Esther, but when she got no answer she banged hard on the door and shouted, "Paul! Are you in there?"

Her mind waged battle with itself like the two sides of Darnell's chessboard. Okay, her practical side said, so Finney is passed out drunk. It's none of your business. Okay, so the weird little asexual monk Darnell is a raging queen. So what? Mind your own beeswax. Get a grip.

She went down to her own apartment and sat in the sunroom, watching for Darnell to return with Finney's car. The streetlight in front had gone out, but once or twice a minute it would blink on momentarily, a sleepy sentry opening its eyes to see if anything was sneaking up on it. A gang of boys skulked by; the streetlight glanced at them for a moment and went back to its slumber.

The practical side of her mind was trying to convince her that everything added up. Apparently Peter had suddenly discovered a taste for men, a deep hunger to judge by the amount of time he had spent up there. He depended on the hot air of his ego to stay aloft, and much of the heat had always come from believing he was God's gift to women, so it wouldn't be easy for him to accept the fact that he was gay. Maybe that explained why he had gone bonkers in the classroom: he wanted to prove to himself that he was still attractive to young women, so he had stuck his hand down someone's blouse.

But another part of her mind didn't buy any of it. Why had Darnell warned her to move out? Why had he raved about the "woman" growing stronger? Why had he said that nobody was safe here? Why did Esther say some men didn't come down? When was Finney going to come down? What was Darnell doing with Finney's car, and when was he going to return?

A knock at the door made Sarah jump and then freeze. Had Darnell sneaked back in? She crept through the hallway and leaned her ear against the door. She could hear someone breathing heavily in the landing.

"Who is it?"

"Peter."

Jeez. Of all the goddamned gall . . .

"Go away."

"I have to see you. I think you're in danger."

Her mind-battle raged. She wasn't sure which side won, the practical side or the weird, but she undid the locks and bolts.

Maybe Howard hadn't exaggerated after all: Peter looked awful, a week-old beard, long red hair in a mad nest of tangles, dark sunglasses staring at her like the eyes of an insect. His face was twisted into an ugly expression she had never seen before.

Sarah tried to slam the door, but his foot was wedged in it, and he forced it back open with ease. His expression crawled into a horrid new shape: he was grinning.

"Go away!" she shouted. "I don't want to see you! Goddammit, I said scram!"

But Peter was already halfway to the living room, pulling her along with him, the door still gaping open. He had a hold of her from behind, or else he would have received his second knee to the groin this week. His breath smelled sour, and the rest of him smelled like cologne dumped over a wino in the gutter. He was gasping, but it sounded more from excitement than exertion.

"Fucking asshole!" Sarah shouted.

Peter clamped his hand over her mouth, forced her face-down onto the sofa, and threw himself on top, crushing the air out of her.

"Cunt!" he said.

He was panting like a dog, struggling to pin her arms and keep her feet from kicking without letting go of her mouth, his cock hard as a hammer against her hip.

Sarah bit his sour-tasting hand and screamed as he wrenched it away, but her face was pressed so hard against the sofa that the scream didn't go far. His fingers slipped around her neck, an iron vice wringing the air out of her windpipe, and her eyes exploded with red shapes.

Her heartbeat pummeled her ears, and through the throbbing noise she could hear Peter swearing: "Stinking gash. I'm going to kill you, bitch, and then I'll fuck you. You'll be a good piece of ass when you're dead."

Red splotches hammered her eyes like fists, bruising and blotting every thought but one: I NEED TO BREATHE!

"I'm going to show you the darkness, bitch," he said. "Darkness like you've never seen. I'm going to poke out your eyes and fuck your eye sockets."

She felt herself losing consciousness and knew that very soon she would be dead. Then a voice came faintly from a mile away: "I giving you 'xactly three seconds and then I gonna give you a new eyehole."

The pressure on her windpipe eased, air at last, though it felt like a fiery fist in her throat as she gasped for it.

"Get yourself offa that girl and lay down with your ugly face flat on the floor, and I ain't half joking."

The room pounded painfully back into focus: Esther with a revolver trembling in her bony hands, Peter crouching down on all fours.

"Get flat down there with your hands straight out, and I plain mean business. There, that's pretty good. Don't have no thoughts 'bout squirming around. My ol' fingers ain't too steady. I see you budge just a little bit, they's likely to start pulling this trigger."
***

First two cops, then four, then six, but once Peter was cuffed and led away the six quickly dwindled to two, and they seemed too absorbed with the difficulties of spelling the words in their report to show much interest in what had transpired. After all, they saw plenty of these domestic cases every week. Likely as not, the woman had provoked her boyfriend's wrath by floozing around.

Her nerves jangling with caffeine and adrenaline, Sarah kept telling the police over and over about Darnell and about Peter's sojourn in the strange love-nest upstairs and about Paul Finney still being up there.

"She took Finney's car," Sarah said. "I mean he. Isn't that a crime anymore?"

"Look, lady, you ever have a guy spend the night with you? You ever borrow his car to get some cigarettes or something? So you want your neighbors to call the police every time that happens?"

"He's pretending to be a woman. Isn't that sorta strange?"

"Lady, half the hookers we pull in are men pretending to be women."

Sarah refused to be taken to the hospital, even though the cops said that having a doctor see the bruises would be helpful in court. She could tell they believed that she, like so many other battered women, would decide not to press charges. Maybe they were right; she didn't want to think about it now. No wonder cops got so disgusted, she thought.

By the time they left, it was nearly 2:00 a.m. Esther looked tired, and Sarah said, "You better go get some sleep."

"I'll get outta your way if you really think you can sleep after all this, but if you want a little company then I'm staying right here. Ain't no one would pay a nickel for the amount a sleep I get no how."

"I don't know how to thank you," Sarah said. "I mean, how do you thank someone for saving your life?"

"Didn't come over here to get thanks. I come over 'cause I heard you say scram and I didn't hear nobody scramming. Ain't the first time I had to pull a gun on someone, but I haven't had to pull a trigger yet. Good thing too. Them bullets must be older'n you. I be plain surprised if they still work."

"Darnell told me to move out," Sarah said, though Esther had already heard her tell the cops the same thing. "He said nobody's safe in this building."

"He's probably right about that. I told you 'bout the strange business I been hearing up there—things falling, things bumping, things moaning, things dragging. Body-sounding things."

"Something happened to Peter up there," Sarah said. "He wasn't like this before. He even looks different."

"Girl, everybody's on drugs these days, and some a these druggies start looking so different you don't hardly know who they are anymore."

"I'm not so sure it's drugs," Sarah said. "I'd give anything to see what's in that apartment."

Esther sat quietly for a while. "Got me a plan," she said.

Chapter Fourteen

Monday morning, Sarah, Esther, and her daughter Marcy were waiting in Esther's apartment when the landlady arrived. Frieda Moskowicz was a small widow in her early 70s with a somber, heavily powdered face. Her thick glasses seemed to magnify the sense of loss that haunted her eyes. She stepped into Esther's bathroom and listened carefully, cocking her head to aim her hearing aid at the ceiling.

"I hear nothing," she said.

"That's cause you ain't got my ears," Esther declared. "There's a bust pipe up there I'm sure."

Marcy nodded in agreement and said, "I sure hear something. Sounds like plaster washing away, doesn't it, Momma?"

Sarah nodded too, thinking how embarrassing all this was going to become in a few minutes. Embarrassing enough that there wouldn't be a broken pipe. Worse, the landlady was likely to find Paul Finney sprawled out drunk and naked. One thing she wouldn't find was Darnell; he hadn't returned after driving away in Finney's car.

Mrs. Moskowicz cocked her head and listened as alertly as a bird. "I hear nothing," she said.

"Sure be something if that whole ceiling comes down on top of our heads," Marcy murmured. She shook her head and added, "Mm mm mm."

Esther's description of her daughter had been true enough: she didn't look her 76 or 77 years. She was still a handsome woman, a full foot taller than her mother.

"I'm not supposed to enter a tenant's apartment without 24-hour notice," Mrs. Moskowicz said. "Except in emergencies."

"Sure seems like an emergency to me," Marcy said.

"Sure does," Sarah said. "I'd hate to see that ceiling come down. If anybody gets hurt there'd probably be a lawsuit."

Sarah's body was dead tired but her brain was wide awake and jittery. She hadn't slept at all last night, and Esther had slept only a little on Sarah's sofa.

"Of course, the woman has never given me her phone number," Mrs. Moskowicz said.

"What's that girl's name anyway?" Esther asked.

"Angela Dietrick," the landlady answered.

"Well, she ain't no woman, I can tell you that," Esther said.

"What do you mean?"

"Nothing. Just speculating out loud."

"Well, I suppose there's little choice," Mrs. Moskowicz said.

"I be happy to come with you," Esther said. "Maybe I can be a some help."

"No, I can't let you. She has a right to privacy."

"She!" Marcy said. "Mm mm mm."

Mrs. Moskowicz started up the stairs clutching her ring of keys. The other three women waited a moment and then crept up halfway up to the first landing. From there they could see the upper landing.

"Maybe she need some help up there," Esther said.

"Don't go poking your nose, Momma."

A few seconds later they saw Frieda Moskowicz emerge from the apartment. She was walking backwards with the weightless, slow steps of a sleepwalker. When she got to the center of the landing, she collapsed with a moan to the floor.

The three women hurried up the stairs and bent over the landlady. Her eyes were open, but she seemed too weak to get up. She was reciting something that sounded like a Yiddish prayer.

"I'll keep an eye on her," Esther said. "Y'all go have a peek."

The bedroom door hung open, and Sarah and Marcy looked there first, drawn by the strange sight of a casket surrounded by wooden candle holders. The lid was open, and they leaned over to look inside. Sarah began to gag; the lining was crusted with vomit and excrement.

"Sure stinks," Marcy said, backing away from the coffin and into the hallway.

Sarah noticed that the closet door was open a few inches. She peered in, but before she could make sense of what she was seeing, she heard Marcy calling from the bathroom: "Lord! Lord! Lord!"

The dark interior of the closet came into focus. Bones. Arm bones, leg bones, rib bones, finger bones and hip bones. A closet heaped with bones.

"Lordy Lord!" Marcy kept saying from the bathroom.

Sarah was getting sick; the room was swaying, and she could

taste the cereal she had eaten for breakfast. She rushed out of the bedroom, needing some air, but before she could get out of the apartment, Marcy grabbed her arm and tugged her into the bathroom.

In the tub was a naked, headless man. Sarah stared at the stuff hanging out of the butchered neck, veins and muscles, a bloody esophagus. Then she looked down at the body, bound with chains, and noticed how fat it was. Fat like Paul Finney.

"Mm mm mm," Marcy said.

Part Three: With a Word like Wind in a Graveyard

Chapter Fifteen

"So many boxes," Howard Goldwin sighed.

Sarah thought he was referring to the boxes she was packing to move to his house. She had already boxed up her computer, books and clothes. The furniture could stay here; it was junk anyway. Now she was filling boxes with piles of paper, trying to decide which ones were essential and which she could throw away. Though Howard had insisted that she stay with him, she didn't want to clutter his house with anything she didn't need. He took such pride in his place.

"I'm sorry," she said. "I really am. Look, I should just get a place of my own."

He looked puzzled for a moment. "Oh no, my love, I didn't mean *these* boxes. I mean every time I glance out the window, I see policemen carrying boxes." He lit a cigarette, his brow pinched into an uncharacteristic frown. "Do you suppose they're all filled with bones?"

"Yeah, probably. Bones, fingernails, hair, all kinds of horrible stuff. You know, I don't think I saw any skulls in the closet. I wonder what happened to the heads."

Sarah shuddered as she pictured the headless body in the old claw tub. Darnell must have boiled down his victims in it, using lye or some kind of acid. She imagined the mess in the drain, the melted flesh in the pipes. She thought of how sluggish her own drains had been, maybe because the main drain was clogged with skin and hair.

"Don't think about it, my dear," Howard said. "You must try to put all this grotesquerie out of your mind." But a few seconds later he said, "And then there's that other dreadful box. The coffin, I mean. I saw them lugging it out a few minutes ago, like pallbearers at a funeral."

He sighed again and moved back to the sunroom for another ghoulish look. Sarah stared at a pile of articles she had photocopied for her thesis—ritual murders and serial killings. Jeez. She threw them into a box and looked through another pile.

Howard returned from the front room. "The rabble!" he said. "All those reporters out there with their cameras like a horde of vulgar Cyclopes staring with glass eyes. And tonight the whole country will be staring at the glass eyes of their TV screens. It's so terribly revolting."

Sarah had noticed, however, that he had dressed for the cameras. He was wearing a natty blazer and a crisp white shirt with gold cuff links—not the best outfit for moving boxes.

"Hope they're getting ready to pack it in," she said. "One of them shoves a camera in my face, they may have a brand new murder to report."

"Perhaps one needs to view it philosophically," Howard said. "Fame is fame. Tell me, Sare, and be quite honest—do you believe I would make a photogenic psychopath?"

"Sure, you were born for the role. You'd be the pinup boy in every loony bin in the whole loony country."

Howard brushed something from his lapel and smiled. "Imagine, all these long years I've toiled for a poor scrap of honest recognition. Better I'd spent those thankless hours dispatching dowagers with the point of my bodkin."

Sarah knew his banter was intended to cheer her up, but it wasn't working. She kept seeing bones, a fat headless body, the icy look in Darnell's eyes when she had torn off his glasses. She peered at a pile of papers: religious belief as an indicator of criminal behavior. She threw them into a box. There was a knock at the door.

"Not another fucking cop!" she said. She stomped to the door and opened it. It was a slender, dapper man, his skin perfectly black, dressed in a gray suit. He pulled a handkerchief from his breast pocket, dabbed his high forehead, and gave her a wide smile.

"Excuse me. I'm Detective Sebastian Okpara. May I please come in?"

"Yeah, sure, like I have some choice in the matter." Sarah turned her back on him and returned to the study to glare at her papers.

Howard was more gracious. She heard him introducing himself and asking the cop to sit down. "Sare," he called from the living room. "Do you have something nice for the detective to drink?"

"No!" she said, more loudly than necessary.

She'd had enough cops and stupid cop questions for one day.

They asked the same things over and over. Maybe before she boxed up her computer, she should have printed up dozens of copies of everything she knew.

"Thank you, but really I'm not thirsty," she heard the detective say. The accent sounded Nigerian. "Miss Temple, I apologize for bothering you. I know it has been a trying day."

"All right, all right," she muttered. She flung a fistful of papers into a box, wiped her sweaty hair off her forehead, and came to the living room. "Look, I've answered so damn many questions already, I don't see how there can be any more."

Okpara rose from the sofa long enough to give her another wide smile. "I understand," he said. "I'm sure it's very frustrating for you, but we are simply trying to do our jobs. I understand that you were acquainted with Darnell Brook?"

She told him what she had already told a dozen other police today but, unlike them, Detective Okpara actually seemed to be paying attention. Soft spoken, polite, nothing like the others who had badgered her all afternoon. He was maybe 40 or 45, his short hair still mostly black around a high, balding dome, his ebony skin smooth and clear, his well-made suit fitted nicely to his trim frame. Unlike the others, he seemed keenly interested in Peter's visit to the upstairs apartment.

"I'll speak to Dr. Bellman," he said. "He was released without charges pending further investigation, which means the department is waiting for you to make the next move. I recommend you press charges against him and seek a restraining order, though if he's deranged he's not likely to pay it any mind.

"Now, please forgive me for adding to your anxiety, Miss Temple, but Dr. Bellman is not your only concern. Darnell Brook may hold you responsible for the discovery of the evidence, so until he's apprehended you must consider yourself a potential target of this highly dangerous suspect.

"And you too, Mr. Goldwin. It's kind of you to help Miss Temple, but be aware that it places you in a risky situation. It's a pity that you came here today. Already the cameras have seen you, and after the evening news everybody in town will have seen you, so the suspect will have a very good idea of where Miss Temple is staying. And so will Dr. Bellman."

"Did you find Finney's head?" Sarah asked.

"The remains haven't yet been identified." Okpara stood up. "I'll be in touch, and please call me if you remember anything else. I'm giving you my cell number as well as my office number. Again, consider your situation vulnerable. I'm going to request round-the-clock surveillance of your house, Mr. Goldwin, but I probably won't get it. Realistically the best you can probably expect is a squad car driving down your street every hour or so. So please be vigilant and don't be afraid to call 911 if you see or hear anything out of the ordinary."

"What a pleasant man!" Howard said when Okpara had left. "A gentleman of breeding. Impeccable manners, good diction—so rare these days."

"You heard what he said. He said I'm going to end up getting you killed."

"He said nothing of the sort, my dear. I heard perfectly well what he said. He said we should call 911 in the very unlikely event there's any trouble. Those were his exact words."

"Now even if I go to a motel they'll *think* I'm at your house," she said. "I've fucked you up good."

"Sare, I won't listen to another word of this foolishness. You're staying with me, and that's final. We're going to have a lovely time together, and we're not going to worry about some scrawny transvestite or that imbecile Peter Bellman either."

Sarah went to the sunroom to see if the news teams were still out there. Some were, but they seemed to be preparing to leave, perhaps catching a whiff of another scene of misery, a family crushed in its car or a baby smothered by its mother.

"Was Peter in that coffin?" she asked. "Is that why he's off his rocker?"

Howard came up behind her and placed his arms around her shoulders. "Let's not think about that," he said. "There have been enough horrors already without trying to dream up new ones."

It wasn't possible, she thought. Not Peter; not someone she had known so intimately. Trapped inside that box of misery.

As she looked out she saw the young boys who ruled the sidewalks looking in. They were staring at the building as if it could teach them some secrets of their trade. Just a few years ago they must have had the same innocence that she had loved in Johnny, but already the world had beaten it out of them.

The hard lump of pain that had been growing in her heart began to crumble, and suddenly she was sobbing it out in jagged chunks.

Howard led her to the sofa and sat holding her, pressing her face gently against his blazer, which grew damp with her tears.

"There, there," he said.

Chapter Sixteen

Angel stood in the shadows beneath the marquee of a defunct strip joint. She was watching a young prostitute work the nearby corner without success. She was too skinny and pimply, drugs written all over her face. The only feature in her favor was the shoulder-length, bright-red hair that shimmered brilliantly in the streetlight. Sometimes a car would slow down, flagged by her hair, only to speed up again toward healthier-looking prospects on the next corner.

After a cop car had crawled past, Angel stepped out of the shadows and approached her. "Ever party with a woman?" she asked.

The girl sized her up and said, "If you got money." She named a price, her brow knitted in preparation for haggling, but Angel wasn't worried about the price.

"Is there a place to go?" Angel asked.

"My place is right up there." The girl pointed to an apartment above a bar just across the street.

They climbed a dark littered stairwell and walked down a narrow hallway. Angel heard the groans of lovemaking through one door, the groans of a fight through another.

The girl fished in her red plastic purse for keys and opened the last door on the right to a tiny room buzzing with flies. There was scarcely enough room for a narrow bed, a large dresser with its veneer peeling off, and a night stand.

"Where's the money?" the girl asked, and Angel handed her some bills. The girl stuffed them into her red purse and began to undress.

Angel placed her hands on the girl's skinny shoulders, kissed her gently on the acne-pocked cheek, and reached town to touch her flaccid little breasts with their silly silver rings. One of the piercings was infected, and the nipple was purple and swollen.

"Love your hair," she said.

"Thanks." The girl lay down flat on the bed. A fly landed on her shoulder and walked toward her armpit.

"You do kinky stuff?" Angel asked.

"Depends. What kind a stuff?"

"I want to do all the work," Angel said. "I want to pleasure you. I'll give you an experience like you've never had."

"I don't take nothing up the back alley," the girl said.

"No, nothing like that. But I need to tie your arms to the bed."

The girl studied her carefully. "Cost 30 dollars more. Just my arms, and not too tight."

Angel laid 30 dollars on the dresser top. She got two neckties from her purse and set to work while the girl watched apprehensively.

"I don't let men do this to me no more," she said. "I learned my lesson the hard way."

No, you haven't learned anything yet, Angel thought. When she was finished tying, she got a rubber ball from her purse and shoved it into the girl's mouth. Fear wiped the drug haze from her eyes, and she kicked with her skinny legs, making the bed rock and squeak. Angel tied her feet to the foot of the bed and got a scalpel from her purse.

"This will only take a minute," she said.

She pinched the girl's nostrils shut, and the girl thrashed violently until she lost consciousness. Angel lifted her head from the pillow and cut carefully and skillfully along the hairline from forehead to temple and around the ear to the nape of the neck. When the cutting was done, she grabbed the hair and gave it a sharp tug. There was a wet snapping sound as the scalp pulled loose.

Angel carried her acquisition to the grimy little bathroom and used a wet towel to wipe the blood from the inside of the skin. She removed her blond wig and stuffed it in her purse for later disposal. She fit the new hair on her head and scrutinized it carefully in the mirror. The girl's cheap cosmetics were strewn on the lavatory countertop, and Angel smeared them lavishly on her face, deliberately doing a sloppy job. In a few minutes she had transformed herself into a gaudy harlot.

She retrieved her 30 dollars from the dresser top and dug through the girl's purse for the rest. There wasn't much money other than what Angel had given her, but it was better than nothing.

The girl had regained consciousness and was pulling so hard on her bindings that her skinny arms looked ready to snap. Angel sat on the bed beside her and studied her pimply face. Already a few flies had discovered their bloody feast. Angel brushed them away and walked her fingertips delicately over the girl's naked skull. Hard to believe that a few millimeters beneath her fingers lay the labyrinth of consciousness, a whole universe throbbing inside its bloody hull. There was an iron sitting on the dresser, and Angel considered using it to crack the skull like an eggshell so she could gaze at the pulsating mystery beneath.

But no—the girl looked as if she'd had such a sad life; surely she deserved a more interesting death. Angel glanced around the tiny room and then stepped into the tinier kitchen. Beneath the old linoleum countertop were a few drawers and one large cupboard about two feet deep, two feet high, and just a bit less wide. Perfect. She pulled its pots and pans out onto the floor and discovered a hammer and some nails behind them.

The girl struggled fiercely while Angel untied her from the bed, rolled her over to lash her arms and legs together behind her back, and dragged her to the kitchen. She started thrashing even more desperately when Angel shoved her into the cupboard. It was difficult to get her crammed in there, fighting the way she was, and then Angel had to force the door shut with her shoulder until she could get it nailed securely.

Even though she had things to do and really couldn't spare the time, Angel fixed herself a cup of coffee and sat on a kitchen chair drinking it and happily contemplating her work. The thuds inside the cupboard grew weaker, and before her cup was empty they ceased.

"So there!" she said.

Chapter Seventeen

Tuesday morning Sarah stood in a gun store staring at a tiny pistol beneath the glass of the long counter. "What's that?" she asked.

"That's a .22 caliber Beretta semi-automatic," the salesman said.

"Is that a good gun?"

"Depends in what you're interested in. Self-defense?"

"Yeah."

"You pull that thing on a thug he'll probably laugh at you. You done much shooting, ma'am?"

"No. Never."

"Then you might be better off with a revolver. Nice and simple—just aim and pull the trigger. And you're gonna want something strong enough to make the guy change his mind."

The salesman led her to another section of the long counter, where the shelves were filled with revolvers of all sizes. Sarah pointed to a small one and said, "What's that?"

He pulled it out and handed it to her. "This is a Ruger LCR," he said. "It's about as lightweight as you can get in a high-power revolver, thanks to the polymer frame. Good smooth trigger pull too."

It felt comfortable in her hand, nice and light, small enough to fit easily in her purse or a jacket pocket. Kind of pretty in a weird way.

"Is this a .22?" she asked.

The salesman grinned. He looked like a biker, burly and balding with a beard, but his manner was friendly. "No ma'am," he said. "This baby holds five rounds of .357 Magnum."

"Jeez," Sarah said. "Isn't that some kind of Dirty Harry small nuclear device?"

"Dirty Harry carries a .44 Magnum Smith and Wesson. Now, .357 will have some recoil for sure, especially in a little gun like this, and you want some training before you try to handle it. But the nice thing is, this'll also shoot .38 Special."

He opened two boxes of ammo to show her the difference in length; they both looked big enough to haul astronauts to the moon. "Now in my opinion .38 Special is the minimum adequate self-defense cartridge, with a pretty decent stopping power, and after a good afternoon of shooting you should be able to make it stand up and sing Dixie."

Stopping power—that meant big bloody holes in people. Sarah had always hated guns and began to wonder if she should just stick with pepper gas. But an old revolver trembling in a pair of 98-year-old hands had saved her life. That was the kind of story one didn't hear very often in the sociology department, the kind of women's lib that NOW never championed.

"Course just showing a gun is usually enough," the salesman said, perhaps sensing her misgivings. "Something like 80 percent of the time when a gun's used to stop an assailant, the trigger's never pulled. But if just showing it doesn't do the trick, then you want something that'll do more than aggravate the bad guy."

She had never heard a statistic like that in school. She decided to check it the next time she was online.

"Where's the safety?" she asked.

"You're the safety," he said. "As long as you don't pull the trigger, this gun won't fire. You can drop it out a window and it won't go off."

Sarah grasped it clumsily with both hands and looked down the sights.

"No, ma'am, you want to keep both hands firmly on the grip. Don't get your hand over the cylinder or you're liable to get a nasty powder burn, and you sure don't want to get your pinky in front of the barrel. Here. Like this." He took the gun and showed her. "Now, hold your arms out like this."

He handed the gun back and she tried holding it the way he had. Yes, it fit her small hand nicely. She imagined the little Ruger waiting in her purse the next time someone tried to strangle her.

"How much is it?"

"Four forty-nine and ninety-nine cents."

"Yikes." She handed it back. "You have anything cheaper?"

The salesman put the gun away and pulled out another that looked just like it. "Three hundred and eighty dollars minus one penny," he said. "It's another Ruger LCR, but this one just fires .38 Special."

"Still too much."

He put it away and handed her another revolver. "This is a Taurus .38 Special Ultralite," he said. "It's a well-made gun and it's just three hundred dollars minus one penny."

It was a bit bigger than the Ruger and felt heavier, but it would still fit easily in her purse.

"Okay, I'll take it. And some ammo."

The salesman put the gun back under the counter and brought a boxed one from the back of the store. Sarah looked it over for scratches, turned the cylinder, and pulled back the hammer with a sense of satisfaction. *Her* gun.

The salesman handed her a form and a pen. "You need to fill this out for your background check," he said. "You have to print or it's no good."

Sarah was almost ashamed at what she was feeling as she filled out the form. In a few minutes she would be as powerful as any man. It would no longer matter that Peter was twice her size. If Darnell intended to kill her, well, she was ready. She would no longer have to depend on squad cars that didn't drive down the street even the measly once-an-hour that she had been promised. Tonight she could walk to the park by herself if she liked. Tonight she would sleep with the gun beside her bed, knowing it would be more than a match for whatever might crawl through the window.

She was making checkmarks on a long list of yes-or-no boxes when she came to question 11.1: "Have you ever been convicted in any court of a misdemeanor crime of domestic violence?"

She glanced at the bottom of the form where it said that making any false statement was a crime punishable as a felony. She reread question 11.1 two or three times, hoping that it asked something other than what it did. Then she marked the *yes* box.

The salesman was watching her. "You marked *yes*," he said. "Is that a correct answer?"

"Somebody filed a charge against me once," she said. "It was a lot of crap, but I was too busy to contest it."

The salesman wadded up the form and said, "I'm sorry, but you're not permitted to purchase a firearm."

Chapter Eighteen

Detective Okpara sat in Peter Bellman's darkened living room and scrutinized the man sitting across from him on the sofa. Bellman wore a soiled bathrobe, his feet and legs bare. Okpara could smell him from across the room. His long red hair was greasy and uncombed, his beard untrimmed, his eyes bloodshot and dilated. One moment they would stare steadily at Okpara like the barrels of two guns; the next moment they'd dart fearfully around the room as if the walls were closing in.

Strung out on meth, Okpara conjectured. That could explain his nervous gestures, his loud, vehement voice, his widened pupils. The circles under his eyes suggested he hadn't been sleeping much. Heavy drapes and even blankets cloaked the windows: people who abused amphetamines too long often developed a sensitivity to light.

Okpara had probed around with a few innocuous questions before asking about Bellman's attack on Sarah. That caused him to leap up from the sofa and prowl around the room.

"Don't believe any rubbish Sarah Temple tells you!" he roared. "She invited me over, she let me in. I mean how the fuck could I force my way through a dozen locks and bolts, tell me that. Do I look like Houdini? She wanted me there. She called me! Hell, she'd invite anybody with a pecker. Need a quick piece of ass, Detective, there you go. She likes it up the back road too, good and hard! So when she found out I didn't want to fuck her, that I just came over to discuss bills, then she threw a tantrum, started screaming bloody murder. She kicked me—I can show you the bruise! Tried to stab me with a fucking corkscrew! Now who could make up something that weird? That's what I told them at the station. I mean, who the fuck could make that shit up?"

Bellman stopped pacing long enough to glare at Okpara. He ran his hands through his wild hair, making it wilder.

"Then she started yelling for some senile friend of hers to bring a gun. 'Bring the gun!' she yelled. 'Shoot his ass!' They had it all planned out beforehand—the old witch was just waiting for her signal. Bam! She was there in two seconds with a revolver, for

Christ's sake! Some half-blind old hag straight from *Macbeth*. I'm going to bring charges against that old gash, I told them so at the station. Bastards threatened to charge me with all kinds of shit, but they couldn't because they know they'd be laughed out of court. Wait'll they hear from my Goddamn lawyer! Haul me down to the frigging station at one in the morning while those two witches cackle with glee! Don't I have any fucking rights? The bitch has even planted rumors at the university—trying to ruin my career now. Well, I've got news for you, Detective. That woman has a criminal record. Domestic violence—just look it up."

The house smelled dirty: rotten food, something dead. A large potted plant near the stereo was withering for lack of water or sun. Okpara wished he could get a warrant to search the place. He was certain he would find drugs if nothing else.

"Miss Temple alleges that you visited her upstairs neighbor, Angela Dietrick, AKA Darnell Brook."

"Shit," Bellman said. "So you believe whatever that woman tells you. Maybe she'll tell you I killed John Kennedy and his fucking brother too. I told you, that woman is a criminal."

"Are you stating that you never visited Angela Dietrick?"

Bellman shot him with a crafty look, no doubt trying to decide what, if anything, Okpara knew.

"Sure, I was there. What of it? But only for a few minutes. Let's see—I'd come to see Sarah because she called and begged me to. Once I got there it was the same old story, begging me to let her move back, begging me to fuck her, all that rubbish. I got fed up and left.

"So when I was leaving the building I met this woman, or this man or whatever he is. How was I supposed to know she was a fucking queer? We struck up a conversation, and I took her to a restaurant. We ate, had a few drinks and a couple laughs. You can ask the restaurant owner, he's a friend of mine. Is that against the law? I mean, did I walk out without paying the fucking tab or something? She seemed nice enough, very intelligent in fact, and she invited me to her apartment. How was I supposed to know about any of this criminal shit?

"So I drove her home and came in, but I only stayed a minute. Place looked funny to me, bare, like she didn't really live there, so I figured it was just some place where she brought men, and I got to thinking about AIDS. I mean, if she rents a place just for one-night stands, she doesn't sound like safe sex, does she? Would you want to screw her? Sarah doesn't give a shit about things like that, she'll screw anybody and anything, but I'm not like that. So I waited till she went to the bathroom and I got out of there. End of story."

Bellman grinned. As he sat down, his bathrobe came open, exposing his groin. He didn't seem to notice. He picked up a bottle of scotch from the coffee table and held it out to Okpara. "Maybe you'd like a drink?"

"No thank you."

"Suit yourself." He raised the bottle to his lips and drank. "Any more questions?"

"Isn't it true that your car was parked there the whole weekend? Until late Sunday night, sometime after midnight?"

"Um, yeah, I guess maybe it was. I'd forgotten. So what?"

He tilted the bottle and drank some more, taking his time with his answer. "As I was leaving the apartment, I realized I was a little drunk. I saw a cab and I took it. No sense breaking the law, huh, Detective? So much for that little mystery. I didn't need the car that weekend, so I didn't pick it up right away. Is that against the law? Maybe it was a no parking zone or something. You want to give me a parking ticket, is that it?"

Bellman grinned and had another drink. "Let me tell you something, Detective. I admire you guys. Devoted seekers of the truth. But tell me, where do you think the truth is hidden? Do you find it in fingerprints, DNA samples, cold semen in some dead woman's cunt? Where do you look? Maybe you find the truth in the morgue, in the cold stiffs laid out on the table? Is it in the cuts and bruises and the gaping holes? Maybe it's written in their eyes—do dead people's eyes tell stories, give you some glimpse? Is that where you find the truth, in the eyes of those cold naked bodies? What do they smell like, Detective? Some of them must get a little ripe, despite the cold storage. I mean, maybe it's a woman who lay rotting in the hot sun for a few days before you found her. What's that like? Are her nipples hard or soft after all that time? What about her pussy? Is it rigid or spongy? You ever fingered one that was pretty ripe? You ever discover the truth there, Detective—in a stinking dead pussy?"

Chapter Nineteen

Sarah was getting iced tea from Howard's refrigerator when the phone rang. She heard Howard answer it in the living room. A few seconds later his tone changed: "Number one, no. Number two, I wouldn't tell you even if I knew. Number three, you are a very sick and pathetic creature. Number four, you are not welcome at my house, and I must warn you that the police are watching this place 24 hours a day."

Sarah hurried to the living room. Howard slammed down the phone and glanced up at her. "Peter," he said quietly. "Wanting to know where you're staying. Maybe that's a good sign, maybe it means he's the only person in town who didn't see my face on the news."

He lit a cigarette with a large gold lighter that always sat on the antique marble-top end table. "Damn, I spoke foolishly," he said. "I shouldn't have mentioned the police. A dead giveaway. Why would the police be watching my place unless you're here?"

He went to the front window and gazed out nervously as if Peter might already be pulling up.

Sarah made an effort to smile. "I can imagine some reasons," she said. "Debauched bacchanals. That great big hookah in the corner."

"Oh that," Howard said proudly. "That is a lovely bauble, isn't it? An old lover gave it to me. It certainly has given me much more pleasure than *he* ever did!"

"Howard, I don't want to put you through any more of this crap. Tomorrow I'm gonna find an apartment."

"Poppycock. I won't hear of it." He smoked his cigarette and stared out the window. "Me and my big mouth. Now he *knows* you're here. Hmm, what's this? Why it's that nice detective! Excuse me, my dear."

He dashed up the stairs while Sarah got the door. Sebastian Okpara touched his forehead with a handkerchief and gave her a wide smile. "Good afternoon, Miss Temple." He stepped into the foyer and peered into the front living room. "Such a beautiful place! So many nice antiques."

Howard appeared at the top of the stairs in a cream-colored silk jacket that he had not been wearing before. "Oh, they're just trinkets," he protested, descending the stairs slowly and regally. "Yard sales and the like. So very nice to see you, Detective Okpara. So good of you to stop by."

Howard steered him to the small second living room, away from the room with the hookah. "Perhaps you'd like some iced tea?" he asked.

"Yes, thank you."

Okpara waited until Sarah sat before seating himself. "I suppose you've heard that we found the remains of twelve victims," he said.

"Yeah."

Twelve heads in the freezer, the TV had said. Eleven piles of bones in the closet and one headless body in the tub. She had spent much of last night dreaming about the body.

"Five have already been identified, including Paul Finney," Okpara said. "That spares you, at least, having to look at some unpleasant photographs."

"Thank God."

Howard entered with the iced tea. "You won't *believe* who just called!" he said, and he related the brief phone call.

Okpara pulled a notebook from his jacket pocket and jotted something in it. "I believe that both of you have known Dr. Bellman for some time?" he asked.

"Too long!" Howard sniffed.

"Two years," Sarah said.

"How would you describe his character?"

Sarah shrugged. "He used to slap me around sometimes. But nothing like Sunday night."

"You never told me that," Howard said. "The next time I see that bully, I shall bloody his nose."

"Is he usually vulgar in his speech?" Okpara asked.

"No, not at all," she said. "More like pompous and pretentious, always wanting to sound like the great intellect."

"I've *always* found him vulgar," Howard said. "Peter Bellman knows nothing whatsoever about literature or the arts. He's a perfect example of everything that's wrong with our educational system these days."

"Would you describe his usual appearance as slovenly?"

"No, just the opposite," Sarah said. "He's super self-conscious about his looks."

Howard let out a sarcastic snort and said, "He *should* be self-conscious. He looks exactly like a baboon."

"Do you know if he has ever abused drugs?"

Sarah wasn't sure what to say. Peter did a few lines of coke once in a while, but should she tell that to a cop? "Not really," she said. "You know, maybe a toke or two at parties."

"Would you say his appearance had changed the last time you saw him?"

"Yes, definitely. He looked like a wild man, hair all over the place. He's always so fussy about his looks."

"I, for one, have *never* cared for his appearance," Howard said. "His taste in clothes is simply appalling."

"I applied for a restraining order today," Sarah said, "but I haven't made up my mind about filing charges. I'm afraid that will just agitate him, and right now I simply want him to stay as far away from me as possible."

"You may be right," Okpara said. "If you press charges, it's very unlikely he'll receive a prison sentence. You let him into your apartment and you didn't seek medical treatment. The only witness is elderly and therefore not highly compelling."

He made a few more notes in his book. "We've pulled up some information regarding Darnell Brook," he said. "I believe it's best for you to know as much as possible about him, in case he should make a move against you. Sometimes an odd scrap of knowledge is the best defense. I must insist upon your discretion, however. The reporters will learn these facts soon enough, but I don't want you to help them. Is that agreed?"

"Of course," Sarah said.

Okpara found a certain page in his notebook, but while he spoke he glanced at it only to verify dates. He seemed to have the whole story memorized. Sarah was fascinated by the cold concentration in his eyes. Despite his soft manner, they looked hard and clinical, as if they were made of glass instead of flesh.

"An important figure in Darnell's childhood was his maternal grandfather, Gustav Dietrick, so let me start there. Gus Dietrick was born in Germany in 1919. His family moved here when he was a child and bought a farm about 40 miles north of Columbus, near Mount Vernon, and that's where Gus Dietrick lived his whole life. He married a woman named Eva Block, another German immigrant, and they had three kids, Ida, Rudolph, and Mariel. Mariel was the youngest, born in 1960. She was the mother of Darnell."

Okpara spoke precisely and grammatically. His accent was definitely Nigerian, Sarah had decided. Though his body scarcely moved while he spoke, his hands made small, eloquent gestures.

"Gus didn't have good luck with his children. Ida, the oldest one, fell into a cistern when she was 11 and broke her neck, and two years later her brother Rudolph was buried under several tons of oats when a grain chute somehow came open in the granary. Somehow young Mariel managed to survive. When she was 16 she ran away from home and ended up in Columbus.

"At age 18 Mariel married a shoe salesman named Robert Brook. That was, let's see, in 1981. Six months later she gave birth to Angela, and a year later Darnell was born. In 1989, Mariel and Robert were killed in an automobile accident. Darnell was six and Angela was seven.

"Old Gus and Eva took the children. There are no records that the children ever attended school while living with the grandparents. Somehow the authorities may have slipped up, never caught on that Gus and Eva had them."

"Darnell struck me as well educated," Sarah said.

"Of course, my dear," Howard said. "His mind was not polluted by public school."

Okpara continued. "We know nothing about them until the evening of August 12, 1992, when Eva called the local police and two deputies found Gus in the barn, dead from a heart attack. They also discovered Darnell buried in the basement in what Eva called the 'bad box.' This was a small homemade footlocker, very sturdy but scarcely large enough to hold the child. It was placed in a four-foot-deep pit dug in the cellar floor. There were a few breathing holes drilled in the lid of the box; they were at the end opposite from his face, possibly so he wouldn't be able to peer out. There are similar holes in the casket that we found yesterday.

"The report states that it had been raining all day and the pit was filling up with water. When the deputies opened the footlocker it was half-filled with water. Another inch or so, and Darnell would have drowned. He was unconscious and didn't awaken until several hours later at the hospital. He apparently didn't remember being put in the box. He was treated for dehydration and was released to an orphanage, where he stayed until he turned 18.

"The deputies noticed more evidence of digging a few feet from the pit for Darnell's box. They got a warrant and dug up another homemade box with Angela's body in it. The body was badly decomposed and had been dead for several months. Cause of death was undetermined."

"How very grim," Howard said. "So very horrible."

"Yes, it is," Okpara said. "I regret having to tell such a depressing story."

"Go on," Sarah said.

"The night Darnell was found was the twelfth of August. He had turned nine the day before. His birthday probably had been spent inside the box. Eva said she thought he'd been in there for two or three days; she wasn't sure and didn't seem very concerned about it. She said Gus put him in there at least once a month, sometimes once a week, whenever he misbehaved. He was usually in the box for a day or two at a time, she said.

"Eva saw nothing unusual about the punishment. She admitted that Gus probably had sex with both of the grandchildren and with his own children before that. She wasn't sure, but she wouldn't put it past him. She was charged with child abuse but was never tried because of dementia, and she died a few months later in a rest home. Her brain was riddled with tumors."

Howard had silently slipped out to the kitchen. He returned with a pitcher of iced tea and refilled their glasses, his face pale and his hand unsteady as he poured.

"It sometimes happens that a child abused so severely will develop a split personality, in some cases even several distinct personalities," Okpara said. "This is called multiple personality disorder. The other personality apparently is a means of escape from an intolerable situation. The other personality, the imaginary one, suffers the punishment, while the real child remains oblivious to the horror. Perhaps one could say it's a great gift of the human mind to be able to create another person to endure the terrible pain.

"But there's a price to pay. Once the torture is gone, the other person doesn't go away. It's possible that this is what Angela Dietrick is: the other person, the one with all of the rage. After his sister died, or maybe even before, Darnell would escape into her personality whenever he was put in the box, and now that personality still lives."

"I don't understand," Howard said. "If her grandfather was such an ogre, why would she take his last name?"

"Possibly it's just a convenient alias," Okpara said. "On the other hand, serial killers sometimes drop clues and riddles as if daring the police to find them. But it's also possible that Angela identifies with her cruel grandfather, the monster who in effect created her. We suspect the casket discovered in Angela's apartment is the one Gus Dietrick was buried in. Seven years ago, his grave in Mount Vernon was robbed. His remains were found at the bottom of the hole—the only thing missing was his casket."

He pulled the handkerchief from his breast pocket and touched it to his forehead. "In order to understand the suspect, we must understand Angela as well as Darnell. That is not so easy. Darnell may be unaware of Angela's crimes, or he may be perfectly aware, we don't know. At this stage of the investigation, we have little more than conjectures.

"But if there should be an encounter, don't believe that you can reason with this creature or appeal for mercy. All of the anger, every memory of every outrage, is locked up inside her. Whatever conscience or empathy may exist, Darnell has kept to himself. Angela has no pity to give you."

***

After Okpara left, Howard sat smoking and brooding in silence. Sarah stared out of the window, trying to convince herself that it was the same world out there that it had been before this nightmare started. For over two years she had been collecting boxes full of articles about child abuse and other crimes, but still the world had seemed reasonably safe and comfortable. Just facts and figures and faceless stories.

"I've never heard a more dreadful story," Howard said at last.

"I shouldn't have stuck you in the middle of this crap," she said. "Tomorrow I'm—"

"Sare, if you say one more word about finding an apartment, I swear I shall lock you in the closet. Sorry—a clumsy choice of words. I need to leave in a few minutes—I have a three o'clock to teach, but I'll be back by 5:00. I have an idea, why don't you come with me and sit in on my class? Nothing very sinister ever happens during one of my classes, except maybe a few students expiring from deadly boredom, and I hate to leave you here alone."

"I'll be fine."

"I have a lovely idea," Howard said. "Whatever you do, don't eat any dinner before I get back. Oh, and one other thing—if that cruel little Adonis should call, tell him that I expressly told you *not* to tell him where I am. I want him to believe that I've quite washed my hands of him."

"Sure," Sarah said.

She had gathered from a couple of Howard's remarks that he hadn't heard a word from his new flame for at least a week. Like most of his infatuations, this one seemed to be woefully one-sided.

As soon as the door shut, Sarah began to wish she had gone with him. She wasn't in the mood to sit here alone. It was a big house with many windows, and each window felt like an eye staring at her. Her throat began to ache again as she remembered Peter's hands clamped around it. She remembered Finney's body, remembered the pile of bones in the closet and the dreadful stink of the box. Gus Dietrick's dug-up fucking casket, for God's sake!

She wished that she had a gun. She would have it right here in the pocket of her shorts, ready to protect her from whatever asshole might be staring in at her through the windows.

Howard's phone rang. Why did he have to be the last person on earth to have a home phone with no caller ID? It kept ringing, and finally she picked it up.

"Hello?"

There was a long silence, then a chuckle. "Hi, Sarah," Peter said. "Are you wearing panties?"

Chapter Twenty

It was a nice day despite everything, still too hot but a bit cooler than it had been, and she decided to take a walk. Surely she would be safe out there in broad daylight, safer than she was in this house. Still, she looked cautiously in both directions before she stepped out. No sign of a bogyman, but no sign of a squad car either.

She liked Howard's neighborhood, a beautifully restored German quarter a few blocks south of downtown. The old brick houses had tiny yards that their owners had crafted into colorful gardens. The narrow streets, also brick, had been built for carriages and pedestrians, and the few cars that travelled them bumped along slowly. There were coffee shops and candy stores, restaurants and bars, an enormous bookstore that she was eager to explore, a park where it would be pleasant to watch the sun set.

She like Howard's neighborhood, she liked his house with its antiques and its clean airy comfort, and most of all she liked Howard's company, so pleasant after the Kafka-bug loneliness of her apartment. He had given her the larger of his two guest rooms, with a luxurious pillared bed and a nice big table for her computer.

In different circumstances he would probably be the ideal roommate; hospitable, cheerful, considerate, kind, he had every trait she had always wanted in a lover without the complication of being a lover. She liked the fact that he didn't look at her the way other men did. It was nice to be able to feel as relaxed around a man as she would around a woman, without the imp of sexual desire to confuse everything.

Apparently the imp was tormenting Howard, needling him to brood over his indifferent Adonis, who probably was a callow brat not worth the fuss. But how many people had seen Peter the same way, back when her heart was still skipping foolishly at the sound of his name? Now that the imp's spell was shattered, she marveled that she had ever wanted him.

Yeah, Howard would probably be the ideal roommate—but not in these circumstances, not when she was likely to get him killed. Despite his protests, she was going to find her own place tomorrow, even if it was just a dumpy room somewhere, and then the Kafka-bug loneliness would be back, but at least Howard would be safe.

It wasn't quite 4:00 when she got back, so of course Howard's car was still gone, and she hated entering the house when he was away. She walked completely around it, checking to make sure the windows and the back door were properly shut, but of course that meant nothing—if Peter or Darnell had jimmied a lock he wouldn't leave the door open to advertise his presence.

The house sounded quiet, too quiet, the foyer holding enough silence to fill a cathedral. The place had enough closets to hide a legion of demons, and then there was an attic big enough for another army of horrors, and then there was the basement . . . She wished she had a gun in her purse.

Grasping her pitiful can of pepper gas, she yanked open the door of the foyer closet. Just Howard's impressive array of coats, but they looked sinister enough, skinny scarecrows on hangers. She stuck her head into the front living room. Had someone moved that hookah an inch or two?

The phone rang.

Jeez. She let it ring five or six times, but it showed no inclination to quit. So what if it was Peter? He already knew she was staying here, and at least if he was on the phone that meant he wasn't lurking in the attic—unless he was up there with his cell phone.

She grabbed the receiver. "Who is it?" she snapped sharply.

"Sarah? Is that you?"

No, it couldn't be . . .

"It's me. Darnell."

Sarah tried to say something, but her mouth didn't work.

"I'm sorry. I know what you must think of me. A monster. Two monsters. But I had to call. I have to talk. I haven't been able to. Angel's much stronger now, she's taking over. But right now she's exhausted. I think she'll be gone for a little while, at least for an hour. I hope."

"How did you get this number? How do you know—"

"*She* knows where you're staying. I found your phone number in her purse. She knows your address too." Darnell recited the street and house number.

"Tear it up!" Sarah shouted.

"Sure. I already did. But it won't do any good. Angel won't forget. She wants to kill you because you know me too well. I mean, you and I have a sort of connection . . ."

"Where *are* you?"

"I can't tell you. The police would come. They'd put me in prison or an asylum. I can't let that happen. I'm claustrophobic, you see—I couldn't bear it. There were experiences in my childhood . . ."

"Yes, I know what happened."

"I thought maybe you would. The police must have told you. So you see, it's just not possible, I can't allow myself to be locked up."

"Darnell, you have no choice." Sarah spoke crisply and clearly, the way she would to a child. "Do you want other people to be killed? Do you want *me* to be killed?"

"No, of course not. I like you. But don't worry, that won't happen. There won't be any more killings. When I'm done talking to you I'm going to put an end to this. I'm going to cut my wrists. I know how to do it, along the veins instead of across, so even if an ambulance came . . ."

"Darnell, you're . . ." No, Sarah thought—don't say you're nuts. "Darnell, you're making a mistake. You need a doctor. A doctor can help you."

"No. A doctor can't help *her*. You don't understand. Angel doesn't want to be helped. She's having too much fun."

"You've got to turn yourself in. Listen to me! If you can't bring yourself to do it, then I will. You tell me where you are, right now!"

"I told you, I can't. I won't let anyone put me in a box again. When I'm done talking to you I'll put an end to this . . . in my own way. But I don't have much time. She's much stronger now, she won't be gone for long. So please listen to me for the little time I have. Someone has to know these things, someone has to write them in a book. The world needs to know."

Sarah listened; she didn't know what else to do.

"I want you to understand, I didn't know anything about her. I knew that I'd once had a sister and I knew she was dead, but I didn't like thinking about her. I tried to keep all that stuff out of my mind, Grandpa and Grandma, the farm, all that terrible stuff. If I thought of Angel at all, it would be back before . . . back when my parents were alive. Sometimes I liked to think of my mother, I'd try to remember her face, and then I'd think of Angel, but I didn't do that too often. Mostly it was like I didn't have a past. If I tried to think of Angel, I couldn't focus. I felt uncomfortable, I felt a wall of anxiety. My mind would drift off. So I just told myself, well, I had a sister once but she's dead and that's that. Do you believe me, Sarah?"

"Yes," she said sharply, impatiently. Darnell was speaking so slowly, babbling on and on, and she was thinking that if he was going to kill himself, then she wished he would get it over with before he changed his mind or before Angel returned to take the reins. She wanted to say, "Shut up and get it done!" but that probably wasn't a good idea.

"But things were foggy and confusing," he continued. "For example, I couldn't figure out where my money was going. I mean, Angel was buying clothes and paying rent for the apartment across the hall, but I didn't know that. I tried keeping a list of my expenses, but the list never added up, and somehow it caused me anxiety just to wonder about it, so I had to stop keeping the list and stop thinking about money. I just told myself, well, money has a way of disappearing and that's that.

"There were blackouts. I'd wake up feeling tired and awful and I couldn't remember anything I'd done the night before. I could remember coming home from work, and then nothing. I'd wake up with dreams sometimes, and they were horrible, but I couldn't remember them clearly. Just images and feelings. I told myself it was depression. I mean, what kind of life did I have? Work, and then I'd come home and eat some macaroni and cheese or a hamburger by myself and maybe I'd read and then I'd go to bed. What was there worth remembering? So I said, sure I don't remember. What is there to remember?"

"Look, Darnell," she interrupted, but he didn't seem to notice.

"And then there was the apartment next door. Every time I stepped out of my apartment and saw that door across the landing, it gave me a bad feeling. I wondered why I'd never met whoever lived there. Just the sight of that door upset me. I felt there was something terrible in there, but I didn't know why I felt that. Sometimes I thought I remembered seeing her going down the fire escape, but I wasn't sure if I'd seen it or dreamt it. So my life was weird. It has always been weird."

"Darnell, you can't just go on talking like this. You need to get help, right now."

He ignored her. "But everything has changed. Your friend had something to do with it—you said his name is Peter. The last time I saw you, I was beginning to get an inkling of the woman next door, like the memory of a nightmare, something too horrible to grasp.

That's because she'd just grown more powerful. Her thoughts were . . . were leaking over, so to speak. I was starting to get a glimpse. I tried to warn you. Before Peter was up there, I knew nothing about her. I hope you believe me. But now I can see some of the things she's been doing. This is weird—sometimes when she's asleep, like now, I can actually hear her dreams. They're not very pleasant. No, not very nice at all. She's dreaming about some woman, a prostitute I think . . . some woman she must have killed . . ."

"*What* woman? Where are you?"

"Never mind. It doesn't matter. I need to tell you about her friend, that's what's important. He's the one who has made her more powerful. He gave her something. It's not the first time—it's happened before. Each time he gives her something she grows more powerful. The first time he gave her something was in childhood. He brought her to life, Sarah. That's what the world needs to know. Before that, she was just . . . she was just my fantasy, so I could imagine I was someone else, my dead sister, because I couldn't stand to be in that box. She was just an imaginary thing that I invented until *he* made her real by giving her the first gift."

"What gift? What are you talking about? Look, Darnell, you've got to tell me where you are. You've *got* to. Please!"

"A name."

"Yes, give me a street name, anything."

"No, I mean her friend gave her a name. And the name brought her to life. And he's given her more names since."

For a minute she had forgotten he was crazy; she had been expecting him to make sense. This new lunacy about the names had caught her off guard.

"You have to let the world know about her friend," he babbled on. "Psychiatrists don't believe in evil. They're materialists. To them everything's just an illness. Dysfunction, syndrome, complex, they use all those words, but they don't know the word *evil*. You commit the worst crimes imaginable, and they say what's wrong with you is just something like mumps or measles except it's in your brain. But I know, and I'm telling you so you can let others know. There is such a thing as evil, pure evil, and it's a living force that can take over your brain but isn't created by your brain. Evil gains power because people don't believe in it. It doesn't want people to believe. It prefers for us to believe that human beings are faulty mechanisms, dysfunctional little animals with measles in the brain."

"Darnell, what the fuck are you talking about? The devil or some kind of shit like that? Look, people are getting killed and all you're doing about it is talking shit. If you don't turn yourself in right now more people will die, but instead you're wasting time talking about the devil!"

There was a long pause, and Sarah was thinking, great, now I've done it, I've got him pondering some kind of theological crap, how many devils can dance on the head of a pin, and any minute *she's* going to take over and the killing is going to continue.

"No," Darnell said at last. "Angel's friend is not the devil, not Satan. It's more like a living darkness. It's a man and yet not a man. The man is alive and yet not alive. Her friend has some connection with that horrible farm where we used to live, our grandparents' farm. I can't tell you exactly what he is, or it is, because I don't know, but it's something malevolent, something that wants to appall the world.

"You have to let people know this, Sarah. Madness isn't just some materialistic dysfunction, like some kind of flu in your brain. It's much worse than that. Listen, I have proof that he's making her stronger. It's right here on my chest." He paused, and when he spoke again he sounded embarrassed. "She's growing breasts."

"What? Darnell—"

"Yes. They're still small, but they're breasts. They're the first female breasts I've ever touched in my life. Isn't that comical? Think how that feels, Sarah. The first breasts I've ever touched, and they're my own."

"Darnell, listen to me—"

"I have to go. She'll wake up soon. There was so much I wanted to tell you, I didn't get to say most of it. Talking to you was all I've had to look forward to, the last good thing for me to enjoy in this life. Now it has gone by so fast. Sarah, I . . . I know you don't want to hear me say this, it must sound almost obscene . . . but I want you to know that I liked you . . . I *do* like you. You were very kind. I suppose it's no surprise to you, but I never had a girlfriend . . . I was always shy."

She thought she probably should say, "I liked you too," but she couldn't bring herself to do it. She just wanted him to hang up, cut his wrists, and get it done.

"I'm frightened of dying," he said. "I've read accounts of near-death experiences, people floating through a tunnel toward the light, people going to the city of light, the city of God. It won't be that way for me, you know. No city of God, no light. Just the box forevermore."

She heard a muffled sound. It took her a few seconds to realize that Darnell was weeping.

"Goodbye, Sarah." He hung up.

***

Darnell hung up his disposable cellphone and sat for a while weeping in the small upstairs efficiency that Angel had rented, thinking that this ugly apartment was the last place he would ever see. No more skies, no more green parks, no more birds or squirrels or dogs or cats.

It was the kind of dump a hooker would rent. Probably she had picked it because it was cheap and because no one would pay attention if she brought men up, but he also suspected that the squalor appealed to her.

He could feel her awakening, trying to wrest control. He was light-headed now and had to struggle to keep from blacking out. He was made weaker by fear and grief.

He wanted to see Sarah once more, wanted one more pleasant evening chatting with her in his old apartment, Sarah looking so pretty and listening as no one had ever listened to him. He wanted her to understand what it was like to be Darnell Brook. He wanted to tell her the story of his strange, sad life. He wanted her to know that he had never intended to harm her or anyone else. In a few minutes he would be dead, and no one, *no* one would have ever truly known him, no one would ever mourn him.

He felt Angel squirming like a fetus in his brain and he knew time was running out. He dumped out her purse on the narrow bed and found her scalpel wrapped in a napkin. He was about to do the job when he thought of the casket that would imprison him from now on, that horrible box, and he realized that he had to leave a note.

He tore a page from Angel's little notepad, where he had found Sarah's new address, but he couldn't find a pen or pencil. He looked desperately around the room. No time to lose; Angel was fully awake now and grappling for control.

Finally he grabbed a tube of lipstick and began to write on the mirror of the vanity. His hand was jerking, wanting to go its own direction, but he managed to scrawl in bright hooker red: "CREMATION PLEASE. NO BURIAL!"

He was almost glad that she was taking over, allowing him no time to think or delay. He grasped the scalpel and tried to bring it to the vein, but his hand wouldn't cooperate. His arm no longer belonged to him. He struggled against the growing blot of darkness until it consumed him.

"Twerp!" Angel said. "I'll fix your shit for good."

She took off her clothes and felt her small breasts with pleasure. They weren't growing as quickly as she wished, but they were definitely growing. A 15-year-old girl would probably be very proud of them. The nipples were plumping up nicely, sticking out like little pink pencil erasers, and she pinched them till they hurt. No one would call them boy-nipples now.

She sat in front of the vanity and carefully threaded a needle with black cotton thread. She got a soup bowl from the kitchenette and placed the needle and thread in it along with the scalpel. She carried the bowl to the bathroom and poured in half a bottle of 91-percent isopropyl alcohol.

At the redhead's apartment she had found a bottle of Betadine and a full prescription of amoxicillin, no doubt intended to treat the girl's infected piercing. She swallowed two of the amoxicillin, slipped on a pair of sterile rubber gloves, and sat on the edge of the bathtub with her feet inside.

The twerp's little scrotum dangled loosely between her legs. She used a cotton ball to coat it with Betadine, lifted the scalpel from its alcohol bath, and made an incision. Not too big, just big enough that she could gently squeeze one testicle out and then the other.

They had been shrinking for months and weren't much bigger than marbles. They were hanging out of her body now on their thin stalks, two ugly purple globs like hemispheres of a little brain, Darnell's stupid little brain, but it wouldn't be thinking its dirty little thoughts any longer.

She pulled the scrotum up tight against her groin to expose the cords as much as possible, then held her breath and cut. The pain was incredible, a head-clearing rush, a bright cascade of agony.

The ugly little globs were lying in the bottom of the tub like purple eyeballs staring up at her.

"So there!" she said.

She was bleeding, but not as badly as she had feared. My first period, she thought. She got the needle and thread from the bowl and began to sew with nice tight overlapping stitches.

The twerp's little penis still hung there, getting in the way of her sewing, but removing it would have to wait. Angel had had enough fun for one day.

Chapter Twenty-One

Detective Okpara was about to leave when Howard came home with several bags of groceries. He stood in the foyer still holding them while Sarah told him about the phone call. At last he set the groceries on the stairs and sat down beside them, his face sagging with dismay.

"How on earth did Darnell get my number?" he said. "It's unlisted."

"Peter has it," Sarah said. "Do you think it's possible—"

She didn't finish her sentence. Surely Peter wasn't working with the killer?

"With your permission, Mr. Goldwin, I'd like put a trace on your phone," Okpara said.

"Yes, by all means. Please do."

"At least one benefit will come of this," Okpara said. "Now I'm sure your house will get the round-the-clock surveillance that I've been asking for. It will be an unmarked car with plainclothes officers, and it may be parked down the street where you won't notice it, but it will be there."

"Good luck finding a parking place on *this* street," Howard said.

Okpara smiled and left, but Howard remained seated on the stairs. The cheerful raconteur's mask had slipped from his face, and he looked older than Sarah had ever seen him, a fifties-something man with a sagging face and dyed hair, his colorful green eyes dulled over with worry. As she bent down to pick up the groceries, she noticed a cigarette burn on the sleeve of his blazer—not like Howard at all.

She carried the groceries to the kitchen and began putting them away: wine, potato salad, cold cuts, bean salad, chips, plastic cups and paper plates. He must have intended a picnic in the park to cheer them both up, and his plan made her feel all the guiltier.

But soon he appeared in the kitchen and said, "Whatever are you doing, my dear? If you put all these things away, how on earth will we eat them? I rather thought we'd go to the park. Unless, of course, you have other plans."

He rummaged in the pantry and returned with a picnic basket. Sarah was amazed; she hadn't seen one like that since she was a child. Schiller Park was only a few blocks away, and they took turns carrying the basket as they walked. The late afternoon sun was still bright and warm, but a soft breeze was promising a cooler evening.

They chose a picnic table, and Howard covered it with a clean red-checkered cloth. Sarah didn't help him because he seemed to be taking such pleasure arranging everything just so. He was beginning to look his old—or rather younger—self again. He had even brought linen napkins, which he placed neatly on the paper plates. He pulled the cork from a bottle of white zinfandel, poured, and handed her a plastic cup.

"To truth and beauty and the occasional naughty little pinch," he said. They drank and he began making sandwiches.

"So we need to figure things out," she said. "I'm moving out tomorrow, but even then you still won't be safe. I'm so sorry about this, but I'm afraid you'll need to find some place to stay until the danger is over."

"Danger? How very silly. Why, I've lived here for years and I've never had the slightest trouble. Ham or turkey?"

"Both please, and try to listen to some sense, Howard. A serial killer knows your address. Doesn't that worry you even a little tiny bit?"

"Not in the least. You said Darnell was getting ready to slash his wrists, and by now he's busy feeding the flies. Mustard or mayo?"

"Both please. What makes you think he's dead? Lots of people claim they're going to kill themselves, but how many really do?"

"Not nearly enough. Pickle?"

"Yes, thank you."

She spooned some potato salad onto her paper plate and began to eat. She was hungry but her mouth felt dry, and she had to wash the food down with wine.

"Sare, my darling, you worry far too much," Howard said at last. "We're going to stick together through this, and we're going to be happy and safe, and that's final."

She smiled. "Howard, if you were straight I'd ask you to marry me."

"And if I were straight you wouldn't need to ask me because I would have married you long ago. May I fix you another sandwich?"

"Yes please."

When they were done eating, Howard opened the second bottle of wine. He apparently felt like getting a bit drunk, and so did she. The sun was nearly down, and the cool breeze from the west felt better than anything she had felt for weeks. Odd that anything could feel so good when everything else felt so bad.

"What we need is a dog," Howard said. He was watching a woman walking past with a beautiful black German Shepherd. "A great big Rottweiler I think, one with fangs all the way down to its knees."

"What I'd like is a gun," she said. "This morning I tried to buy one, but they wouldn't let me."

"Why not?"

"Once upon a time when Peter was slapping me around I gave him a good sharp knee to the nuts, and the bastard was so pissed off that he pressed charges. Before I could do anything about it I learned my parents were dead and had to leave town. Now I'm a criminal."

"Well, I hope you kicked him really, really hard."

"Not hard enough."

"I used to own a brace of dueling pistols myself," he said. "The most gorgeous things, as big as blunderbusses—they would have terrified an elephant. Though not very practical, I suppose, by modern standards. I haven't the faintest idea how you were supposed to load them, I guess you had to pour some powder in the barrel and stick a ball in there somehow. I wish I still had them, but some perfidious young rascal pilfered them."

"That's what lovers do," she said. "They steal our blunderbusses and make us feel like shit. To hell with all lovers."

"I'll drink to that."

He refilled their cups and they drank without talking until the sun was gone and so was the wine. They were repacking the picnic basket when suddenly he said, "Sare, my dear, I believe I have just solved our little problem. Imagine a nice safe place in the country that Peter Bellman and Darnell Brook can't possibly know anything about. Imagine a place just far enough out of town that no one can follow us without being spotted, but close enough that I can easily drive back to teach. And then imagine a nice big gun in your hand, just in case."

"What are you talking about?"

"Do you trust me?"

"Of course I do."

"Then let me do the thinking and don't ask any questions. I'll make arrangements as soon as we're home, and by tomorrow night we'll be we'll be as safe and snug as two cooties in a rug."

***

Howard awoke with a small cry. He had been dreaming that he was giving a dinner party for a dozen other men at the big table in his dining room. Most of the guests were past lovers, men whom he had not seen for years, but the man seated at the head of the table he had never seen before. Already the dream was fading, and Howard could no longer remember the stranger's face, just his long flowing hair and the fact that he was the most gorgeous man Howard had ever seen.

For some reason he felt sad, though he couldn't imagine why. What he could remember of the dream seemed festive; he wondered why it should disturb him so. He rolled over and tried to go back to sleep, but the strange sadness of the dream wouldn't let him. He wanted a glass of wine; perhaps that would put him to sleep. He and Sarah had drunk some Burgundy before going to bed, and he was sure there was some left in the bottle.

At last he got up, put on his silk robe, and stepped out to the dark hallway. He heard Sarah's noisy fan as he crept past her shut door, and he hoped she was sleeping soundly. Since she had moved in, her comfort and safety were on his mind more than any other concern, and he thought with pleasure of the brilliant plan that had popped into his head during their picnic. Tomorrow night they would both be safe and secure, far from the reach of any psychotic hooligan.

It was only tonight that he had to worry about—and of course the police were out there somewhere watching, so there was really no need to worry. Still, he found that he was tiptoeing.

As he crept down the stairs, it occurred to him that the dream might have a religious meaning, the Last Supper and all that. Possibly that explained the sadness it had left him with. He had been raised a Roman Catholic, and he had never stopped believing in his childhood faith, though he had stopped attending church. He found it impossible to take comfort from a church that didn't accept him and wouldn't allow him to marry, not that he had ever wanted to. But perhaps some part of him missed attending Mass, and that was why the dream had left him with a sense of loss.

He went to the kitchen and found the half-empty bottle of Burgundy. He poured a full glass and took it to the big living room so he could sit in his favorite chair. The only light was the dim glow that seeped through the front window, and in the near-darkness the wine looked as opaque as blood.

As he gazed at the glass, it occurred to him that one didn't age gradually, but rather in fits and starts. Suddenly one was aware of being much older than the last time one had noticed. It seemed to him that he had recently become much older. Perhaps Sarah's presence had stirred something in him that made him aware of the new accumulation of years.

He was surprised by the pleasure he had been finding in thinking about someone other than himself for a change. Odd how loneliness could creep up on one like age. He wondered what it would be like to have a true mate, a lifelong partner whom he could care for as he currently was caring for Sarah.

The house was filled with quiet unsettling sounds, a creak here, a rustle there. Probably his imagination, but Howard was glad they would be getting away for a while. He no longer felt safe here, though he tried not to let Sarah see his anxiety.

A sound from the back of the house caused him to pause in mid-sip. *That* hadn't been his imagination. There it was again—a scratching sound or maybe a rustling in the privet hedge out back. Probably a cat or raccoon had gotten itself caught in the hedgerow somehow. He sat motionless with the glass to his lips and listened.

He heard it again, and finally he forced himself to get up and pad quietly in his slippers to the dark kitchen. There was a shadow on the glass behind the curtain of the back door. He stopped, and a second later the shadow moved—maybe the shadow of a man, but he wasn't sure. Then he heard rapid wheezing breath, like a mad dog panting or a mad man. He crept closer to the door and the shadow moved again.

Suddenly there was a loud, metallic tapping, like a huge steel beak pecking at the wood, and the door shook. Howard was unable to move. His thoughts were on Sarah—should he call out and warn her or run to the front door and yell for the police? Maybe they weren't even there. It was a moot question anyway, because he was frozen with terror.

The tapping ceased and the shadow vanished from behind the curtain, but he remained petrified for a long minute. At last he snatched up a long chef's knife from the counter, ran to the door, and yanked the curtain aside.

Nothing was there. He unlocked the door and jerked it open. Nothing there. He stepped out onto the stoop and peered into the shadows of the small back yard. Nothing moving, but then the corner of his eye caught something dark ducking behind the corner of his neighbor's house.

When at last he turned to go back in, he saw a sheet of paper attached to the door by a nail driven into the oak. He tore off the page and squinted.

Someone had scrawled in big childish letters: A DEAD WHORE AND A DEAD QUEER LIVE HERE.

Chapter Twenty-Two

The noisy fan in Sarah's room drowned out other sounds, even the sound of the police talking to Howard downstairs at 4:30 in the morning, and she was so exhausted that she slept peacefully until almost 11:00. She showered, and when she came downstairs she found Howard in the kitchen making sandwiches with leftovers from the picnic. He looked tired.

"Did you sleep well?" he asked.

"Like a baby. You?"

"Like a very old baby," he said. "I hope you don't mind leftovers for lunch. I have a class from 2:00 till 3:20, and then we'll hit the road. Just pack what you'll need for a couple three days."

"I guess I'll do some housecleaning while you teach."

"No," he said rather sharply. "I don't want you here by yourself any more, not till all this blows over."

This didn't sound like Howard's usual blithe attitude. "Did something happen while I was asleep?" she asked. "Another phone call?"

"No, nothing happened. I just think we need to be more careful, that's all. Oh, and there's a very rare parking place right out front at the moment. I want you to move your car there."

"Why?"

"It will be bait, my dear. We're going to leave your car parked in front of the house so every psycho in town believes you're still here. Meanwhile the police will be down the street watching in case anyone tries to break in. It was my idea, and Detective Okpara thinks it's a brilliant plan."

"You spoke to him?"

"I called him this morning to tell him where we're going, and he thinks that's a brilliant plan too."

"Well then, he knows more than I do. Where *are* we going?"

Howard smiled. "Mum's the word. You know, loose lips sink ships and all that."

"Yeah right, like I'm gonna run out and make an announcement on the news."

"Just trust me, Sare. And move your car before someone grabs the spot."

As she was walking to her car she noticed the unmarked car with two plainclothes cops inside it parked a few houses away. She waved, but they pretended they didn't see her.

When they got to the university Howard gave her some money, a grocery list, and the keys to his car so she could pick up food while he taught. Charcoal was on the list, so presumably there was an outdoor grill wherever they were going. Maybe he was borrowing a friend's vacation cabin in a woods somewhere, and she doubted she would feel any safer stuck out in some woods in the middle of nowhere. She wouldn't even have her car. What was she supposed to do while Howard was away teaching, sit out in some damn cabin all by herself?

She didn't like Howard's secrecy and had a hunch she wouldn't like his plan, and the only reason she was going along with it was to protect him: if she insisted on staying here and renting her own place, then he would be all alone in his house, and his house was probably the least safe place in town right now.

When she picked up Howard he took over the wheel and headed southeast out of town.

"Are you going to tell me where we're going now?" she asked.

"Yes. We're going to stay with my friend Benjamin Easton. He lives on a farm near Lancaster, all alone in a huge old house."

"No we're not," she said. "I absolutely refuse to deal with a stranger right now."

"Benjamin Easton is certainly no stranger, my dear. I've known him for ages, and he's a lovely man. He told me he'll be delighted to put us up until the police get everything sorted out. It will be fun."

"So this is why you were being so secretive," she said. "You knew I wouldn't agree to stay with some damn stranger."

"Guilty as charged. Forgive me, Sare, but you agreed to trust me, and you need to trust me now. I intend to keep you safe whether you want me to or not."

Sarah stared angrily at the blur of trees and houses and wished that she were driving back to childhood, to Iowa, to Johnny and her parents. She wondered why Johnny's ghost hadn't come to her like a comforting cloud of sunshine to help her through this mess. Probably because his ghost was a figment of her mind, like Darnell's Angel, just a wish-fulfilling escape from ugly reality.

Howard was talking about Ben Easton. Sarah scarcely listened, but she gathered that Ben was a psychologist—"a brilliant man, my dear"—who taught at the Lancaster Branch of Ohio University. She pictured one of those empty-headed gay hunks that Howard favored, the kind with thick golden hair and no brains underneath it.

At least if the house was as huge as Howard claimed, she would be able to hide in one of the rooms while he pursued his lust. Tomorrow when he drove in to teach she would ride in with him no matter what he said, and then she would get her car and get her own place, and that would be the end of that.

About half an hour out of town, Howard turned off the highway onto a narrow road. The land was gently hilly out here with the sweet smell of fresh hay. He drove a mile or two past a few farms, cattle staring at their car and two horses capering in a pasture, and turned into a long gravel driveway.

The sun was low enough behind them to cast shadows pointing like dark accusing fingers at the house. It looked deeply uninviting, sitting a good fifty yards off the road and half-hidden behind tall trees. It wasn't so huge as Howard had claimed, just a forlorn-looking farmhouse with white siding and on the other side of the driveway a weathered barn and some outbuildings.

The enormous front yard needed mowing and was dotted with white-headed dandelions and other weeds. Here and there were some fruit trees that needed pruning, and scattered among them were a few neglected flower beds. Obviously whoever had lived here before had tried to make something nice of the yard, but just as obviously Howard's brilliant friend was letting the place go to hell. A shame, she thought.

Howard parked beneath a tall elm with two dead branches hanging from it like ghostly hands preparing to snatch the car. They got their suitcases from the trunk, Howard's huge one and her tiny one, climbed onto the front porch and knocked. Surely Ben must have seen them heading down his driveway, but he seemed to be in no hurry to greet them.

At last the door opened, and a tall lanky man nodded at them with a faint smile that didn't look particularly happy. He didn't look like a psychologist or like anyone who should whet Howard's appetite. Older than Sarah had expected, forty at least, with a lean square-jawed face and sandy brown hair combed straight back and graying at the temples, he wore old blue jeans and a plain gray outdoors shirt that had seen some wear. And cowboy boots, for Christ's sake, scruffy-looking brown cowboy boots with squared toes.

Just some phony academic wanting to look like Clint Eastwood in one of those spaghetti westerns, Sarah thought. *The Good, the Bad, and the Bogus.*

"Benjamin, you look lovely, lovely!" Howard exclaimed. "And this is my dear friend Sarah, a most delightful young lady!"

She extended her hand and Ben shook it with no enthusiasm. His cold gray eyes met hers for only an instant, and in that instant she saw quite clearly that he didn't want her to be here, didn't want either of them here.

"Nice to meet you," he said in a voice that didn't seem to mean it, and Sarah smelled alcohol on his breath. "Come in." He reached for Sarah's small suitcase, but she rather rudely jerked it away.

He hadn't done much to clean up the place for them: books and magazines cluttered the living room sofa and the coffee table. Ben led them into a dining room, its table littered with more books, and opened a door to a stairway.

"I'll show you your rooms," he said as he started up the creaking stairs.

"Benjamin, it's been so long," Howard was saying. "How have you been? What on earth have you been doing?"

"Just a little private practice," Ben answered quietly. "I just keep a few patients, kick out the ones I don't like. That's most of them."

"Are you teaching?"

"I have the summer off."

"How I envy you."

He led them along an L-shaped hallway to a small bedroom with a brass bed, an oak washstand, and an old oak dresser with a large mirror. There were two windows, both open with screens, and in one of them a fan was blowing in fresh air.

"This okay for you?" he asked Sarah.

The room looked quaint, not the deliberate quaintness of Howard's house, more like the unintentional old-fashioned plainness of the house where Sarah had grown up. She placed her suitcase on the cedar chest at the foot of the bed and said, "It's very nice."

"Go ahead and get settled in," Ben said. "I'll show Howard his room."

"I know this is an imposition—" she began, but he had already stepped out of the room.

Howard chattered as the two men moved down the hallway. Sarah closed the door, sat on the bed, shut her eyes, and tried to imagine she was in her own apartment somewhere far away.

Long after the men had gone downstairs, she went to the bathroom. Ben had placed clean towels and washcloths on the wicker hamper. She washed her face, trying to scrub away her sour mood with the sweat. Since he was putting her up, she should make at least some effort to look friendly, but it took a lot of scrubbing before she felt able. She put on a bra, which she rarely bothered with, and then a blouse with a higher neckline and went downstairs.

The men were in the kitchen. Ben was husking the corn she had bought, and Howard was brushing marinade on the chicken. He was no longer chattering, and there was a gloomy silence that she didn't know how to break.

"There's beer and whiskey," Ben said at last. "And I see you brought some wine."

"Beer sounds good."

She got one from the refrigerator and stood there feeling awkward until Howard said, "Those coals should be getting hot." He picked up the tray of chicken, and she opened the screen door for him and followed him out back to a picnic table with a grill smoking beside it.

"Your brilliant friend doesn't want us here," she said quietly.

"Of course he does," Howard said. "I think he's just a little depressed."

"That makes two of us," she said.

Howard didn't answer. He put the chicken on the grill and stood with his back to her, poking it with his long fork. Sarah sat at the table, sipped her beer, slapped mosquitoes, and felt ashamed of herself. Howard was going out of his way to help her, and all she wanted to do was strangle him.

Eventually Ben came out. He ambled more than walked, a lanky, all-the-time-in-the-world gait that Sarah found somehow irritating. She couldn't tell if he was being insolent or was just annoyingly comfortable in his own skin.

"Corn's ready whenever the chicken is," he said in a quiet Western drawl, as if he were saying something about cattle rustlers in them there canyons. "We better eat inside, mosquitoes will be out soon."

They ate at the kitchen table. Howard's grilled chicken was good, and so was the rice Ben had fixed with tomatoes and hot peppers, but they mostly chewed in silence despite Howard's sporadic efforts to get a conversation started.

After dinner they moved into the front living room. Ben seated himself across from her in a rocking chair, his long legs seeming to stretch halfway across the room. To avoid looking at him, she stared at one of the many paintings that covered the walls, a dark landscape of jagged desert mountains, distant and aloof like Ben, and she wondered if he had painted it. Even Howard seemed to have run out of things to say.

"Tell me about Darnell," Ben said at last.

He watched her with no expression while Sarah told him what she knew. His gray eyes were like mirrored sunglasses: maybe they were paying attention, maybe they weren't, and it was none of your business anyway. She disliked him more and more, his coldness, his imposing tallness, his whiskey-abetted ease. He said nothing when she finished, and she wondered if he had even been listening.

"Do you believe this dreadful young man has done away with himself?" Howard asked.

He was slurring his words. Both men had been refilling their glasses pretty often from the bourbon bottle on the coffee table, but Howard looked trashed while Ben still looked sober and cheerless.

"I doubt it," Ben said. "Darnell said Angel is becoming dominant. If he was telling the truth, then Angel wouldn't let him kill her. If he was lying about that, then he probably wasn't telling the truth about suicide."

"What do you make of this poppycock about growing breasts?" Howard asked. "Do you think he's been taking hormones?"

"Maybe not," Ben said. "When I was a grad student I studied a criminal with multiple personalities. Some of his personalities were female, and I talked the psychiatrist in charge of the case into doing blood work when the patient was in a female phase and again when he wasn't. Turned out when the patient was in a female phase, his estrogen level shot way up. Besides, it's no great trick for a man to grow breasts. There's a small epidemic right now of men doing just that, especially guys who make birth-control pills. There are plenty of estrogen-like chemicals in every polluted river, partly because women who take the pills pee just like the rest of us. There's one chemical called diethylstilbestrol that'll send a guy to Victoria's

Secret in a hurry."

"Can Angel take over completely?" Sarah asked. "I mean sort of shove Darnell out permanently?"

"Yes," Ben said. "She's probably had the upper hand for a long time. Think of it this way: the mental models we fabricate as children are with us the rest of our lives. Imagine what strange models a child cobbles together when the world he perceives is monstrous. Young Darnell locked in a box a few feet from his dead sister—he identifies with her because she's his sister and because they share the same punishment. She's close to him, just a few feet away, but she's also separate. She's a girl, with all the otherness that entails. She's a year older, giving her the superiority of age that kids are so sensitive to. But more than that, she's *dead*. Death gives her the ultimate otherness, a kind of supernatural superiority. Darnell can't see her, but he imagines she can see him, like a ghost peering into his box.

"That's probably been his relationship with Angel until recently. They're close, but separated by a wall. She's superior to him. She knows more than he does. After all, he has locked up his pain inside of her, and that's a box he doesn't care to open. After he returns from an Angel-phase, he has no memory of what she did, at least until recently, if we can believe what he said over the phone. On the other hand, Angel always knows what Darnell is doing and thinking. It's a mental construct created in childhood, still defining his reality today. The two apartments side by side, just like the two adjacent boxes. He needed that other apartment next to his, the other box as a means of escape."

"Does that mean he's renting two places now?" Howard asked, slurring his words quite badly.

"I doubt it. Till now he has used Angel to bury his pain and anger. She acts out the anger by killing people, and Darnell remains innocent. But now the crimes have been exposed, so there's not much purpose to the innocent, ignorant side. That's why Darnell says she's pushing him out—he has become extraneous. I think they'll fit comfortably into one apartment now. The little family's getting smaller."

"What do you make of this stuff about Angel's friend?" Sarah asked.

"Darnell doesn't want to accept blame for his crimes," Ben said. "Until recently they were all Angel's doing, but now he knows she's really just a part of himself so he needs to invent a new character to take the blame. Some dark devilish 'friend' who stands behind Angel and makes her do all this. Notice he told you it was this 'friend'—not innocent Darnell—who brought Angel to life. He's Darnell's *deus ex machina*, god from the machine, or in this case a devil from the machine, creaking down from the theater ceiling on a pulley to rescue Darnell's drama of innocence."

It made a kind of sense, Sarah thought, but she wasn't convinced. It didn't fit with the feeling she had gotten from Darnell's voice and words, and he had made a point of saying that this "friend" wasn't Satan.

"You said Darnell was preoccupied with religion," Ben continued, the whiskey not slowing him down. "Religion is a common excuse with psychotic killers, God's voice in the head telling them to kill, and that's probably all this 'friend' amounts to. Other religious trappings are pretty obvious too, the candles he placed around the casket and the timing of his crimes."

"What timing?" Sarah asked.

"You said the men followed Angel home on Fridays and left on Sunday nights. Jesus was buried in the cave on Good Friday, and on Easter Sunday the rock was rolled away and Christ emerged from his tomb."

Snazzy, she thought, but a more likely explanation was that Darnell worked during the weeks and couldn't go out and play till the weekends. Of course a theory like that wouldn't get you published in *Headshrinker Quarterly*.

"There are often ritualistic aspects to these cases," Ben continued. "Religion's an excuse to these killers, and they may think of the killings as sacred religious rites. On the other hand . . ."

He stopped talking and stared at something behind her head.

"On the other hand what?" Sarah asked. She was getting tired, and Howard was dozing beside her on the sofa.

"On the other hand, everything I've been saying is probably just crap. Like the killers themselves, psychologists have invented a pseudo-religion to persuade themselves that the voices in the head aren't really there, that the dark figures in the soul are just neurons acting up."

It felt like a cynical prank, as if he had been teasing her all night with his analysis just to say ha ha, the joke's on you.

"Well, what *do* you think?" she asked. "Is Angel's friend real or not?"

Ben stared at her, his gray eyes hard as tombstones, and Sarah wondered if she was any safer with him than she would be with Darnell.

"All I know is that mental illness is probably the ugliest damn trick God ever pulled on mankind," he said. "You're much better off with cancer. Whether there's something even uglier standing behind it I don't know. It's late and I need to go to bed now."

Chapter Twenty-Three

Sarah was aware of birds chirping over the drone of the window fan before she came fully awake. One of them sounded exactly like R2-D2, squeaking and hooting while Darth Vader pursued it with a ray gun.

When she opened her eyes, it took her a moment to recognize where she was. However much she disliked Ben Easton, she liked this bedroom, the homey old furniture, the sunlit outdoorsy air blowing in through the fan, the cacophony of birds outside.

She showered and dressed and came downstairs. There was no one down there, but through the kitchen window she saw Ben sitting out back at the picnic table by himself, reading a newspaper and drinking coffee. She had been hoping that Howard would be up to insulate her from him.

There was a note on the table: "Cereal, milk, coffee. Help yourselves."

Sarah poured a cup of coffee and went to the dining room, not wanting Ben to see her through the kitchen window. The paintings on the walls were impressionistically sunny landscapes, light playing delicately on a ripe cornfield, a colorful woods, a sparkling creek wandering through bright autumn trees.

She recognized the barn in one of them, so apparently Ben was the mystery artist after all, and in fact when she looked closely she saw the name Easton in tiny letters in the bottom right corner. It was a good painting with a sort of Andrew Wyeth feel, two trees in the foreground with the barn behind them, its weathered siding glowing warmly in the sun. He had some talent at least.

There were two other rooms downstairs in addition to the kitchen, the bathroom, the dining room, and the living room where they had sat last night. One of them had its door shut, maybe Ben's studio, and the other was a second living room.

She received an unpleasant surprise when she stepped into it: the paintings in here were downright macabre. The palette had darkened, the brush stokes were jaggcd and crude, the trees and buildings were distorted, and shadowy faces with leering eyes peered through bushes that resembled bones.

A painting hanging above an old upholstered chair appeared at first to be a purely black canvas. She moved closer and discerned deep grays amidst the black, a hulking shape emerging from the gloom, a dull gleaming of sinister windows, the suggestion of a roof like a monstrous forehead.

It was the barn, transformed by the eyes of nightmare into an emblem of death.

The painting struck some ugly chord deep inside her, and she never wanted to see it again. She went back to the kitchen, fixed a bowl of corn flakes, and sat at the old fashioned wooden table. A moment later the screen door opened, and Sarah's spoon paused halfway to her mouth.

She and Ben stared at each other like two gunslingers in a saloon. "Draw, you varmint!" she felt like saying.

"Morning," he said, and headed for the coffee pot.

"Morning," she said. "Where's Howard?"

"Asleep I guess. I don't think whiskey agrees with him."

"Anything in the paper about Darnell?" she asked.

"Nothing interesting."

Ben poured some milk into his coffee and went back out, screen door banging behind him.

Goddammit, Howard, wake up, Sarah thought. All that whiskey must have half-killed him. She rinsed her bowl and glanced out the window. Ben was back at the picnic table, arms crossed, long legs sticking out like two telephone poles.

Try to be friendly, Sarah thought. He *is* putting me up. She poured some more coffee, stepped out and headed for the picnic table. The grass was still dewy, soaking her sneakers. Last night she had noticed that the grass was neatly mowed back here. She figured he probably kept the front looking awful just to scare people away.

He didn't say anything when she sat down, but he handed her the paper. He was busy staring at the barn as if waiting for it to collapse. The weathered building looked as if it might oblige any minute.

Small article in the front section about the manhunt, nothing helpful. Sarah turned to the rentals and had read most of the way through them before Ben spoke.

"Did you sleep okay?" he asked.

"Very well, thank you."

She noticed a furnished efficiency that was cheap: "AC, kitchen, laundry, $425/mo incls all utilities. NS environment."

"You rent this place?" she asked.

"It's mine. I rent out the fields to a neighbor."

"Have you lived here long?"

"Seven years. I was born in Texas, came here to teach."

Sarah thought about the flower beds and fruit trees out front. They looked neglected, but definitely hadn't been neglected for seven years. She wondered why he had cared for them once and no longer did. She glanced at him and saw he was still staring at the barn.

"I like the barn," she said.

"I hate it. I'm thinking I should have it torn down."

"Looks like it just needs some paint," she said. "I love old barns. I love fields and country air. It's very nice here."

"It's nice if you like privacy," he said.

Ouch.

"Well, as to that, I'll be getting out of your hair today," she said. "I'm going into town with Howard and I'm renting a room. But I do thank you for your hospitality."

He stared at her as if he had no idea what she was talking about.

"You misunderstood me," he said at last. "That's not what I meant. I very much want you and Howard to stay here until Darnell is safely behind bars."

She didn't say anything.

"Howard is probably my best friend, and you're his friend," he said. "I want both of you to be safe."

"Thanks, but I don't like to be nuisance. Like I said—"

"You don't understand," he said. "I'm very aware that my social skills aren't exactly at their peak right now, but that has nothing to do with you and Howard. It's too much country air I guess, too much privacy. Right now I could use some company, so you'd be doing me a favor."

His gray eyes didn't look so hard and chilly at the moment. She saw pain behind them.

"Well, if I get in the way please let me know," she said.

"Howard tells me you want to buy a gun," he said. "Have you ever shot one?"

"No."

"Guns are dangerous if you don't know how to use them. Why don't I bring out a couple and you can try them. I've got a shooting range behind the barn."

Great. Not only was he a nut, he was a fucking gun nut too. It figured. His barn was probably full of fertilizer bombs.

"Thanks. I dunno."

He ambled to the house and returned in a while with a big duffel bag strapped over his shoulder. She followed him to the barnyard, where there was a rough wooden shooting table and some targets at varying distances with bales of straw piled behind them to stop the bullets. Beyond the shooting range were cornfields on either side of a weedy lane that led to a woods.

He set his bag on the table, pulled out a plastic gun box and opened it.

"Let's start you off with something simple, a .22 revolver. This is a Taurus, six-inch barrel, holds nine rounds. You can see that it's empty, but the first thing you need to know is that a gun is always loaded, even if you know it's not. Sometimes the things we're most certain of turn out not to be true. You never ever point a gun at yourself or anyone else unless you mean business. You load it like this. Put on these glasses and ear protectors."

He showed her how to hold the gun. She aimed carefully, but when she pulled the trigger the barrel moved and the bullet ended up nicking a bale of straw two feet above the target.

"Don't pull the trigger," he said. "Squeeze it."

She hit the edge of the target on third try, and after a while she was aiming at a more distant target and hitting it not too far from the center. He pulled out a .22 caliber Browning Buckmark semi-automatic, showed her how to load it and how to jack the slide, and pretty soon she was making five-inch groups on the 20-yard target.

"You're good at this," he said. "Let's try a bigger caliber."

He opened another box and removed a small revolver that looked familiar. "This will shoot .357 Magnum, but I think that's more kick and flash than you'll want, so I'm going to load it with .38 Special. Try this on the 20-foot target. It's not made for long range."

She examined the gun more closely. It was the same Ruger LCR she had looked at in the gun store, the one priced way out of her budget at $450. It kicked and spat some fire, even loaded with .38 Special, but she didn't mind, and pretty soon she was printing fairly tight groups on the target.

Howard handed her a tiny leather holster. "This will protect the gun when you carry it in your purse," he said.

She stared at the holster, then at him. "If you're thinking of selling it, I'm not sure I can afford it," she said.

"I can't very well sell it because I just gave it to you."

"No, I can't possibly accept it."

He turned away rather coldly, as if offended.

"Whatever suits you," he said. "If you want to give it back after Darnell is locked up, that's your business. But until then I want you to keep it with you at all times."

Howard emerged from the house and shambled toward them with uncertain steps. He was showered and groomed but didn't look well.

"Thank goodness it's you two," he said. "I was certain that Armageddon had erupted. Benjamin, what on earth did you put in that whiskey? Today I shall take the pledge of temperance. Never shall Beelzebub's venomous sour mash pollute these lips again."

Ben grinned. It was the first time Sarah had seen him smile.

"Must be that dead raccoon I tossed in the still," he said. "Howard, I want you to do the same thing she's doing—learn how to use these things."

"Not now, dear friend, not now!"

"Tomorrow then," Ben said. "You guys ready for lunch?"

"How can you even think of food?" Howard said. "I'm going to toddle back inside, curl up on the sofa, and hope it doesn't spin around too much. Somehow I must repair myself. Tell me honestly, is it really Thursday? If so, I have a class to teach this evening. Oh, the horror." He headed for the house.

"Hungry?" Ben asked her.

"I guess. Maybe I could just try a few rounds of .357 first."

"Fun, isn't it?" He handed her the box of ammo.

"It's interesting," she admitted.

Sarah loaded the revolver and took careful aim at the 20-foot target. The gun kicked like a jack hammer and fire seemed to shoot two feet from the barrel.

When she was finished, Ben removed his ear protectors and gathered up the guns. "Hell of a cartridge," he said. "If what's after you is flesh and blood, this will do the trick."

He looked back at the barn and she did too. It did look rather creepy, she thought, the once-white siding weathered gray and the glassless upper windows staring down at them with the deep darkness of the hayloft. Their gaze reminded her of Ben's eyes.

"Of course, some things aren't flesh and blood," he said. He strapped the bag over his shoulder and headed for the house.

Chapter Twenty-Four

Peter Bellman stood at his bathroom mirror and trimmed his beard. The Big Truth was what really mattered, but mundane details were also part of the scheme, and keeping up appearances was part of the detail work. The High Priestess of the Solitary One had no patience with sloppiness. He had been sloppy at first, before his brain had time to adjust to the Big Truth, but there would be no sloppiness tonight. Tonight was for keeps, and he wanted the details to be perfect.

He wished now that his beard had been neater and his clothes cleaner two days ago when the detective had paid his visit. The ignorant heathen were obsessed with appearances, and Okpara even more than most. Such nonsense: if only Peter had shaved, then there wouldn't be plainclothes cops parked down the street watching his house right now. They were easy to spot, coffee in one hand and donut in the other, sitting there for hours as if their car were a new house on the street, easy to spot but still a nuisance.

Now his beard looked perfect and his living room was nice and spotless, in case the detective showed up again. The rest of the house was a mess, but he preferred it that way.

This benighted age belonged to appearance-freaks, number-crunchers, detail-worshippers, and fact-mongers like that slut Sarah. They had grown powerful in the days of the Industrial Revolution, and each new toy wrought by capitalism had abetted them in their battle against truth. Now truth was plastered over with billboards, repudiated by glossy magazines selling expensive crap, painted over with expensive cosmetics and facelifts, drowned out by smiley-faced fools on TV, and smothered beneath the weight of useless gaudy junk.

The hypocrisy of our time was like the falsehood of modern funerals, the beautiful truth of death painted over with mortician's makeup, the coffin gilded so our eyes wouldn't notice the dark dirt it was being lowered into. Peter of course had been aware of this even before his Awakening, but then he had doubted there was any great truth behind the phony facade. Now he knew there was. The squalor of his house was a kind of *memento mori* to keep his mind on the rich dirt of truth.

Another *memento mori* was Sarah's stupid cat rotting on the bathroom counter. He probably should toss it out before the maggots turned into flies, but he liked the smell.

He had shaped his beard into a neat respectable Vandyke, and now he painted it jet black with liquid shoe polish. He cut his long red hair until it was just above his collar, then he painted it black like his beard and slicked it straight back until it was plastered flat against his head.

Even Okpara wouldn't recognize him now. He grinned at the mirror and said, "Ooo, who is that handsome young man!"

He went to his bedroom to put on a freshly laundered shirt, khaki pants, and a nice pair of boat shoes with soft quiet soles. In the kitchen he slipped a pair of rubber gloves into his hip pocket and selected a boning knife with a thin seven-inch blade. He had read somewhere that a boning knife was ideal because it would give slightly to slip past bone. It was an expensive piece of German cutlery, and he was certain it wouldn't break. He felt the blade for sharpness, slipped it into the cardboard sheath he had made, and taped the sheath to his leg near the ankle. When he pulled up his sock and dropped his pants leg, the knife was perfectly hidden.

He went to the living room, lifted the drape and peered out. The cop car was still there, halfway down the block where the fools thought he wouldn't notice them. That was good—he was afraid they might have sneaked away to get some more donuts. Dumb bastards were earning their pay at least.

He stepped out onto his front porch so they could see that he was at home, and just to be sure they noticed him he yelled loudly at a little kid walking past: "Hey, you dumb fuck, get your ass outta my yard!"

Then he realized that he didn't want the cops to see his black hair dye, so he ducked back inside. Details, details.

It was 4:15, time to get moving. He had checked the schedule of summer classes and knew that Howard had a class from 5:00 to 6:20, which meant a certain sleazy ho was going to be home all alone pretty soon like Little Miss Muffet. He turned on the TV with the sound cranked up loud, turned on a couple lights to fool the cops after the sun went down, put on a pair of dark sunglasses, swigged some scotch from the bottle, and slipped quietly out the back door.

There were many things these dumb cops didn't know, like for example they probably didn't know that there was a gate in the back of his privacy fence that opened to his neighbors' back yard on the next street over, and they surely didn't know that those neighbors were his friends, and they sure as fucking hell didn't know that those neighbors were on vacation and had given him their house key so he could take care of their tropical fish.

He used their key to open their back door and then used their phone to order a taxi. While he was waiting for it, he stared at the dead fish floating in their aquarium. Details, details.

He had the cab drop him at a bar not too far from Howard's house, but not too near either. The street he strolled casually down was the one just west of Howard's, where there wouldn't be any unmarked cop cars.

One more thing these dumb cops didn't know was that he had found a secret passage to Howard's back yard. The old brick houses in this neighborhood were jammed so close together that some of them didn't even have side windows, just a skinny little path between them to the back yard. A couple nights ago he had discovered the path between two houses that led to the backyard that adjoined Howard's backyard on the next street over, with just a hedge to separate them.

That night he had chickened out and just left a cheerful little note, but the High Priestess had no patience with cowardice, and he wasn't going to chicken out tonight.

He arrived at his secret path, peered casually at the two houses beside it, and couldn't see any signs of life in either of them. It was better to do this sort of work after dark, of course, but there were some advantages to this hour of day. For one, the people who lived in this neighborhood were mostly white collar types, which meant most of them were still at work. Secondly, people who sneaked down a skinny path between two houses looked suspicious at night, but when the sun was still up they just looked like normal folks going to visit a friend's back yard.

In the unlikely event that someone noticed a stranger with black hair and a black Vandyke, so what? Before he went to bed tonight both beard and hair would be shaved off. Details, details.

He took one last look at everything and hurried down the narrow concrete path. The danger was that there might be someone in either of the backyards, but there wasn't, so he hurried to the hedge in back and peered through it to make sure no one was staring out one of Howard's back windows. No one was, so he wriggled through the hedge into Howard's dinky little backyard and sprinted to the back of his old brick house.

This was fun.

He pressed his toe against the basement window, intending to give it a swift kick, but realized he didn't need to when the bottom of the window budged. The damn fool hadn't remembered to lock it. The window, hinged at the top, swung upward easily, and Peter slid down noiselessly to the basement floor.

It was dark and musty down here, a furnace and some junk furniture and countless shadows. The shadows, the shadows. The bright toys that glittered in the light changed every year, new, improved, better-than-ever gizmos that tempted the heathen away from truth, but these shadows always remained the same. These were the same shadows that Solomon had gazed on; these were the shadows that had danced on the walls of caves while hunters huddled beside their fires. The truths in these shadows were the same ones that the ancients had glimpsed, truths that the earliest men had seen, their restless brains piercing the deep riddles with apelike eyes before glittering toys had blinded them.

Peter stood in the shadows and pondered the Big Truth that the Solitary One had given him. A word, but more than a word, a word worth more than all the tinsel of this world, a word that gave sight to the blind. A clash of clattering consonants with the ghosts of vowels whistling and wailing between them like wind blowing past the iron fence and carved stones of a graveyard. The sound reminded him of Hebrew, but he knew it was made of a language that had died before Moses was born, a jagged shape of sound that couldn't be transcribed in the Arabic alphabet. Not that Peter would ever need to write it down—it was written indelibly in his memory, it had altered the convolutions of his brain, it was a fingerprint stamped on his mind.

Now it was time to give the Big Truth to Little Miss Muffit. He pulled the boning knife from its cardboard sheath and crept up the basement stairs.

Chapter Twenty-Five

Howard's class was supposed to meet until 6:20, but he let them out at 6:00. His hangover had settled down from tidal waves of agony to a stagnant lagoon of malaise, but he was still in no shape to teach.

Besides, he was eager to get back to the farmhouse. He knew that Sarah wasn't comfortable around Ben, and he knew she would feel better with him there. It was exhausting to keep up a show of good spirits for her when in fact he was frightened out of his wits, but he didn't intend to let her down. He was going to help her through this. It was so rare that he had an opportunity to care for someone.

He was surprised by how fond he had become of Sarah. It was sad to know that when this dreadful crisis was over she would return to being just a friend. They would meet occasionally for coffee, and she would find him pleasantly amusing, and then they would go their separate ways.

All day he had been entertaining a bittersweet daydream that she would continue to live with him. They could have such fun together, little parties and picnics and strolls and many happy stories shared over wine. But it was just a daydream: soon she would be gone.

Howard eased his car out of the faculty parking lot and headed toward his house. He needed to pick up a few things to bring to the farm.

Straight men with their wives and children had no inkling of loneliness, he thought. If only he were attracted to men his own age, perhaps he could find a stable relationship. But older men appealed to him no more than women, and the lovely young butterflies he chased merely took his gifts and then fluttered off to other foolish old sugar daddies. He had been robbed and even beaten up by them, but he had never been loved.

When he got to his neighborhood, it occurred to him that a nice gift might cheer Sarah. He drove around for a while on the bumpy brick streets, trying to think of what she would like. There was a candy store that made divine fudge, but she didn't seem like a candy-person. He parked and stepped into an antique store, hoping that something would catch his eye. A vase? No, she wasn't a vase-person either. Perhaps a nice old book. No, she had too many already.

At the jewelry counter he spotted a lovely pair of earrings, simple globes of gold, but the gold had a mysterious hue that reminded him of what his grandmother used to wear. The woman at the counter explained that it was rose-gold, an old-fashioned look, unusual these days. Howard asked her to gift-wrap them, and as he carried them to his car he thought of how splendid they would look on Sarah's ears.

In his small front yard he stooped to pull a couple of weeds from his ornamental herb garden. He detested weeds like pimples or wrinkles and found it difficult to pass by his garden without pulling a few. He spotted a big, slovenly dandelion that had taken up residence in the center of the lavender, a barbarian ensconced in the royal court, but evicting it would have to wait until he was dressed for gardening.

He had set timers to turn some lights on and off automatically, and the lamp glowing through the front window was comforting, but his big brick house no longer felt dependable or secure. He was tempted to follow the cobblestone walk around back to examine the rear windows, but he told himself that if he gave in to paranoia it would soon consume him. Besides, the police were supposedly parked somewhere on the street, though he hadn't seen them.

He let himself in and glanced cautiously into the two living rooms. Everything looked as it should. Even so, he tiptoed up the stairs and crept along the hallway to Sarah's room.

Feeling like a trespasser, he searched through her closet and dresser for things she might want. The mysteries of women, their frilly little underthings, their perfumes and cosmetics like witch potions—really they were a different species altogether, enigmatic daughters of the moon.

He placed a few items in a shopping bag and gazed with trepidation at her computer. It would be nice to bring it along, but he was certain that if he unplugged it some strange electronic genie would wipe out its micro-widgets for good. He considered himself the last Victorian, quite out of place in this sordid modern world, and electronic gadgets seemed to dislike him as much as he disliked them.

He went to the bathroom to find his hair dye and made the

mistake of glancing in the mirror. Last night's whiskey seemed to have shot the clock forward several years. His face was so baggy and sunken that he could discern the skull beneath.

Nothing frightened Howard so much as aging, and he hurried to his bedroom and searched through his closet. Which tie goes best with this jacket? he wondered. Where on earth did I put that set of cufflinks?

He froze, a colorful silk tie in one hand, a blue linen jacket in the other. There had been a soft noise downstairs, like the sound of the front door easing shut. But that was impossible—he had locked it behind him when he came in.

He stood still for a minute, hearing all sorts of things and hearing nothing. Very quietly he placed the jacket and tie on his bed. There was no phone upstairs to call the police. Maybe he should stick his head out the window and yell for them, but he hadn't seen their car anywhere when he was searching for a parking place. Besides, one shouldn't call the police about every little squeak or creak.

He glanced around for a weapon. Though the fireplace in his bedroom was unusable, he kept antique wrought-iron implements leaning in front of it. He crept over and grasped the heavy iron poker. It would stop anything that walked.

Emboldened by the weapon, he moved quietly to the top of the stairs and called down, "Who's there?" His voice sounded frail in the silence.

"I'm coming down," he said at last. "I'm armed. I have a big gun, a .352 Magnum."

He had gotten the number wrong, he realized. What did they call those things?

"It's loaded," he said, his voice a kind of wail in the damnable hush.

Each step down the stairs was a battle against muscles gelatinous from last night's whiskey and tonight's fear, but at last he made it to the foyer. From here he could see into both living rooms, and nobody was there. He disliked massive sofas and instead had delicate loveseats and settees that no one could hide behind.

He took a quick look at the kitchen and then the dining room. There sat his big oak table, gleaming with lemon oil and waiting for a banquet. There was the beautiful sideboard that he had purchased so cheaply at an estate auction. The windows on either side of it were neatly shut behind their white lace curtains. It must have been his imagination after all, just nerves.

He was stepping back into the foyer when he heard what sounded like the jangle of coat hangers—and then the door of the coat closet burst open and someone dashed out of it so quickly that Howard had no time to react.

In the next instant the back of his head banged hard against the dining room floor, and he was lying flat on his back with someone sitting on his belly. He had dropped his iron poker, and the assailant snatched it up before Howard could regain his senses.

It took him a few seconds to recognize Peter. He looked so different, his hair plastered straight back and painted black, the dye or whatever it was trickling down his sweaty forehead. He wore sunglasses and had a ridiculous pointy little black goatee. It was very badly trimmed, cut an inch higher on one side of his face than on the other. And for some reason he was wearing Howard's barbeque apron.

He sat there on top of Howard's aching belly and grinned down at him. "Hey, old Howie, it's great to see you," he said. "Why don't you ever invite me over for dinner? You got this nice dining room and all. Maybe I'm not queer enough for you, is that it?"

He was wearing bright yellow rubber gloves and held the fireplace poker in one hand and a kitchen knife in the other. He began to rub the knife blade against the poker as if honing it.

"Well, aren't you at least going to say hi? And by the way don't try screaming or I'll knock your fucking teeth out. Okay then, if you don't want to be friendly let's get right down to business. Just tell me where she is, and I'll leave you alone."

"Who?" Howard said.

Peter jabbed the tip of the poker hard into one of his ribs.

"Come on, Howie baby, don't make me get rude. We're friends and colleagues, aren't we, so let's keep this all nice and friendly. You know who I mean, our mutual friend with the big gaping vagina."

"How would I know where she is? You can see, there's no one here but me."

Peter jabbed Howard's Adam's apple with the tip of his knife.

"You fucking liar. Here I'm trying to be nice and friendly, and all you do is lie to me. Her fucking car's parked right out front. Where is she?"

"I don't know, I swear I don't. It's true she was staying with me, but she went out for a walk last night and never returned. The police are looking for her. They're afraid Darnell has nabbed her."

"You fucking liar." The tip of Peter's knife pressed deeper into Howard's throat, and he thought he felt blood trickling down the side of his neck. "Truth is all that matters, and the whole world paints it over with lies."

"Peter, try to listen to reason. You won't get by with this. The police are watching my house, they're parked right out front. I promise you if you leave right now I'll keep my mouth shut. I promise that as a gentleman."

"I said, where the fuck is she? Tell me now or lose an eye."

Howard yelled for help, and an instant later the iron poker smashed his face.

When he regained consciousness, his mouth was a raging cavern of pain. He tasted blood and when he moved his tongue he felt something like pebbles in his mouth. He spit them out onto the hardwood floor and stared at them. They were teeth, chunks of teeth and whole teeth lying in a little puddle of blood.

His beautiful teeth, which he had always taken such good care of. He tried to picture himself with false teeth. It was impossible, and with that thought he realized he was going to die.

A sound emerged from his throat, not really a scream, a sort of keening, and Peter smashed his shoulder with the poker.

"Shut up with that fucking noise," he said. "I don't want to hear another peep out of you."

He threw something down on the floor beside Howard, a notepad and a pencil. "Write down where she is, and I'll do you a great favor. I'll cut your throat, and you'll be dead in a moment. Otherwise, you're going to die more slowly and horribly than you can even imagine. Now write! And don't tell a fucking fib. I want her cell phone number too. I'm going to call, and if it's not her number I'll string out your death inch by stinking inch."

It's impossible, Howard thought. I can't die today. So many things to do.

"Write!"

Howard's shoulder seemed to be broken, and it was painful to roll into a position where he could press his pencil against the pad. He waited a moment for his eyes to focus and then scrawled, "Peter Bellman did this to me."

Peter read it and chuckled. "Cute," he said. "Tell you what, I'm getting a little sick of your behavior. I've tried to be nice, and you treat me like shit. Unbutton your shirt. I said, unbutton your fucking shirt."

Because of the shoulder, Howard had to undo the buttons with one hand.

"Theologians used to argue that Adam had no navel, not being born of woman," Peter said. "Think of the nonsense they've wasted their time on, just to avoid the big truths. Well, I'm going to turn you into Adam, Howie old boy, and then maybe you'll know some truth."

The pain was appalling. Howard tried to lose consciousness but couldn't. When it was done, Peter held the bloody hunk of flesh in front of Howard's face.

"Is it an inny or an outy?" he said. "Aww, it's an inny. I cut out your inny, and now it's an outy."

He rubbed the bloody mess against Howard's nose and sniggered like a dirty-minded schoolboy.

"This is only the beginning, my friend. You're Adam now, and this is the beginning of your paradise of pain. Unless you start writing."

Mother of God, Howard prayed silently, comfort us now in the hour of our death.

"You'll change your mind," Peter said. He began doing something down there, probing with his gloved fingers. "You want to string this out, we'll do just that. Look look look! Oh, look what I have!"

Howard looked: it was a loop of his intestine, pulled a foot or so out of his body.

"Every fifteen seconds, a little more comes out," Peter said. "One, two, three . . ."

The pain squirmed and crawled like a brutish tomcat digging into Howard with sharp claws. It occurred to him that Sarah would never get her earrings, and his eyes began to blur.

Peter pulled. "This is your shitty life, Howie, coming out foot by foot," he said. "We're getting to the truth now. One, two, three . . ."

The tomcat snarled and clawed. Howard pictured Sarah wearing the earrings. They glowed like rose-hued moons. She's still young, he thought. She'll get through this. Fortune will shine on her again.

Peter pulled. "Oh, Howie, you stink! Look at you, guts hanging out. Weren't you ever potty trained?"

Howard felt embarrassed, so dirty. He could smell himself, even over the pain. Mother of God, he mouthed, his tongue writhing against broken teeth.

What was Peter doing? Lifting something. Mother of God, now in the hour. He was lifting the leg of the dining room table, looping the intestine around the leg.

"I'm going to let you do the work," Peter said. "In 15 seconds, you either write or you crawl. One, two, three . . . "

Ben will take care of her. She's in good hands. Mother of God, pray for us now.

"Crawl."

Howard wouldn't. He lay there. He had crawled and kowtowed before plenty of men, men half his age, but he wasn't going to crawl now, not this late in the day.

He felt Peter lifting him to his feet, holding him up on watery legs. The brutish alley cat seemed to be withdrawing its claws and slinking away, leaving behind it a deep embarrassment even worse than pain. So uncouth—his clothing soiled with his own insides.

"Let's dance, my dear," Peter said. "I'll lead."

Howard felt himself being moved around the floor. He thought he heard a band strike up a Viennese waltz, something by Strauss the Younger. In Peter's arms he whirled, and he saw that people were seated at the table, lifting glasses of wine to applaud their dance.

He saw faces he recognized, and he thought how nice of them to stop by. There sat John, that boy with hair like wheat—Howard hadn't seen him in years! He was aware that his shirt was hanging open, that he had clumsily spilled something down his front, and he hoped his guests wouldn't notice. Oh, and there was Mark, that shy young man with the charming stammer.

They all looked so happy, and as the room grew darker and he and his partner whirled faster, Howard suddenly noticed the gorgeous man seated at the head of the table, the man with the long flowing hair and the gentle eyes. The man smiled at him, and Howard realized that the man was going to ask him for the next dance.

Yes, he thought, I've waited all my life to dance with him. Such a lovely face, such a pleasant party, I believe I shall dance all night.

Part Four: A Ghost of Other Light Flutters

Chapter Twenty-Six

"I'll be back in about four hours," Ben said.

Sarah didn't answer and scarcely even nodded to show that she had heard him. She was sitting on the porch swing, her hand resting on the Ruger LCR in her lap, her eyes on the long driveway scarcely blinking. She had been sitting there a lot for the past three days.

Thursday night when Howard didn't come back she had called Okpara, and when he called her back an hour later with the terrible news she went out to the front porch with her gun and apparently had sat out there the whole night without sleeping, though Ben couldn't be sure because eventually he had drifted to sleep on the sofa in the front living room.

Yesterday she had eaten two donuts and an apple, an improvement over the day before. Now it was Monday, and her eyes were still glazed with an inward look, as if she was watching something inside her mind more than anything in the material world.

It was a look all too familiar to Ben, a look that frightened him more than an open wound. Flesh wounds were much easier to treat.

He hated to leave her like this. He had canceled his appointments with most of his patients, well-to-do neurotics inventing problems because life hadn't provided them with enough, but there were a few patients he didn't feel comfortable canceling, those who really needed some help. The irony didn't escape him: dreading to leave Sarah in order to go see patients, when in fact he was the last person on earth who could help any of them.

"Physician, heal thyself," he muttered as he opened the garage door.

Sarah's car was parked in the garage beside his. Yesterday he had gotten it with the help of a friend. Ben had dropped him off at the park near Howard's house. From there the friend had walked to Sarah's car and had driven it to a parking lot a mile away and had waited there until he was certain no one was following him. Only then could he bring the car to Ben's place.

Ben backed out and shut the garage door. At least Sarah would be safe here, he thought. No way anyone could slip down that long driveway without her noticing. And despite her state of shock, she was certainly alert, like a coyote. But he knew that the deadliest foe was the enemy within.

He headed up the driveway. The last thing he had wanted was a house guest, especially a woman with Sarah's troubles. If anyone except Howard had requested the favor, he would have refused. But Howard had been such a help during Ben's darkest time, offering better remedy with his bottles of wine and hours of company than any psychiatrist could have done with his meds. It seemed impossible that the gentle, kind man was dead. And now that Sarah needed help, Ben couldn't abandon her.

In his rearview mirror he could see her sitting there and watching. God save you from my help, he thought.

***

Sarah watched Ben's car pull out of the driveway. If she was sorry to see him leave, it was only because four eyes could watch better than two.

He no longer annoyed her. His quiet aloofness didn't matter to her one way or another. All she felt toward him was gratitude for providing her with a place to stay, a place with such a long safe driveway. Aside from that, he was merely a body, something that walked around and banged cupboards and doors and tried to get her to eat sandwiches that she didn't want.

She didn't have any room in her mind to think about Ben because all the room was taken up by grief, remorse, and anger. She would gladly trade her life for a chance to turn back the clock a few days and undo her idiotic mistake of moving into Howard's house. What had she been thinking? She had placed her needs above his safety, and now Howard's blood was on her hands, and she knew she could never wash it off.

Avenging his death wouldn't wash her hands, but at least it would give them something to do. She watched the driveway hoping that his killer would head down it toward the Ruger waiting in her lap or the .30-30 Winchester lever rifle waiting in the living room. Would it be Peter or Angel? If the cops had noticed any clues to link one or the other, Okpara hadn't shared them with her.

Sometimes she imagined driving to Peter's house, ringing his doorbell, and blowing out his brains. Then she would comb every street of the city looking for Darnell or Angel or whoever the two-brained monster was pretending to be at the moment. But she wasn't entirely crazy, not yet at least, so instead she sat and watched and waited.

The driveway remained empty. At last she went into the house and hunted through Ben's duffle bag for ear protectors and ammunition. She went to the range, stood in the blazing sun and shot until her wrist ached.

Amazing how purpose improved one's aim. She left a large ragged hole in the center of the target, a few stray holes surrounding it like flies buzzing around the body of her prey.

***

Matthew Hamelin sat alone in the back booth of a bar. He was making every effort to look as if he shunned attention, knowing that this was sometimes the best way to attract it, and in fact he wanted attention very badly. He hadn't had sex in months, actually years, in fact only twice in his life, and those two times were way back three years ago when he had attended Warren G. Harding High and they were with the second-fattest and first-ugliest girl in his class. Not exactly the love-life of Shelley or Byron.

So he huddled in his booth hunched over his notebook, in which he had started to write a poem, though in fact he had written only one line and was unable to think of another because the bar was unusually busy and noisy for a Monday night. Even though it was pretty far from campus it had been invaded by a mob of brainless drunken students who were shouting dumb jokes and hooting with laughter over the blaring jukebox.

Hamelin huddled and frowned and hunched and chewed his pencil and tried to blare just as loudly with his posture that he wanted no attention whatsoever, that he was far too serious to be bothered by half-dressed women and their silly breasts. Unfortunately, nobody seemed to notice.

Hamelin reread his line, wondering what should follow it: "The tethers of time shall tick with tedious tyranny . . ." Until when? he wondered. Until the end of time, of course, and he tried to find words to capture the end of time. Bones rocketing out of the hills. Yes, that was good. "The tethers of time shall tick with tedious tyranny / Until bones rocket out of the hills and . . ."

But wait, hadn't he read that phrase somewhere—Dylan Thomas, maybe? Sure, everything had been said before, and he hunched down further, bitterly envying dead poets, whose jobs had been easier because in their day everything hadn't already been said.

A shadow fell over his page. Hamelin looked up at an attractive woman, a bit older than most college students maybe, a bit too heavily made up for his taste, but attractive nonetheless, her brilliant red hair shimmering mysteriously in the dim bar light.

A Pre-Raphaelite enchantress, he thought. A lovely haunter of tombs and ruins, pale of skin with pale blue eyes, a beauteous muse of poets and painters.

"What are you writing?" she asked.

"Nothing," he stammered, suddenly ashamed of the single line he had written, so silly with all that ridiculous alliteration.

"Please, let me see."

Hamelin reluctantly handed her the notebook. She furrowed her pretty brow and studied the line. At last she smiled.

"I like it," she said. "The tethers of time shall tick with tedious tyranny / Till the box, unlocked, bequeaths its darkness to all."

"Yes!" he exclaimed. "Pandora's box! The end of time! May I write it down?"

"Sure," she said, handing him the notebook. "But why don't you come with me, and I'll teach you some different words. Words you've never even dreamt of."

Chapter Twenty-Seven

Howard's funeral was the next day, and the melancholy reality brought Sarah a step or two out of her withdrawal.

"I can't go," Ben said. "I don't want anyone to see me there and say, yeah, that's one place I haven't looked, I'll bet Sarah's staying with that guy."

"I'm going," Sarah said. "I need to."

"I figured you would. I'm going to follow you and try to find a place to park where I can keep my eye on the funeral home."

"You don't need to do that," she said. He didn't answer, and she said, "It's not fair that you can't go. He was your friend too."

"Yeah, he was my friend, maybe my best friend, but I can honor his memory best by keeping you safe. That's what he'd want me to do."

He said it with no particular affection, just stated it as a fact, and she knew he meant it.

"There's one other thing," he said. "I know you'll resist my advice, but I want you to listen to it. I think you're feeling guilty for his death, and I know from long experience that guilt mixed with grief is deadly poison. It's essential that you stop feeling guilty."

"That's not so easy."

"No, but there's a method that helps. Every time you feel guilty, the instant you know you're feeling it, you need to repeat something like a mantra until you've blocked the feeling. Maybe the mantra should be 'Howard wouldn't blame me, so I won't blame myself,' or whatever works for you, just so it's short and to the point. Say it out loud if you're alone, otherwise sound it out in your mind. Maybe for a while you'll need to repeat it hundreds of times a day, then after a while not so much."

"I'll try that," she said.

She had nothing appropriate to wear, her only black suit still hanging at Howard's place or maybe even impounded as evidence at the police station, so when she got to Columbus she stopped at a store, bought the first dark dress she saw, and put it on in the dressing room.

When she came out to the parking lot she saw Ben watching her, his car parked some distance from hers. She liked his wariness. The mind of a warrior, she thought, or maybe an outlaw, and she wondered who he was, this stranger who was sheltering her.

The viewing room at the funeral home was nearly full, many people whom she recognized from the department, many others whom she had never seen. He'd had so many friends that it seemed odd she thought of him as a lonely man. The dignified silver-haired woman sitting in front she had met a couple of times—it was Howard's mother, and she thought she should go up and offer her sympathy, but she was afraid that if she did something might break inside. The smell of flowers and the cloying sound of the piped-in organ music were making her feel sick, and she wished she hadn't eaten the food Ben had forced on her before she left the house.

She went to the front of the room and stood at the closed casket. Another smothering box, she thought. How many boxes had already been spawned by Gus Dietrick's grim original, evil begetting evil like a malignant cancer, and how many more boxes would there be?

Over the casket she mumbled some lines from Blake, Howard's favorite poet:

So I turn'd to the Garden of Love
That so many sweet flowers bore,
And I saw it was filled with graves,
And tomb-stones where flowers should be . . .

She tried to pray, but found herself talking to Howard instead of God, hoping that something remained of him to hear her thanking him and giving him her love and begging his forgiveness.

She hardly noticed that someone had come up beside her until he spoke: "How's it going, Sary baby? I've been looking high and low for you."

She could scarcely believe this was Peter. He looked like a punk rocker from Bedlam. His head and face were shaved and dotted with pink razor nicks. He wore sunglasses, dirty khaki shorts, and a garish Hawaiian shirt. She recognized it as one he used to wear sometimes at his parties as a gag. "The loudest shirt in the world," he used to call it—just the thing for a funeral.

"Such a tragedy he said," he said. "I loved him like a brother. Or maybe like a sister. Poor Howie, not quite a man, not quite a woman, and now not even quite all there. I read that somebody gutted him like a pig. Imagine how that must have smelled!"

It took all of Sarah's self-control to keep from moving away. But Peter sounded so deranged, scarcely aware of what he was saying, that she believed it was possible he would let something slip.

"Nice crowd of gawkers," he said, looking around the room and grinning at everyone he saw. "I'll be Goddamned, there's that old tosspot Hoffmann. Surprised the DTs haven't carried him off to his great reward. Yes sir, everyone loves a good funeral. Too bad it's not open casket, give the folks their money's worth. Such rubbish, all this embalming and fastidiousness. We want the flies, we want the flies! So, Sary baby, how ya been? You gettin' any?"

She didn't answer. She was trying to keep her food down. She was aware that half the people in the room were staring.

"Jesus H. Christ, it's hot in here!" Peter said. "These thieving morticians charge enough you'd think they could afford to crank up the air conditioning. I mean, do these corpse fuckers want their goodies to rot before they get 'em planted?"

Everyone was looking. A priest was walking up the aisle toward them, and he stopped and stared.

"You know what I always think of in this hot weather, Sary baby? I think of your sweaty snatch. Yes sir, the mercury shoots up and I can't get my mind off that sopping wet gash. Bet you're not wearing panties in this heat, either. Tell ya what, sweetheart, let me know where you're staying and I'll come by tonight and suck the juices right out of you. I'll bet funerals get you horny too."

Sarah suddenly felt so sick that she tottered and nearly fell against the casket. A hand clasped her shoulder to steady her, and she looked around and saw Detective Okpara. Peter grinned at him and slunk away.

Okpara took her arm and steered her gently out of the room. In the hallway he said, "Do you need the restroom?"

She nodded. He led her to the door, and she stumbled through it and knelt at the toilet. Another prayer, she thought—this one brutally honest and sour in her mouth. When she was done, she rinsed her mouth and returned to Okpara waiting in the hallway.

"Where is he?" she asked.

"He already left. Would you like a stick of gum?"

"Yes, please."

He gave her one and they stepped outside into the heat. Peter was sitting in his Volvo, grinning at them. They went to Okpara's car, and he started it to run the air conditioner.

"I came to see who would show up for the funeral," he said. "Sometimes a killer is so proud of his work, he cannot resist returning to view it."

"Did that asshole do it or was it Darnell?"

"Mr. Bellman seems to have a good alibi," Okpara said. "At the time of the murder, two policemen were watching his house. Still . . ."

"Still what? Still you don't know who killed Howard. Still you can't find Darnell. Two fucking cops can watch Peter's house, but still maybe he can slip away. Cops can supposedly watch Howard's house, and still he can be murdered inside it while they sit there on their asses."

"I understand your anger, Miss Temple. The department gave less priority to watching Mr. Goldwin's house after the two of you left. This was not my wish, but I don't run the department."

Sarah chewed her gum and didn't say anything. She suddenly became uncomfortably aware of the gun that was hidden in her purse. All she needed right now was to be arrested for illegal carry.

"I'm angry too, Miss Temple, but this case has top priority. The FBI is involved, and it's only a matter of time, but terrible things can happen during that time. Did Mr. Bellman say anything to you that may be useful?"

"I don't think so."

But just in case there was some shred of a clue hidden in Peter's deranged peroration, Sarah recounted what she could remember, even the comments about her body, which embarrassed her no more than if Peter had been describing a rock. The only thing that could cause her shame was to allow the guilty to go unpunished.

"Are you aware that Ben Easton is sitting in his car across the street in a McDonald's parking lot?"

"Yeah, I know. How did you know it's Ben?"

"We ran his plates."

"So I guess he's so obvious that anyone would notice him?"

"No, not obvious to anyone but a cop casing the immediate area. Do you intend to stay at his house for a while?"

"Don't have anywhere else to go."

"Are you carrying a gun?"

"Um, I'm planning to get one."

"That would be wise."

Mourners began to file out of the funeral parlor to their cars. Pall bearers carried out the coffin and placed it in the hearse.

"Do you wish to go to the cemetery?" Okpara asked. "You may ride with me."

"Let's see what he does," she said.

Peter's Volvo was flagged along with the other cars, but when the procession began to move, he waited in the parking lot.

"He's waiting to see what we do," Okpara said.

"Pull out," she said.

Okpara joined the line of cars, and Peter pulled directly behind them.

"Mr. Bellman does not appear to be intimidated by the law," Okpara said. "That's good. It may work to our advantage."

The procession of cars moved slowly down the street, a motorcycle cop leading them through red lights and stop signs. Sarah glanced back and saw Peter staring at her and grinning. He was jerking his head back and forth, and she could hear a rap song blaring from his radio.

"Can you U-turn?" Sarah asked. "I'm not going to the cemetery if he's going to be there."

Okpara smiled and said, "Cops can do anything." He waited until there was no oncoming traffic, then pulled out of the procession and headed back toward the funeral home.

"He's not following us," she said.

"That's a shame," Okpara said. "I was hoping he would make a U-turn. Then I would be able to arrest him."

"How soon can I get my stuff from Howard's house?" she asked.

"Whenever you wish. The forensics work is finished. You'll want to make arrangements with Mrs. Goldwin. I believe it's her house now."

For some reason the words struck her with more finality than the funeral itself. Soon there would be a for sale sign in front of Howard's house; soon it would be owned by people who had never met him.

Okpara looked in his rearview mirror and said, "We seem to have picked up a tail."

"Peter?"

"No. I see Mr. Easton's car following us about half a block behind." Okpara smiled. "You seem to have found yourself a very vigilant watchdog. That is good."

Chapter Twenty-Eight

W ednesday evening Ben grilled two T-bone steaks, and Sarah was surprised to find that she ate all of hers. She ate all of her baked potato too and her salad and even a slice of store-bought cherry pie.

She realized that she was feeling a bit better, and she had no idea why. She had been reciting Ben's mantra every time she started feeling guilty, and maybe it was helping. Even Ben seemed happier than he had that first night she met him; he was still taciturn, but he seemed warmer and he even smiled occasionally. She noticed too that he hadn't been drinking much, maybe just one beer during the day and a glass of whiskey after dinner.

He poured himself one now and asked her if she wanted anything. "Some wine," she said, and he poured a glass for her.

"I don't have any appointments tomorrow," he said. "I'm thinking of driving to Mount Vernon, but I don't want to leave you here alone, so I'm thinking of asking a friend to come over and help you keep an eye on things. Is that okay?"

"What's in Mount Vernon?"

"A good friend of mine lives there. He's a folklore collector and local history buff, wrote a book a few years back about haunted houses in Ohio. He called me today, and I asked him about the Gus Dietrick place because if anything awful has ever happened in Ohio, Ed Hardin knows about it. He says it's the most haunted house in Ohio—he has a bunch of stories about it. He says it's still standing, sort of. After Gus died the land was auctioned for back taxes, and the farmer who bought it never bothered to tear down the house. Ed says teenagers go there to make out and come back with stories that don't have anything to do with sex. He knows the owner and thinks he can get permission for me to see it. I know it sounds crazy, but I'd like to look at the place and try to get some sense of it. I want to know what makes Darnell tick."

Sarah pictured a bleak, rotting house, and it seemed to fit right into her gallery of horrors, along with Gus Dietrick's coffin, the bones in Angel's closet, the headless body in the tub, the casket she had seen yesterday. But she also remembered the Philo Vance mysteries she had enjoyed reading as a kid: the way to find a murderer was to understand him psychologically. Even a decaying house and some old ghost stories might be helpful.

"I want to go too," she said.

"No, I don't think that's a good idea. I think the place will just depress you more."

"I want to go," she said.

***

Matthew Hamelin staggered down the stairs and out the door into the transfigured night. His van was parked near Angel's apartment, but his head was exploding with so many images that he didn't believe he could drive, and he chose to walk the many blocks to his apartment though his achy legs moved jerkily like rotting bones wired together.

He wanted to pick up a few things, clean clothes and a pair of sunglasses and all the cash stashed under his mattress, and then he would walk back if his jerky legs could do it. But he would make them do it—even if his legs fell off he would somehow walk back to his beauteous Pre-Raphaelite muse, his lovely haunter of tombs and ruins, his mistress and queen for now and evermore.

Headlights burst like grenades in his head even if he shut his eyes. To avoid them he reeled into alleys and dark narrow streets, hugging the shadows. Every shadow was a poem woven of darkness. He was astonished that he had never noticed this before, but he realized that until now he had been nothing more than a blind poseur. There were poems everywhere, holy litanies whispering from every puddle of darkness, and while he plunged through the alleys hearing dogs bark at him and seeing the flicker of TV screens through the windows of the blind, the strange poems of the night rushed through his head on a river of ebony:

Brain staring blankly at blank dumb matter dancing for the moment with a dying fire's flicker—the night is ill in the alleys where she wanders—flames beating wings of shadow on walls scribbled with holy graffiti this shadow show of animal teeth and breath—each place where she lies down to sleep is his grave— flames beating wings of shadow against a cave wall a TV screen flickering secrets in the dark—stones hushed over her dead give her sweet poison for succor—a cave drawing etched in the first moment of time glimpsed in the dying fire's ballet of flame before walls return to darkness and primordial goblins suck your bones—drink deep of his dark poison and be free—a ghost of other light flutters and murmurs with hidden whims where his old bones wait—see, see again, see anew, see with altered eye—then the graffiti's secrets are hidden in the dancing darkness the lips of death pressed against your eyes to shut off the world each eye the planet's dying ember—then go to worship where old bones lie.

***

Angel watched from her window as the poet stumbled away. She let the drape fall and turned back to the box surrounded by black candles in the center of the room.

One reason she had chosen this small apartment was the old refrigerator, with a latch instead of magnets to hold the door shut. She had removed the shelves, dragged it to the middle of the room, laid it on its back and punched a few air holes in it.

It had done its work. It had given her the last key, the seventh name. Her years of toil would soon bear fruit.

In the beginning her job had been almost impossibly difficult because then she had been weak, able to overpower Darnell for only a few hours at a time and only a few times each year, but with each new key she had grown stronger and wiser. After receiving the fifth key, she had become more adept at choosing men who had the ears to be name-bringers. Instead of toiling through several failures for each success, she had recognized Peter Bellman at once as a name-bringer, and likewise Matthew Hamelin.

The other one, Paul Finney, had been a mistake. He had gone mad in the darkness.

Angel stepped inside the ring of lit candles, knelt before the box, and began to speak each name in succession. They were names but more than names, words but more than words. They were three-dimensional shapes in space that unlocked realms the uninitiated knew nothing about. They were seven incantations, the seven seas of occult knowledge, the seven keys to the seven doors of the soul, the seven runes for the seven stigmata.

As she spoke the new name, the seventh and final key, she felt its power sweep through her as swiftly as a wind. The candles guttered and blew out.

Then she heard her loved one's voice clearly at last, not as vague sounds in her ears but as sharp ciphers in her brain, a secret placement of hermetic symbols, a sacred pattern of augury sticks, an omen of entrails, a language of dancing crows, a whisper of dried leaves rustling along the furrows of her brain.

She strained to hear the beloved voice, and it showed her an image of a house that she recognized from childhood, a brick mansion with a tall watchtower in the center of the roof.

It told her what she must do.

Chapter Twenty-Nine

By Thursday Sarah had recovered enough to enjoy the country drive, the green farms sprawling on either side of the road, the smell of hay and field corn blowing in through the windows of Ben's car.

She had never seen Mount Vernon before, and she liked the attractive town square surrounded by a quaint downtown, the old courthouse and old churches, the pleasant streets lined with big Victorian houses that seemed to belong in New England. She decided that when all of this was over she was going to make an effort to be happy again. But that would be a while.

After a long hot dry spell, the sky was trying to rain but seemed to have forgotten how. It darkened and roiled and brooded and occasionally even grunted with thunder, but it couldn't produce a drop. When Ben parked in front of Ed Hardin's big gabled house, the clouds that strained above it echoed the gray-blue paint on its wood siding and the lilac and purple that accented its gingerbread.

Ben banged the bronze knocker, and a moment later several images of a man appeared in the leaded-glass window as he unlocked the door. The door opened, and Ed Hardin smiled at them, a white-haired man about 70 with a neatly trimmed white beard.

While Ben introduced them, Sarah could see that Ed was under the impression she was Ben's lover. He seemed to approve heartily, giving her a welcoming smile and a warm handshake. Then he winked at Ben and said, "Ben, you're looking so much happier!"

If Ben looked happier now, Sarah hated to think what he had looked like before. But come to think of it, maybe he had been looking a bit more cheerful lately, and she wondered what there was to cheer him up.

"Well, I got permission to look at the house," Ed said. "Your timing is good. The owner said he's planning to knock it down this fall. He's afraid some teenager will fall through the floor and sue him. You sure you really want to see that dump?"

"We're sure," said Ben. "But first let me see your bathroom." He headed down the hallway.

Ed smiled at Sarah and shook his head. "A brain surgeon

couldn't change that man's mind. Would you like a Coke or something?"

"No thank you."

"Well, let's sit down."

The foyer was so regal with its crystal chandelier that Sarah almost hated to leave it, but the living room was even more magnificent. She sat on a sofa that Victoria herself might have sat on.

"Nice," she said, glancing around at display cases and shelves filled with curios.

Ed smiled, his blue-gray eyes warm and merry. "I suppose it's a bit excessive for a single man, but I enjoy it. Have you known Ben long?"

"No, just a few days."

"I'll bet he's not told you a word about helping me with my book."

"He said you'd written one."

"But I'll bet he didn't tell you that he wrote a long introduction. Very interesting, too, the psychological significance of ghost sightings. Really the best part of the book. Without his introduction, it would be just another collection like a thousand others. He wouldn't take a dime for doing it, seems almost embarrassed if I mention it. That's the way Ben is. He never beats his own drum."

Sarah wondered if Ed was trying to play matchmaker.

"I've known him for many years," Ed said. "We belong to the same shooting club. Did he mention that?"

"No."

Ed certainly didn't resemble what Sarah had always pictured as a gun nut. Funny world, she thought: a gun-control zealot like Peter trying to strangle her and a shooting enthusiast sitting here looking as dangerous as Santa Claus.

"Of course Ben wins all the trophies," Ed said.

"He seems so, I don't know, so shut off," Sarah said. "Sometimes I wonder what shut him off."

Ed frowned. "You mean he hasn't told you? No, come to think of it, I suppose he wouldn't. Not like Ben to talk about his problems." He heard Ben returning and said, "Well, shall we go before this storm hits?"

Ed insisted on sitting in back so Sarah could sit up front with Ben. "I didn't put any stories about the Dietrick house in my first book," he said, "because I'm devoting an entire book to the place. I'm almost finished writing it. They're not the usual tales. Usual ghost story goes something like this: old woman murdered in her house so people who go there see her ghost moaning and banging around. So in this case you'd expect people to see ghosts of the children who died there, or maybe creepy old Gus, but almost no one has reported seeing them, and the few who have don't sound convincing, just some kids who want to sound interesting but probably haven't even been there. I always try to verify their stories by questioning them on details of the house."

"So you've been inside it?" Ben asked.

"Yes, but I don't believe I'll ever go inside it again. If you don't mind, I think I'll just wait in the car. And I won't be very happy waiting there, either. Turn left up here."

They were already out of town, and Ben turned from the highway onto a narrow road lined with woods. It was beautiful countryside, sparsely populated and gently hilly. Storm clouds hung over the knolls and valleys, still keeping their dark burden to themselves. Sarah remembered that it had been raining the day Darnell was found in the box, and she hoped it wouldn't rain while they were in the house.

"Sounds like you've got your own story to tell," Ben said.

"Maybe so, but I'm not telling it. Ruins the scientific objectivity of the collector, you know."

"If they didn't see ghosts of children, what did they see?" Sarah asked.

"Nothing remarkable, most of them. A dark presence, a suffocating shadow, an evil mist. Some of them say they saw a shadow moving like a man. Pretty vague and unsensational, I know, but the remarkable fact is the number of people who've experienced it. And the number who say they'll never go back, not for love or money. You hear other ghost stories calmly recounted, sometimes even humorously, but not the Dietrick stories. When people tell you about their experiences there, I tell you, the sweat breaks out on their foreheads."

"Any place where bad things happened will provoke people's imaginations," Ben said. He was driving slowly because the road was pocked with chuckholes.

"Sure," Ed agreed. "Every ghost story takes place where something creepy happened. But, Ben, you should hear some of these people tell their stories. I have tape recordings, and you can hear it right over the tape. Big macho teenage bullies with their voices shaking like scared schoolgirls. They tell some doozies, too. Some of them say they saw more than scary shadows, but they didn't see ghosts of children. This might interest you, Ben. What they saw was always a ghost from their own past, not from the history of the house. One young woman saw her mother, who had died of cancer, saw her walking in the dining room, emaciated and naked. The tumors were *outside* of her body, hanging onto her white skin like enormous purple leeches. Turn right after this hill."

They turned from the narrow road to a narrower one. There was a woods on one side, a field of soybeans on the other. Ahead, Sarah saw a small boxy house that looked empty.

"Is that it?" she asked.

"No. There are a couple other deserted houses on the road," Ed said. "That's another thing: no one seems to like to live on this road."

Ben chuckled. "Think you just stretched it a little too far, Ed. You had me half believing you for a minute."

"Well, it's true. A family named Siskens used to live in that one back there. They live in town now. They say they couldn't stand the place. They say it drove their daughter insane. Something sure did, she's a raving lunatic now."

"So you're saying the whole road's full of haunted houses?" Ben asked. "Maybe you can get a movie contract on this."

"Maybe they're all haunted, but none of them are as haunted as the Dietrick house," Ed said. "Okay, here's one. A man, and he wasn't a teenager either, he was a crusty old farmer, nobody's fool. He was driving by the Dietrick place when his dog jumped off the bed of his pickup truck and ran into the house. The dog was in there barking its head off and the man couldn't get him to come out, so he went in after him. The dog was upstairs, barking at something in the hallway. It was the man's brother, who'd been killed a year before when he fell into a hay bailer. I'll let you imagine what he saw, all mauled up, pus and blood dripping from the wounds. But here's the interesting part. This farmer and his brother had always been as close as that, but since this experience he's repudiated his brother's memory. He's burned all his brother's things, even photographs. He says his brother is damned and in hell. No one can change his mind."

"You love ghost stories, Ed, and like any good storyteller you're building us up for the moment when you leap up from the campfire and say 'Boo!'"

"I'm just a collector, and I'm just telling you what I've collected. Here's an interesting story for you. A young guy saw his murdered girlfriend in there. He was so shaken up that he went straight to the police station and confessed that he'd killed her a year before. He's sitting in prison right now."

There was a large red barn on the left and past it an enormous brick house with curtains in the windows and a car in the long driveway.

"Doesn't look like those people moved out," Ben said.

"That's the Stonebrenner place," Ed said. "A young couple live there, probably because the rent's cheap. That place has an interesting story too. Now, the Dietrick house is on the right just past this hill."

Sarah gazed at the Stonebrenner mansion, which sat nearly as far off the road as Ben's place. It looked out of place on this forlorn road, darkly majestic with a round belvedere or watchtower in the center of the roof that rose a story above the rest of the house. About 100 yards past it was a small family cemetery inside a grove of trees. She had seen places like this in the east, estates belonging to families who had gained their prominence back in the days of the pilgrims.

The Dietrick place, when it appeared on the right, looked anti-climactic, a plain two-story farmhouse, its rotting wood siding utterly devoid of paint, its front porch roof caved in, its yard a field of thistles and milkweed. Almost not a house anymore. With every door open and every window broken, it looked as if its secrets would have escaped long ago.

Ben pulled into what was left of the driveway, and Ed pointed to a pile of wood and tin to their right. "There's the barn where Gus Dietrick was found. We'll, now you've seen it. Why don't we get back before these clouds break."

"Sarah, you stay here with Ed," Ben said. "I'm going to step in for just a minute."

She stared at the gray windowless hulk, the dark clouds brewing above it.

"I'm coming too," she said.

Chapter Thirty

Unable to see, hear, smell, or move, he was a rock seething with panic and pain and plans. For a while, so very long ago across a black, soundless chasm of time so wide it was meaningless, he had still been able to feel the crawling things and the stifling air, but those sensations too had faded as the last of his nerve endings flickered out, and when they were gone he missed even the itchy inching of the worms on his skin.

Many times his mind had roamed into the farthest reaches of madness, and many times returned, until it was impossible to tell any longer what was madness and what was sanity, so that even now, as his hour seemed to be drawing near at last, he couldn't know if the rescue he anticipated was real or merely another delusion.

But he had learned to treat each delusion as if it was reality, believing that if he exercised his powers to control the elements of each lunatic scenario, then eventually his will would prevail and would shape the means of his escape. And now, if this unlikely scenario should prove to be real, his escape was close at hand, the final key delivered at last to the one he had groomed and tutored to unbolt the dark.

But even now, with the climax of his lunatic plan approaching, he sensed enemies wandering into his realm intent on sabotaging his work. He would not allow them to succeed. For endless years he had roamed through the farthest reaches of madness, so no one better understood its bottomless terrors, and madness was the weapon he would use against them. He would snuff their sanity like candlelight and bathe the intruders in the pure blackness of their own souls.

In the blackness, they wouldn't have a chance. Black always wins.

***

Ben got a flashlight from his trunk. The front porch didn't look safe, so he and Sarah entered through a side doorway near the back, its door rotting in the weeds beside the house. This must have been the dining room. There was nothing much to see: no furniture, just a sagging wooden floor bare except for beer bottles and cans, cigarette butts, broken window glass, and other rubbish. The walls were riddled with holes and scrawled with graffiti. A closet door gaped open, revealing nothing but tangles of dust and an animal's nest.

They moved to the front room, where a condom and a pair of panties on the floor suggested that some couple had been brave and crude enough to have sex here. Birds had built a nest in the ceiling chandelier and wasps' nests clung to ceiling corners.

There was a small room behind the dining room which must have been Eva's bedroom. The skeleton of a metal bed remained, its bare springs littered with leaves. They went to the kitchen: a filthy old sink with a small hand pump; pieces of a smashed wooden table on the floor. Some joker had stuck a scarecrow in the broom closet. Sarah could feel the floor give a little beneath the weight of her body.

"I think Ed may have oversold the place," Ben said. "I've seen better haunted houses."

"It's not much," Sarah agreed, not sure if she was relieved or disappointed. They certainly weren't going to find anything useful here.

"No point in going upstairs," Ben said. "We might fall through the floor."

"There's the basement."

"Yeah," he said without enthusiasm.

The door to the basement was in the kitchen. It was the only door that remained securely shut, as if even the drunken teenagers who vandalized the place had wanted to keep whatever was down there sealed in. It was stuck, the frame warped from water and settling, and Ben had to yank hard to get it open.

A stench of damp dirt and worms and fungus and rotting animals belched up from the dark bowels. He aimed his powerful police-style flashlight down the stairs. Its narrow white beam looked strong and bold for a few feet, but then seemed to be swallowed by darkness.

Sarah followed him down the creaking stairs. She had descended only two or three steps when she felt cobwebs clinging to her face. When she reached the dirt floor, it felt damp and slippery. Odd that it would still be wet after this long dry spell.

She thought she could feel bugs crawling on her bare arms and legs—surely her imagination. She wished she were wearing shoes instead of sandals; snakes or rats might be waiting in the muck. The stench of mildew and dead animals was overpowering.

Shelves with buckets and cans seemed to sway in the puny beam of Ben's flashlight. Sarah glanced up at the doorway glowing faintly at the top of the stairs. Its light seemed to stay up there, unable to penetrate this reeking gloom. There *were* things crawling on her feet and ankles. She lifted one foot and then the other, slapping them again and again, but the invisible crawlers weren't deterred.

"I'd rather be in Philly," Ben said.

His voice, like the light, seemed to dissolve in the darkness. He swept his flashlight across the floor, searching for the graves.

"There they are," he said, his voice crumbling so quickly that Sarah wasn't certain he had said anything.

They moved carefully on the slippery dirt toward the two adjacent holes. The light seemed unwilling to enter them; the most the flashlight could do was make them glow vaguely. Surprisingly, teenage wits had not filled them with beer cans—the gaping graves were immaculate in their muck. Black water lay at the bottom of each hole.

Sarah heard a deep rumble, followed by the hiss of rain. Time seemed to collapse, annihilating the distance between this moment and the rainy day when Darnell had been found in one of these holes, the rotting body of Angela in the other. It seemed to her that two powerful fists had compressed all the sadism of history into two wads of black horror that gaped hungrily at her feet, wanting her too, wanting her and Ben, one wad of horror for each of them. She felt the basement's darkness press heavily against her shoulders, weighing her down, absorbing her strength and giving it back as despair.

"Let's go," Ben said, but his words were scarcely audible, shaped of heavy darkness instead of air.

Sarah tried to move, but her legs felt like rocks. Lifting one and forcing it away from the hole was too much work. The effort was sapping her strength, and the despair that replaced it seemed to be saying: Join us in the sanctuary of the dark. We've been waiting here just for you.

A clap of thunder shook the fetid air. The flashlight died, and in the darkness she absurdly couldn't remember where the graves were. She felt something on her shoulder, Ben's hand, and he said, "Let's go."

Or had he spoken? Another voice, deeper than his, was speaking more clearly. "This is your home," it said. "This has always been your home. One bed for each of you, now lie down and sleep."

Ben had a hold of her arm now and was tugging her toward the stairs. She resented his meddling. She wanted to stay. A dark figure standing beside the graves was speaking, its deep voice quiet and crackly as if the vocal cords were dead.

"Your name is Angel, and this is your home," it said. "It has always been your home. All else is delusion."

Ben was also speaking, saying something about staying in focus, but his words decayed as soon as they were spoken. They were dust in her ears. The other voice was saying, "Who has a right to live in a world that tortures children? All of them must die. This is the true world, Angel. The world is woven of darkness and pain, and you shall lie in the darkness and sleep in the box forever."

"Try to keep in focus," Ben was saying, but he seemed to be somewhere miles away even though he had a hold of her hand and was tugging her toward the stairs.

Sarah tried to think of Johnny, but Johnny, too, had suffered and died and was buried in a little box. What right did she have to live? But Johnny had loved her, and love was a beacon of light.

She lifted rock-heavy legs and trudged in the direction Ben was pulling her. Johnny, Johnny, she repeated as a mantra in her mind. Lead me out of here, Johnny, lead me back up to the light. She pushed through the heavy air as if walking underwater.

At last they were at the foot of the stairs, but Sarah could see only a stain of filthy light in the doorway above them. Ben was behind her now, trying to urge her up, but she weighed too much to climb stairs, the gravity of history crushing her, the misery of millennia muttering in her ear, "You can't leave because you belong here, Angel. Truth is the grave and the box is your home."

"It's not easy for me either," Ben said. "You've got to help. Climb, climb."

She made it up one step and then another. Ben's hands pressed against her back, forcing her on. She conquered another step, and thunder roared its disapproval, making the air tremble and ring like a tuning fork.

The faintly glowing rectangle of doorway was not so far away now. She believed she could make it. Another ponderous step, and then another.

The doorway was just in front of her now, but as she gazed at it she saw with horror that the rectangle wasn't above her but beneath her. And it wasn't a doorway but a grave.

Her grave.

Ben was struggling and panting behind her, trying to push her down into the hole. But it wasn't Ben—it was something heavy and monstrous and reeking of death.

The thing behind her pushed her to her knees and pressed her face down closer and closer to the grave. The puddle of water at the bottom was glowing pale like swamp gas. It was squirming and growing like an embryo, sprouting arms and legs and a head.

The embryo grew into Johnny, his naked skin death-white and glistening. No longer a child, he had grown into a man, but his grown-up face simpered perversely like a child's.

"It's not fair," Johnny said. "You left me here all alone. There's no one here to play with me now. Come back and stay with me, Angel. I need you."

His bone-white hand reached up and touched her face, and cold water trickled from his fingertips down her throat to her breast. "We can play our old games together," he said. "Come home, Angel, and be my friend."

His cold wet fingers grasped her wrist tightly and were tugging her down into the grave when she heard Ben let out a terrible cry from somewhere behind her. Then it sounded as if he was falling down the stairs, and he cried out, "No! No! For God's sake, leave me alone!"

Ben needed her help, so she jerked free from Johnny's grasp, pushed herself up heavily from the edge of the grave, and stumbled through the dark toward the sound of his cries. She found him sitting on the wet floor at the bottom of the steps, shaking and sobbing with terror. She grasped his sweaty arm and tried to pull him up, but he jerked his arm away and yelled, "No! No! For God's sake, leave me alone!"

"Come on, Ben, get off your fucking ass!" she yelled. "Let's get the hell out of here!"

The fear that had sapped her strength a moment before now gave her vigor. She wrestled him upright and started pulling him up the stairs while he struggled weakly and moaned like a madman. She saw a dark shape standing in the doorway, but she kept going. She felt its watery fingers groping her face and breasts as she pushed her way through it, pulling Ben along behind her.

Ben seemed to snap out of his madness as soon as they were

upstairs. "Thank God it's you," he said. "I thought it was something else."

But Sarah scarcely heard him. Already she was running out of the doorway, running out of the house into the heavy rain that was drenching the graves of children and adults alike.

Chapter Thirty-One

Sarah sat silently beside him while Ben steered the car through the rain toward Lancaster. Ed Hardin had wanted to collect their stories, but they had told him nothing. The horror was still too raw and frightening to be shaped into folk tales.

They were halfway back to Ben's house before he said, "Do you mind telling me what you saw?"

Ben listened carefully to her story, his respect for this tough-spirited woman growing. She had lost her brother, her parents, and her friend. The sense and predictability of her life had vanished. Yet she had somehow found the strength to help him an hour ago. If she hadn't pulled him up the stairs, Ben believed he would have ended up permanently mad or even dead.

"What do you think happened down there?" she asked.

Ben stared through the wipers at the rain pounding the pavement. Lightning still split the sky, but it was some miles behind them now.

"You know what a psychologist is supposed to say," he said. "All this stress, a new trauma every day, Howard's death, and the house like a symbol of it all. Add to that Ed's stories to heighten our suggestibility. Then the darkness of the basement and those stinking graves. Even the thunder played its part. Any shrink worth two cents of his inflated fee would say it was irresponsible of me to let you go down there. Though if you hadn't been there I—"

"So that's what you think? You think it was all delusions?"

"No. It was something more."

"Then what was it?" Sarah asked.

"I don't know. There's nobody stupider than someone who knows all the answers. The night I met you, you asked me if I thought Angel's friend was real. I said then I didn't know, but now I say yes, Angel has a real friend, and we just had an encounter with it. Who or what it is I don't know, but I do know it's dangerous."

"What did you see down there?" she asked.

"I thought I heard you fall," he said. "I tried to help you up, but you were unconscious, so I picked you up and started carrying you up the stairs. But when I got about halfway up, the light from the doorway fell on your face, and I saw that what I was carrying wasn't you after all. That's when I tumbled down the stairs and went completely insane. She was on top of me then, trying to strangle me."

"Who's she?" Sarah asked.

"My wife."

Ben tried to put the bloated purple face out of his mind, the bulging eyes that stared at him reproachfully, the lip pulled up in a cat-snarl, the noose wrapped tightly around her neck. Worse even than that were the things she said, hateful accusations, horrible curses.

He focused on the road. The rain made driving difficult. Now wasn't the time to explain more, and he waited until they were back at his house and had both showered and eaten dinner and were sitting out back at his picnic table watching the sunset, he with a whiskey and she with a cold beer, the grass dry because the rain had not extended this far south, and as they watched the daylight condense and sink into a dark purple bruise he told her about Isabel.

"She taught for the Ohio University art department, a painter. Maybe you noticed some of her paintings in the house."

"I thought they were yours," Sarah said. "They're good."

"Yeah, she had talent. I saw her paintings before I ever met her, a show in the OU art building in Athens. I kept driving back down to Athens to have another look at them. One afternoon I noticed a woman watching me as I stared at them. Tall, dark hair, dark eyes, pretty damn beautiful. Somehow I knew she was the painter."

Ben could still clearly see the first glimpse he'd had of Isabel, standing in the corner with a trace of a smile, her dark eyes radiating genial pleasure, enjoying this man gazing at her paintings as some women enjoyed men gazing at their bodies. He had said, "These are yours, aren't they?" and when she nodded he said, "I like the way you see things."

"There wasn't any getting-to-know-each-other phase," he continued. "No sweaty nervous first dates and all that. We just fell into step as if we'd always been together. I don't mean we made love right away—that waited a while. But we were together like twins from the day we met.

"It's a funny thing, because we were very different. Her perceptions were turned up so high that any little thing could thrill her, maybe a clump of goldenrod or a cloud in front of the moon.

But there's a downside to that—things most people would find a little irritating she found downright painful. There's no way to describe her, really. There's no one else like her."

Ben drank his whiskey and poured another. It was getting dark now and the mosquitoes were out. He asked Sarah if she wanted to go inside, and she said no. He listened to the cricket-filled silence, seeing Isabel's face wherever his eyes fell. She was everywhere, she was nowhere. His world was still filled with her and empty too.

And here was this auburn-haired woman watching him and listening to his deepest feelings, this woman who had saved him from madness or maybe death. He didn't know what to think of her, he didn't know what he felt about her, but he was glad she was sitting here beside him. He ground his boot heel into the grass and continued.

"I don't remember ever proposing to her. I guess we both just assumed that we'd get married. A month or two after we met we were already talking about how many kids we wanted and when we'd want them. Not right away—we'd wait a few years. Guess it was maybe three months after that day in the art building, we were married at St. James here in Lancaster. This farm was hers—she was raised here and had always lived here except when she was getting her degrees.

"When she got pregnant a few years later we weren't really expecting it—I was fighting for tenure and she was busy teaching and putting shows together. But we didn't complain. It was the most exciting thing that had ever happened, for both of us."

Ben saw what he didn't want to see, still couldn't bear to see, Isabel's rounded abdomen making her sexier and more womanly than ever. He shut his eyes, trying to squeeze out the image.

The rest he told quickly, in a spare summary, the brutal rape, the two men springing like panthers from bushes near the Athens campus, her miscarriage, her depression turning to madness, her doctor wanting to place her in an institution for a while, his own absurd, inexcusable belief that he could help her, that she was better off at home than in an institution, that it was safe to allow her to wean herself from the over-medication the doctor had prescribed, that love and time and her paintings were therapy enough, and all the while as Ben struggled to help her he had to fight the department for the tenure that one person on the committee sought to deny him because he didn't walk the walk, and while he fought for his academic survival he had too little time for Isabel, too little attention to see that she was sinking further, that she needed her medication, needed in fact to be institutionalized, any idiot should have seen it, there was no excuse to pardon his arrogant blindness . . .

"The day I was given tenure I came home with two bottles of champagne, but I couldn't find her. All her things were here, her car was in the garage, but she was nowhere. At last I looked in the barn. She was in the haymow, hanging from a beam. Just a little over a year ago now."

Only the crickets spoke.

Chapter Thirty-Two

Puddles beside the road showed that it had rained earlier, but now the country sky was clear and glittering with stars. Angel sat in the front passenger seat of Matthew Hamelin's old Dodge van. Though she had given him 24 hours to recover from his ordeal, he was driving very badly. Perhaps he always did. The van weaved precariously on the country road while the poet struggled to wedge his weak timbreless voice into the few pauses that punctuated the loud harangue issuing from Peter Bellman, who sat in the back and leaned his shaved head forward to bray like an ass in the driver's ear.

They were both insane, their brains melting down like wax, too weak for the single name that each one had learned. The deterioration of their minds caused them to behave like adolescent boys as they vied for Angel's attention.

She tried to ignore them so she could focus on the voice in her head. She had forgotten so much, roads and directions along with the rest of childhood's debris, and she was depending on the voice more than her memory to navigate them along the narrow country roads. It spoke in words as well as images now, saying, "Follow the compass in your mind. I am the lodestone that draws you to me."

It was difficult to heed the voice with her two brain-damaged suitors arguing. Angel told them to shut up. They did for a minute, shamed like scolded dogs, but soon Bellman was at it again, leaning forward and braying tediously above the whispers in her mind.

Name-bringers usually didn't last long after they had done their job. She knew that one of her earlier helpers was in a mental institution, another in prison, a third dead by his own hand, another dead from a brain aneurysm. She had to make do with these two.

"Shut up," Angel said. "Turn right up here. Stay on the road." The van had veered onto the grassy shoulder, a foot from the ditch.

"Let me drive this fucking thing!" Bellman roared.

They were close now, the voice growing clearer and Angel's memory beginning to recognize this road, and she knew that a little farther up they would turn left, yes, there it was. She ordered Hamelin to turn, and with a rush of excitement and pain she recognized the road where she had lived as a child. Once as an adult she had gone to Mount Vernon with a name-bringer to dig up Gus Dietrick's grave, but never had she returned to the house.

They drove half a mile, and there it was, a few yards ahead on the left, the filthy old house falling to ruin and stinking of Grandpa, and the sight of it was deeply horrible and wonderful.

"Slow down," she said. "Turn out your lights."

The van coasted slowly past the ruin, the place of Gus Dietrick and the damp grave, the place of Angel's death and her rebirth, the place where she had met *him* who had given her new life, who spoke even now in her head, saying, "My love, my love, you are close, be careful now, let nothing go wrong, let each step be perfect that brings you to me, let your feet not falter, let your mind not stray, let nothing cause you to fail."

"Slowly, quietly," she said as they drifted beyond the Dietrick house. "Just a little farther."

The big house with the watchtower came into view on their right. About 100 yards before they got to it she saw the narrow weed-covered lane leading to the cemetery.

"See that little lane?" she said. "Turn into it and drive to the grove of trees. Good. Turn off the motor. Now no one speaks, not a single word or I'll kill you. Get out very quietly and ease the doors shut without a sound. Get the tools from the back. If anyone makes a noise I'll kill him."

The two men did as they were told, fearing her as intensely as they worshipped her. They followed her with their tools into the little cemetery, stepping carefully over the iron fence that had fallen in the weeds.

The voice in Angel's head was almost mad with excitement now, saying, "I've waited so long, I cannot wait any longer!"

She aimed her flashlight at the few old grave markers. "Here! Here!" the voice cried.

It was just a mound overgrown with grass and weeds, no marker except for the lodestone that pulled her.

"Dig," she whispered.

The two men set to work with their shovels. Amidst the brilliant stars, the moon was only a sliver, a sharp silver sickle hanging in the clear black sky. That was good. She could see lights burning in two of the windows of the big brick house. Probably the occupants were in bed this late despite the lights, but better the night was dark.

The dirt was soft from the recent rain, and it piled up in mounds on either side of the grave. A dog began to bark in the distance across a field.

"Hurry!" she whispered.

Bellman started to say something, but Angel shushed him. She saw one of the lights in the house go out, and a few seconds later an upstairs window lit up.

"Stop, don't move," she whispered.

They all three stood still. The dog barked again and then howled like a wolf. The sharp sickle trembled over their heads. At last the upstairs light went out.

"Dig!" she whispered.

The voice in her head had ceased speaking, but she could hear it making sounds. It seemed to be weeping. A shovel hit wood, and the weeping ceased as if the suspense was too great even for weeping.

At last the casket was uncovered, and the men struggled ineptly to get ropes underneath it. Then they scrambled out of the grave and stood at either end of the hole, straining clumsily with their ropes and puffing like clowns.

"If you drop it, I'll kill you both," she whispered. "But first I'll castrate you. I've done it before."

They pulled and strained, and when they finally got it above the ground, each one tried to move it to a different side of the hole. But they didn't drop it, and at last it rested solidly on the grass.

The voice in her head had started up again in a frenzy of weeping and screaming. She understood: after having stilled his panic for so long in the box, now that the moment was so near he had lost all control. Angel knew the panic; she had died with it swelling like a fist in her throat.

The heavy casket lid was secured with many long screws made of dull metal that looked like lead but seemed to be as strong as steel. The men pried at it with the tips of their shovels while the voice howled and cried—but only in Angel's head. The box itself was silent. Then the edge of the lid splintered and, with the loud groan of screws pulling from wood, it came open.

She shone her flashlight into the coffin, and her heart sank. He was dead, dead beyond recovery. The voice in her head must have been her imagination.

She touched the corpse's face, its eyelids sunken, its blackened upper lip contracted in a rictus revealing long yellow teeth and black gums. The body looked like an emaciated mummy so shrunken that its rotting clothes were several sizes too big for it. The skin was dark gray and stiff beneath her fingers, but it felt slightly pliable like tough saddle leather, and as she looked closely she saw that the worms crawling across it hadn't been able to penetrate it.

"I'm here!" the voice screamed. "I'm alive! Give me the names!"

Angel knelt, filled her lungs with air, and lowered her face into the coffin. She pressed her mouth against the grinning black lips and breathed through them the first word, a crackle of harsh consonants with strange vowels howling through them like wind through a broken window.

She filled her lungs again, and forced the second word into the gaping, reeking mouth. The voice inside her head howled with pain as she forced in the third word and the fourth. At the fifth word she felt something stir, felt the stiff emaciated torso shift, heard appalling cries of agony in her head, and a lungful of putrid air groaned out of the cadaver's throat.

She filled her lungs, breathed the sixth word into the mouth stinking of death, and again it exhaled its pestilence back at her. As she breathed the final word into the mouth, all the pains of hell seemed to burst out in one shattering cry inside her head. The leathery chest seized and heaved, and a loud gurgling rattle issued from the corpse's mouth.

Baby Beddybye was coughing.

Part Five: Bequeathing Seven Swords of Pain

Chapter Thirty-Three

Angel lay in Matthew Hamelin's bed with Baby Beddybye, kneading the ropy muscles beneath his leathery skin. Last night she had brought him to the poet's apartment from the cemetery.

He lay naked on his back, motionless except for the spasmodic jerking of his chest as he breathed, each breath a hoarse, rasping wheeze followed by a thick gurgling from deep inside his lungs.

There was so little flesh left that she could plainly see his bones, and whatever flesh was left smelled like something dead. No longer dark gray, his skin had bloomed purple-blue, splotched in places with deeper purple, as if bruised from head to toe. His muscles were no longer stiff like dried wood, but rather like green saplings, and Angel could feel them give beneath her fingertips. Though they had shrunk to hard cables, she thought that he had once been burly and powerful, and she thought he would be again.

His torso was marked with seven deep scars, four on his chest and three on his back. Six of them were shaped like crescent moons, but the scar carved above his heart was a deep ragged X. Angel had known of these seven stigmata only from whispers and dreams, and she wondered what they signified.

Baby Beddybye was completely bald with a high impressive forehead, though now it was bony like a skull. A wiry gray beard covered his face. The rictus had relaxed from his upper lip, and his mouth was nearly closed now with only a glimpse of yellow teeth showing, but he was still unable to speak except with the voice in Angel's head. The voice spoke rarely and only to direct her where and how to massage, and when she did so a painful groan would pour out of his throat, the breath still reeking of the grave.

The voice spoke now. "I thirst," it said, and she reached for the glass of cat's blood and let some trickle into his mouth. The poet had brought the cat home late last night, and now he was out looking for another cat or a dog, anything with blood.

It scarcely seemed possible that Baby Beddybye was here, lying in bed with her. For most of her life he had been merely a memory of a phantom. Angel's mind went back to the last time she had seen him, under a storybook sky in a school playground that she now knew was only a place in her imagination, a place dreamt into being so she could forget that she was locked in the box.

But she knew also that then even *she* had been imaginary, a figment of Darnell's mind that he invented so that he wouldn't be the one lying in that cramped darkness—a figment in her brother's mind until the man beside her had miraculously made her real, somehow mixing the clay of her remains in the nearby coffin with the living spirit of Darnell in his box, and into that mixture breathing the Word that gave her life.

"Lower," the voice whispered in her mind. "There." She dug with her fingers, and a groan rumbled out of Baby Beddybye's throat.

Angel remembered the cold blue sky and the warm jacket he had given her. She remembered his words: "I know one of your secrets."

She remembered swinging while she listened to his soft whisper: "You're thinking about an ogre and a witch. What you'd like to do to them."

She had stopped swinging. "Now you haveta tell me a secret," she had said.

"I will, if you promise you will always be my friend."

"Okay."

"Forever and ever. You have to swear."

"I swear, cross my heart and hope to die."

Baby Beddybye had smiled. "Okay. Listen very, very carefully. I'm going to give to you a magic word. It will make you powerful."

He could give her only one word, he had said. A person could receive only one word directly from him because two words from his lips would overpower anyone's mind. But as she got older, she would be able to gather more words, until she had all seven. She would have to find name-bringers to bring the words to her, one by one, one name-bringer for each word.

To receive a word, each name-bringer would need to be locked in a box because all people locked in boxes are metaphysically (she hadn't understood the word at the time) in the same dark place, lying side by side so to speak, so only in a box could name-bringers hear

Baby Beddybye whispering in their ears.

The instructions he taught her sounded not so different from dark fairy tales that her father had read to her, and not so different from the punishment that Grandpa had established as an ordinary part of her life. Nothing very strange.

"You must promise," he had said, "that when you have all seven words you will use them to help me, as I'm helping you today."

Angel promised. Baby Beddybye placed his beautiful manly lips on hers and breathed the word into her lungs. The blue sky darkened, a bitter wind swept over the playground, and thunder boomed. A bolt of lightning set a tree near the schoolhouse ablaze. Darnell's mind screamed with outrage as a new mind was planted inside it, a mind that eventually would overpower and bury his.

The wind eventually died down and the sky lightened, not to its childish storybook blue, but to a complex palette of hues, no longer a child's sky. It was an adult's sky now. The tree burning beside the schoolhouse crackled and hissed.

"Now," he had said, "what would you like to do to Grandpa?"

"Break his heart!" Angel said at once. "Squeeze it like a balloon and make it pop."

Baby Beddybye had smiled, pleased with her wish. "It's done," he said. "You have just torn his heart in two. It has burst like a rotten tomato. Now, what about Grandma?"

Angel had needed to think for a minute. "Put worms in her brain," she said. "Big squirmy worms to eat her brain."

"There," the voice said.

She kneaded a softening, quickening muscle beneath the purple skin.

Baby Beddybye groaned and his eyes sprang open, black and shiny like polished stones.

***

Mathew Hamelin returned to his apartment, and Angel was surprised to see that he had a man with him, a bearded man with dirty clothes.

"This is George," the poet said. "I'm going to give him a hundred dollars to paint my bedroom."

"Show him the bathroom first," Angel said. "He can have two hundred if he paints it too."

"What's wrong with him?" George asked, staring at the naked emaciated purple-blue man wheezing on the bed.

"He's sick," Angel said.

"Boy, I'll say," George said. "I never seen nobody that sick. If it wasn't I can hear him breathing, I'd say he was way past ready to bury. I won't work 'round sick people if they have anything catchy."

"Show him the bathroom," Angel said.

Hamelin led George to the bathroom, and while they stood with their backs to the doorway Angel slipped in behind him and slit his throat. George collapsed to the floor jerking and gurgling, blood spraying everywhere, and Angel said, "Get his throat over the tub, you fool."

The poet grasped him under the armpits from behind and struggled until his torso was leaning into the tub, his legs hanging out and still jerking. His precious blood was running down the drain while Angel searched for a stopper. Hamelin reached past her and plugged the drain hole with a wadded washrag.

"Where did you find him?" Angel asked.

"He was standing on a sidewalk with a sign that said, 'Will work for food.'"

"Well, I guess he'll work *as* food instead."

"So what is he anyway?" Hamelin asked. "Is he a vampire? I mean, will we have to find blood for him from now on?"

"No. He told me that once he's recovered he'll be able to eat normal food again."

"Well, if he's not a vampire, just what *is* he?"

"He's your lord and master. That's all you need to know."

Chapter Thirty-Four

The next day Baby Beddybye was able to take a few steps with Angel and Matthew Hamelin supporting him. His muscles seized up in spasms, his bones ached like rotten teeth, and his eyes throbbed as if nails were driven into his skull. He was naked because the scraping of fabric against skin would still be intolerable.

He collapsed into a chair, ordered Hamelin out of the room, and looked at himself in a mirror. The purple was fading from his skin leaving behind the dark blue of an old bruise. He touched his beard; it looked as if it had grown for a month or longer in the tomb before the follicles had shut down.

"Shave it off," he told Angel, manipulating his tongue and lips with great difficulty. His vocal chords were still stiff as reeds, making his voice a harsh rasp. "It's the hair of the grave. But get a bag and collect every tiny piece. Burn it when you're finished."

The shaving cream felt like ice, but the razor felt like fire scorching his skin. He watched Angel closely, making certain she got every bit of the beard-filled lather into the sack. He wasn't going to allow Charles Newman to get his treacherous hands on any scrap that came from his body.

"I don't even know your name," Angel said.

"The last name people knew me by was Isaac Stonebrenner," he answered. "Henceforth those who must know anything about me will call me Jacob Stonebrenner. I'm going to become my own son. After I recover my treasure I'll be able to pay very good money for impeccable identification to prove it."

"How long were you buried?"

"Forty years. Since before you were born."

Stonebrenner watched this register on Angel's face—impossible for her to grasp, impossible even for him.

"How old are you?" she asked.

"Older than most. Younger than a very few."

She shaved under his chin without speaking for a minute, and needles of pain pierced his traumatized nerves. Stonebrenner regarded her face critically, watched her small breasts when she leaned forward and the loose shirt she wore hung partly open. So this was the one he had waited for, not man, not woman—but his.

He could hear a question hanging in her mind, though she hesitated to give it words. "What are you?" she asked at last.

He could hear the name in her mind that she was afraid to voice. She wanted to know if he was Satan. His lip curled into a grin, causing a painful cramp to grip one side of his face.

"Just a man," he answered.

She carefully slapped a glob of lather and whiskers into the sack and stooped to pick up a small drop from the floor. "Who did this to you?" she asked. "Who buried you?"

"Another man," Stonebrenner answered. "A man whom I had helped and trusted. A man who taught me a great deal and then betrayed me. I'll tell you all one day."

He drank from his glass of sweet refrigerated blood while Angel finished shaving him. She placed a warm wet towel on his face, and his nerves did a frenzied dance. He held up his hand and looked at his fingernails; they were long yellow-brown cracked claws.

"Trim them," he ordered. "Collect them in the bag too. My enemy must not find a single whisker or nail."

Angel left the room and returned with a pair of nail clippers. She began with his left hand, and it felt as if she were snipping off his fingertips.

"I used to call you Baby Beddybye," she said.

"I know."

"I've loved you all my life."

"I know. And I've loved you too."

"May I call you Baby?" she asked. "Would you mind terribly?"

"You pulled me from the tomb. You may call me what you like."

When she had finished with his fingernails, she knelt to trim his toenails. Each snap of the clippers sent a hot poker plunging up his leg. He could hear the name-bringer moving around in the next room.

"Tell me about him," he said.

"Hamelin? He's just some silly college student. He believes he's in love with me. Each day he writes me a love poem."

Stonebrenner considered this for a moment, amused and not amused that this puny interloper begrudged the attention that Angel was giving him. He could sense the poet's resentment radiating from the other room.

"We may need him for a while," he said. "Tell me about the other one."

"His name is Peter Bellman." She snapped the nail clipper, and the pain shot clear to his groin. "His brain is going fast. He could be trouble. The police are watching him."

"I'll have a word with him," he said. "Can he be called on the telephone?"

"Yes, but only from a pay phone or a prepaid cellphone. The police are probably tracing his calls."

"I know nothing about the world today," Stonebrenner said. "What are cellphones?"

Angel told him about cellphones and other innovations. He asked her many questions about computers. The materialists, he thought, struggling to make genies out of electricity because they believed in no other sort of genies.

"Where can I find one of these computers?" he asked.

"Hamelin has one. He can show you how to use it."

When she had finished his nails, Stonebrenner studied his face in the mirror. His color was still not right, not nearly right, but maybe by tomorrow he would be able to go out.

He told Hamelin to show him how to use his computer, and he played with it with great interest until the pixels dancing on the monitor made his eyes throb so badly that he had to stop. He spent the rest of the afternoon lying naked on the sofa in front of the television, drinking blood and painfully stretching each limb until it hurt too badly to stretch it any more, then stretching another. He had learned self-discipline like no ordinary man. It had saved him in the box, and it would speed his recovery now. He used the remote control to shuffle through the channels, watching bits of new movies, commercials, news programs, music videos, all of them fascinating. He was amazed that the rabble had managed to invent new music even uglier than rock and roll.

By evening he was able to walk a few feet on his own and keep down a few tablespoons of beef broth mixed with blood. Before long maybe he would be able to eat normal food. The dark blue was draining from his skin, leaving a sickly blue-gray that felt less painful. He ordered Hamelin to go out and buy him a walking cane and some clothes.

Stonebrenner loathed sleep because it was too much like his long ordeal, but his body needed it, so he forced himself to take naps throughout the night. His dreams were haunted by faces, Charles Newman's especially, the deceitful visage that had tormented him for so many years, and after an hour or less he would awaken with an agonized cry, believing himself back in the coffin.

Angel was always beside him in the bed, trying to comfort him with her voice and gentle fingertips. Even now he sometimes believed that this was an illusion, lying here with her, free at last— believed that it was just another long fugue of madness that would end with him back in the box. He was relieved when at last the sun leaked through the curtains.

The calisthenics had paid off: today he could walk without Angel's help, stiffly but surely, using the cane only a little. He drank a large breakfast of blood and beef stock and dressed himself in the dark gray suit that Hamelin had bought for him. It was exactly what he had ordered, light-weight wool, conservatively cut, not much different from what he had been buried in.

He looked in the mirror and wanted to look away. His blue-gray skin was stretched so tight that his face looked like a death's-head. The teeth were the worst: they were yellow-brown and had grown so long that they looked like fangs. He had been in the grave too long, and he wondered if he would ever resemble a normal man again.

He put on a pair of dark glasses and called for Hamelin. "You're taking me for a ride," he said. "Bring your money."

"Where are you going?" Angel asked.

"I'm going to find a gift for you," Stonebrenner said. "I'm going to bring you centuries of time."

Chapter Thirty-Five

Stonebrenner and the poet were gone for several hours. Finally they returned with grocery bags full of weeds and dozens of little boxes and sacks.

Angel followed Baby to the kitchen and watched him unpack beakers, flasks, retorts, and Bunsen burners, turning the poet's kitchen into a chemistry laboratory. He lined the counter with vials of herbs, pills, powders, and liquids. When she asked what he was doing, Baby glanced impatiently at her and said, "Don't interrupt me. I'll explain when I'm ready."

Angel found Hamelin sitting in the dining room, staring gloomily at his frail hands. "What's going on?" she asked.

He looked up at her with a tragic expression. "First he made me drive him to pharmacies and health-food stores, where he purchased countless poisons and quack nostrums and flasks and whatnot. Then we went to the riverbank and he picked toadstools and unsavory weeds. Deadly nightshade, hemlock, and who knows what other noxious tares."

"What are they for?"

"To kill me," the poet muttered morosely. "Maybe to kill both of us. He's envious of our love. Though he can tyrannize our mortal bodies, he cannot abolish our love. I've seen how he enslaves you, forcing you to serve the unnatural needs of his cankered flesh. Like a perfidious puppeteer, he can jerk the strings of our tendons to his pleasure, but he cannot overrule what the heavens have ordained. He knows our love was writ in the stars in the infancy of time, and therefore he sulks with spiteful and lethal schemes. But do not fear, milady. In the shadow-land of death, beyond the black river Styx, our love bed awaits us, already bedecked with flowers. There, beside the gentle banks of Lethe shall we rinse away all sordid remembrances of his malignant tyranny. Prepare yourself, milady, for the blessed journey."

"Can't you just speak English once in a while?" Angel said.

The poet slunk sullenly away to the bathroom, and soon she heard him working on George's body with his handsaw, cutting it into parts small enough to carry out of the apartment inconspicuously.

Angel returned to the kitchen and watched Baby grind something that looked like chalk with a mortar and pestle. He poured some of the white powder into a beaker. Flasks were bubbling above Bunsen burners, and a retort fitted with copper tubing was distilling a greenish liquid. Herbs and weeds simmered in two big stockpots on the stove.

Again she asked him what he was doing. This time he glared at her with his black-button eyes and said nothing. She retreated to the bedroom, but by now the whole apartment was filled with nauseating odors, bitter, sweet, acidic, ammoniac, sulfuric.

Baby was still working in the kitchen when Angel went to bed. Several times she awoke choking from the fumes and crept to the kitchen to find him toiling over his flasks. When she got up in the morning, he was still in the kitchen. Presently he came to the living room and ordered Hamelin out of the apartment.

The poet stared resentfully at the floor, unable to meet Stonebrenner's eyes. "'Dead flies cause the ointment of the apothecary to send forth a stinking savour,'" Hamelin quoted. He gave Angel a significant look and left.

"Come to the kitchen," Baby told her. "I'll answer your questions now." He spoke in a hoarse whisper, his vocal cords still not recovered.

The Bunsen burners were turned off, and the flasks and beakers had been emptied. All of the liquids and powders apparently had cooked down to a cup or so of thick green-brown syrup simmering in a saucepan on the stove. Angel sat at the kitchen table.

"I'm four and a half centuries old," Stonebrenner said. "I would like you to share the rest of my long years with me."

Angel simply stared at him.

"You must understand the dangers before you consent," he whispered. "The strongest medicines are also deadly poisons; they can kill as easily as cure. The medicines I'll treat you with would kill most ordinary people—but you're not ordinary. Over the years you have ingested all seven of the words needed to release me from my paralysis. For most people, even one of these words would cause brain damage, and two of them would kill. You've built up a tolerance, and that's why I'm confident you will survive the treatments. But be warned—the treatments will be horrendously painful and will make you sick unto death."

Angel thought of her castration, its scar still not fully healed. She still needed to apply Betadine each day to keep infection away.

"I'm used to pain," she said. "It doesn't scare me. I'll put up with pain to be with you. But I wouldn't want to be immortal if I couldn't be with you."

"Don't say immortal," Baby said. "Not even the stars are immortal. They'll burn out in time. And even the angels that rage in hell will have their last day. I'm not an immortal, nor shall you be. I'm a Longevital."

A nice word, Angel thought. The accent fell on the second syllable: lon-GEV-i-tal.

"We are told that Adam lived 930 years," he rasped, his voice as dry as parchment. "His son Seth lived 912. Methuselah lived 969 years. It would be your genetic birthright to live this long, except that in those ancient days the Nephilim were born of human women."

"What are Nephilim?" she asked.

"The sons of God had intercourse with women," he answered. "Fallen angels, what Christian theologians call demons."

"Angels?" she asked.

"Angels are just creatures from another place," he answered. "A different race, as much like people as horses are like donkeys. But they bred with humans, and their offspring were the Nephilim. Genetic hybrids, like the offspring of the horse and the ass. The human gene pool was corrupted, and death was planted in our chromosomes. Modern man is genetically degraded like the poor mule. But the treatments I offer will destroy the death gene, and your rightful genetic heritage will be given back to you."

"How long will I live?" she asked.

"You may live for centuries, as long as Methuselah. Ordinary poisons and diseases and wounds won't kill you. There are a few ways to kill a Longevital, and those I'll teach you when you're a Longevital yourself. Until that time, I mustn't trust even you with those secrets."

"You know you can trust me, Baby. I love you."

Again he smiled. "I know many recondite mysteries," he said. "But the mysteries of the human heart I have yet to fathom. Still, in due time I'll put my fate in your hands and trust you with secrets that could injure me. In the meantime, know that the path to Longevity is painful, and that a Longevital is not invulnerable. You saw, for example, the state of paralysis that was inflicted on me. I might have existed like that for several more miserable years if you hadn't unlocked the spell with the seven words."

"Who did it to you?" she asked.

"Another Longevital named Charles Newman."

"Who's he?"

"An enemy who was once my friend. A fiend who was once my mentor and is now my nemesis."

"Why did your friend become your enemy?"

"Some men have much wisdom but are ignorant of love," he answered. "That's the gnosis I seek to learn. I'll teach you many powers, and in return you'll teach me the power of love. Is your answer yes or no?"

"You know my answer."

Stonebrenner got up and stirred the mixture simmering in the saucepan. "There are seven treatments altogether," he said, "each one more poisonous and painful than the previous. Each treatment will harden you for the next. The remaining treatments will have to be administered after I've reclaimed my house. I have ingredients there, powders made of rare fungi that I grew in my basement, rare weeds that I planted long ago in the woods, which should still be growing wild. Some of the ingredients are from plants and insects long extinct, but I possess them in dried powders. In two days I'll reclaim my house, but I want to start your first treatment at once. There's no time to waste."

"We waited so many years to be together, why do we have to hurry now?"

"Because Charles Newman may already realize that I've been released. If not, he's bound to find out soon. I have woven a veil to hide myself from him, but his powers are equal to mine, and soon he'll penetrate the veil if he hasn't already. Sooner or later there will be a contest between us. I want to give you your birthright before that happens, in case I should prove the loser."

"But I don't want to be a Longevital unless I can be with you," Angel said. "I've had too many years already—alone."

Baby sniffed the mixture, then looked at her carefully, his stone-black eyes seeming to weigh and measure her.

"Longevity is for the courageous," he whispered. "You mustn't be weak or cowardly. If it turns out that your long years are spent apart from me, then bear them bravely. Besides, who can know how the contest will turn? You may have another chance to rescue me before it's over."

"If there's a chance I can help you, I'll do it," she said. "But I want to spend my years with you."

He smiled and turned off the heat beneath the pan. "Take off your shirt and lie on the sofa."

Angel went to the living room and removed her shirt, relieved that Hamelin was away so that he couldn't gaze at her breasts with his sad weak eyes. They had grown; they had become the breasts of a young woman. If Hamelin were to see them, he would no doubt write a dozen stupid poems about them.

She lay down on the couch, and Stonebrenner came in with the hot pan. He put it on the coffee table, knelt beside her, and said, "When the treatments are complete, I want you to be my wife."

With his words in her ears, Angel scarcely noticed the pain when he began to cut her with the scalpel just above her stomach.

"The first treatment is to the liver," he explained. "It will give you some immunity against the next treatments, which would otherwise kill you."

He cut deeply, and blood pulsed from the wound. The incision was semi-circular, like six of the seven stigmata on Stonebrenner's body, and Angel realized they were the scars of his own seven treatments.

He scooped some of the mixture from the saucepan with a spoon, held open the incision, and filled it with the hot ointment. At first there was just a scalding sensation, which she could bear. He added another spoonful of ointment and another.

"Just relax," he said. "Try not to be afraid. It will begin soon."

It did—reeling sickness and excruciating agony like being turned inside out. Before long there was a new discomfort: Baby was sewing the wound shut with a darning needle, sealing the poison inside.

"Try to be brave because it will soon get worse," he said. "Later, while you're in the deepest throes of your sickness, I'll lop off your penis. You'll be in so much pain by then that you'll probably not even notice."

Chapter Thirty-Six

Monday morning, after Ben left to see his patients, Sarah filled the riding mower with gas and got to work on the front yard. She had already mowed it on Friday, but then she had set the blade as high as it would go so the tall grass wouldn't stall the mower, and now she was redoing it with the blade set lower. Ben had put her up for nearly two weeks, and since he refused to take any rent money she had been trying to repay his kindness by mowing, pulling weeds, cleaning house, buying groceries, cooking meals, and whatever else she could find to do.

The grass needed a good dose of fertilizer with weed killer, but a yard this size would take a lot of fertilizer. She wondered how much the farmer who rented Ben's fields would charge to spray it with his tractor. She should ask Ben.

As she mowed around the fruit trees and the stone-edged flower beds, she could see how much loving care he and Isabel had put into the place in happier times. She thought of how brutality infected everything in its victims' lives, Isabel's paintings growing darker with each canvas, the yard becoming overgrown with weeds, the neglected barn weathering into a monument of misery. She thought of how long the effects could last, Gus Dietrick's evil still haunting the present two decades after his death.

It was so hard to undo the damage, but at the very least she could fix up these flower beds to look nice again. Of course she should okay it with Ben first.

She liked the farm, liked the long secure driveway, liked her old-fashioned bedroom, liked the shooting range and the backyard. And—uncomfortably—she was beginning to like Ben.

She stepped on the brake and sat there with the mower idling, feeling deeply ashamed of herself. Howard had died because he helped her. What if Ben ended up dying for the same reason? She had been staying here for purely selfish reasons, and now there was a new selfish reason—the imp of sexual desire.

She put the mower back in the barn, took a quick shower, and wrote a note for Ben because some things are easier to write down than to say out loud. She folded it, wrote his name on the front, and left it on the kitchen table where he would be sure to see it. Then she got her car out of the garage and left.

    ***

When Ben got home he wondered where Sarah was, and for some reason he was reminded of that awful day a year ago when he had come home and wondered where Isabel was. Probably she was buying groceries, and he wished she wouldn't do that. It wasn't likely that the wrong person would see her at a grocery store in Lancaster, but it was possible, and he didn't think groceries were worth the risk.

He didn't notice the note on the kitchen table because he went straight to the computer in his bedroom, wanting to check on an issue involving one of his patients. There was a long email from Ed Hardin:

Hey, Ben, I have some local news that should interest you. Do you remember that brick mansion with the interesting watchtower that you saw across the road & just a little north of the Dietrick place? Maybe you noticed a small old family cemetery on the property? Well, somebody recently robbed a grave in that cemetery!

The young couple that lives in the brick house discovered the vandalism yesterday, but there are shoe prints in the ground that make the police believe the grave was robbed while the ground was wet. It hasn't rained here since that big storm Thursday when you and Sarah were here, so my guess is that the grave was robbed Thursday night, maybe just a few hours after you were here.

Police say the shoe prints belong to three people, two men & the third maybe a man or woman. Could the maybe man or woman be Darnell/Angel? You told me the casket they found in his/her apt probably was Gus Dietrick's. Has this 2-sex psycho now dug up another grave just across the road?

The casket was still there, but the body was gone. The casket looked like a homemade job built of very thick oak with steel rivets & screws, sturdy enough to keep the dead from rising on Judgment Day. Even stranger, this was an unmarked grave & apparently nobody knows who was buried in it. Maybe now you'll believe what I've said about strange things occurring on that road. The whole road may be haunted after all!

The Stonebrenner house, as the place is called, has its own

interesting history. It was built in 1891 by a wealthy railroad magnate named Fenton Brown. Brown's son & family lived there after the old man's death & later the grandson & his family. The small cemetery that was vandalized contains the family cadavers, though no family bones were known to be resting where the vandals dug their hole.

The grandson's fortunes declined & the house being costly to maintain, he put it up for sale in 1962. The property was purchased by a stranger named Isaac Stonebrenner, who remained equally a stranger after moving in. He kept entirely to himself, his needs from town taken care of by 2 servants, a husband & wife who, by all accounts, were pretty strange themselves. Rumors & legends circulated that he was some sort of witch or warlock, but the villagers never stormed the castle to discover a Frankenstein monster or a coven of devil worshippers engaged in a spicy sex orgy.

Stonebrenner disappeared in 1973. Maybe no one would have noted his absence if the 2 servants hadn't appeared at the McClosky law firm with a letter in Stb's handwriting requesting that McClosky initiate some pre-arranged trust proceedings. The letter said that urgent business matters required Stb's attention in Europe & he'd be gone indefinitely. The 2 servants, by the way, proved unable to care for themselves with Stb. gone & were placed in a mental institution. Both were diagnosed as suffering senile dementia, though they were only middle-aged. They were both dead within the year.

I told you, it's a strange road.

The details concerning this trust are supposed to be privy, but the current McClosky, son of the attorney who drew up the original agreement, has a tongue that's easily loosened by a few glasses of wine & I confess I've learned several interesting secrets about our little town by wining & dining him, more wine than dine. He's a harmless & likable fellow, though rather piteously lonely & melancholic, which is maybe why he takes so readily to the cheering fruits of the vine. (Folks around here rather snidely call him Son because he's too cheap to change the McClosky & Son sign, even though his father is long dead.)

I've gathered from his loosened tongue that Isaac Stb. prescribed very unusual arrangements regarding the property. In the case of Stb.'s death or disappearance, both the farmland (500 acres) & the house were to be rented, together or separately, & these monies, together with interest from a separate fund, were to be applied toward taxes & upkeep so that the property could be maintained indefinitely by the fund, to be claimed (& this is the interesting part) at any time by any person meeting certain secret criteria (which criteria, to his credit, no amount of wine will loosen from McClosky's tongue).

In other words, this mysterious man Stb. must have anticipated that he would eventually disappear & wanted the property to be maintained for some unknown heir or for his own return.

Am planning to invite McClosky for dinner soon to see if I can learn more. Also I have many notes and stories I've collected over the years regarding the Stb. house & I'm going to spend the next few days poring over them, trying to see if there's any possible connection between Stb. & Darnell/Angel aside from the obvious connection that he/she lived right across the road.

Ben, when will you meet me at the club for some shooting? I've recently acquired a .22 caliber Anschutz Silhouette that I believe will put your beloved off-the-rack Savage to utter shame. Let's see who wins the trophies now! Or better yet, why not come up & stay for the weekend? & bring that charming Sarah by all means! She's pretty & smart & pleasant. I hope you won't be offended by some well-intentioned meddling from an old friend, but it's time, Ben, to stop licking your wounds and latch onto her!

Keep your powder dry,

"Bullseye" Ed

Ben looked at his watch: after 5:00 already. It shouldn't take this long to buy groceries, and he realized he was feeling very uneasy. He went downstairs, and while he was pouring a glass of iced tea he noticed Sarah's note on the table.

Ben,

I'm off to look for an apartment in Lancaster. I think an apartment here makes sense—I don't think Darnell or Peter or any other creep will find me this far from Columbus. I should be back by 6:00 or so. I guess you'll have to put up with me again tonight, but if I can find a place today I'll move my stuff tomorrow and get out of your hair. I'll bet you were wondering is that girl ever going to leave?

Ben, I'm no good at saying this sort of stuff. You've probably saved my life, and you've also kept me sane (sort of). I don't know how to say thanks for all you've done. Words aren't enough. I hope I can somehow repay you some day. At the very least I'll buy you some better bourbon than that swill you drink.

–Sarah

Ben called her cellphone and she picked up.

"Where are you?" he asked.

"I'm looking at an apartment right now. It looks pretty nice for the money. I think I'm going to take it."

"Have you put down any money yet?"

"No."

"Please don't."

"Why not? I'm afraid if I wait somebody else will snatch it up."

"Sarah, just come back and let me talk to you before you do anything."

"Well, okay."

After she hung up, Ben wondered exactly what it was he wanted to tell her. He filled a big pot with water and put it on the burner. He dumped a jar of pasta sauce into a pan and put it on low heat. He peeled some garlic and onion and sautéed it in a skillet. When it was starting to turn color he added some ground beef and stirred it around. The beef had already cooked and he was adding it to the sauce when he finally heard her bad muffler pulling up the driveway. He was surprised and a bit ashamed at the excitement he felt.

"Smells good," she said when she came in. "Want me to set the table?"

Ben had cleared the magazines and books off the dining room table a few days ago, and that's where she set the plates and wine glasses. Ben had told her that he wanted to talk, but he couldn't think of much to say while they ate. He considered telling her about Ed's email, but that wasn't what he wanted to talk about. When they were done eating they drank Chianti and she talked about the apartment.

"It's nice and sunny," she said. "It has two big window air conditioners—I think I'll be pretty comfortable there. Since I'll be right there in town, maybe we can meet for lunch sometimes."

He looked at her green eyes, which seemed to catch the light even in this dim room; he looked at her delicate chin, which gave her face a lovely cat-like shape; he looked at her lips, which maybe frowned more than they smiled but the smile was always worth waiting for.

They weren't smiling now. They wore an odd expression that Ben couldn't read.

"I don't blame you for wanting to get out of here," he said. "It's a gloomy house with a gloomy barn and some very gloomy paintings in the second living room. And I guess maybe I've been pretty gloomy myself."

"In fact I think you've been looking rather cheerful lately," she said. "I've been meaning to say something about it." She stood up and picked up the dirty plates.

"I want you to stay here," he said.

"Well, are you really sure you want to put up with a roommate?"

"I don't mean as a roommate," he said. "I mean I want you to stay because I'm in love with you."

"Oh."

She put down the plates, took his hand, gently pulled him up from his chair, and kissed him. Her lips felt very different from Isabel's, so soft and warm.

"Well then, maybe we should take the wine up to my room," she said.

Chapter Thirty-Seven

Tuesday while Angel was still too sick to be moved from her bed, Stonebrenner ordered the poet to drive him to the public library.

The city was even uglier than when he had last seen it, grotesque hamburger and pizza dumps wherever he looked. How idiots loved ugliness, he thought, like insects crawling over one another in their struggle to make the planet repulsive. It was a pity that the Third Reich hadn't conquered the world. The riffraff that he saw through Hamelin's van window would be dead or toiling in the factories where they belonged.

The library building was a welcome relief with its Grecian pillars and marble facade. But Stonebrenner soon saw that brainless scum had invaded its sanctuary as well. Fat sow-like women clutched thin plastic boxes in their blubbery arms. He went to the room that stored the plastic boxes and saw that they were the movie DVDs Angel had told him about. A glance at the boxes showed him what garbage they were. Stupid movies for people too stupid to read, but determined to take advantage of any free trash that the government stooped to provide.

He went to the periodical room and read dozens of news magazines cover to cover, his eyes aching like rotten teeth. History was the same foolish blunders repeated over and over, and the only event that surprised him was the fall of the Soviet Union, though even that he should have anticipated—an inefficient system based on hopelessly misguided principles laid down by a corrupt and idiotic Jewish intellectual.

Next he found books on cosmology, physics, and quantum mechanics and raced through their pages as quickly as he had read the magazines, his eyes aching even worse now. Interesting how Schrödinger's wave equation and Heisenberg's uncertainty principle affected the research being done in modern particle accelerators.

The plethora of big bang theories fascinated him, but the anthropic principle fascinated him more. Of course it was implied in Heisenberg's principle. If it was true that human observation affected whether something was a particle or a wave, then even dull-witted scientists must begin to realize how closely linked the fabric of the universe was to the human brain that watched it. Science was plodding ever closer to the truths of magic, but only a handful of scientists had the imagination to recognize how close they were.

Stonebrenner wanted to read more, but Angel was too sick to be left for long in the inept care of Hamelin. He asked a librarian where there was a pay phone so he could call a cab. She stared too long at his blue-gray skin, and he planted a deep pain in her stomach that might soon turn to cancer.

After he called the cab he remembered another small chore that should be done—he wanted to have a word with someone. He dialed the phone number that Angel had given him.

"Hello?" Peter Bellman said. "Hello? Who is it?"

Stonebrenner spoke one word into the receiver. Only one was necessary.

***

The single word that the Solitary One spoke over the phone was not English or any other tongue Peter Bellman had ever heard, yet he understood the meaning at once, or at least part of the meaning, because as the word expanded in his mind its meaning grew ever deeper and more profound. The word was a sphinxlike riddle and also a command, a command so imperative that it could not be disobeyed.

Though it was a single word, its meaning couldn't be fully expressed in a whole paragraph or maybe even in a whole book, but boiled down to its simplest essence the meaning was: "Find the Truth."

He knew the Truth he was ordered to find had nothing to do with trivial details or facts and figures; it was Truth with a capital T, the essential Truth of the Universe. And *find* meant something stronger than discover, something more like expose or reveal.

Peter sat in front of the dresser in his bedroom and stared at his reflection, hoping he could find the truth there. Every man's mind is a microcosm of the universe, he reasoned, and therefore he was looking at whatever Truth he could ever hope to know of the universe.

But Truth is an elusive thing, so after a while Peter dragged in another dresser from a spare room so that it faced the first dresser, and he sat between the two large mirrors. Now his face and the back of his head were both visible in the mirror in front of him, the kind of comprehensive perspective that he needed to solve the riddle, a picture of the whole rather than the fragment that the ignorant heathen see.

But the two mirrors added a maddening complexity: above and to the right of the reflection of his face, there was the reflection of the back of his head, while above and to the right of that was another reflection of his face, then another reflection of the back of his head, ad infinitum. He knew that the infinite reflections were part of the riddle, a reminder that if he got beneath one false image of himself he would find another false image, and beneath it another, and no matter how assiduously he might peel away the layers of appearance, he would never get to the Truth.

Like many profound riddles, this one sounded easy but was damnably difficult.

Then it dawned on him where the truth was hidden and what the single word had commanded him to do. The idea terrified and sickened him, but the Solitary One was not to be disobeyed, and seekers of the Truth must not be cowards.

It was going to be thirsty work, so he brought a pitcher of cold water from the refrigerator and set it on the dresser, and then went to the basement and brought up his rotary power tool and a whole package of diamond-edged cutting discs.

He set the tool to spin at its slowest speed, but still the disc kept getting hot because bone is a hard substance. Whenever the disc got too hot he would dip it in the pitcher of water to cool it. By now the water was red with blood, but the work was so arduous that he drank from the pitcher every 15 minutes or so, not caring about the blood.

First he sawed a shallow groove all the way around his bald head an inch above his eyebrows and ears, sopping up the blood with a towel when necessary, and after he had made the initial groove he kept going slowly around it, cutting a bit more deeply with each pass.

His head hurt horribly, maybe as much from the heat of the disc as the cutting itself, and many times he set down his tool and wept with horror and dismay. But the Solitary One's word could not be disobeyed, so after a few minutes he would turn the tool back on and continue his work.

The job became more difficult and exacting when the cutting disc finally made it all the way through the skull in places. Blood and fluid would ooze out whenever the disc touched the lining of his brain, and he would carefully move on to the next place that still needed cutting.

It was very difficult now to keep from losing consciousness, but the command was so authoritative that it pushed him onward. Concentration was the key, the perfect mental focus of a Zen swordsman or a fakir handling hot coals. The trick was to put aside all useless conventional thoughts and emotions: the Truth would forever hide from conventional minds.

At last the sawing was finished. Peter placed the bloody power tool on his dresser and regarded his work with grim satisfaction: a clean cut, good craftsmanship. Amazing what the human mind could do once it put aside its squeamish qualms.

He lifted off the top of his skull and gazed with amazement at his naked, pulsating brain. He had cracked open the riddle like a walnut, and the meat of the nut was revealed. But where in that meat was the Truth?

He cautiously prodded the side of his brain with a fingernail, and instantly he was bathed in a memory so vivid that it seemed he had been whisked back to childhood by a time machine. He was nine years old, playing in the backyard, and his mother was calling him to dinner. His mother, his beautiful mother who had always doted on him, who had kissed away his every hurt and had praised his every deed.

Her voice was as clear as if she were in the room with him—"Petey! Petey, darling!"—and he had a sudden spasm of horror and remorse. He had done something very naughty, he realized, taking off the top of his head like this. What would Mommy say? Would she be able to kiss it and make it better?

No, he thought. This is no time for Mom and all her conventional thinking, Sunday school and Cub Scouts, macaroni casseroles and cherry pies, birthday parties and Easter egg hunts. Goodbye to Mom and all that rubbish.

He reached in with both hands, a prospector digging for Truth.

Chapter Thirty-Eight

One of Gerald McClosky's rules was never to drink in his office, but today he was sorely tempted to break it. In fact he had been wanting a drink since early this morning, when someone called the office saying he intended to lay claim to the Stonebrenner estate. The Stonebrenner trust was his largest account, going back to the days when the business was his father's, but there were a few irregularities that put McClosky in an uncomfortably compromised position.

It was natural enough, after so many years of managing such a peculiar trust, to begin to believe that it would never be claimed, that it had become by default as much the property of McClosky and Son as of Isaac Stonebrenner, who by now must surely be dead. An eccentric recluse leaving instructions that seemed the product of a less-than-sound mind, the decades elapsing with money rolling in and no one coming to claim it, the trust fund growing fat with the great succession of bull markets that had begun in the eighties: all of this might tempt even a highly ethical man such as Gerald McClosky to begin skimming a little here, a little there, just borrowing really, and covering the loans with inflated expenses and cooked figures in the account book, strokes of the pen that had seemed subtle at the time, but now McClosky feared that any two-cent accountant would find them with his eyes shut.

The appointment was for 11:00, and the clock that McClosky had inherited from his father said 10:58. McClosky wondered if he had time for just a swallow of the vodka that he kept locked in his desk for emergencies. Highly unprofessional, drinking at the office, but vodka wasn't likely to tell on his breath if he sucked one of the antacid mints that he used for his dyspepsia, and besides it was his fucking office and his sanctimonious prig of a father was long dead and gone, God rest his soul. Just one. McClosky unlocked the drawer, took a large swallow from the bottle, and locked it back up. That felt better.

The clock began to chime, and before the first chime faded the door opened. A tall man entered, and McClosky sucked in his breath so hard that he nearly inhaled his antacid mint. The man was completely bald and wore a pair of dark glasses and a nice gray suit, but aside from those everyday features he almost didn't look like a man. His skin was cadaver gray and so sunken that his face looked like a skull. His shoulders were broad, but beneath the suit his body seemed to be as shriveled as his face.

"My name is Jacob Stonebrenner," the stranger said in a hoarse whisper. "I've come to claim my father's property."

There was a hint of an accent that McClosky couldn't place, maybe German. He hurried toward Stonebrenner and grasped his hand. It felt icy cold and bony, and the lawyer was shocked when he glimpsed the cracked yellow nails. Then a fetid odor made his head reel; it reminded him of a dead animal in a moldy cellar.

"May I see your identification?" he asked.

"Identification is irrelevant," Stonebrenner said.

He sat down in the chair facing McClosky's desk, and McClosky hurried behind his desk and sat down too, nearly falling into his chair because his legs felt weak.

"It's true that identification isn't needed according to the terms of the contract," he said. "But I'll need a social security number for taxes."

"I'll supply identification in due time," Stonebrenner said. "Right now don't waste my time with these questions."

"Of course not. Well then, I have all the necessary materials right here. The conditions prescribed by your father are a bit unusual."

"I'm perfectly familiar with my father's conditions," Stonebrenner said. "Don't waste my time talking about them."

"Of course not. Well then, we'll need my secretary to witness and notarize. She should be back any minute now. She had to deliver some papers to a nearby office."

Stonebrenner let out something like a hoarse snarl, and McClosky called his secretary's cellphone. "Miss Berger," he said, "could you please get back here as soon as possible? Yes, it's urgent."

McClosky put several more antacid mints in his mouth and said, "All of your father's furniture, by the way, has been carefully put away in the attic and a safe storage unit. The young couple that live there now also farm the land. According to the terms of the rental agreement, you're to pay them fair market value for this year's crops or else allow them to continue farming till harvest.

"Now, perhaps you're aware that when they rented the place they had to sign an agreement, as per your father's instructions, which allows you to take possession one week from tomorrow. That means the tenants are required to vacate the premises no later than midnight next Wednesday. You have every legal right, of course, to insist on this clause, though to be honest with you I don't look forward to evicting them. They're a nice young couple, and I regret to say they have suffered bad fortune recently. This spring their only child died of a rare disease. I dread that another disruption so soon on the heels will be hard on them."

Stonebrenner's upper lip twisted into an ugly smile, revealing long yellow teeth. "I'll have a word with them," he said.

His voice sounded like the dry rustling of a fly's wings, and the smell of a dead animal was stronger now. McClosky opened a ledger on his desk so quickly that he nearly tore a page.

"The books are in order," he said, speaking in a nervous rush. "You'll be pleased to know that the trust is very nicely in the black. There have been a few expenses, of course, repairs and fees and taxes, all in the normal course, everything perfectly accounted for with receipts and so forth. Everything is shipshape and neat as a pin. You'll be very happy when you see what the estate is worth. Of course you're welcome to double-check the figures, though quite unnecessary I assure you. We're scrupulously careful with such matters."

"Look at me," Stonebrenner said. He leaned forward and removed his dark glasses.

McClosky was transfixed by glossy eyes so black he couldn't tell which part was iris and which part pupil, more like polished stones than eyes. The pungent stench of death was overpowering, and for a moment McClosky saw something grotesquely inhuman, something like an enormous cadaver-gray insect with a skull for a face.

The grinning insect jaws opened and Stonebrenner said, "You'll pay back a dollar for every penny you've stolen from me. Be grateful if the payment isn't in flesh."

"Yes, of course," McClosky said. "A dollar for every penny is more than fair. I thank you for your kindness."

There was a light tapping at the door, and Miss Berger entered, late middle-aged and skinny as a scarecrow. When she saw Stonebrenner she gasped softly and fell into the chair beside McClosky's desk. Her notary seal slipped out of her hands into her lap, but she didn't seem to notice.

"Miss Berger, this is Jacob Stonebrenner," McClosky said.

She nodded quickly and tried to scoot her chair farther away from Stonebrenner, but its legs apparently were caught in the carpet.

The lawyer opened his safe and got out the thick envelope that Isaac Stonebrenner had sealed with wax in this very office when Gerald McClosky was only nine years old. He handed it to Miss Berger and said, "I want both of you to examine the seals."

They both did, and he said, "Very well, I need both of you to sign this document certifying that the seals haven't been broken."

They did, and he said, "Miss Berger, please notarize the document."

"I need to see Mr. Stonebrenner's identification to verify his signature," she said.

"I will supply it in due time," he said.

He stared at her with his black polished-stone eyes, and this time she succeeded in getting her chair to scoot back a few inches. She reached for her seal, which had tumbled from her lap to the carpet, and quickly notarized the document.

"Well then, I'll go ahead and open the envelope," McClosky said.

He broke the seven red wax seals with his letter opener and removed three smaller envelopes, each one also sealed with wax, and a sheet of parchment.

He read the parchment carefully and said, "This instructs the applicant to write a message on a sheet of paper before the envelope marked number one is opened. Both myself and one witness must agree that your message perfectly matches the message sealed in said envelope. If we agree that it does, the estate will be transferred to you at once. If we don't agree that there's a perfect match, you may appeal the decision to a judge, but otherwise you have no right to a second chance. The other two envelopes contain different messages and are to be opened only if the first applicant fails the test and a different applicant wishes to claim the property. Miss Berger, please give this to Mr. Stonebrenner so he can examine it."

Miss Berger took the piece of parchment in her trembling hand but didn't get up from her chair. Apparently she was reluctant to approach Stonebrenner.

"I know perfectly well what it says, I don't need to see it," he said. "I've brought my own pencils but I need a piece of paper."

McClosky pulled a clean sheet of paper from a desk drawer, and both he and Miss Berger scooted their chairs back when Stonebrenner brought his own up close to the desk so he could write. He pulled several colored artist's pencils from his pocket and began, but McClosky saw that he wasn't writing but instead drawing some sort of picture.

"Mr. Stonebrenner, I believe the instructions say that you must write some sort of message," he said.

Stonebrenner ignored him. His hand skimmed across the paper, crafting an elaborate multi-colored mosaic of serpents and insects and signs of the zodiac and strange hieroglyphics. In a few minutes he slid the drawing across the desk to McClosky and said, "Open the envelope."

McClosky broke the seven seals and pulled out a similar drawing. Not just similar, he realized as he compared the two—they were identical to the tiniest detail. For some reason the twin images made him feel sick, or maybe it was Stonebrenner's putrid breath, and he quickly handed them to Miss Berger.

"My word!" she exclaimed quietly.

"Do you agree that Mr. Stonebrenner's drawing resembles the original?" the lawyer asked her.

"They're exactly alike," she said. "Exactly."

"Well then, there are some papers to sign, of course," McClosky said. "I'll send them to the courthouse and the recorder's office will issue a new title."

He slid the documents one by one across his desk to Stonebrenner, who signed them and slid them back. As the lawyer leaned his head down to add his own signature to the first document, he thought that his eyes were playing tricks.

Two inches above Jacob Stonebrenner's signature was the signature that Isaac Stonebrenner had penned decades ago. Never before had McClosky seen two signatures so alike. Illegible but fascinating, they resembled some ancient script of a dead language, the calligraphy of a lost time.

Chapter Thirty-Nine

Hamelin was waiting in his Dodge van in front of the lawyer's office. He sat in the passenger seat with his face pressed against the window.

As Stonebrenner climbed into the driver's seat, he noticed drool hanging from the poet's mouth and oozing down the window. It was a bad sign; it meant he wouldn't last much longer, and Stonebrenner might need him for a while.

Hamelin was muttering quietly to himself, voicing his feeble hatred in half-coherent phrases that slobbered from his mouth as meaninglessly as the strings of saliva. Stonebrenner knew that the frail young man plotted constantly to kill him, but at the moment he was too preoccupied to be amused by this absurd conceit.

Stonebrenner started the engine and pulled away. He was getting used to driving again. He missed his beautiful 1952 Bentley Continental, superior in every way to the wretched junk people were driving nowadays, trash made by trash to be driven by trash.

The roads turned hilly as they got out of town, and the hills brought memories. He had lived here for 11 years before he was entombed, and there was something to be said for those years, even though so many of their hours had been spent in sleepless vigilance, gazing from the watchtower, not free to drive through the pleasant countryside or enjoy the blessings of his wealth.

But things would be different after Charles Newman was conquered. Together, he and Angel would triumph against the monster.

He didn't recognize the road until he was nearly upon it. He turned right and stared past the drooling poet at the deep woods. He steered the van through a dipping curve and recalled the first time he had seen this road, a few days after fleeing Boston. The sense of déjà vu was overwhelming, the same anxiety gnawing at him now as then.

But today the anxiety was tempered with exhilaration. He was free from the box, breathing country air again and coming home at last.

There it was on the left, the big barn and the magnificent brick fortress beside it. He pulled into the long driveway, got out, and stared at the yard, the trees, the windows, the steep slate roof with the tall belvedere standing watch in its center. This was his castle, the place of his secret chambers.

Off somewhere past the house was the cemetery. He couldn't bear to look at it.

He went to the front door and knocked. It was opened by a tall sandy-haired man in his mid-twenties, a gangly bumpkin smelling of hay and sweat who stared at Stonebrenner's face with astonishment.

"My name is Jacob Stonebrenner. I own this house and the land. You'll have to move out at once."

The young man just stared at him, his mouth gaping. At last he said, "That ain't gonna be so easy to do."

"Did you read your rental agreement? It says one week."

The man swallowed, stared, and swallowed again, his big Adam's apple bobbing. "Well, yes, but . . ."

"But what?"

"But that ain't gonna be so easy to do . . . My wife . . ."

"What about your wife? I don't believe the contract has any special clause about your wife, does it?"

"Well, no, but . . ."

"Is your wife here?"

"She's upstairs."

"Is anyone else here?"

"No."

"Good," Stonebrenner said. "Maybe we can work out a deal."

He pushed past the gape-mouthed young man, through the foyer and into the large front living room, God-awful junk furniture strewn everywhere he looked. If there was a single piece of his own furniture missing, that bucktoothed lawyer was going to pay with more than dollars. He stared at the massive stone fireplace, the sadness of forty lost years lying cold in its hearth.

"What kind of deal?" the young man asked.

Stonebrenner turned from the fireplace, stepped up to the farmer with two cat-quick strides, and placed his hands on the young man's temples. Warm tingling current surged along his arms to the balls of his thumbs. It was a simple technique based on the same voltaic principle used by faith-healers. The only trick was knowing when to stop—a moment too long and the synapses would melt like ice cream.

The man slipped out of his grasp and collapsed to the floor with a loud moan.

"Eric?" a voice asked from the foyer. "Who's here?"

Stonebrenner turned and saw a young woman rushing into the room. She knelt and grasped the farmer's shoulders. "Eric! What's wrong?"

A perfect wife, Stonebrenner thought, loving and loyal, her long smooth hair the color of wheat, a nice figure, not too thin or too plump, freckles on her pretty young face like splashes of sunny innocence. He peered into her mind and glimpsed her grief over their son's recent death, glimpsed her husband trying to console her with vapid phrases that he had heard in church.

The farmer moaned, opened his eyes, and tried to sit up. "God, I'm sick," he said. He threw up on the floor.

The wife shot a suspicious look at Stonebrenner. "What's going on?"

"Your husband seems to have fainted."

The perfect wife helped her sick husband to the sofa. "I'll get some water," she said and hurried out of the room. The man moaned again, his head lolling weakly against the back of the sofa.

"Go fetch a mop and clean up your vomit," Stonebrenner said.

The man groaned and touched his forehead. "Feel so sick," he said.

"What's your name?"

"Eric Beers."

"Eric Beers, I don't believe you understand your circumstances. You belong to me, body and soul. When I tell you to clean something up, you do it. God may grant free will, but I don't."

Beers stared at him with an angry, wary expression. He was putting up a remarkable fight, but he got up and tottered out of the room to get a mop. His anger was good; that meant the synapses hadn't been badly burned. A bit of resentment was fine, so long as obedience followed it.

The pretty wife came in with a glass of water and a wet cloth. "Where's Eric?" she asked.

"Getting a mop. He's going to clean his vomit off my floor."

She glared at Stonebrenner and said, "Who are you, anyway?"

Stonebrenner grinned and said, "I'm your lord and master."

Fear and anger kneaded her innocent face into something less pretty, and she started yelling for her husband and ordering Stonebrenner out of her house.

He grinned and transfixed her with his eyes. She stopped yelling then and stared at him with a different expression, something like religious awe.

She was a spirited woman with strong resistance, but his eyes were stronger, and he realized that even though his ordeal in the tomb had weakened his body, it had significantly strengthened his will power. A sorcerer's greatest tool is the power of his will, and all the rituals and disciplines of his training are whetstones to hone it. What greater discipline can there be than 40 years locked in a box? It occurred to him that by now he might very well be the most powerful man on earth, more powerful even than Charles Newman.

Eric Beers had returned with a mop and bucket and was staring gape-mouthed at his wife.

"Get to work," Stonebrenner said, and the young man started mopping.

"Put down your glass of water and come here," he told the wife, and when she did he touched her temples very gently. He liked her, liked her fight, and he didn't want to burn all of it out of her. She knelt and was sick for a minute, adding her vomit to the puddle her husband was mopping up, but she didn't pass out, and after a minute she was able to stand with Stonebrenner's help.

"Good," he said. "Now have a drink of water and rinse out your mouth."

He held the glass to her lips and she drank. He set the glass on the coffee table and kissed her, pressing his tongue into her mouth.

"What's your name?" he asked.

"Kathy."

He unbuttoned her pink sundress, removed it, and pulled off her pink panties. Her body was nice, only a faint trace of stretch marks on her softly rounded belly, her breasts still shapely with pretty nipples the same color as her freckles.

Eric Beers was leaning on his mop staring at them, his lips curled in an impotent snarl, and Stonebrenner told him to get back to work. He led Kathy to the sofa and told her to lie face down over the arm of it. A bit of her fight came back when he entered her, and he pressed her face against the sofa cushion while she struggled and moaned.

The thoughts that he glimpsed in her mind now were sexual,

memories of her first fumbling high-school dates with Eric, his wet lips pressed nervously against hers, his rough farm-boy hands slipping awkwardly into her brassiere, but behind the clumsiness of their youth Stonebrenner glimpsed something else, a strange and mysterious emotion called love.

He thought about the gnosis of love. In his whole long life he had always been too busy and too driven to explore its mysteries. His monkish dispassion hadn't saved him 40 years ago, but this time the power of love would be his ally against Charles Newman, and he believed that love would prevail. His love must be for Angel, of course, but this too was a form of love, and it had its undeniable pleasures.

When he was about to finish, he grabbed her hair, yanked her face up off the sofa cushion, and slapped her hard to put some fight back into her, and she howled with indignation as he ejaculated.

Eric Beers was staring at them again, his lips twitching with anger, and Stonebrenner told him to take his mop bucket out of the room. Kathy was still lying over the sofa and sobbing softly as he zipped his trousers and went outside to the van where Hamelin was waiting.

"Drive back to town," he said. "If there are still any body parts in the apartment, clear them out. Then bring Angel here. She'll be very sick and you'll have to help her to the car. Bring whatever essentials you'll need because we'll be staying here from now on."

The drooling poet cursed under his breath but backed out of the driveway to do what he was told. Stonebrenner returned to the house, where Eric Beers was helping his wife get dressed.

When her sundress was buttoned he sat with her on the sofa and kissed her forehead.

"It's all right, Kathy," he said. "Everything is all right."

Her eyes were open, but she seemed to be staring at nothing.

"I told you to get that bucket out of here," Stonebrenner said. "This is my oak floor, and I don't want a wet bucket sitting on it."

He climbed the wide stairs to the second story, and then climbed the narrow spiral stairs that led to the belvedere. He looked out of a cobwebbed window, as he had looked for countless hours so many years ago. He cleared his mind and made every sense alert.

He couldn't detect Charles Newman in any direction he turned, but that meant nothing. He hadn't been able to detect him 40 years ago either.

Chapter Forty

Stonebrenner eased Angel's wheelchair down the basement steps. The jostling made her head reel, and she was trying not to vomit. It was embarrassing to throw up in front of Baby, and she always tried to wait until he was out of the room.

He had allowed her only two days to recover from her first treatment. The second procedure, performed just hours after she had arrived at his house yesterday afternoon, made her even sicker than the first one because this time he had administered three treatments all at once. He had cut three deep incisions on her back, one for each kidney and another for her pancreas, and had filled them with three different poisonous concoctions. All three sites burned with fires that shot like blazing bullets all the way through her body.

Her groin also burned, because there was a sutured wound where her penis used to be. There was still a plastic tube stuck in her urethra to help her pee, but Baby said it probably could be removed in a day or two.

Angel wondered if he was speeding up the treatment program so it would be finished before his enemy could find them. She tried not to harbor such suspicions because she needed to trust her physician, her teacher, her fiancé. Even if he was rushing things, she was willing to take the risk if it meant having a chance to help him in his fight against Charles Newman.

At the bottom of the steps, she forced herself to lift her head and sit upright in the chair, wanting to appear alert and interested. He had promised to show her his treasures, but nothing she could see looked valuable, just a large basement with stone walls, a furnace, a hot water heater, shelves and cobwebs. He pushed her chair to the far end, but there was nothing to see here, not even shelves, only a dead spider stuck on a dirty wall.

"Watch closely," he said. "Down here where no one can possibly see us, I'll show you how I crafted the lock that keeps our enemy from being able to set foot on this property."

He stretched his arms in front of himself and began weaving his hands around in a strange way, as if caressing an invisible object.

Angel thought she wasn't seeing clearly, the bad light and her illness making it appear that first one hand and then the other would flicker out of view for a moment—vanish completely and then reappear.

But it wasn't her eyes: his hands really were disappearing; they seemed to be dipping in and out of some strange convolution of nothingness in the basement air.

"There," he said when he was done. "You see, I keep my lock hidden in a parallelism, where no one can possibly find it."

"Parallelism?" she asked weakly.

"Yes, a parallel domain. There are many kingdoms, more than one could count. To craft my lock I make use of a nexus where another domain intersects ours."

"I feel so dizzy."

"I'm aware this isn't the ideal time to teach you," he whispered sternly, "but lift up your head and pay attention. There's much you need to learn in a very short time. Two of us are stronger than one, but not if one of us is ignorant.

"The lock that I just showed you protects this house, the yard, and the barn against Charles Newman. Many years ago, even when I still trusted him, I collected bits of his hair and nails whenever I had an opportunity. They contain his DNA, of course, and so I was able to craft the lock specifically for him. You and I may come here, even the mailman may come, but Newman is irrevocably locked out. He may be able to wander around in my fields, but he won't be able to enter my house or my immediate property."

"Then you're safe," she said.

"Here I'm safe. But until I find him and kill him I'm a prisoner because I can't safely leave this property."

"Where is he?"

"I don't know. Newman is a traveler, so he could be anywhere. He likes Europe, but he could be in Tibet or Africa searching for potions and spells and talismans. Or he could be much nearer. I've put out my feelers for him, but he seems to have woven a veil around himself so dense I can't penetrate it. But wherever he is, I'm certain he's coming closer. By now he knows I'm out of the grave, and he wants to put me back in.

"But let's turn to a pleasanter subject. Let me show you a much simpler and cruder lock. To open this one, all you need to do is push hard on these two stones at the same time."

Baby pressed two stones, and part of the basement wall groaned inward, making a doorway into darkness. He wheeled her chair through it, and the air inside was cool, damp, and musty. He pushed the stone doorway shut behind them, switched on a flashlight and handed it to her.

"Aim it down the stairs," he said.

The flashlight shook in her hands, and Angel saw steps hewn out of solid rock. Baby eased the wheelchair down step by step until they came to a stone floor. The trembling circle of light showed walls of rough stone and stalactites hanging from a low ceiling. They were in a long, narrow cavern, and Angel felt an ugly thrill of terror. Her time in the box had made her deeply claustrophobic, and she very badly wanted out of this tight place.

"These are natural limestone caverns," he said, his hoarse voice echoing. "The room we're in is the largest chamber. They extend under the property for a little ways, out toward the woods. Fifty years ago I hired contractors to build the stairs down from the basement and build the door in the basement wall, and I paid them very well to keep their mouths shut. They dynamited the only other entrance and sealed all the cracks and crevices with concrete to keep the caverns watertight. The only openings are a few waterproof shafts to keep the air fresh. No one else can get in. We're always safe here."

He pushed her chair farther into the cavern, where it widened a bit. This part was set up as a laboratory, wooden tables cluttered with flasks and retorts, wooden cupboards wherever they could fit into the recesses of the walls. He lit a kerosene lantern on a table and opened a steel trunk nestled in an alcove in the wall. He reached into it and scooped up a handful of gold coins.

"We'll never worry about bills," he said, grinning like a skull with long yellow teeth.

He shut the trunk and opened a cupboard, its shelves lined with jars and beakers. He removed a small jar and held it carefully, as if it were a priceless vase.

"Dried venom from an extinct snake," he said proudly. "This is one of the ingredients that's making your pancreas hurt so badly right now. Once this irreplaceable powder is gone there will be no more Longevitals, unless science catches up."

He replaced the jar carefully and pointed to others. "I have specimens of eight extinct insects, and I ground some of their precious carcasses to treat your kidneys. I have dried leaves from the

Egyptian Sekem tree, which hasn't been seen for centuries, though it's rumored that some Sufi adepts possess living specimens. My Angel, the contents of these shelves are priceless. Who wouldn't torture his own mother for such treasures?"

Baby shut the cupboard and pulled a dull metal box from a cranny in the wall.

"This contains one of our vulnerabilities—Hermesium. It's a metal invented by alchemists, and it's deadly to Longevitals. The screws Charles Newman used to seal my coffin were made of it. You must never handle it without rubber gloves—the poison may leach through your skin."

He opened another cupboard and showed Angel another treasure. She had never seen him like this, so filled with enthusiasm. For a while his excitement nearly made her forget how sick she was, but her scalp itched and whenever she scratched it a clump of hair came out in her hand. It had been falling out since the first treatment, and soon she would be bald.

Baby had thrown away her beautiful red hair, and she wondered if he wanted her to look as terrible as possible. Maybe it was because he wanted to love her spirit rather than her body—he had talked many times about the marriage of spirits.

"There's so much to teach you," he said. "Today we'll work on the etymology of the ancient words. I know very little about computers, but they make a useful analogy. Each word your name-bringers collected was like an intricate digital download. When you breathed the seven words into my mouth, you were reinstalling seven operating programs to restore me from the spell Newman had planted in me, a spell no doubt similar to a computer virus."

Angel tried to concentrate on his teaching, wanting to learn the skills she would need to help him, but the poison he had given her yesterday turned his words into a dizzy delirium, a sour spew of sickness.

Chapter Forty-One

Late Friday afternoon Ben and Sarah were lying in his bed—their bed now—enjoying the soft afterglow of lovemaking when his cellphone rang. He saw that it was Ed Hardin and picked up, even though Sarah grumbled and made a face.

"Well, Ben, it cost me three of the best bottles from my cellar, but I learned some interesting news from Gerald McClosky. Stonebrenner is back, his son supposedly."

"What do you mean 'supposedly'?"

"Well, this supposed son's signature is identical to his father's, for one thing. I've learned some other things too."

"What things?"

"I don't want to tell you over the phone. You already think I'm a crazy old coot with my ghost stories, and this stuff will sound just plain nuts if I can't show you the evidence I've dug up. Why don't you and Sarah come up here for the weekend?"

Sarah was running her fingernails over Ben's chest. He didn't want to go to Mount Vernon for the weekend; he was having too much fun here.

"I don't need to see any evidence," Ben said. "I already know you're nuts. I'm trained to see things like that."

"Let's just say I've collected a hell of a lot of folklore over the years, and the last few days, since that cemetery was vandalized, I've been looking through my files and piecing some of the stories together like a quilt. And believe me, it's a pretty crazy quilt I've come up with."

"I smell another book in the works. Guess I better get started on the intro."

"Maybe so. But I'll tell you something, Ben, I'm pretty sure this supposed son of Stonebrenner is old Isaac himself."

"Yeah? He'd be pretty old, wouldn't he?"

"Yeah, he was probably in his mid-fifties when he disappeared, which would put him in his 90s now. McClosky said he doesn't look that old, but he does look awful. He said he looks like something that crawled out of a grave—I believe those were his exact words."

"So he's the son and he's sick. Not a very good ghost story."

"It's not that simple, Ben. Poor old McClosky seems to be in a bit of financial embarrassment, so I offered him a little loan, and in return he let me examine a drawing made by Isaac and one made by the son. Now, you know I collect art and I know something about recognizing forgery. These drawings were done by the same man, Ben."

Ben wasn't paying much attention. Sarah had gotten out of bed and was slipping on a very small pair of light blue panties. Then she slipped on a white T-shirt that didn't quite cover the panties, stepped into a pair of sandals, and left the room.

"You've read too many Sherlock Holmes stories, Ed. Besides, who cares if it's the old man or his son?"

"Ben, I'm sure this has something to do with the Dietrick case. I have evidence."

"Yeah? What evidence?"

Ben didn't want to think about the Dietrick case right now. He and Sarah had been trying to put it out of their minds.

"I told you, I can't explain this over the phone. If you want to know how all this fits together, you'll have to come here and see for yourself. I want you to look at the materials I've found and then make up your own mind. Bring some guns and we'll do some shooting. Does Sarah know how to shoot?"

"Better than you. I'll ask her what she wants to do and get back."

Ben hung up, got dressed, and went downstairs. Sarah was in the kitchen peeling asparagus; chicken breasts were sautéing on the stove. He stood behind her, held her close, and smelled her hair. To hell with the Dietrick house, with Darnell and Angel, to hell with everything except the smell of Sarah's hair.

The past few days had been happy, maybe even happier than the days when he had gotten to know Isabel. Wednesday after his appointments they had hiked through the valleys and caves of Hocking Hills. They had rented a cabin for the night, and since he had no appointments Thursday they had rented horses. Sarah hadn't ridden one since her childhood in Iowa, and he could still see the smile on her face as she rode her brown mare through the hilly forest trails.

But maybe the best times had been spent right here, hours of laughter and lovemaking and secret-sharing. The ugly situation out there beyond the long driveway had left them alone, and they had begun to believe that Darnell was dead and the danger was past. Why bring back that darkness now?

"So wha'd he want?" Sarah asked.

"He wants us to come up to Mount Vernon and listen to his silly stories. Ed loves to have people listen to his stories."

"What's this old man and son stuff?"

Ben told her. At first Sarah seemed to take it no more seriously than he did, but by the time dinner was on the table, he could see she was stewing over it. She had been smiling like a little girl for several days, but now her frown was back. He wished he hadn't told her.

She chewed her chicken breast slowly with her brow furrowed. "When we were leaving that horrible house, you said you didn't think what happened there was just our imagination," she said. "Well then, what was it?"

"Let's not think about it."

Sarah frowned some more and sipped her wine.

"Just because nobody's been killed for a few days doesn't mean it's all over," she said.

Ben ate his asparagus without speaking. He had a bad feeling that they were going to be driving to Mount Vernon tomorrow.

Chapter Forty-Two

Angel lay in bed unable to lift her head. Whenever she tried to move it, the bedroom whirled like a carnival ride. Last night she had received her final three treatments.

There was a deep poison-filled incision above each lung, making each breath ache and rattle as she struggled against suffocation. But the worst incision was the big X that Baby had carved above her heart, and she could feel that organ fluttering weakly in her chest like a trapped bird.

She smelled her own sepsis, smelled her flesh rotting beneath the bandages. She kept shutting her eyes, wanting to sleep, but having nothing to focus on made her even dizzier, so she forced them back open and stared at the ceiling chandelier.

Baby was standing at one of the bedroom windows, staring out, watching. Sometimes he did that for hours on end. His anxiety made her feel worse, and she tried to ignore it, tried to ignore everything but the chandelier.

Someone entered the room, and the room spun as she turned her eyes to see. It was Kathy Beers, the farmer's wife. Whenever she had no direct orders to occupy her, she wandered from room to room like a wraith haunting the house. Her pale freckled skin, her spectral hair, her empty blue eyes, and the white nightgown she always wore made her look all the more like a ghost.

Angel turned her eyes away. She hated the ghost and wished that Baby would kill her.

Instead, he turned from the window and led Kathy to Angel's bed. The ghostly weight caused the room to tilt and sway. From the corner of her eye, she saw Baby undressing, carefully folding his trousers, laying them on the chair and unbuttoning his shirt. She thought he was undressing so slowly and deliberately to torment her with his striptease.

It wasn't the first time he'd had sex with Kathy beside Angel in her own bed, soaked with the stench of her illness. At first it had shocked her, even through the muffling layers of nausea, but now she told herself that it was his way of symbolically making love with her, using this pale zombie as a surrogate beside the sick body of his fiancée.

Still, she looked away as Baby climbed into bed and pressed his naked body against the ghost. The whole room seemed to rock and gyrate with the bed. Vertigo brought vomit to Angel's throat, but she kept swallowing it, not daring to ruin Baby's lovemaking with her illness. The swaying room, the glittering chandelier, the sounds of intercourse all seemed even more hallucinatory than the visions she had experienced as a child in the box.

She knew the sense of delusion wasn't caused entirely by her illness. It came from Baby's presence, his sorcery leaking into the air around him. Where Baby walked, a trail of hallucinations followed in his wake, as if he warped the texture of reality around him.

She knew his powers were evil, but what kinship did she have with virtue? Born of iniquity in a box of depravity and nursed on insanity, she had no objection to his evil so long as the two of them shared it together.

Kathy's ghostly moaning reminded Angel of her own anatomical inadequacy. When her illness was over and she and Baby were married, could his sorcery give her what other women were given at birth? Of course there were sex-change clinics, and while she listened to the bedsprings squeaking, she imagined having the most beautiful vagina to offer him, labia like pink petals of a flower, genitalia so alluring that they would thrill him for centuries while they walked the world together.

Her fantasy was interrupted by the sound of someone entering the room. Angel turned her eyes painfully. It was Matthew Hamelin, glaring at the three of them. She knew what thoughts were swimming through his damaged brain: he was furious that Baby was in bed with both women.

Such a feeble, absurd little man, pale and weak like her brother Darnell. But unlike Darnell, who had been sweetly innocent, the frail poet was constantly seething with hostility.

Baby stopped his lovemaking and stared at him. "You're jealous, are you?" he said.

Hamelin shrank back but didn't leave the room. Angel could almost hear the two halves of his brain warring: one side terrified, one side vengeful.

"Well then, take off your clothes," Baby said. "Join the fun."

The poet stiffened, obviously sensing a trick. He tried to back out of the room but couldn't. Not possible to disobey the lord and master. He unbuttoned his shirt, pulled it out of his trousers and took it off, revealing a narrow, hairless chest. He removed his shoes and tried to undo his pants, but his fingers began to convulse, jerking up and down on the zipper like a TV picture gone bad.

"Control your excitement," Baby said. "Open your fly and show us what you've got."

The pants came off and the socks, and Hamelin stood there trembling in a pair of stained cotton briefs.

"Take those panties off too," Baby said.

Hamelin's white face reddened as he pulled them down. Angel felt almost sorry for him, pathetically naked, a frail white shivering twig revealing his laughable inadequacy to his mistress.

"Now take off the rest of your clothes," Stonebrenner said.

The poet looked down at himself, confused—there was nothing else to take off.

"Come here," Baby said, "I'll help you."

His face blazing with hostility and terror, Hamelin stepped shakily to the side of the bed. Baby got the scalpel off the night table and used it to cut the outlines of a shirtfront on the poet's naked chest. He cut a V-shaped incision beneath his neck, and from the bottom of the V he cut a bloody red seam straight down the chest where the buttons would go, and then cut another seam around his abdomen.

"Now, open up your shirt," he said.

Bitterness and fear consumed the poet's face, but he worked his fingertips into the long incision from neck to belly button and began pulling the cut pelt away from his flesh.

Angel watched from the corner of her eye, thinking that this must be part of her delirium. It had to be. Surely no one could do what the poet was doing, peeling the skin of his chest open like a shirt and baring the bloody meat beneath it. It wasn't possible.

She shut her eyes and looked at the spinning darkness instead.

Chapter Forty-Three

Saturday started out well enough. Ed Hardin bought them lunch and then took them to a shooting range near Mount Vernon. They all took turns firing his new Anschutz .22 caliber rifle, which looked very fancy and expensive though Ben was able to outshoot it, or at least outshoot Ed, with his inexpensive Savage .22 bolt action.

Ben had brought his customized Springfield 1911, so for the first time Sarah tried shooting a .45 caliber pistol. She had brought her Ruger along, and Ed made a fuss over it as if were a Rolls Royce.

They all tried their hand with Ed's Hammerli target .22 pistol, and both men were impressed with her skill. Though Ben's groups were much tighter than hers, sometimes just one ragged hole in the center of the target, she found she could shoot nearly as well as Ed. His age showed; his hands trembled a little when he aimed.

For a couple of hours Ed drove them around to show them the beautiful old campus of Kenyon College a few miles outside of Mount Vernon and the pleasant rolling Amish farmland beyond it. They returned to his house in the late afternoon, and Ed showed them his wine cellar and selected several bottles for them to enjoy before, during, and after dinner. Then he showed them the new reloading equipment he had added to his basement workshop. He opened box after box of custom target ammo he had loaded, holding up the brass cartridges for their inspection as if they were jewels.

Sarah began to wish that she and Ben weren't spending the night; an elderly man's hobbies can grow old pretty quickly. His cooking, at least, was one hobby that she could appreciate. He served sautéed veal scallops with mushrooms, Amish noodles, sautéed eggplant, and a delicate chocolate mousse for dessert. After dinner he opened yet another bottle of wine and led them to his front living room.

"Okay, I'll lay out my evidence," he said, "and you, the jury, can decide if I'm insane or not. Sarah, as Ben can tell you, for many years I've been threatening to write a book about the most sinister sorcerers of the last 100 years. I'll probably never get around to writing it, but I've done a good deal of research. Probably the most sinister of them all is a shadowy figure named Elden Becker.

"Becker lived in Boston in the 40s and 50s, and there are many ghastly rumors surrounding him, lurid tales of hypnotized women used as sex slaves and later found floating in the river or wandering through the streets in a state of lunacy. People he came in contact with had a tendency to disappear permanently, and others ended up in mental institutions in a zombie-like state.

"Unlike Aleister Crowley and some of the other well-known hocus-pocusers, Elden Becker shunned publicity. It seems not many photographs of him exist, and I've only been able to dig up two. Here's one of them."

Ed had piled enough books, clippings, and scrapbooks on his coffee table to keep them entertained for a week or more, and he dug through one of the piles and produced a page from a 1939 copy of the *The Baltimore Sun*. A headline read, "Elden Becker questioned about disappearance of heiress," and above it was a photograph of a broad-shouldered bald man trying unsuccessfully to cover the camera lens with his large hand.

"So what?" Ben said.

"So a couple days ago I discovered something pretty remarkable," Ed said. "Isaac Stonebrenner had already disappeared from Mount Vernon by the time I moved here, so I've never seen him. But when I started looking into all this stuff that's been happening, I asked around for a photograph of him, and here's what I found."

He pulled a glossy color snapshot from one of his stacks. "This was taken right here in town in 1972, not long before Stonebrenner disappeared."

The man in the photo, walking past the Mount Vernon courthouse and looking toward the street with a wary expression as if sensing a camera nearby, certainly looked like the man in the newspaper photo, and not a day older.

"Okay, so two men in a world of billions look alike," Ben said.

"Apparently three," Ed said. "That is, if you want to believe that Isaac and Jacob Stonebrenner aren't the same person. I showed this 1972 picture to the lawyer McClosky, and he swears this is the same man who was in his office a few days ago. He's lost some weight, McClosky said, and he looks really sick and horrible, but it's the same man!"

Ed pulled a small battered black-and-white photo from one of his scrapbooks. "Here's my only other picture of Elden Becker," he said. "If you look closely at the picture of Stonebrenner you can see a little triangular spot on the right side of his forehead, like a birthmark or something. Now look at this picture—the mark is very tiny, but you can see it."

"It's probably just a spot on the print," Ben said.

"Elden Becker disappeared from Boston in 1962, the same year that Isaac Stonebrenner showed up in Mount Vernon."

"Maybe so, but they're not the same person," Ben said. "That newspaper picture is from 1939. So how old would Becker be today?"

"Well, this is the part that I didn't want to tell you over the phone," Ed said. "I'll just show you the evidence and let you decide. I started digging through my collection of books on the occult, and here's what I came up with."

He picked up an old book from the stack on the coffee table, opened it to a bookmark, and handed it to Ben.

Ben glanced at it and said, "My Latin's about good enough to read an old Roman stop sign."

"Okay then, here's one in English."

Ed found another book, opened it to a bookmark, and began reading out loud something about an alchemist treatment that could allow a person to live for centuries.

"Ed, this is ridiculous," Ben said.

But Ed wouldn't shut up. He droned on and on, reciting more passages about magicians and Longevitals from his dusty old books and then playing tape recordings of stories he had collected about the Dietrick house and the Stonebrenner mansion.

Sarah wasn't sure what she had hoped to learn from Ed's folklore, but this wasn't it. The wine was good, but old and complex and heavy in her mouth, and really she would have preferred a beer or a Coke. Two antique pendulum clocks ticked on the walls while a big grandfather clock ticked in the corner of the next room, and Ed, with his white beard, began to remind her of Father Time.

She tried not to yawn, but it was difficult. When her eyelids grew too heavy, she got up and strolled around the big room, looking at his paintings and the two glass display cases full of curios.

"What's all this supposed to add up to anyway?" Ben asked.

"You tell me," Ed said. "A man who doesn't age. Wherever he goes, the people he comes in contact with either disappear or are found wandering around like zombies. He lived next door to the

Dietrick house, and that house and every other house on the road churned out enough ghost stories that I couldn't collect them all if I tried. He disappears for 40 years, leaving a bizarre legal arrangement that suggests he plans to return. A child unfortunate enough to live near his house grows up to be a psychotic killer. An unmarked grave is robbed on the Stonebrenner property, and a few days later Stonebrenner himself shows up at McClosky's office and reclaims his property. You tell me."

Ben grimaced. "Come on, Ed, you don't really expect us to believe that Stonebrenner came out of that grave?"

"You can believe whatever you want, I'm just showing you the evidence. Maybe it doesn't tell you anything, but it tells me that Stonebrenner is a Longevital. Furthermore, he's a magus, a sorcerer, a warlock, the kind of person they used to hang in Salem. Maybe they knew what they were doing."

"You've been collecting these spook stories too long," Ben said. "You need to find a different hobby."

"Okay, fine, I won't say another word. But let me ask you one thing. When you two visited the Dietrick house, what did *you* see? Was that just another stupid spook story?"

Ben didn't answer. Sarah started to say something but stopped. She didn't want to revisit the Dietrick house right now, even in conversation.

"Well, that's my sermon for tonight," Ed said. "Want some more wine, Sarah?"

"No thanks. I'm getting pretty sleepy."

"So am I," Ed said. "You two want separate rooms or will one be enough?"

"One," Ben said.

It was the first sensible word Sarah had heard all night.

Chapter Forty-Four

It was the X-shaped incision that almost killed her. Angel seemed to hover above her body. She could see it lying beneath her in the bed, white and wasted, naked except for the bandages covering its wounds, one bandage for her liver, one for each lung, and one for the big X that Baby had carved above her heart. The other three wounds were on her back, two for her kidneys and one for her pancreas.

They were seven swords of pain plunged deep into her body. If she let go of the swords she believed she could float away, painless and free. The emaciated body languishing beneath her already looked dead, waiting only for her to let go so it could give up this miserable battle against the poisons oozing through its veins. She could feel its heart flutter and stop, flutter and stop, a palsied fist too weak to clench. Only love forced her to hold on, but even her love fluttered and wanted to stop.

She tried to tell herself stories of what she and Baby would do when this ordeal was over, the places they would go with all the time in the world to see them, the secrets he would teach her, the ways they would love each other for centuries to come, as no other lovers ever had.

But she was too sick to believe in anything, even in Stonebrenner. If he loved her, how could he put her through this agony? Surely his intent was to kill her, as slowly and sadistically as possible.

Flutter and stop, flutter and stop, the pale body beneath her with its seven stigmata looking dead already, a shrunken cadaver. Flutter and stop.

And then there was a new trouble. With Angel nearly absent from her own body, floating above it like a ghost, she felt something else trying to move in, trying to take over.

It was Darnell, squirming and wrestling, fighting for control.

* * *

Ben and Sarah made love quietly, not wanting to be overheard by Ed, whose room was across the hall from theirs, and Sarah found the slow stillness exciting, Ben's body moving like warm waves over her tingling nakedness, his hands lapping softly at her breasts, his lips teasing hers like ripples of salt water. She reached orgasm twice, and each time she wanted to cry out; but containing the cry, clutching it inside her as an ecstatic secret, made it even more intense. None of her other lovers had ever felt so good.

When they finished, she could see the sounds that Ben had wanted to make written on his face. She laughed quietly and held him against her.

He murmured sleepily and curled up against her, his hand still cupping one of her breasts. Sarah heard his breathing slow into slumber, felt his hand loosen and slip away, but still she lay awake, staring at the dark ceiling and thinking she should try to make sense of Ed's strange stories, but her mind kept wandering off to think of Ben instead.

She thought of the horses they had rented Thursday. She hadn't been on a horse since childhood, and she hadn't enjoyed a better day since she was a child. It seemed impossible that such happiness could come in the midst of such trouble. Finally she closed her eyes and drifted, imagining the sound of hooves, Ben's horse clopping alongside hers through curvy forest trails above lush valleys.

She heard a voice beside her. "Sarah. It's me. Darnell."

She sat up so quickly that Ben grunted and rolled over. Darnell was standing naked a few feet from the bed, glowing whitely in the dark.

His hands were primly in front of him, covering his groin. He looked emaciated and sick and was nearly bald, with just a few thin tufts of hair still clinging to his scalp. On his skinny torso were three ugly sutured wounds shaped like crescent moons, and over his heart was a wound shaped like an X. He had the small breasts of a young woman.

Sarah let out a sharp cry and grabbed the sheet to cover her own breasts. Ben made another slumberous sound and stirred.

"Please don't wake him," Darnell said. "I won't hurt you, I promise. I don't know how much time I have. You have to listen."

He moved a step closer to the bed, and Sarah shrank back against the headboard.

"Angel's very sick right now, but I don't think she's going to die," he said. "She's with her friend, whose name is Stonebrenner. He's not an ordinary man, he's some kind of monster. He's been teaching her black magic. Now that she's too sick to resist me, I'm using the powers he's taught her. That's how I'm here—it's a trick he taught her. He calls this an astral body."

Darnell reached out his hand to the dresser, and it passed through the wood. "You see, I couldn't harm you with my hands even if I wanted to. But there are *other* ways, and I won't be in control for long.

"He's giving her a treatment that has made her sick, but when she's better she and Stonebrenner will kill you. You know too much about me, so she thinks you're a threat.

"And if I can find you, so can she. I don't even understand how I found you, but she probably does. It must be another trick he taught her. It's like something drew me here."

Sarah poked Ben with her elbow and called his name.

"No, don't wake him," Darnell said, but it was too late. Ben's hand was already darting to the floor at the side of the bed, where he usually kept a gun, but it was downstairs in his bag.

"Ed!" he shouted. "Intruder! Bring a gun!"

"It's Darnell," Sarah said.

"Ed!" Ben shouted again. "Intruder!"

Sarah could hear Ed stirring in his room across the hall.

"He's trying to warn us," she said. "He's not really here, it's some kind of magic trick."

The apparition raised his hands in a pleading gesture, and Sarah saw that there was only a sutured wound where his penis and testicles should be.

"Please listen," he said. "I can't be here much longer, I'm too sick. Stonebrenner won't be easy to kill. Neither will she by now. There's a kind of metal called Hermesium. It's one way you can kill them. There may be other ways, but he hasn't taught them to her yet."

The door burst open: Ed with a pistol grasped in both hands.

Darnell ignored him. "Hermesium," he repeated. "It's some kind of special alloy. I don't know where you'll find it, but somehow you have to, and you have to kill them with it or else they'll kill you."

His pale blue eyes gazed at Sarah, two blue flames flickering in the dark.

"Sarah," he said, "this is agony, beyond anything you can imagine. I want to die. You have to kill me. Swear you'll kill me and the evil thing that lives in my body. And kill her friend too."

The white apparition faded like an ember. Only the two

flickering blue flames of Darnell's eyes remained. Then they went out too.

"So maybe you don't think I'm crazy anymore," Ed said.

Part Six: Dealing Death in the Dark

Chapter Forty-Five

Half an hour later, while she was drinking coffee in the front living room with Ben and Ed, Sarah could still see the flickering blue flames of Darnell's eyes. They seemed to have left stains on her retinas.

"It could have been Angel pretending to be Darnell, trying to lure us into some sort of trap," Ben said. "Maybe it was even Stonebrenner."

"I don't think so," Ed said. "Why would Angel or Stonebrenner tell you about Hermesium?"

"That's probably just some mumbo-jumbo made up to confuse us," Ben said.

"Ben, I'm disappointed in you," Ed said. "I know I'm a tedious old man, but really you ought to listen to me once in a great while. Three hours ago I was sitting right here on this sofa telling you about Hermesium, and I could have sworn you were sitting just a few feet away from me."

"Sorry, Ed. I guess I must have been getting sleepy."

Ed pulled a book from the pile on his coffee table and opened it. "Yep, I could have sworn I pointed to this very page and told you to look at it. It's a formula for making Hermesium. It's an old alchemist metal, one of the countless steps toward producing the philosopher's stone. Sarah, you heard me, I hope?"

"Yeah, sure," she said, not exactly lying. She had heard him say something about a poisonous metal, but she hadn't paid much attention.

"So what?" Ben said. "So some old book has a recipe for something called Hermesium. That doesn't prove it's harmful to Stonebrenner."

"But it *is*, Ben. I told you that too." Ed pulled another book from the pile. "This is the book I was showing you that discusses

Longevitals. It says Hermesium will kill them, especially if it's delivered to the heart or the brain. So will decapitation. The book doesn't mention fire, but it stands to reason they're not made of asbestos."

"Fine," Ben said. "So where do you get Hermesium? Local hardware store?"

"I told you that too. My basement. I cooked up some two days ago, after I started investigating this Stonebrenner business." Ed closed the book with a sigh. "How's your coffee, Sarah?"

"It's good."

It was some fancy gourmet bean, dark and strong. She would be awake all night, but that was all right. She had no intention of shutting her eyes in that bedroom again.

"Okay, so what are we supposed to do?" Ben asked. "Bake it up in brownies and get him to eat it?"

Ed smiled. "Simple. I'm going to cast some Hermesium bullets, make some of my very special reloads."

"Wait a minute," Sarah said. "I mean, we can't just go busting into Stonebrenner's house and start shooting up everyone. Don't you have any laws here in Mount Vernon?"

"Let's try to be a little more serious, both of you," Ed said. "A little while ago you didn't take a single word I said seriously, but now I want you to. This isn't a game."

Ed's usually merry blue-gray eyes didn't look so merry as he glanced back and forth at both of them. They looked tired and frightened and a bit angry.

"The bullets are for your personal protection," he said, "and unfortunately you may need them. If Darnell found you, do you think Stonebrenner can't? I'm going to cast some bullets this morning, and you're going to load your guns with them, and you're going to keep your guns with you everywhere but the shower until this business is settled. And that reminds me—I have something else to protect you, something you can keep with you even in the shower."

He went to one of the display cabinets where he kept his curios. He unlocked a drawer beneath the glass case, got out a little wooden box and brought it to them. Inside the box were two identical gold medallions on gold chains.

Sarah picked up one and examined it. A dark red stone was set in the center with undecipherable symbols inscribed in the gold around it.

"This looks old," she said.

"They are old, much older than you think. They're also priceless, so when all of this is over I would like to have them back. But until that time, I want you to wear them 24-7, awake or asleep."

"What are they?" Ben asked.

"They are Seals of Solomon," Ed said. "Only four are known to exist, and I have two of them. They are the most potent protection known against the spell of a sorcerer."

Ben placed his on the coffee table and said, "Ed, this is the twenty-first century."

Ed's eyes had lost all their merriment; now they just looked angry.

"Ben, you're the psychologist here," he said, "so please explain yourself. A little over a week ago you visited the basement of the Dietrick house and apparently saw something so horrible that you still won't tell me what it was. One hour ago you saw a horrid apparition in your bedroom, and it was talking to Sarah just as clearly as I'm talking to you. And now you're making wisecracks about what century it is."

"I'm sorry, Ed. Of course you're right. I really don't want to believe this stuff, but I guess I'd better start trying."

He put the gold chain around his neck and slipped the medallion inside his shirt. Sarah did the same with hers.

"As soon as the sun comes up, I'm going to call Okpara," she said.

"What are you going to tell him?" Ben asked. "That some apparition told us that Angela Dietrick is shacked up with a sorcerer who maybe she dug up out of a grave? Maybe he'll want to give the police force some Hermesium bullets too."

"I'll tell him the truth," she said. She was becoming annoyed with Ben's attitude too.

"Well, I don't know about you two," Ed said, "but I could use a few hours of sleep."

They said good night and watched him plod wearily up the stairs. Sarah was embarrassed: last night they had both felt smugly impatient with the old man and his silly old books and newspaper clippings.

She stretched out on the sofa and, despite the coffee, soon drifted off to sleep. She awoke when someone kissed her forehead, and she let out a loud gasp thinking it was Darnell.

It was Ben. "Sorry to startle you," he said, "but the sun's coming up and you said you wanted to call Okpara. I thought of calling him myself, but he knows you, maybe he'll listen to you."

"I thought you said calling him was a stupid idea."

"I was wrong. I guess it's best to let the sober eyes of the law look at this before we get any deeper into weirdness. I made you some coffee, thought you might want it before calling."

"Thanks. Is Ed up?"

"Not yet."

"Did you sleep?"

"No. I relaxed in a chair and kept my eyes on things."

She smiled, thinking he probably hadn't relaxed very much. While she drank her coffee she tried to imagine what she would tell Okpara, but by the time she dialed his cell number she still hadn't come up with anything that sounded sensible.

He answered, and without any preamble she told him about Darnell's apparition and everything he had said about Angel and Stonebrenner. She even told him about the grave robbing and a few bits of the occult lore Ed had told them. If she spoke quickly enough, she didn't have time to feel silly.

Okpara listened in silence. When she finished, he said, "Miss Temple, I do not altogether discredit what you've told me. The department isn't above hiring psychics in some tough cases, though we try not to let the reporters know. I've seen two cases solved in that way. Also when I was a boy in Nigeria, I knew of a woman possessed by demons. She could make stones fly through the air, and she spoke in languages she'd never learned. Once she spit a poisonous snake out of her mouth. So I'm not entirely skeptical."

"Can you do something?" Sarah asked.

Okpara sighed. "Miss Temple, do you know what my two favorite days are? Saturday and Sunday. I believe this is Sunday."

"Well, maybe tomorrow."

"Impossible. Mondays I work, and though the department sometimes hires psychics, they're not going to authorize me to drive out of my jurisdiction to question a warlock. No, today, my day off, my favorite day of the week, I'll have to drive there myself, unofficially. Maybe Stonebrenner will let me in if I invent the right story. Possibly I can get a sense of things."

"Thanks. I don't suppose when you're done you could let me

know what you learn?"

"Yes, Miss Temple, I'll call and let you know if I see any rocks flying through the air like birds or any vipers darting out of the man's mouth. You'll probably hear from me in about three hours. I'm going to leave right away, so maybe I'll have time for a round of golf when I get back."

Chapter Forty-Six

Stonebrenner stood in his watchtower, his keen senses like antennae alert to all four directions, searching for a sign of Charles Newman. Of course Newman had probably woven a veil around himself to hide from Stonebrenner, just as Stonebrenner had done to hide from Newman.

On the other hand, it was possible that Newman was far away, in Europe or Africa or any other corner of the planet. It was possible that Newman didn't yet realize Stonebrenner had escaped the grave. It was even possible that Newman was dead.

Not knowing was intolerable; there is nothing an adept prizes so highly as knowledge, for knowledge is the father of power. Not knowing meant that Stonebrenner had no choice but to remain constantly vigilant despite his exhaustion and the other matters that demanded his attention.

Angel, for example. All of last night he had stayed by her bedside holding her cold, nearly lifeless hand and begging her not to die. Last night perhaps he had learned more about the mysteries of love than he cared to know. He had administered the treatments too rapidly, giving her new treatments before she'd had time to recover from the previous ones, and it had caused an alarming fibrillation, making her heart tremble between life and death. All night long he had cursed Newman, because it was fear of his old enemy that had compelled him to speed up Angel's treatments.

An hour before the sun came up, her heart had finally steadied itself, and now all danger was past. Already she was a Longevital with the great powers of recovery that Longevity bestowed. In another hour she would be healthier than she had ever been, and today they could marry.

Stonebrenner wondered if he had ever been married before. Memory is one of the Longevital's vulnerabilities: eventually there were too many years for the brain to store. His memory reached back for nearly two centuries with clarity, but events and faces before that grew progressively more obscure, like dreams half remembered. Certain kinds of knowledge, such as the many languages he had learned, stayed with him longer, but experiences disappeared into the ever-darkening tunnel of forgetfulness.

Anything that had happened to him more than 300 years ago, he could know only from his journals. He knew that his Bavarian mother had borne him in 1560, in the reign of William IV, son of Duke Albert IV the Wise, but his mother existed for him now only as a few scribbles in a journal and as a black and white photograph he had taken decades ago of a painting of a beautiful young woman, a painting that he had sadly lost in his flight from Boston in 1962. Sometimes he awoke with an image of being a child held in a woman's warm arms, but this was more likely a dream than a memory.

Even the circumstances of the treatment that had transformed him into a Longevital were lost except for a few cryptic notations. He knew the name of the man who had treated him, but the name meant nothing, and why the man had chosen to give him the gift of Longevity he could only guess. Stonebrenner sometimes wondered if the treatment had been a favor from a homosexual admirer; the coyness of the brief journal entry seemed to hint at things left unsaid. He had been 32 years old when it happened. The 20-some years that his appearance had aged since then were in fact centuries.

Apparently he had not developed an interest in sorcery until much later. On the contrary, his early journal entries showed an embarrassing predilection for the most conventional Catholicism. They made no more than a dabbler's reference to the occult until the eighteenth century, when he had made the acquaintance of Count Alessandro di Cagliostro in Paris. Later he had studied with Eliphas Levi, whose face he could still remember though Cagliostro's was beginning to fade into the tunnel of darkness. In England in the 1880s an obscure teacher had helped him to master the complex magical system of the Elizabethan John Dee. Soon after, he had been initiated into the Unseen Guild.

He still remembered with delight his victory over James Matthews, whom he murdered in 1937 for the man's invaluable collection of grimoires and texts of alchemy, including the lost book of Trithemius, Abbot of Spannheim, who raised Mary of Burgundy from the grave at the bidding of her husband, the Emperor Maximilian. But tucked among the books was a manuscript written by Matthews' own hand, which proved to be of far greater interest than the rest of the library, for it told in detail a story that

Stonebrenner had known only by vague rumors.

According to Matthews' manuscript, the great magician Cornelius Agrippa, who had supposedly died an ignoble death in 1535, had in fact staged his own death, ensorcelling an unfortunate impostor to die in his stead. Agrippa, in fact, had become a Longevital in 1534, at the age of 48, and had since lived under many names in many places, becoming more powerful in his magic each year that he lived. According to Matthews, Agrippa was still alive but had been paralyzed and entombed by a rival adept in 1897. His body still lay hidden somewhere in Romania.

The information was exciting to Stonebrenner because he had learned the seven words that could undo this spell of paralysis. He was certain that if he could find Agrippa's grave, he would be able to revive the great magician, bind him to his service, and learn from him the most profound Hermetic secrets.

In his manuscript Matthews named his informant, a Longevital who owned a map showing the location of Agrippa's grave. Stonebrenner's search led him to Baltimore, where the map's owner was living under the name Philip Masterson. A penniless and dissolute man addicted to opium, Masterson was employed as a gigolo by an elderly heiress. To persuade Masterson to give him the map, Stonebrenner had found it necessary to murder the heiress.

So in the spring of 1939 Stonebrenner traveled to Romania to unearth the master. It was a difficult and risky time for an adept to travel incognito. All of Central and Eastern Europe was swarming with adepts and initiates thronging to Germany, where Hitler was making plans to invade Poland and begin the thousand-year triumph of magic over reason. On every train and bus, Stonebrenner sniffed out an initiate of the Vril Society or the Thule Group or the Golden Dawn or, most dangerous of all, the Unseen Guild. But Stonebrenner had woven his veil with care, and none of the occultists recognized him for what he was.

Agrippa was buried in Transylvania, where his raging spirit tormented the inhabitants with horrors and apparitions, which they attributed to their old bogeyman Vlad the Impaler, also known as Dracula. With the help of two ensorcelled peasants, Stonebrenner disinterred the mummy from a mountainside cave. Agrippa had been entombed for 42 years, and there was nothing left of him but dry leather stretched over bones. Stonebrenner's confidence sank: even if this corpse could be revitalized, surely it would have suffered such extensive brain damage as to be useless.

But he was mistaken. Agrippa was even more powerful than his legend. Not only did the seven words cause him to breathe again, but within days he was strong and alert. Agrippa took the name Charles Newman, and he and Stonebrenner (at that time known as Elden Becker) fled the complications of Europe and rented a house together in Boston.

The next 23 years were the happiest of Stonebrenner's life. Newman, apparently grateful to his rescuer, taught him more gnostic and Hermetic powers than Stonebrenner had imagined could exist. But perhaps even more importantly, the two Longevitals shared a friendship that seemed to Stonebrenner to deepen into love. From Newman, Stonebrenner learned the mysteries of love between two men, just as now he sought to learn from Angel the mysteries of love between man and woman.

But a sorcerer who could weave such mighty illusions could also weave an illusion of love. One night in 1962, while Newman slept heavily from an overdose of opium, Stonebrenner sat up experimenting with telepathy and penetrated the sleeping man's veil. What he discovered in Newman's mind was not love at all, but the most abominable treachery. He saw what Newman planned to do with him. He saw the true motive behind Newman's teaching.

That night Stonebrenner wove a web of silence around his sleeping mentor so that he could gather his most valuable belongings without awakening the man. He hastily packed his vials of precious substances, his irreplaceable books, his hoard of gold, and he fled Boston and the monster who lived there.

He drove to Ohio, thinking that the Midwest would be an unlikely place for Newman to search for him. He found the quiet town of Mount Vernon, a sleepy and obscure haystack to hide in. He was charmed by the New England ambiance, and when he found the big brick house with its watchtower and its caverns, he bought it at once.

He had then focused all of his training toward one project: to weave a veil so impenetrable that even Newman wouldn't be able to pierce it. Newman had taught him well, and for 11 years Elden Becker, now known as Isaac Stonebrenner, remained hidden in his Mount Vernon fortress. But they were tense and terrible years, each waking hour spent in fearful vigilance, countless hours of gazing from the watchtower even as he watched now, each hour seeming it might be the one when Newman would suddenly appear. Even worse than the fear was the sense of betrayal. The one man whom he had loved planned to bury him alive!

How Newman had found him, Stonebrenner still didn't know. One night as he sat sleeping in a chair, the monster was suddenly upon him, binding him with paralysis and then using two ensorcelled thugs to haul him out of the house to the tiny cemetery, where a coffin already awaited him beside a freshly dug grave.

The horror that followed, Stonebrenner still couldn't bear to contemplate: the years of suffocation and madness and despair. But it's said that the greatest teachings learned by the greatest adepts are those that they teach themselves. There was truth in the saying, for even in the grave Stonebrenner continued to learn and grow more powerful.

He sent his astral body to haunt the people who lived in the neighboring houses, trying to teach them the words that would revive him. But using an apparition to deliver even a single one of the seven words was as impossible as delivering a complicated computer program in a crude telegram. What he needed was someone trapped in his own horrible circumstance. Likeness is the crux of all sympathetic magic, and a likeness of circumstances might allow him to deliver his message.

At last his chance arrived: two young grandchildren came to live with a stupid and depraved old man named Gus Dietrick. Stonebrenner penetrated Dietrick's mind and found out his filthy secrets. Two of his own three children he had raped and murdered, and he lusted for the two grandchildren as he had for his own offspring.

Hour after hour, Stonebrenner would whisper suggestions into the old man's diseased brain. "Your grandchildren have been naughty," he would say. "Bury them in the basement for a while. Teach them a lesson. Put them in boxes. Drill a few breathing holes in the lid so they won't suffocate. Let them lie there and think about their badness. Put them in the bad box, the bad box!"

At last Gus Dietrick began to do as he was told. And there in her box, while little Angel suffered the same horror as Stonebrenner, he would visit her as a friend, preparing her to receive the first word. But a child's mind is a fragile thing, and Stonebrenner was impatient—he delivered the word before she was ready. A blood vessel burst in her brain, and when Gus opened her box he discovered that she was dead.

Only one more chance: the boy. This time Stonebrenner didn't dare to fail. He had to be patient and take his time. A plan came to him. While Darnell screamed and wept, Stonebrenner would whisper to him, "It's Angel's turn. Let Angel take over. She knows how to leave the box."

The terrified boy did as he was told; he created in his mind another personality, that of his dead sister, and this alternate personality, being emotionally more remote, was easier to mold and train. Stonebrenner worked carefully and slowly, becoming her friend, her beloved friend in the box, and at last he believed she was ready. He sent her the first word, and she received it.

In that moment the first key of his rescue was established, and in that moment Angel became something more than a mere alternate personality. The word had given her an independent life. Stonebrenner needed for her to live and in time to grow stronger than Darnell. It was impossible to deliver more than one word directly to her, so he depended on her to find new name-bringers.

The years that followed were endless in their uncertainty. He couldn't even know for certain that Darnell Brook existed, much less Angel. Countless bouts of madness had brought him many delusions, and perhaps Darnell and Angel were also figments of his disintegrating mind. But this madness had proven to be reality, and here he stood, freed from the grave, staring out of his tower.

Suddenly his radar-senses sounded an alarm. Someone coming from the south, looking for him. A minute later a car came into view. It slowed and turned into his driveway. There was only one person in the car, a black man, and for a moment Stonebrenner believed it was one of Newman's minions.

But as the man emerged from the car, Stonebrenner realized he had been mistaken. He knew how to smell a cop.

Chapter Forty-Seven

Sebastian Okpara would sooner stare into the barrel of a loaded gun than into the eyes of a rich person's lawyer. At least with a gun, one had a chance. Stonebrenner's enormous yard and magnificent house made him painfully aware of the flimsiness of his pretense for this visit. Out of his jurisdiction, without permission or knowledge of the department, he was here to snoop around on the basis of a young woman's half-coherent tales of witchcraft. Not the sort of thing one wanted to explain to a review board under the high-power scrutiny of a rich man's attorney.

Fortunately he was alone. Okpara didn't like his partner, Christina Child, and particularly didn't like the bullying style she used when interviewing a suspect or a witness, and whenever possible he conducted his interviews alone. During every interview he tried to keep in mind one of the lessons his mother had taught him: Never let your manners slip. Okpara tried to show the same courtesy to prostitutes and heroin addicts that he showed to the mayor or the district attorney, and he hoped that politeness would serve him as well this morning as it usually had in the past.

He knocked on the massive carved-oak front door and waited. The humid air was oppressive after his air-conditioned drive, and he touched his forehead with his handkerchief. The door was opened by a lanky young man with sandy hair. The man said nothing, and Okpara noted his strange gaze and dilated pupils, much like Peter Bellman's eyes, clearly indicative of drug abuse.

Okpara showed his badge and said, "Is Jacob Stonebrenner here?"

The young man just stood there staring, mouth gaping, as if not sure what he was looking at. Okpara looked past him into the large foyer and saw someone descending the stairs, a broad-shouldered man, perfectly bald, wearing a gray suit.

When the man reached the light at the bottom of the stairs, Okpara sucked in his breath. He had never seen such a face on a living person, blue-gray and cadaverous with strange black eyes that reminded Okpara of eyes he had seen in the morgue.

"You may return to your work, Eric," the man said, his voice a strange harsh whisper, and the young drug addict shuffled slowly away into the back of the house. "I'm Jacob Stonebrenner."

He smiled in a decidedly unfriendly manner, his yellow teeth long and so slender that there were ugly gaps between them. He stood blocking the doorway, his arms crossed in front of him, and his fingernails were shockingly yellow like his teeth and cracked. His dank odor reminded Okpara of a body recently found in the river.

"I'm Detective Sebastian Okpara, Columbus Police Department. I regret disturbing you on a Sunday morning, but I was hoping I could ask you a few questions."

"Concerning what?"

"Concerning the abandoned house just down the road. We are interested in knowing if you've noticed any unusual activity there, anyone coming or going."

"I've seen nothing," Stonebrenner replied. He stood utterly motionless, a nerveless sentry who feared Okpara no more than a housefly. It was Okpara who fidgeted, shifting his weight from foot to foot, dabbing his forehead with his handkerchief, trying to find something to do with his hands.

"Not even teenagers?"

"I said I've seen nothing. I've not been here long."

Stonebrenner's stance appeared to soften, but Okpara believed it was the kind of feint a boxer displays right before he delivers a knockout punch. "Perhaps you'd like to come inside and have a cold drink," he said.

"Yes, please," Okpara said. "I've always been interested in beautiful old homes."

Stonebrenner grinned sardonically and stepped aside, allowing Okpara to enter. All the doors facing the foyer were shut, as if the house was unwilling to give up any of its secrets. Stonebrenner opened one of them and ushered Okpara into a large living room.

"I've not had a chance to bring down my furniture," he said. "This trash belongs to the tenants. They wish to remain until the crops are harvested, and we've worked out an arrangement."

So the drugged-out young man was a farmer? What was he growing, Okpara wondered—opium poppies?

Okpara admired a stone fireplace that covered much of one wall, its ornately carved mantle probably worth a months' mortgage on Okpara's small house. He wondered sadly how soon every valuable house in the country would be owned by drug dealers or the corrupt politicians who enabled them.

He heard a sound behind him. A tall young woman with long blond hair and freckles had entered the room. She wore a soiled white nightgown that trailed the floor, transparent as gauze. Her eyes suggested that she too was wrapped in a narcotic dream, floating soundlessly in a world of her own.

"This is Kathy Beers, one of my tenants," Stonebrenner said.

Kathy seemed not to notice Okpara as she drifted through a wide doorway into another living room like a spirit of the dead.

Okpara tried to piece Sarah Temple's story together with what he was witnessing. He knew that some producers and traffickers of narcotics were involved with Satanism, in the belief that occult rites would protect them from the authorities. He wondered how Darnell Brook might fit into this. The grisly murders he was suspected of committing had the look of Satanic ritual killings. Was it possible Brook was involved in a drug operation run by Stonebrenner? That could explain Peter Bellman's erratic behavior after visiting Darnell. Possibly the FBI had been compiling the wrong profile on the killer all along.

"A lovely fireplace," Okpara murmured.

"Perhaps you'd enjoy seeing more of the house," Stonebrenner said.

"Yes, please, if it's no imposition."

Stonebrenner ushered him back to the foyer and shut the door on the cloud-wrapped young woman, who had wandered back into the front room. While Okpara gazed at the elegant staircase, he suddenly felt a crackling warmth on his temples, like an electric current. Stonebrenner, he realized, was standing behind him and touching the sides of his head. How very odd.

A dizzy nausea swept through him, and he felt his legs lose their strength. Stonebrenner caught him and held him upright until the nausea subsided.

"Thank you," Okpara said. "It's so hot today." He reached weakly for his handkerchief and touched it to his forehead. "I feel better now."

"Would you like some water?" Stonebrenner asked.

"Yes, please."

As he followed Stonebrenner down a hallway, Okpara had to grasp the wainscoting a few times because his legs felt so weak. This happened on a hot day sometimes, he thought, especially if he ate a sugary breakfast. He should mention it to his doctor; maybe he had a touch of hypoglycemia.

He followed Stonebrenner into the large kitchen, and Okpara's legs nearly buckled again when he saw what was lying on the counter. It was a human carcass, its arms removed and most of the skin peeled off the torso. The young farmer, wearing a bloody butcher's apron, was busy sawing off one of the legs. In the second that it took for Okpara to see this, his hand had already pulled his Glock from its shoulder holster. Obviously Stonebrenner wouldn't want him to leave alive after seeing this.

"Freeze," he said, aiming the gun at Stonebrenner.

"No, you freeze," Stonebrenner said. "And put your gun away. As you can see, there's no need for it. We have already butchered one pig this morning and have no desire to butcher another."

Okpara saw that the human carcass in fact was a slaughtered hog. He put his gun away and wiped his forehead with his handkerchief.

Stonebrenner grinned and said, "We make our own sausage here. It's so much better than what you buy in the store, no preservatives or nitrates. Maybe you'd like me to send you some?"

"That would be very nice," Okpara said, pleased by Stonebrenner's courtesy, and again he decided he should make an appointment with the doctor. Too much stress, too many long hours, and if one wasn't careful one's health could collapse. Stonebrenner gave him a glass of water, and he drank it gratefully.

"You're a dawdler, Eric," Stonebrenner said. "You should have finished this job long ago."

The young man rudely ignored him and continued to saw the meat with a sullen expression. Such disrespect for his betters, Okpara thought. The young these days have no manners.

He heard something behind him and turned to see a skinny pale woman coming into the kitchen. She wore a bathrobe and was utterly bald except for a few tufts of pale hair. She stared at him, and as Okpara stared back he suddenly realized that he was staring at Darnell Brook.

"Detective, this is my daughter Jane," Stonebrenner said. "I'm sorry to say she's been ill with cancer, and the treatments have caused her to lose her hair."

Okpara smiled at her and said, "I'm very pleased to meet you."

"Are you feeling better, Jane?" Stonebrenner asked.

"Much better," she said. "In fact, I've never felt so good. But I'm very hungry."

"Fresh meat is what you need, my dear," Stonebrenner said.

For just one moment, Okpara saw him take a cleaver from the counter and lop off the carcass's penis; and for just one moment he saw him grinding it in a hand-cranked meat grinder clamped to the counter, expelling strings of bloody human flesh onto a plate; and for just one moment he saw Darnell Brook devouring the horrid mess, licking blood greedily from his lips as he chewed.

But then in the next moment he saw Stonebrenner's daughter delicately munching some very tasty-looking ground sausage. Such a caring father, Okpara thought, and he hoped Jane would recover from her cancer.

"Well, there's no point in my taking up any more of your time," he said. "You've been very gracious. Here's my card, and if you happen to see anything suspicious, please call me."

"Certainly," Stonebrenner said with a smile.

As Okpara drove back to Columbus, he wondered what had possessed Sarah Temple to manufacture such outrageous stories about a respectable man. It occurred to him that possibly Miss Temple's role in this case was not so innocent as he had believed.

Look at the facts, he thought. Miss Temple seemed to be at the center of everything. She admitted she was acquainted with Darnell Brook. Had they been involved together in a drug operation that performed Satanist ritual murders to protect them from the law, and then had she turned on him when the bodies were found?

No doubt she had urged Paul Finney to visit Brook's apartment, where he was murdered in one of their rituals. And then another man had been brutally disemboweled while Miss Temple was living with him. Her ex-boyfriend, a respectable professor whom she had viciously attacked with the help of another woman, a woman who possibly was also involved with the drug operation, was now behaving strangely and was unable to teach. Quite likely Professor Bellman was a victim of poisoning—perhaps he had learned about the drug operation and needed to be silenced. And now Miss Temple was shacked up with a man whose wife had been found hanged in his barn just a year ago.

Yes, it all fit together. But why was she now spreading accusations against a respectable country gentleman? If all citizens were as decent as Jacob Stonebrenner, Okpara thought, our society would have no need for policemen.

Okpara drove slowly, thinking of the man's exquisite manners, his beautiful clothing and immaculately groomed appearance. Even his fingernails, Okpara thought—they were so elegantly manicured.

Chapter Forty-Eight

Ben sat in Ed's front room loading the magazine of his Springfield 1911 with the .45 caliber hollow-points that he and Ed had cast from Hermesium. It was an awkward job because he was wearing rubber gloves. There were eight cartridges, seven for the magazine and one for the chamber. When he finished with his Springfield, he loaded Sarah's Ruger with the five cartridges they had made for her. Five and eight would have to do: Ed didn't have much of the metal, and he wanted to keep a few rounds for himself in case Stonebrenner knew where he lived, as Darnell did.

"These are .38 Special, but we loaded them plus P, so they'll have a little kick," Ben said.

"That's okay," Sarah said.

"And remember, if you unload this thing you need to wear gloves. Ed says if this stuff kills Longevitals, it may not be too healthy for us measly mortals."

"Probably not EPA-approved," Ed said. "Well then, let's have some lunch."

They were eating ham and Swiss sandwiches with potato chips at the kitchen table when Sarah's phone rang. "It's Okpara," she said.

She stepped out into the hallway, but Ben could hear her voice. She wasn't doing much of the talking, but a couple of times he heard her say, "This is nuts!"

When she came back to the kitchen her face was pink with anger. "Unbelievable!" she said. "Un-fucking-believable! Okpara just accused me of every damn thing you can think of. Maybe I was in cahoots with Darnell, some kind of drug-running operation or something like that. Maybe I even killed Paul Finney, just like I killed Howard. Oh, and you hanged your wife, Ben. He's lost his damn mind."

"He's been ensorcelled," Ed said.

"What does that mean?"

"It means Stonebrenner has cast a spell on him. Your detective will certainly be no help to us from now on."

"Oh yeah, I forgot," Sarah said. "He also said Stonebrenner's the world's perfect gentleman, an outstanding example of civilization. He even raved about how nicely he manicures his fucking fingernails!"

"McClosky mentioned his fingernails," Ed said. "He said they're yellow and cracked."

"Well, they're not the only thing that's cracked," Sarah said. "So now what do we do?"

"Reconnaissance," Ed said. He got a sheet of paper and began to draw a map. "Coming from Mount Vernon, we approach Stonebrenner's house from the north. If you remember, it's on our left, on the east side of the road, and set pretty far off the road."

He drew a rectangle for the house.

"There's a large barn about 50 yards before we get to the house, and it's set the same distance off the road. And maybe 80 or 90 yards past the house is the little cemetery. A dirt lane leads to it from the road, and it's inside a grove of trees that will hide a car pretty well. Teenagers park there to make out, and later on I get to hear their spooky stories."

"So we park there and do what?" Sarah asked.

"We window peep with binoculars, and if we see Darnell that's probably enough for the cops to get a warrant. Better yet if we can get a photo. I have a good camera with a telephoto lens, and I'll pick up some super-fast film for night shooting. Ben, do you have a decent camera?"

"Just a plain-Jane digital one."

"Bring it anyway—just be damn sure the flash is shut off. And don't you have some sort of night viewer thingy?"

"No."

"Too bad, but of course bring your binoculars. I have an extra pair Sarah can use. Fortunately my car is black, and with the lights out it should disappear pretty well behind the trees in the graveyard. Unfortunately your car is silver."

"Gunmetal gray," Ben said.

"Whatever. Sarah, what color is your car?"

"Bright red."

"You young people love to be flashy. Okay, here's what I have in mind for you, Ben. There's a cornfield about 20 yards before you get to the barn, and between the cornfield and the barnyard there's a dirt lane so a farmer can drive his tractor all the way from the road to the fields that are back there east of the barn and the house. So I'm thinking you could drive your flashy silver car a little way down this lane until you're hidden behind the barn, and then no one in the house can see it."

"Sounds like the barn would also be hiding the house so I couldn't see it."

"True. But if you get out of your car you can duck into the corn field just to the north and walk through it till you're east of the barn, where you'll have a good view of most of the windows that I won't be able to see from the cemetery. The corn is as tall as you, so it will keep you hidden, but bring a can of pepper spray in case Stonebrenner has dogs."

"Ed, I think this may be the dumbest idea I've ever heard," Ben said. "What if Stonebrenner calls the cops?"

"In the first place, he won't," Ed said. "I think the last thing Stonebrenner wants is more cops sniffing around. In the second place, I'm very well respected around here, and the police are going to believe me a lot quicker than they'll believe some stranger who looks like a Halloween decoration."

"Tell that to the judge," Ben said.

"I think it's a great idea," Sarah said. The two men stared at her, and she said, "Look, Ben, Darnell knows how to find me wherever I am. So just how safe do you think I'm going to feel as long as he's walking around free?"

"I guess you're right," Ben said. "Okay, Ed, I'll do this under one condition. I want Sarah to stay home."

"No way," she said. "Besides, what makes you think I'd be any safer at home?"

"She's right," Ed said. "Right now she's not safe anywhere."

"Okay," Ben said. "If you insist on going, I want you to go in Ed's car. That's because if I have to sneak around through a cornfield, that either leaves you all alone in my car, which I don't want, or else sneaking through a field with me, which I want even less. You two should be pretty safe hidden in the cemetery—but, Ed, I want you to be right there beside her all the time, and if you need to step out of the car to get a good view, I don't want either one of you to be more than ten feet away from it at any time. And at the first sign of any trouble, I mean even if a raccoon farts, I want both of you back in that car immediately with the pedal to the metal, hightailing it back here as fast as you can. Agreed?"

"Agreed," Ed said.

"Don't I get any say in this?" Sarah asked.

"No," Ben said. "You're already outvoted two to one. And before you say I'm some sort of domineering sexist pig, let me say that getting you killed isn't a very good way of protecting you."

"All right," she said. "I'll go with Ed and try to be good if you promise not to go any farther from your car than absolutely necessary to see around the barn."

"Fair enough," Ben said.

"Don't forget to turn your dome light off so it won't come on when you open the door," Ed said. "Set your cell phones to vibrate— you don't want them suddenly blasting out Beethoven's Fifth while you're sneaking around. Go home now and put on black clothes and get all the stuff you need. I think half an hour after sunset should be dark enough, so meet me back here no later than sundown. And whatever you do, don't forget to wear those medallions I gave you, or I swear I'll skin you alive!"

Chapter Forty-Nine

While Angel stood naked in the kitchen eating more of the delicious raw ground meat, Stonebrenner stripped off her bandages. All of the wounds were healed, even the big X-shaped one, leaving scars of pink new skin. Using a small pair of scissors, he began removing the stitches.

Lovely pink stigmata, she thought, and she felt ashamed of the suspicions she had harbored toward Baby during the worst of her illness.

He smiled and said, "Welcome to the long future, my love. You're a Longevital now."

"What day is it?" she asked. "I've lost track."

"Sunday, the eleventh of August."

"Darnell's birthday," she murmured. The thought troubled her for some reason. She reached for her glass of water and sipped it thoughtfully.

"Is something the matter?"

"No." She smiled at him. "I feel so good today, better than I've ever felt. Baby, I love you."

"I hope you'll love me for the many years to come," he said. "For today we shall be married."

Her hand reached instinctively to her bald head.

Baby smiled. "Don't worry, I've bought you the best wig that money will buy. But don't imagine that you'll remain bald like me. When your hair grows back out, it's certain to be nicer than ever. I've also bought you a lovely white gown, as befitting a virgin."

Angel was suddenly aware of how bad she smelled, long days and nights of sickness having coated her skin with a film of sweat and disease. As hungry as she was, she wanted to take a shower at once.

She put down her plate, but Baby said, "Eat more and drink more. You're hungry and probably dehydrated. And there's plenty of time before you need to dress. Now, my love, let me see your hand."

She gave him one of her hands, embarrassed by its bony emaciation. Baby examined it carefully, then placed it gently on the kitchen counter and picked up a butcher knife.

Suddenly Angel screamed. Her hand was pinned to the wooden table by Baby's knife.

He pulled out the knife carefully and said, "Just testing. If your treatments were completely successful, it shall heal within the hour. Now I'll leave you alone to enjoy your food and drink." He kissed her forehead and left.

Angel held up the injured hand. It blazed like fire, but it wasn't bleeding as much as she expected. No doubt he was right: it would soon heal. Still, she wished he had found a gentler way to test her condition.

She stared at the food. Despite her hunger, she had lost her appetite.

She thought of Darnell again and murmured, "Happy birthday."
***

But her hand did heal within the hour, the wound fading into a pink blush of new skin, and she realized that a less dramatic demonstration might not have convinced her. Her appetite returned after she bathed, and she ate some more of the meat. She felt much more attractive wearing the luxurious wig of long straight black hair. The color suited her, she thought.

Baby joined her in the kitchen and inspected her hand with satisfaction. He kissed it and said, "One hour from now, sweet Angel. Two o'clock in the front living room. And until then, I'll observe the old propriety. A groom shouldn't visit his bride before the ceremony." He left.

After eating, Angel went to her bedroom and sat at the dresser putting on her makeup and painting black eyebrows to match the wig. She liked the leaner look of her face. Her next meal, she decided, would be much smaller; she wanted to be slender and pretty for her husband.

The wedding dress he had bought for her was a beauty, white lace and embroidery, a long train that she lifted when she moved around the room. The meal seemed to have given her vigor; never had she felt so strong, and never so excited.

The hour arrived at last. Kathy Beers appeared in Angel's chamber wearing a pretty flowered dress and, as bridesmaid, she escorted Angel down the long staircase and into the front living room, which was filled with flowers. Stonebrenner, dressed in a black tuxedo, waited with Eric Beers, who was wearing a cheap black suit, its sleeves too short for his gangly arms. No doubt it was the best he owned.

Eric Beers officiated, stumbling awkwardly over the words Stonebrenner had written. Though Angel had little experience with weddings, the words seemed to her fairly standard, except there was no reference to God: "Dearly beloved, we are gathered together here in the presence of the Shadow of the First Moment to join together this man and this woman in matrimony . . ."

The room was dark, its windows shrouded by thick drapes, but the roses and chrysanthemums glowed pleasantly in the light of the black candles blazing on the mantle. Angel stared at them and wondered if the strange mood she was feeling was what people called joy. After all the years of horror and pain, she clutched at last like a bouquet of flowers a solemn promise of love.

She heard the farmer say, "Jacob Stonebrenner, wilt thou have this woman to thy wedded wife . . ." She heard Baby answer, "I will."

Then it was her turn. "Angela Dietrick, wilt thou have this man to thy wedded husband in the estate of matrimony? Wilt thou love, comfort, honor, and keep him in sickness and in health, and, forsaking all others, keep thee only unto him, giving him power and strength, and aiding him howsoever possible, so long as ye both shall live?"

"I will."

Baby placed a gold band on her finger.

"Those whom the Shadow of the First Moment hath joined together let no man put asunder. I pronounce you man and wife."

If there was something in the mysteries of love that Baby hadn't understood before, Angel believed he understood it now. She could tell by the way he kissed her, deeply and tenderly, as a loving husband.

He led her out of the living room. Instead of heading up the stairs, he said, "As you are the heart of my life, so my caverns are the heart of our house. I should like to consummate our marriage there, in our secret chambers, where we'll always be safe."

She thought of the cool air of that hidden sanctum, and it seemed the right place for them make love the first time. As he led her to the basement, she worried again about her anatomical deficiency. Despite it, she was determined to please him as no other woman ever had.

After he pressed the two stones to unlock his secret door, she said, "Maybe someday I'll have every attribute of a woman, but today I'll use other ways to satisfy you."

Baby looked slightly puzzled. Then he smiled and said, "Sweet Angel, you're a virgin, and I love you best that way. Let ours be the purest kind of marriage, a wedding of our spirits."

His words disappointed her, but as he carried her over the threshold, through the darkness of the doorway, Angel thought even that kind of marriage could be exciting, lying together naked, their deep longing never diluted by carnal knowledge.

Then a question troubled her thoughts. If Baby didn't intend to make love to her, what had he meant by the word "consummate"?

***

Stonebrenner set Angel down, lit a lantern, and shut the door behind them. He believed she would consent to their wedding of spirits, but he dreaded the minutes ahead.

As they descended the stone steps into the cool darkness, he said, "You've taught me much about love, and I hope you'll teach me even more. I hope you'll teach me about the most perfect love, that which places another before oneself."

"I will," she answered, as if continuing her wedding vow.

"I've never told you why Charles Newman paralyzed me and buried me alive," he said. "It's a practice known to adepts as 'cradling.' When Newman cradled me, he gained some of my spiritual energy. I was for him like a storage battery hidden away, a source of energy he could tap into.

"Newman himself had once been cradled by another adept, who wished to draw upon his immense powers. The more powerful the one you cradle, the more power you can draw from him, and that's why the deceitful Newman spent years teaching me his Hermetic secrets. When you released me, Newman's strength must have dwindled accordingly, and though he's still dangerously powerful, he'll rage until his battery is buried again."

Though he didn't look at Angel's face, he sensed her stiffening with apprehension. She was beginning to understand.

"Until Charles Newman is defeated, we must join our strength against him," he said. "I believe you know what I'm going to ask you to do. You understand now what I mean by the wedding of our spirits."

Angel stopped walking. "I can't," she said, her voice tiny and terrified in the dark cavern.

"You vowed to help me any way you can," Stonebrenner whispered. "I likewise pledge to you that once I've defeated Newman I'll release you from your cradle. I'll sacrifice that much of my power as a proof of my love for you."

"I can't," she repeated, her voice prickling with panic. "I'll do anything else to help you. You can torture me, you can even kill me. But not *that!*"

"Killing you wouldn't help me in the least," he said. "Only one kind of sacrifice will help."

"No! I can't!"

Angel stood coiled in her long white gown, breathing hard, ready to spring away from him, but there was nowhere to run.

"You must," he said. "You're my wife. Just a few minutes ago you solemnly vowed to give me power and strength and aid me howsoever possible. Did that vow mean nothing?"

"I can't!" she cried. "I can't be locked in the box again!"

Stonebrenner grabbed her, and her cry echoed in the cavern, drowning out the sacred vow she had spoken in the living room only minutes before. The noise was intolerable. He clamped his hand over her mouth, but the cry still echoed in the hollow darkness.

Angel fought with the strength of a Longevital as he wrestled her through the tunnel at the rear of the cavern. Where the ceiling was too low for standing, he crouched down and dragged her. The tunnel ended in a chamber much smaller than the workshop, its ceiling no more than an inch above Stonebrenner's head, its walls only a few feet from his shoulders. He had left the lantern back in the workshop, and though he had trained his night vision with herbs and spells, his eyes could just barely penetrate the thick darkness of this small cave.

She kicked and clawed as Stonebrenner lifted her into a coffin-shaped cavity carved out of a ledge in the wall. He climbed in on top of her, pressing her down inside the rock tomb with the weight of his body while he chanted the words of the cradling spell above her noises. He caressed the air above her forehead, weaving the dreamy, hypnotic passes that, along with the chanted lullaby, at last began to still her struggles.

Her arms and legs slowed and stiffened. Her chest shuddered and clutched for air, and then he felt its fierce spasms diminish to feeble tremors, and then the tremors stilled and even her lips stopped writhing.

Angel had moved her last.

Stonebrenner was still lying on top of her, panting like a husband exhausted by lovemaking. He climbed out of the tomb and leaned against the rock wall until he had regained his breath.

A dreadful honeymoon, he thought. He imagined her terrified eyes staring at him in the darkness, so he bent over and shut them with his hand. He placed his lips next to her ear and whispered.

"There's a saying about digging your own grave, my unfaithful Angel, and that's what you've done. If you had given yourself to me willingly, as an act of love, I would have released you as soon as Newman is dead. But since you were unfaithful to your vows, here you shall lie until time at last, in its slow mercy, releases you to the torments of hell."

Though her lips were as still as stone, he could still hear her cries ringing in his brain. He stood for a long time, pressing his hands to his ears in the darkness.

"I still hear you!" he shouted, and his words echoed back at him mixing with her keening howls. At last he passed through the tunnel to his laboratory and searched through cupboards and crevices for tools he had stored away four decades ago.

Angel's voice rang in his brain: "Baby! Help me, Baby!"

Her words dissolved into a shrill sound that Stonebrenner recognized, the sound of sheer terror that had raged in his head for so many dark years, a noise so horrible that he couldn't bear to hear it again. He tore open cupboards, their jars falling and breaking, their irreplaceable substances wasted on the floor. At last he found what he needed.

He hunkered back through the tunnel and shone the lantern on her face. It was as still as marble, and yet her lips moved in his mind.

"Baby, help me!" they said.

Stonebrenner fumbled in the vague light to thread the thin copper thread into his needle. As he pierced her upper lip, it twitched and seemed to struggle to form a word. He stitched it tightly to her lower lip.

The sewing, he knew, could serve a purpose only symbolic, but much of magic is symbolism. As he pushed the needle through her upper lip again, her teeth flashed white in the lantern light. He pierced the lower lip, stitched tightly, and the voice seemed to grow quieter.

"Baby," it murmured softly.

He stitched again, sealing the paralyzed lips together. The voice was hushed and muffled, its words no longer distinct, but he could still hear it as a faint moaning, a maddening mumble in his ears.

Somehow her eyelids snapped open, and their frozen stare was a kind of speaking more visceral than words. He stitched both eyelids tightly shut.

Then at last there was silence, except for the roaring of his ears. Even so, Stonebrenner knew that her infidelity would haunt him for many years to come, until it too receded into the tunnel of forgetfulness.

The lid was a heavy slab of rock. Yesterday he had propped one end of it up against her tomb, but the slab was so heavy that he had to use a long steel bar as a lever to lift the other end and slide it over the opening. But before he completely sealed her in, he leaned over and stared bitterly at her face.

"Beddy-bye," he whispered.

***

Stonebrenner climbed the basement steps to his kitchen with a heavy sense of despair, but as he was climbing the wide stairs to the second floor he felt a tremendous force rush through his body and mind. It was Angel's fury surging through him, and her fury was power such as he had never felt before, the strength of two human spirits joined in one body.

The power grew even stronger as he climbed the spiral stairs to his watchtower. It came in great waves that felt like rushes of cocaine mixed with something else, maybe a hint of mescaline to fuddle the brain. He realized that hatred was at least as strong as love, and just as his own hatred had once given strength to Newman, Angel's hatred would give him strength over Newman, who now was weakened because he had lost his cradling.

Stonebrenner felt like a superman, felt that he could do anything. There was a remarkable skill that Newman had tried without success to teach him, and Stonebrenner felt that now he could accomplish even that. It was a skill called levitation, though Newman had called it climbing out of the well of gravity. There were vectors of gravity everywhere, vectors pulling from the sun and moon and planets, even from the stars, and a true adept could use these vectors to swing through the air like a monkey swinging through trees on vines.

A great rush of Angel's fury surged through him, and he lifted his feet off the floor and climbed up the air until he could touch the ceiling. Amazing. He climbed down and climbed up again. It was easy—anything was easy now.

He opened a window and stared out. Did he dare try it? He sat on the windowsill, his feet dangling out—and then he walked. He was walking above the steeply sloped roof. Did he dare move past the edge of the house, with the yard three stories below?

Angel's anger swept through him, and using its power like a sail he soared to the nearest tree and perched in one of its high branches like an owl.

Chapter Fifty

The sun was already setting when Ben and Sarah got back to Mount Vernon. Sarah called Ed, and he told her he would be waiting for them in his car out front. Ben stopped just long enough for Sarah to get into Ed's car, and then he followed the black Mercedes out of town.

By the time they reached Stonebrenner's road, the sky had faded to near black. When they came to a little rise in the road, Ed shut off his headlights and Ben did the same. The big barn came into view just past the rise, and the Mercedes stopped for a moment so Ben would see the narrow lane beside the cornfield. He turned into it, and the Mercedes continued silently past the house to the cemetery.

Ben parked directly north of the barn, got out and checked to make sure he couldn't see the tower. He couldn't, so no one in the tower should be able to see his car. The only sounds came from the crickets in the distance; the ones near him were silenced by his presence.

He stood still for a moment, getting used to the scant light of the rising quarter moon. Too bad he had never ordered the Russian night-vision binoculars he had noticed so many times in his surplus catalogs, but at least the ordinary ones that were slung around his neck had powerful 20x50mm lenses. He shoved the Springfield into the waist of his black jeans, stuck a small LED flashlight in a hip pocket, and eased the car door shut silently without latching it.

It was a muggy night with a rustling of hot breeze that made the leaves of the tall corn wave like arms of a thousand dancing scarecrows. He climbed the rusty wire fence into the field and walked along the fence line until he was past the east corner of the barn, then he pressed his way a few feet into the dense corn for cover. He could see the house now, and there were lights in a few of the windows, but no one was visible through them.

But someone was standing in the tower. It looked like a man, but he was facing east, and even with his binoculars Ben couldn't tell if it was Darnell or Stonebrenner.

He saw that the field he was in joined another cornfield that lay about 50 yards east of the house and probably continued south past the cemetery. From that field he should be able to see the man more clearly. So he forged his way east, moving against the rows of corn, and the sharp edges of the leaves seemed to mutter and gossip as he fought his way through them.

When he reached the east field it was much easier to make his way south because now he was walking along a row instead of against them. Directly east of the house he stopped and looked at the tower again with his binoculars. There was just enough moonlight shining through one of the high windows to illuminate a ghastly white face staring back at him with button-black eyes.

It was a frightening face, and Ben ducked back into the corn and headed north, back toward his car.

***

Stonebrenner stood in his watchtower, but instead of gazing out like a sentry, he gazed inward.

His initial elation had turned into anger, and whether it was his anger or Angel's he couldn't tell. It was true that her anger gave him power, but it also made him feel ill. Her wrath was more concentrated now, and when it surged it jabbed him like a spike in his brain, fuddling his thoughts and giving him a pounding headache.

How much better it would be if she would give her power to him in love instead of hatred; then they would be two inseparable allies bound in one body, together invincible against the enemy. Had he not given her life itself, bringing her spirit back from the dead to live again in her brother's body? Had he not given her the great gift of Longevity? Had he not nursed her through her illness, saving her from a second death when her heart fluttered weakly and wanted to stop? Had he not loved her faithfully ever since she was a child, with the warm devotion of a parent as well as a husband? And had she not turned on him like a viper not even one hour after they were married?

Angel, thy name is treachery, he thought.

Twice within the range of his memory he had experienced love, and twice his love had been turned against him. Treachery was the essence of sorcery, the art that twisted the nature of reality against itself.

Stonebrenner pictured the long chain of treachery stretching from him to Charles Newman, to the sorcerer who had cradled Newman, to whoever stood behind that one, each adept sucking his power from another who in turn sucked it from another, like elaborately crafted Chinese boxes, box inside of box, stretching back long before Simon Magus, long before Solomon himself, even before Lucifer was locked raging inside the box called Hell, for even Lucifer's dark power derived from the earliest moment of time, a fraction of a second so brief that one needed 34 zeroes to express it, that moment of inflation when the single unifying force split into three and a shadow fell on the texture of spacetime, and from that moment came entropy and the decay of the proton and all murders and all wars and all sorcery and all treachery.

But Angel's treachery was the worst of all. So I'm alone, he thought. Alone in my high tower. The two whom I loved now hate me.

He told himself that he was better alone. The man who stands alone stands strong. He has no friends to deceive him.

Stonebrenner saw a glint of light in the cornfield east of his house and peered carefully out. Yes, there was a man dressed in black standing out there in the field watching him with binoculars.

The man ducked back into the corn and vanished. Stonebrenner turned to a south window and saw a black car parked in the cemetery and saw another intruder dressed in black standing in front of the car.

He cursed his carelessness. Angel's treachery had caused him to let down his guard, and now his enemies were closing in. On this his wedding day.

And now a new distraction: he heard someone climbing the spiral stairs to the tower. It was Kathy Beers, still wearing her flowered bridesmaid dress, emerging from the stairs at the floor like a ghost from its grave.

Angel's fury suddenly stabbed him like a dagger in his heart.

"Viper!" he hissed.

He clamped his hands against Kathy's temples and forced his anger through the balls of his thumbs in a crackling fury. It was his anger and Angel's anger joined together in holy matrimony, and within seconds Kathy's melting brains were leaking out of her nose like snot.

He put his arms around her and embraced her as she went limp. He placed his mouth roughly against hers and tried to suck up her soul as it escaped past her lips. Some magicians claimed to have done so, but most likely they were liars. There was nothing but the last exhalation of her lungs.

He let her body fall and turned back to the window. He felt better now, having righteously vented his anger against another vessel of treachery, for indeed that's what all women were.

Invigorated, he opened the window and swooped out of it like an owl.

***

Ed was standing beside his car on the side away from the house with his camera sitting on the car roof to hold it steady while he occasionally snapped a photo. Sarah was maybe 20 feet in front of the car, half hidden behind a tree in the cemetery, watching the tower with her binoculars.

There was a man up there, and by the ugly bald head she knew it was Stonebrenner, but there was no sign of Darnell or anyone else.

She put down her binoculars because they were hurting her eyes. She glanced around the big yard and then looked at the cornfield that lay east of it, and for a second she saw some cornstalks moving in an odd way, and then she saw two glints of light that looked like binocular lenses. She put her own back to her eyes and for a split second she saw Ben crouching there in the corn, watching the tower, and then he ducked back into the corn.

"Goddammit, Ed, Ben's back there in that field," she said in a loud whisper.

"Shh," Ed said. "Not so loud."

"Well, Goddammit, I saw him. He promised he wouldn't go any farther than the corner of the barn, and now he's back there in that fucking field."

"Call him and tell him to go back to his car," Ed whispered.

She tried to call, but his phone went immediately to voice mail.

"Goddammit, he's shut off his fucking phone," she whispered.

Ed didn't seem to be paying much attention to her—he was snapping another photo.

"Goddammit!" she whispered again, this time to herself, and she scurried east from tree to tree toward the field.

And then something big fell out of the sky behind her and grabbed her around the waist. She tried to scream, but it clamped a bony claw over her mouth and then soared up into the dark air with her like a mammoth bird.

Chapter Fifty-One

Ben was walking north through the field, back toward his car, when the corn leaves started talking to him.

The corn glowed pale green in the moonlight and gestured in the breeze. Though it didn't seem to him that the wind had picked up, the sharp leaves whipped and slapped against him, cutting his skin. At first he paid no heed to the words he seemed to hear, thinking his imagination was running wild. He hurried faster, the leaves clawing his face, and their rustling became a roaring whisper, a chorus of sharp, dry tongues speaking in unison.

"Where are you going?" they seemed to be saying. "Do you want him to kill Sarah?"

Ben stopped and listened. They couldn't be ignored, the crisply whispered words rustling through the field.

"Look up at the tower," the thousand tongues said.

Ben looked and saw that there were two figures up there now, what appeared to be a man and a woman, and they seemed to be dancing. He looked through his binoculars, but the moon was too high now to shine through the windows, and the figures were just dark silhouettes. They swayed and shifted, the two melding as one and dividing again into two, and it seemed the woman was limp in the man's arms.

"That's not Angel he's dancing with," the corn leaves whispered. "That's Sarah."

The voice in the corn could be coming from Darnell or Stonebrenner or maybe from his own imagination, but the figures in the tower were real.

"He enjoys having her body pressed against his," the leaves said. "He likes her body, so slender and small, but when he's done dancing with her he'll kill her."

Ben pulled his cellphone from his jeans pocket and saw it was shut off—his pocket must have pressed against the button. He booted it up and tried to call Sarah. Her phone rang eight times and went to voice mail. He punched in Ed's number, and Ed picked up.

"What's wrong with your phone, Ben?" he said. "I've been

trying to call you."

"It was shut off. Is Sarah there with you?"

"No. That's why I've been trying to call. I'm stumbling around out here in the dark hunting for her, but I'm afraid Stonebrenner has her. You're not going to believe this, Ben, but I think I saw something like a big shadow fall out of the sky and then swoop away with her. I think she's up in the belvedere with him."

"Ed, I'm going to have to go in the house. I'm going to try to be silent if that's possible, because I need the element of surprise. I want you to stay where you are and keep looking for her in case we're wrong. She could be lying on the ground hurt somewhere."

"Will do."

"One other thing, Ed. If you find her I want you to get her in the car and get the hell out of there ASAP."

Ben hung up and looked up at the tower. The silhouettes were still up there dancing. He clambered over the wire fence and ran to the back of the house. He tried the back door, but it was locked. He wanted to kick it in, heedless of noise, but he wouldn't be helping Sarah if he got himself killed.

He noticed a bulkhead entrance to the basement slanting out from the foundation. The rotting door lifted easily, and he hurried down leaf-strewn steps and tried the door at the bottom. It wouldn't budge. He switched on his little flashlight and examined it. There was no lock. Peering through the narrow gaps between the planks, he saw that it was barred on the inside with a horizontal wooden beam.

He opened his pocketknife, stuck the blade through a gap, and tried lifting one end of the beam out of its bracket. It was heavy, but it moved. He raised it higher and at last felt it sliding, slowly at first, then suddenly in a hurry. It crashed to the floor, the noise shockingly loud in the dark silence.

Ben pushed the door open and shone his beam around the basement looking for the stairs, but before he found them he saw a dismembered human carcass lying on a wooden table, most of the flesh stripped from its bones.

No time to worry about that now—he found the stairs and quietly climbed them. At the top he switched off his light and pulled the Springfield from his jeans. It was cocked and locked with his thumb resting on the safety lever; he knew from practice that he could flick down the safety and squeeze the trigger in a fraction of a second.

He eased open the door to a mammoth kitchen, vacant. The other kitchen doors were shut. He crept to one of them, pushed it silently open, and followed his gun into a spacious dining room where no one was dining but the shadows.

Its doors, too, were shut. There was an oppressive odor in the dark air, like the smell of a thousand dead flies. Ben opened one of the doors and found a parlor, its doors also closed, and he kept opening more doors until he found the foyer with the staircase.

He listened for Sarah's voice—surely she should be screaming or crying?—but there was just an abominable silence. He didn't want to think about what that might mean.

As he mounted the wide staircase, the air seemed rotten with the odor of a sickroom. Darkness gathered in a thick clump at the top of the stairs, ripe with the stench of disease.

Ben could barely make out the two hallways, one leading to the front of the house and a longer one stretching north and south, but he didn't dare switch on the flashlight. The few doors that he could pick out of the gloom were shut, and the entrance to the tower apparently was hidden behind one of them. Then he noticed what seemed to be an open doorway at the end of the hallway—hard to tell in the murk.

As he crept toward it, something suddenly came racing toward him through the doorway. It was a woman, naked and ghastly white, but she wasn't coming through a doorway after all—she was a reflection in a full-length mirror on the wall.

Ben whirled around, his gun up and the safety off, but there was no one else in the hallway, nothing moving toward the mirror. And yet the flickering reflection in the mirror kept rushing toward him, floating rather than walking, speeding toward him but drawing no closer.

The woman was emaciated and bald, her face contorted with malevolence or terror, her lips and eyes sewn shut, the sealed eyelids staring blankly while her stitched lips writhed as if trying to rip themselves open.

Sheer terror caused Ben to kick the mirror and shatter it to pieces. He shouldn't have done that—he had made too much noise— but even now, even with it broken, he could barely keep his legs from buckling.

And breaking it hadn't helped, because fragments of the woman's features still flickered in the shards of glass scattered on the floor, a white breast in this piece, a clutching hand in that piece. In one of the fragments Ben saw an eyelid rip free of its stitching, and a pale blue eye peered at him.

He recognized the eye of the phantom-Darnell he had seen at Ed's house. It blinked, its torn lid bleeding, and stared at him like a chunk of blue ice. Ben was transfixed; he couldn't remember where he was or what he was doing here.

How long this lasted he couldn't say, but eventually he thought he heard a man's voice faintly singing. With difficulty he tore his gaze away from the eye and forced his attention back to the dark hallway.

"La dee da da, la dee da," someone somewhere was singing, the sound so hushed that Ben couldn't locate it.

He hurried back toward the stairs, and it seemed that the singing was coming from behind one of the shut doors there at the center of the house. He turned the knob, eased the door open, and found a little room with iron stairs spiraling up. The voice was coming from the tower. It must be Stonebrenner, singing while he danced with Sarah, so maybe Ben wasn't too late.

He started up the stairs, the twisting stairwell so narrow that he had to stoop so his head wouldn't hit the steps above it. The singing was clearer now: "La dee da da, la dee da, la dee da dee da dee da . . ." It was a song that Ben faintly remembered, an old dance tune.

He stuck his head through the opening at the top of the stairs and peered into the tower. It was larger than he had expected, maybe 20 feet in diameter. A man and woman were dancing, but the woman wasn't Sarah, and the man wasn't Stonebrenner: it was a gangly young man with sandy hair.

Holding the woman close to his body, he led her slowly around the circular floor while he sang in her ear. Her head hung limply against his shoulder, and her bare feet weren't moving—the young man was dragging her. She was dead or unconscious. Behind them, the quarter-moon peered into the top of one of the windows.

The man was too preoccupied with his dance to notice Ben until he emerged the rest of the way into the round room and said, "Where's Stonebrenner?"

The young man knelt to lay the woman's body gently onto the dusty floor. As he straightened up, Ben aimed his Springfield at the center of his chest and repeated his question, but the man just watched him with a vacant, fearless look.

Ben moved a step closer, and the man stepped sideways. Ben moved another step and so did the man. At first Ben couldn't make

sense of his movements—he didn't seem to be trying to get away—
and then he realized the man was trying to keep himself between
Ben and the woman's body. He was protecting her. His expression
wasn't malevolent, just stupidly wary, like a determined but feeble-
minded dog.

Ben got a hold of his arm and pressed the gun against his temple.
"Talk. Where's Stonebrenner? Where's Sarah?"

The man began to weep. The wary look left his face, replaced by
grief.

"He killed her," the man said at last. "He killed her."

"Killed who?" Ben asked.

The man didn't answer. Sobs racked his body.

"Look, I'll blow your fucking head off if you don't tell me where
Sarah is."

But the man was crying too hard to speak. Ben stepped away
from him and glanced out one of the windows. Maybe they were
down there in the yard? A reflection moved in the glass: the man
was lunging at him.

Ben stepped aside, and the man fell clumsily against the window.
The wary, canine expression had returned to his face. Ben grabbed
his shirtfront and shoved the gun into his throat. The wariness fell
from his face, and he started weeping again.

The Hermesium bullets, Ben realized. When the gun was close to
him, the Hermesium broke Stonebrenner's spell.

"Tell me who Stonebrenner killed," Ben said.

"Kathy. He raped her the day he came here. He made me watch."
The man whimpered like a puppy, and a trail of mucus oozed out of
one nostril.

"Who's Kathy?" Ben asked.

"I couldn't do nothing, I couldn't do nothing."

Ben pressed the muzzle deeper into his throat, and his Adam's
apple bobbed up and down. "I said, who's Kathy?"

"My wife. He killed her tonight. I found her up here." A shudder
rippled through his body, and he let out a mournful howl. "Can you
hear me, Kathy? I couldn't do nothing to help you."

"Where's he now?" Ben asked.

"In the barn. I saw him flying through the air like a big ugly bird
with a woman clutched in his claws. He took her to the barn."

"Where's the other one—Angela, Darnell?"

"You mean Angel? I don't know. Maybe he killed her too."

Ben dropped the gun's magazine into his left hand, slid out a cartridge, and handed it to the young man. "Keep this with you," he said. "It messes up Stonebrenner's power."

The man stared at it for a moment and then swallowed it.

Ben heard a scream from the direction of the barn. It sounded like Sarah. He raced down the narrow twisting stairs, no longer caring how much noise he made.

Chapter Fifty-Two

Sarah stood at the edge of the south hayloft, trying not to sneeze in the chaff-filled air. Stonebrenner had carried her up there and then had disappeared somewhere into the shadows, maybe hidden behind the stacked bales of hay. One story beneath her was a wide threshing floor, and above the floor to the north was another dark hayloft. She felt her hip pocket and realized the Ruger was gone—it must have fallen out.

There was a built-in wooden ladder leading down to the threshing floor, and she grasped its rungs and started climbing down. A hoarse chuckle from deep inside the barn made her freeze.

"Fe fi fo fum," said a voice as dry as the hay chaff. "To bloody hell shall you come!"

She started climbing down again, and the voice said, "Come to me, said the spider to the fly."

The voice seemed to be coming from below her now, maybe hidden behind the tractor on the threshing floor, and she scrambled back up to the hayloft.

Stonebrenner chuckled again, and his laughter was a raspy scratching sound like an animal's feet racing over the straw.

"And who might you be, little girl?" he asked from somewhere behind her. "And what are you doing on my property?"

"I ran outta gas," Sarah said, her voice sounding small in the big barn. "Just down the road by a little cemetery. I was hoping I could use your phone."

"Liar!" the voice rasped.

Now it seemed to be coming from the north hayloft. She peered into darkness over there and thought she saw a clump of shadow shift.

Suddenly the shadow darted across the floor of the north hayloft. It scuttled up the barn wall to the high ceiling and scurried across the rafters toward her. It was Stonebrenner, dressed in a gray suit like a banker but crawling across the steeply pitched ceiling like a spider, clinging upside-down to the beams.

He scuttled closer until he was directly above her, grinning down. She closed her eyes and whimpered.

"There's someone else here too," he said hoarsely. "There's a man in my house, but I don't think it's Newman. Who is it?"

"I don't know."

"Liar! All women are filthy liars and most men too. You and the man are both working for Charles Newman, aren't you?"

"No. I told you, I ran out of gas."

"Liar! I could melt your brains in a few seconds, and they would pour out your nose like snot. But not yet. Live bait will be more useful than dead. Let's see what you're afraid of. People who are afraid tell the truth."

Sarah felt something brushing against her arms like cobwebs wrapping themselves around her. She tried to brush them off, but they were binding her arms to her sides, wrapping her like a mummy. Her legs, too, were being bound by invisible thread.

Suddenly she was jerked up off her feet. She dangled a few feet above the floor of the loft and spun slowly, as if hanging from a rope. Another jerk, and she was yanked a few feet higher. Then invisible thread tugged at her ankles, tilting them up behind her until she was lying face down and horizontal in the air. She floated up and out of the loft, and then she was staring at the threshing floor far beneath her.

She screamed.

"Ah, I believe you're afraid of falling," Stonebrenner said. "You're afraid of falling and snapping your pretty neck, aren't you?"

Spinning slowly, she stared at the floor sinking deeper and deeper beneath her. She was too frightened to move a muscle, afraid that struggling might snap the thread.

Up and up she went. Now she dangled just a few feet below the center of the high-pitched ceiling, and the floor was slowly spinning far, far below her. She swayed like a pendulum and spun slowly, almost afraid to breathe. She shut her eyes.

"You dangle by a thread spun from sheer imagination," Stonebrenner said. "*My* imagination. So you understand the problem you'd face if any harm came to me. If Charles Newman should do anything to weaken me, my imagination would weaken too, and so too the imaginary thread. Thus our fates are bound."

Sarah made herself open her eyes and saw that Stonebrenner was standing on some bales of hay stacked in the south hayloft. He was looking out of a high window toward the house.

"Now talk to me," he said. "Who is the man in my house and where is Charles Newman? Is Newman somewhere on my property too?"

Sarah tried to say, "I don't know," but she screamed instead. It was a high-pitched shriek that didn't sound like her own voice at all.

A terrifying minute or two passed in silence, and then Stonebrenner said, "Ah, here your man comes now. I see him leaving the house. Your screams have drawn him like sirens. Thusly do women's lying voices sing their men to their graves. Scream again, young lady, and let him know where you are."

She clamped her lips tightly together.

"Then I'll do it for you," Stonebrenner said, and he let out a hoarse shriek maybe not so different from hers. "Help me! Help me!" he shrieked.

Sarah forced her eyes open and saw him shaking with laughter.

"Did I sound like you?" he asked. "Did I have the precise tone a woman uses to lure her man over the abyss? Does this man love you or is he only your partner in crime? Do you suppose he will sacrifice himself to save you? Oh, I do hope he loves you—it will make things so much more interesting."

***

Before he left the house Ben called Ed and said, "Stonebrenner's in the barn with Sarah."

"Meet you there in a minute," Ed said.

Ben unlocked the kitchen door and ran to the barn. It crouched above him like a monstrous, mocking sphinx. It was the setting of his worst nightmares, an emblem of time doubling back on itself to repeat his darkest hour of grief. A year ago he had found his wife hanging from a beam in a hayloft, and he dreaded what he might find tonight.

The side door opened easily. The hot air was itchy with chaff and smelled like hay and ancient horse manure. This end of the barn was horse stables, though there weren't any horses. Something ominous was hanging on the wall, ready to pounce, but when he aimed his flashlight at it, it transformed itself into an old saddle.

He saw a couple of barrels, some feed bags, and something straight in front of him that looked like a man standing perfectly still. He eased toward it, aiming his pistol at it with one hand and his flashlight with the other, and it turned out to be a pitchfork propped against the wall with an old straw hat resting on top of its handle.

He passed through an open gate from the stables to the large threshing floor, empty except for a tractor parked at the far end. Above him on either side was a dark hayloft. A barn owl strummed his nerves with its cry, and then a very human cry came from straight above his head.

Ben aimed his light at the high ceiling. Something was hanging up there, twisting slowly, and for a moment he saw Isabel dangling from her rope. But it was Sarah, floating up there horizontally, face down, her mouth wide open with terror.

Something moved in the south hayloft, and a bald head peered down at him from the edge. Ben aimed his gun, and the man ducked out of sight.

"This gun's loaded with Hermesium bullets, Stonebrenner," Ben yelled. "But I'm not interested in killing you. I just want Sarah, and then we'll get out of here and leave you alone."

Stonebrenner's hoarse answer came from the darkness of the loft: "Ah, but if you shoot me, the woman falls to her death. Look carefully—do you see any ropes holding her? Here, I'll move her around a bit to show you."

Sarah screamed as she suddenly started to fall, and then she was jerked back up to the ceiling.

Stonebrenner appeared at the edge of the loft again, this time holding a gleaming sword in his right hand.

"There, you can see for yourself," he said. "There's nothing holding her up there but the power of my mind, and if you even so much as scratch me with one of your bullets she shall plunge like a rock. So I hold one card and you hold one. Give me your card and I'll give you mine."

"What card do I have?" Ben asked.

"Don't waste my time on games. Even I'm not powerful enough to hold her up there forever. Your card is Charles Newman. I know he's here somewhere—I can smell his vile stench. Somehow you've managed to unlock my property so he's free to roam around on it like a hyena. Bring me his head and you can have the girl."

"How do you expect me to do that?" Ben asked.

"You're his ally, so it should be easy," Stonebrenner said. "You said yourself that your gun is loaded with Hermesium bullets. He trusts you, doesn't he? Then go outside and shoot him. Do you see that machete leaning against the wall down there? Take it with you—it should remove his head easily enough."

Since they were playing cards, Ben decided he may as well bluff. "Okay, I'll do that," he said. "But let Sarah down first. As soon as she's safe beside me, I'll bring you his head."

"Don't waste my time on idiocy!" Stonebrenner shouted hoarsely. "Bring me Charles Newman now or she'll die!"

"I'm here, Becker," someone said.

It was Ed, stepping out of the shadows of the horse stables.

Chapter Fifty-Three

Ed also had a sword, and Ben recognized it as the ornate sabre that usually hung on the wall of his front room.

For a few seconds nobody moved, and then three things happened almost all at once. Stonebrenner dove out of the hayloft and swept down through the air straight toward Ed with his sword extended in front of him. In the next instant Ben heard Sarah screaming and looked up to see her plunging down from the ceiling. And in the next instant he saw a man soaring up into the air and catching her in his arms.

The man drifted down slowly with Sarah and landed softly on his feet beside Ben. It was Ed. He handed Sarah to Ben, snatched up the sword that he had dropped on the floor, and swooped up to the north hayloft.

"You never could fight worth a damn with a sword, Becker," Ed yelled. "I wasted many hours trying to teach you, but you were a dull and stupid student."

"We'll see who's stupid," Stonebrenner answered, and Ben saw him standing in the opposite loft. "You've lost your cradling, Newman, and you're weak as a kitten without it. But I have my own cradling now, and her power surges through me like lightning."

"Ah, so you need a woman to help you," Ed said. "Well, let's see what one weak woman and one stupid man add up to."

Ed swept out of his loft and Stonebrenner swept out of his, and there were brilliant flashes of light and sharp cracks of thunder as they clashed their swords together in the dark air above Ben's head.

But Ben wasn't paying much attention to them. He was holding Sarah tightly in his arms and asking if she was all right, and she was holding him just as tightly and saying yes.

The men were darting toward each other through the air above their heads, clanging their swords together to make loud bursts of light and then darting away again. Stonebrenner swung his sword at Ed, and he summersaulted out of its path.

Ben let go of Sarah and tried to aim his gun at Stonebrenner, but it was hard to tell one man from the other. They looked more like bats than birds, hurtling this way and that way, difficult to see in the darkness.

One of them flew into the north hayloft with the other in pursuit, and for a while Ben couldn't see them, but he heard the clanging of their swords and short blasts of thunder like gunshots, and then he heard a sharp cry of pain that sounded as if it probably came from Ed.

"Get out of here," Ben told Sarah, handing her his car keys. "Get the car and hit the road."

"Not unless you're coming," she said. She had grabbed the machete and was holding it with the handle against her thigh and the blade pointing out, its tip waving slowly back and forth like the head of a cobra.

Stonebrenner flew out of the loft with Ed in pursuit, and now they were fighting directly above Ben's head, lunging and parrying and feinting and slashing while they tumbled and summersaulted through the air. Blood was dripping down, and most of it seemed to be coming from Ed.

Ed swooped into the south hayloft, and Ben fired two shots at Stonebrenner as he darted to the other loft, but even as he fired them he realized he had missed. Now he had only five rounds left, and he regretted having given a cartridge to the man in the tower.

"Do you have your gun?" he asked Sarah.

"No, I lost it."

Ed was standing at the edge of the south loft. He raised his sabre high in the air and began chanting words that sounded like nonsense. Suddenly a bolt of lightning shot from the tip of his sword to the peak of the ceiling, and something like a small swirling black hole appeared up there. As the hole grew wider, creatures flew out of it, screeching like insane children on a carnival ride.

They were dark gray and shaped like little naked men, but they had bat-like wings and grotesque half-human faces with red rat eyes and wide grinning mouths filled with long pointy teeth. They flew around in a confused manner, bumping into one another, until Ed shouted a sharp command, and then they swooped toward the north loft where Stonebrenner was hidden.

Ben couldn't see Stonebrenner, but he heard him chanting his own strange words. There was a flash of lightning, and a moment later the creatures flew out of Stonebrenner's loft and attacked Ed in the opposite loft.

Ed swung his sword, trying to fend off the winged monsters, while Stonebrenner laughed. "You want to fight with demons, I'll give you demons," he said.

A dozen bolts of lightning exploded from the north loft, and wherever one struck the ceiling or a rafter a swirling black hole appeared. Creatures began to tumble, squirm, and wriggle out of the holes, some of them flying or leaping into Ed's loft and others falling onto the threshing floor where Ben and Sarah stood.

Gigantic eels with human faces were flopping on the floor, toad-like creatures the size of large dogs were squatting or hopping, centipedes six feet long were scooting up and down the walls. The barn was filled with strange hoots, cries, screeches, hisses, howls, and yelps.

"Let's get the fuck outta here," Sarah said.

"I don't think we can," Ben said.

Baboon-like things with red skull faces were guarding the gate to the horse stables, and other misshapen ogres were blocking every other possible exit.

"I can open hell-holes all night long," Stonebrenner said. "I learned many things in the box. I spent so much time in hell that I can draw you a map."

Something big landed on the floor several feet in front of Ben and Sarah. It slithered around for a few seconds and then pushed itself up from the dirt with two long thin arms. When it was standing upright on two legs it looked like a pale green lizard-man with a long neck hooded like a cobra.

Ben fired two shots at it, and it backed some distance away but seemed to be unharmed. It stared at him with little round eyes and showed cobra fangs dripping with venom.

"Don't waste your ammo," Sarah said. "I don't think you can hurt these things. Anyway, they seem to be staying away from us."

It was true. The floor was crawling with mammoth centipedes, spiders, vipers, lizards, and grotesque mammals, many of them vaguely humanoid, but around Ben and Sarah a circle of the floor about eight feet in diameter was bare. The air was filled with shrew-faced harpies and bat-winged goblins and giant dragonflies with the pudgy faces of human babies, but they also kept their distance. Some of the things falling from the black holes landed near them on the floor, but they soon walked, squirmed, or scuttled away.

"Maybe it's these good-luck charms," Ben said. "Ed said they'd protect us."

Something like a huge grinning octopus fell out of the air right in front of them. Sarah cleaved it in two with her machete, and the two halves crawled away in different directions, one half with five legs and one with three.

Ben heard Ed yowling with pain or horror, and he floated slowly out of the south loft covered with monstrosities. A snake-thing with three heads was coiled around one of his legs, biting ferociously; a huge scorpion-thing was clinging to his back, jabbing him with its stinger; leech-things were hanging from his face; and a harpy with a hideous female face was riding on his shoulders and clawing his throat with talons.

The leech-things made slurping sounds as Ed pulled them off his face one by one. He reached back and managed to throw off the scorpion-thing, but the harpy and the snake wouldn't let go.

Stonebrenner swooped out of the north loft and jabbed him under the right arm with his sword before Ed could cartwheel out of the way. Then they were at it again, fighting furiously up there, thunder cracking and light flashing as their swords clanged together. One of them suddenly swooped down, and Ben was about to shoot when he saw it was Ed. Then the other darted down and pierced Ed's thigh with his sword.

Ed yelped and swept up to the ceiling. As Stonebrenner was flying up after him, Ben aimed and fired three rapid shots. Stonebrenner let out a screech like an owl, flipped over in the air, and began to fall.

Ben was stepping out of the path of his fall when Sarah ran in front of him and swung her machete like a ball bat. Stonebrenner's body hit the dirt floor, and a split second later a big hard ball smashed down beside it. It rolled and stopped between Ben's feet.

It was Stonebrenner's head. Ben looked up and saw Sarah standing in front of him. She was holding the machete tightly in both hands, its edge dripping with blood.

Part Seven: To the World That Waits Above

Chapter Fifty-Four

Lightning flashed from Ed's sword and made a spinning black hole appear in the barn floor. He barked out some strange words, and the demonic creatures began to walk, squirm, scuttle, hop, fly, or slither into the hole.

Something like an enormous praying mantis standing on two legs was reluctant to go. It stood and stared balefully at them with green insect eyes until Ed barked another word, and then it too leaped into the pit.

Ben peered into the hole. It looked like a bottomless well. A terrible stench like excrement and burning flesh fumed out of it, and he heard cries, screams, whimpers and moans seething with hatred but pitiful in their agony. Even after the hole puckered shut like an anus he could still hear the frenzied howling in his brain.

Ed's clothes were shredded. The right leg of his black trousers was soaked with blood where Stonebrenner's sword had pierced his thigh, his black shirt was soaked beneath the right armpit, and he was bleeding from dozens of smaller wounds. His face was covered with open red sores where the leech-things had been sucking.

"You're bleeding badly," Ben said. "You need to get to a hospital."

"No, I'll be fine," Ed said. "These wounds will heal in a couple of hours. His sword wasn't tipped with Hermesium."

"So you're one of those?" Ben asked.

"Yes, I'm one of those."

"Who are you really?" Ben asked.

Ed smiled. "It doesn't really matter. I've been called Charles Newman and many other names. I apologize for the deception, but it was necessary. You see, Stonebrenner cast a very powerful spell to lock me out of his house and grounds. It wasn't possible for me to come any closer to his property than that little cemetery where I parked. The only way for me to break the spell was to bring a key into his house, where he had built his lock. But you see the problem—how could I do that if I couldn't enter his house? So it was essential for either you or Sarah to enter his house with my key to melt his lock."

"What key? What are you talking about?"

"The medallions I gave you. They truly are invaluable, and I'd like to have them back now."

Ben and Sarah took off their medallions, and Ed slipped them into his pocket.

"You needn't worry about Angel anymore," he said. "She's buried deep beneath the ground. You'll remember that, and you'll remember what happened here, but you won't remember this conversation. After I leave, you'll remember Charles Newman as a tall slender stranger with long black hair and a black beard. Let's make the black beard neatly trimmed—I detest slovenly facial hair."

"Ed, this is ridiculous," Ben said. "Sarah and I are going to remember this conversation and everything that happened here for the rest of our lives."

Ed smiled, and Ben heard footsteps approaching behind him. It was the young man with sandy hair, wandering in from the horse stables. Ben aimed his gun at him, but he seemed to offer no threat. Ignoring them, he came up to Stonebrenner's body, stared at it, and then went back to where the tractor was parked.

"Who's that?" Sarah asked.

Ben started to explain what had happened in the tower, but a moment later the man returned with a large red gas can. He doused Stonebrenner's head and body, stepped back and set down the can. He pulled a book of matches from his pocket, struck one, and tossed it at the body.

There was a stink of gasoline and burning flesh, and Ben could see the corpse writhing and shrinking inside the ball of fire. The young man watched Stonebrenner burn for a moment, then picked up his can and strolled out of the barn. Already flames had started consuming the loose hay on the floor, and a long red tongue began to lick its way up to one of the haylofts.

As Ben and Sarah left the barn, they saw the young man heading toward the house with his red can. They ran to Ben's car and started backing out to the road.

"I wonder what happened to Ed," Ben said. "He told me he was coming to the barn."

"Better call and see if he's okay," Sarah said.

Ed picked up on the first ring and said, "Are you all right, Ben? I can see the barn's on fire."

"Sarah and I are fine. Stonebrenner's dead, and Angel is too. Where are you?"

"I'm sitting in my car. It's embarrassing, Ben, but when I was coming to help you a man stepped out of the bushes beside the barn He was tall and had long black hair and a black beard. I've never seen him before."

"We saw him too," Ben said. "His name is Charles Newman— he's Stonebrenner's enemy."

"Well, here's the embarrassing part—he told me to go back to my car, and for some reason I found that I had to obey him. I think he's some sort of sorcerer, just like Stonebrenner."

The barn windows were beginning to burst, flames shooting out of them and black pillars of smoke rising to the sky. Ben headed south down the road, since they were going to Lancaster instead of Mount Vernon, but then he stopped in front of the house. It was on fire too.

"Ed, I'll call you tomorrow and tell you everything that happened, but right now Sarah and I are dead tired. We're going to go home and try to get some sleep."

"Sleep well," Ed said. "You've earned it."

"He's safe in his car," Ben said after he hung up.

"Well, he sure wasn't much help," Sarah said.

"He's an old man," Ben said. "He would have just been in the way in the barn."

He and Sarah stared at the house. The young man must have doused the downstairs with gasoline and then poured a trail of it up the stairs, because flames were already showing through the second-story windows.

But it was the tower that Ben was watching. All of its windows were open, and two dark silhouettes were moving up there, dancing like the bride and groom figures on top of a wedding cake. A few flames appeared in the tower and grew bigger, but the couple kept dancing as smoke poured out of the windows. Then their clothing caught fire, but they continued dancing. They turned and whirled and clutched each other tightly, growing brighter as they spun, two dancing sweethearts embraced by flame.

They looked like the happiest lovers in the world.

Chapter Fifty-Five

As Sarah drifted to sleep, she was worried that she would have nightmares, but she didn't. She dreamt that she and Ben were riding horses along a beautiful forest path early in the morning, the grass fragrant with dew.

Ben rolled over beside her, and she opened her eyes. He was facing her with his eyes open too. The sheet was down by their waists, and the fan was blowing cool air across their naked bodies. Through the window curtain she saw that the sky was beginning to brighten with dawn.

"Did you sleep?" Ben asked.

"Yeah. I was dreaming that we were riding horses."

Ben smiled. "Our old barn has been very unhappy lately," he said. "Maybe we should buy a horse to cheer it up."

Our, we. They were nice words, and Sarah liked the way they sounded.

***

Charles Newman sat in his study polishing his sword and sipping a glass of old Burgundy that he had been saving for a special occasion, and occasions didn't get much more special than this.

When Elden Becker AKA Isaac Stonebrenner fled Boston half a century ago, he had wrapped himself in a veil so seamless that it had taken Newman 11 years to trace him to this town. Newman found him more by detective work than by magic.

Even after paralyzing him and burying him, Newman wasn't able to trust him to stay in his box. Becker seemed to grow more powerful in the grave, adding clever nuances to the skills Newman had taught him. He wove his veil around himself so tightly that even though Newman could tap some of his cradled power, he couldn't overhear what Becker was plotting from his grave.

Newman's magic was of little help. The only way he could keep watch over this restless grave was to remain here and resort to the same detective work that had led him here in the first place. So for 40 years he had played the role of the harmless folklore collector, trying to intuit Becker's schemes in the grave from the spook stories that people told him.

The stories held plenty of hints and clues, at least in retrospect, but Newman's age was finally showing, and he had misread all of them until it was too late. By the time he understood Becker's plan, his enemy was already disinterred and back in his house, gloating from his watchtower while Newman was helpless to get past his lock.

For many years he had known that Ben Easton would someday be an important ally. The cards and charts and all his other tools of augury had told him that, and so he had carefully cultivated Ben's friendship over the years and had waited for the time when he would be needed.

But when the time came, Ben seemed oddly stubborn and reluctant to help, so Newman had found it necessary to nudge him along occasionally like a chess piece. When Ben didn't take his stories about Longevitals and sorcerers seriously, Newman had found it necessary to draw Darnell's astral body to Ben's bedroom in order to persuade him. When Ben was in the cornfield heading back to his car, Newman had found it necessary to make the corn leaves talk in order to lure him into the house.

And so Ben had gone where Newman was unable to tread, and he was glad that Ben and his charming young friend had survived. Newman knew nothing of love, but he had developed a kind of affection for them.

At last he could leave this town, and leaving was long overdue. When he had moved here he had dyed his hair and used other methods to make himself look as young as possible, and over the years he had gradually allowed more age and white hair to show, but now people were beginning to ask him what his secret was.

There were rumors of a magus buried somewhere in Latvia, and there were the secret alchemist caves of Egypt that he had never explored. So many places to see, but for some reason the prospects didn't stir his blood as they should. He had been nearly half a century old when he received his Longevity treatment, and nearly five centuries had passed since then. Age was creeping up on him quite noticeably now, and his powers were waning like a once-mighty fire feebly clinging to its embers.

And he knew that somewhere, perhaps somewhere close by, a much younger and more powerful magus was waiting to pounce, a new enemy who would be stronger and more effective than Elden

Becker.

The Burgundy had been bottled in 1972, the year that Becker was cradled, and Newman had looked forward to drinking it, but the wine was disappointing. It was complex and interesting and probably had been noble in its time, but it had turned a bit sour in the cellar.

***

Stonebrenner's cradling spell had lost its potency the moment he died, and Angel was able to move again. Already she had torn open her stitched eyelids to stare at the darkness, and already she had torn open her stitched mouth to scream.

Now that she was no longer paralyzed, she urgently needed air. The stone slab that sealed her tomb was terribly heavy, but by using her feet as well as her arms and using desperation for strength, she finally got it to slide just enough to make a small gap for air.

She was too exhausted now to move it any farther. But she would regain her strength and she would try again and, no matter how long it took, eventually she would move it far enough to escape the box.

And then there would be trouble.

Thanks!

Thank you for reading my novel. I hope you enjoyed it, and if you did I hope you'll tell others about it. As an independent author, I have no publishing house to promote my work. Horror fans learn about my novels from other horror fans who mention them on social media or post online reviews.

Also by Harvey Click

Demon Mania
The exciting sequel to *Demon Frenzy*!
Amy Malone thinks she and Shane are safe living in a desolate area of New Mexico, but after she encounters a mysterious sorcerer she's plunged into a demon-ridden nightmare even worse than what she faced in Blackwood. Pursued through moonlit wilderness by grotesque grimsnuffers and hunted by hideous jabber-suckers that suck out their victims' flesh through pulsating tentacles, Amy must survive a deadly maze to confront the most fearsome monster of hell: a demon so deadly it can kill with just a look.

Mixing horror with dark fantasy, *Demon Mania* is a wild whirlwind of sword and sorcery, witches, warlocks, black magic, telekinesis, spirit-travel, deadly assassins, eerie prophecies, breathless action, and demons—lots of demons.

The House of Worms

Dexter Radcliff's elderly great-aunt owns an ancient Native American artifact called the Talking Horn that allows one to speak with the dead, and when Dexter's carelessness causes the Horn to be stolen he is plunged into a nightmarish struggle with the Lost Society, a vast narco-terrorist network of occult assassins led by a dead sorcerer. But Dexter's problems have just begun—soon he will have to contend with parasitic brain-eating worms, sinister Longevitals who can live a very long time thanks to a hermetic treatment, a "Twisted Zoo" containing among its horrific exhibits Dexter's murderous atavistic twin, "spectreholes" that open spectral doorways to other worlds, and a hellish monstrosity older than mankind that is preparing to return to earth and return earth to primordial chaos.

This grisly novel is not for the timid. The first chapter entices the readers like a bloody fishing lure, and each following chapter drags them deeper and deeper into a swirling maelstrom of horror.

Demon Frenzy

Sometimes going home again is a lot like going to hell.

Searching for her lost brother, Amy Jackson returns to her isolated hometown in the Appalachian Mountains. But Blackwood has changed. Now it's run by a mysterious drug lord who has something more lethal than guns to protect him. He has demons—more vicious, venomous demons than even Hieronymus Bosch ever dreamed of—and after Amy witnesses an unspeakable atrocity he unleashes all the frenzied furies of hell against her. Soon she is stalked by snakewalkers, herky-jerkies, toadfaces, listeners, harpies, centicreepers, and the sinister crying man, who weeps while he torments his victims.

Magic Times

Everybody wants a little magic—but just a little can do a lot of damage!

A young man not overly burdened with brains hitchhikes to Ohio in search of his runaway girlfriend, but he finds a lot more than he's looking for. Soon Jason is chin-deep in a bizarre and perilous predicament involving a witch, a crippled magician, a sinister businessman, a mysterious stalker, and a book of magic that could bring about the end of the world.

Harvey Click, best known for his lurid horror tales, explores a different genre with this darkly comic coming-of-age novel. He mixes a tablespoon of black magic with a teaspoon of zesty sex, a sprinkle of savory satire, a dash of dire danger, a splash of spicy suspense, a pinch of pungent irony, a cup of coarsely ground comedy, and a full measure of sheer madness.

Manufactured by Amazon.ca
Bolton, ON

31875182R00153